DOLLAR SERIE$

by

New York Times Bestseller
Pepper Winters

OTHER WORK BY PEPPER WINTERS

Pepper Winters is a multiple New York Times, Wall Street Journal, and USA Today International Bestseller.

Her Dark Romance books include:

New York Times Bestseller 'Monsters in the Dark' Trilogy
"Voted Best Dark Romance, Best Dark Hero, #1 Erotic Romance"

Multiple New York Times Bestseller 'Indebted' Series
"Voted Vintagely Dark & Delicious. A true twist on Romeo & Juliet"

<u>Grey Romance books include:</u>
USA Today Bestseller
"Voted Best Tear-Jerker, #1 Romantic Suspense"

<u>Survival Contemporary Romance include:</u>
USA Today Bestseller Unseen Messages
"Voted Best Epic Survival Romance 2016, Castaway meets The Notebook"

<u>Multiple USA Today Bestseller 'Motorcycle Duology'</u>
"Sinful & Suspenseful, an Amnesia Tale full of Alphas and Heart"

ROMANTIC COMEDY written as TESS HUNTER
#1 Romantic Comedy Bestseller 'Can't Touch This'
"Voted Best Rom Com of 2016. Pets, love, and chemistry

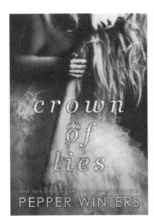

EROTIC ROMANCE DUET
Truth & Lies Duet
5 weeks on the USA Today Bestseller lists

ELDER

I BELIEVED WHEN I was younger that hard work resulted in the ultimate pay-off. That the rewards gained from obsession were enough to justify hurting those I loved.

I always knew I lied to myself.

I always understood what the hidden frowns and unhappy glances meant when I became wrapped up in unhealthy addictions.

However, it wasn't until they banished me that I finally came to terms with just how terrible one-tracked mindedness could be.

I was the reason for my loved one's deaths, and being ostracised from my family was the least I deserved.

I was a monster.

I knew that.

Until Pim.

Until one woman gave me love despite all my flaws. She showed me I could have a life if I only harnessed myself better. If I learned how to stay in control for longer. If I finally replaced the heart I'd long since destroyed.

I started to believe her.

I grew that fucking heart.

Only for her to shatter it when she copied my family and left.

ELDER

ONE, TWO, THREE times, I paced the second bedroom.

One, two, three times, I strode to the door and almost turned the handle to return to her.

One, two, three times, I sat on the bed and clutched my aching skull, willing myself to stay in control until Selix arrived.

I gritted my teeth as the driving demands muttered ceaselessly in my head. There was no reprieve. No help. I'd run out of marijuana and just the knowledge that Pim was outside that door—waiting to ask more questions, to interrogate me with a sexy fierceness in her eyes and gorgeous bravery in her spine—made it that much harder to stay away.

Christ!

Even with a wall and locked door between us, I struggled to keep my distance. This morning was fucking taxing, but last night had been the longest I'd ever endured.

I'd told Pim the truth about how hard I'd fought to stay away. The only thing giving me strength was thinking of my baby brother. Of the atrocities I'd caused and the many more I might make if I gave in to the malicious chatter inside my head.

I winced all over again, recalling her face as I deliberately broke her heart.

My awful slur of *'You're not worth it,'* echoed sickly, making me suffocate with self-hatred.

She'd been right to call me a liar.

I was a fucking falsifier who couldn't keep his story straight. Even to himself. So many instances I'd told her the truth, only to cover it up immediately with deceit.

One moment, I told her I didn't want her body, only her mind.

The next, I admitted I couldn't breathe without touching her.

One day, I told her she owed me every penny I placed on her self-worth.

The next, I retracted the hypocrisy and delivered her freedom free from any debt.

Yet, she didn't take it.

She stood before me and accepted my forgeries as if she didn't hear what I spoke but only what I was desperate to keep hidden.

She'd swum into my veins and infiltrated my soul without me knowing. By the time I understood what she'd done...it was too late. She'd reached inside my chest and fished out my heart. She'd gutted it, filleted it, and slapped it on a goddamn frying pan.

I had the power to stop my pain.

All it would take was six steps to the door and a twist of the lock to sink into the addiction I despised. If all I cared about was myself, then fine. I wouldn't be sitting here rocking like a junkie, counting down the seconds for Selix to arrive to fix this. I would be out there, balls deep in Pim.

But unfortunately, by taking my heart, she'd given me something I'd been lacking since the flames ate my childhood and family.

She'd given me culpability.

And an even larger dose of self-control to *never* put myself first again—no matter how loud the whispers howled.

I wouldn't put her in danger again. I would drive a stake

through my heartless chest before I let that happen.

She was worth it.

Ten times, no, a *thousand* times fucking worth it.

She was worth more than any fortune or vengeance. And that was what sealed my deal with the devil plotting on my shoulder.

I couldn't do this anymore.

Nothing in the world would seduce me into marching back to her, pushing her onto the bed, and ripping off every piece of clothing between us. I wouldn't admit that the only way I could continue living was either with her naked and under me for the rest of our days or far, far away where she turned back into a stranger and I could return to my strictly regimented life.

Both options weren't healthy and sure as hell weren't acceptable.

But…she's worth it.

And that was the lie I'd never rectify.

She had to believe she *wasn't* worth it.

She had to hate me for what I'd done.

She had to accept my lies as truth—had to see me as the addict I was and not the quixotic lover she hoped.

Despite the morbidness of my thoughts, one piece of sanity remained. A knowledge of how my mind worked and a tentative hope that two solutions might save me as they had before.

Distance and time.

There was such a thing as cooling off, and I was in desperate need of it.

In my past, the way to 'cure' me of my current obsession was brain boredom—where my mind suddenly decided it had conquered all it needed to, and the fog lifted, letting me see the world without addiction again.

A universe of sensations existed past that one compulsion, and it always seemed as if I'd stepped from a vortex of nothing but origami, origami, or fight, fight, fight to breathe a deep sigh of relief and be sane.

It took a while. It wasn't guaranteed. But it could happen with Pim. I could grow bored of her...

I rolled my eyes.

Bullshit.

The more time I spent with her, the more fascinated I became.

Okay, time might not work...but perhaps distance could.

The second way of breaking my OCD was separation from the cause. To ignore the screaming demands to over focus and indulge. To ride through the detox no matter how agonising.

Some obsessions only took a day to overcome. Simple things like a song that'd captured my attention only for me to play it repetitively, hour after hour, until I physically couldn't listen to the beat without wanting to kill myself while at the same time, unable to stop pressing play.

In those cases, all I needed to do was throw away the CD, or burn the iPod, or turn off the internet even as my cello called to me.

A few days cold turkey and the storm summoning me to drink its venomous rain and live in its rancid clouds dispersed into clear skies once again.

It's worked before.

It can work again.

If I could avoid Pimlico for a few days...a week maybe...then I could forget the nirvana of being inside her and go back to the way things were. Platonic things. Rescuer and recovering things.

All I need is time.

Checking my watch, I ignored the twitch to check it one, two, three, and noticed an hour had gone by since I'd yelled at her.

Guilt chewed caverns inside me.

I'm a bastard to say she wasn't worth it.

She was worth so much more than what I had to give, and

that fucking terrified me. I'd hurt myself before I hurt another person I love—

My spine shot straight.

Love…

For the second time, that sneaky word snaked into my thoughts.

I knew sibling and parental love. I understood what it was like to give someone my heart unconditionally because of blood and obligation.

But to go from strangers to friends…to *in* love.

To hand over my everything and be happy that I had the ability to fall instead of freak out about what this meant.

Am *I in love?*

Was that what churned inside my chest? The sickening knowledge that I would throw myself out of the window if it meant it was the only way to keep Pim safe, or was it yet another layer of guilt knowing what she'd lived?

The question hissed through my blood, twisting the need for physical intimacy into something entirely different.

She was the one making me hurt.

But she could also be the one to make me better.

All my previous rationales vanished.

Glancing at the door, I stood before I gave myself permission. I'd tell her exactly what had to happen. That for the next week, she'd have to stay in quarantine for her own protection. If we crossed paths, a minimum distance would be recognised at all times with staff present. And above all, no touching.

If she obeyed, I could get myself under control again, and we could go back to being friends.

I could continue to love her. Care for her. Cherish her. And she would be given everything she ever wanted.

My hand clamped over the door-knob while my mind entered a fugue, desperate to earn Pim's laugh again, to watch her steal something inconsequential all the while stealing my heart.

That was what I needed.

She was what I needed.

We can make this work.

We could sail side by side as cohabiters until we arrived in England. There, I'd set her free because it was the right thing to do.

I would forever be her No One, and who knew? Perhaps we could remain pen friends while I sailed the seas searching for redemption and she slotted back into the life she was stolen from.

The idea warmed my aching heart while at the same time crushing it beneath its vicious shoe.

Wishing I had a joint to take the edge off, I yanked open the door and stepped into the suite's lounge.

My eyes fell to the carpet where she'd stood and begged me to talk to her.

Nothing.

The thick floor-covering held no indents of her feet, no sign she'd been there at all. Of course, she wouldn't remain standing for over an hour. She'd return to somewhere far more comfortable.

The bed.

I couldn't approach such a thing—especially after we'd had sex on it—but I gritted my teeth and stalked toward the bedroom we'd shared. To the crumpled sheets and the lingering scent of sadness and lust.

Empty.

Instantly, I missed her presence.

There was no rustle of femininity. No prickle of her eyes on my body.

No silent mouse or brave Pimlico.

The room was bare.

My stomach turned to lead as I spun slowly, peering into the bathroom, believing any second she'd come out and I'd stride forward and gather her in a bone-crunching hug.

A hug that would turn to kissing.

A kiss that would turn to touching.

A touch that would turn to fucking.

A nightmare

that

I

could

never

fucking

stop.

Inhaling hard, I pinched the bridge of my nose, shoving aside those thoughts and focusing on the vacant room.

She was gone.

Which was probably a good thing. An excellent thing. But the knowledge she'd snuck out while I sulked in the other room tore my skin from my skeleton.

Then my gaze fell on the folded note on the bed.

Ah, shit.

Raking fingernails over my scalp, I shook my head as if denial would change the finality of the white paper.

"No." I backed away rather than shot for it.

I already knew what it said. This was my fault. I'd scared her off. I'd hurt her. Through my actions and harshness, I'd told her to leave. I'd *wanted* this to happen even though I'd negate such a claim.

"Fuck."

She'd been too strong for her own good. She'd ignored her distrust of strangers and choosen a corrupt world over me.

Forcing myself forward, I picked up the letter.

The penmanship was familiar from reading her notes to No One. My eyes skimmed the text—absorbing the theme but unable to fully soak in her crippling message.

Sentences like *I always knew our time together was temporary— just like you.*

And *This is goodbye, Elder.*

They were too violently excruciating to accept.

Instead, I looked at the scribble over *Pimli-* at the bottom and froze.

Goddammit, could the pain get any worse?

I crumpled up her note, doing my best to hide what I'd seen—what she'd given me—but the six little letters of her signature burned upon my retinas.

Not the name given to her by misfortune.

But her *true* name.

The name Selix had told me yesterday when he'd informed me of the location of Pim's mother. The name I'd known and hadn't told her—even as I demanded more of her heart than I could ever deserve.

Tasmin.

"Fuck." I hung my head, balling the letter tighter with rage. She hadn't enlightened me on her last name, but it didn't matter.

I knew that, too.

I'd stolen her right to tell me, and it made me a shitty human being.

Tasmin Blythe.

The psychology student from West London with good grades, a lonely existence, and perfect behaviour as a role model daughter to one of the most prolific criminal psychologists in the United Kingdom.

Selix had been the one to find out, but I hadn't stopped there.

I'd turned to Google, and instead of asking Pim everything I wanted to know, I once again stooped to stalking. I'd read her letters to No One, and now I'd read facts written about her online by third parties.

No matter what information Google gave me, it hadn't given me an ounce of what I'd learned by living with her. Google could tell me about the night of her abduction. It could deliver missing person reports, newspaper articles of this shining rising star, and how police had no leads. But it couldn't tell me what she smelled like, laughed like, moaned like. It couldn't teach me the way her eyes widened when I gave her a compliment or how her teeth indented her lower lip as I kissed her throat.

But Google had told me things Pim didn't know herself. A few months after her kidnapping, more documents appeared, but this time, they focused on her mother. The mother who was suddenly thrust into the limelight, eclipsing her daughter's disappearance with her own heinous actions.

I had it all wrong.

I thought I wanted information. That I wanted every secret and hidden agenda. However, gaining that knowledge from a computer screen was hollow and woefully unsatisfying.

What I truly wanted was Pim. I wanted the beauty of her voice as she told me about her studies. I wanted the perfection of her face as she reminisced about childhood pets or favourite places.

Pim had started as my charity case and ended up meaning so much more. She left before I could tell her why I needed her so goddamn much.

You could go after her.

I knew her home address.

I'd used Google Earth to study her old apartment. I'd used street view to walk the same cobblestone alleys she had before she'd been taken.

I could go there and wait for her. Or I could march through Monaco and find her and tell her the truth about what her mother did and what it meant for her future.

But if I did, there was no way in hell I could let her go again. There would be no safety net in sight. No happy ending. Only me living a life of sexual frustration while she remained lonely and rejected.

She'd left.

If I could somehow do the same, it might be exactly what we needed to survive each other.

I stood by the bed, waiting for an epiphany on what to do.

Chase her.

Forget her.

Claim her.

Abandon her.

One, two choices.

One, two decisions.

One, two potential disasters.

I wished I had a third option just to balance out the tic inside my skull.

The crazy counting wouldn't stop; I rubbed my temples. Pim had done this to me. I wished I had the ability to turn off emotion. I wished I could walk away from her as she'd just walked away from me.

My legs screamed to hunt her down and drag her back— kicking and screaming if it came to that. But even as I entertained the idea of chasing her through downtown Monte Carlo, an irrefutable depression settled.

She'd made the decision for both of us.

She'd been the one to have the guts and look into the future and only see decimation.

It was over.

Done.

Finished.

That's the way it has to be.

I hated it. I mourned it. I already felt myself breaking apart.

Throwing her letter across the room, I pulled my phone from my pocket and dialled Selix.

He answered on the first ring. "I know, I know. I'm running late. Almost there."

"Doesn't matter anymore." My voice was shattered glass.

Selix paused. "What's happened?"

That question couldn't be answered in my current state. "I hope to God you got the tin I asked for from my bedside drawer."

"Got the tin."

My shoulders slouched, already tasting the sickly smoke of a joint. I didn't have the power to calm my riotous thoughts, but weed surely would.

"Good," I said. "Tell Jolfer we're leaving the moment we return."

"Already ahead of you. The captain has the yacht fully stocked with food and fuel. He's ready to leave when you are."

"Fine."

When I didn't hang up or give more instruction, Selix asked, "Anything else?"

"Yes, Pimlico ran off."

Christ, I didn't mean to sound so fucking gutted. Stupid voice betraying me. Stupid heart screwing me over. Stupid fucking universe putting her in my path.

"You going to find her?" Selix's tone was quiet...unpresumptuous, but it still set my hackles on edge.

Yes.

No.

I don't fucking know.

"Just...come get me. I've waited long enough. I need to be on the ocean."

"I'm literally two streets away. Traffic was a bitch." He cleared his throat, about to over step the line he loved testing. "Look, if my opinion is worth anything, I think it's a good thing she's gone. No longer your problem."

Now that I've tasted her, she'll forever be my problem.

Selix didn't need to hear that. "I never liked your opinions. This time is no different. Shut up and drive. The sooner we're off this godforsaken soil, the better."

"Guess I'll let the Hawks know your plus one is no longer needed."

"Fuck you."

Selix chuckled. "Hey, I could always go as your date." A car horn sounded before he added, "Look, here's another opinion you probably won't like. You're still sailing to England. Want me to find her and stow her on board? You wouldn't have to see her. I'd keep her away. At least then you'd know she's back where she belongs and you could truly forget about her. Your part would be done."

I shook my head even as Selix's proposal spread like wildfire. "You know as well as I do she has no one there to take her in. Her mother—"

"I know," he interrupted. "But fuck that. I'm sure she has other family."

She doesn't.

Same as me.

And that was yet another crucifix to bear.

I didn't want to hear any more.

Pim had made her choice.

I was making mine.

She was on her own.

It didn't matter I would forever carry a hole where she was concerned. I wouldn't hurt her again. She'd earned her freedom. England or Monaco—her fate would be the same in any country as she no longer had a home.

She would make a new one somewhere far from me.

From Alrik.

From everyone.

"Enough of your damn opinions, Selix. Bring me that tin. Never mention her name again, forget she ever existed. I expect to set sail within the hour. You can't do that? You'll be swimming with the goddamn fish."

Pimlico

TWO DAYS AGO, walking the streets had been an adventure.

I'd had Bill and Lance shadowing me—giving me courage because they worked for Elder, and Elder was my guardian angel. When someone jostled me, I didn't get scared. When a man stepped in front of me, I didn't panic.

Today had been completely different.

I'd spent the day all alone.

Vulnerable, lost, afraid.

Men smiled, and all I saw were monsters.

Women laughed, and all I saw were victims.

Morning had turned to afternoon, and I'd walked listlessly, heart-bruised, and happy-broken, second-guessing my rash decision to leave Elder.

No matter what street I took or direction I chose, I couldn't stop myself from looking over my shoulder...hoping.

Hoping he'd stalk around a corner and scold me for leaving such a note. Wishing he'd appear around a bend and kiss me stupid for ever thinking I had enough willpower to stay away.

Minutes had turned to hours, and those silly fantasies went unanswered.

He never appeared.

And I never turned back.

I'd left for his sake. I'd run away to *heal* him. I thought I was selfless enough to do it, but as afternoon morphed to evening and evening darkened to midnight, I wondered what new level of imbecility I'd risen to.

Didn't I deserve to be safe and cared for?

Didn't I earn the right to love and be loved in return?

He doesn't love you.

I rubbed at the ice freezing my skin. Elder had never told me how he felt. For all I knew, I was still just a conquest, and my leaving would be met with relief instead of misery.

You know that's not true.

But I had no willpower to convince myself because if I did…what would prevent me from running back to him and forcing him to live in agony all because I couldn't imagine my life without him?

No.

I won't do it.

My thoughts (no matter how scattered) were the only possessions I had as I continued to wander the streets of Monte Carlo. I had no luggage, no blankets, no money to trade unwelcoming footpaths for sympathetic beds.

This was my penance for telling a man he'd earned my heart only to walk out the door without a goodbye. My empty stomach daren't growl because it deserved to have no fuel. My arthritic bones daren't complain because they brought such discomfort on themselves. And I definitely didn't allow the piercing laments of my heart to earn a single tear from me.

This was my fault, and I would pay the price to prevent Elder from doing so.

For an entire twenty-four hours, I lived in limbo.

As the streets emptied of law-abiding holidaymakers and were replaced with alcohol-fermented partiers, I kept to the shadows and out of sight.

Security guards patrolled outside their nightclubs and the police presence increased—protecting the rich and famous from bad decisions and terrible consequences.

It was the longest night of my life. Not only because I had nowhere to sit down and rest, but because I never stopped moving to avoid the beady eyes of other night-walkers.

This part of town had no homeless, and the glitz and finery wore down a piece of me I didn't know I harboured: a certain kind of hate for wealth.

I might've been brutalised, but my captivity had been in a beautiful mansion dripping with money. Then I'd been rescued and stowed on the Phantom where its very creation was all thanks to Elder's underhanded dealings.

I loved my bedroom on the Phantom, but until tonight, when I finally earned some grit beneath my sandals and dirt upon my hands, I'd forgotten what it was like not to have everything.

To be surrounded by shop windows full of thousand-dollar dresses and not be able to afford them. To smell the scents of pricey dinners in exclusive restaurants and not be able to eat.

Yet again, something else had been stolen from me: the value of things. Not that I ever took my living on the Phantom and all its luxuries for granted, of course, but for once, it was nice to worry about normal things—things Tasmin used to constantly fret over while Pimlico had forgotten by being kept as a toy.

Things like hours passing and no way to tell the time. Concerns like itineraries and no way to get to where I needed to go. Problems like the mundaneness of life and being responsible for my own person.

My thoughts kept me distracted from my flat feet and sore back as dawn slowly approached and prettily made-up women turned to tipsy makeup-smeared consorts, and men went from handsome devils to morally-corrupted scoundrels.

Ducking out of the way of a domestic, and staying to the shadows to avoid the eyes of security guards, I poked at the open wound by leaving Elder. All night, I'd been a game of roulette as my mind spun the wheel and my choices between staying away and returning became the little white ball.

Sometimes, that ball landed on red. Red...the colour of love, of passion, of blood and rage and lust.

But sometimes, it landed on black. Black...the colour of desperation, of grief, of wrongness and hate and confusion and pain.

Neither gave me an answer I could live with.

Dawn crept to daybreak.

I looked at the horizon and saw how far I'd walked.

My heart hiccupped at the amount of distance I'd placed between Elder and me. My feet turned mutinous, wanting to go backward rather than forward.

All I wanted to do was kneel before him and promise I'd never again ask him to touch, kiss, or bed me. If that was the sacrifice for his friendship and protection, then so be it. I would pay it lifetimes over.

If I did that, I could be with him right now.

I could be sailing out to sea.

Safe.

Warm.

In love.

Who cared if he never touched or kissed me again?

He was *safe*.

And safe was worth so much more to me than romance.

Isn't it?

I hated that my answer was no longer clear cut.

He'd spoiled me. He'd shown me that safety only came from trust, and trust had the unnerving ability to create affection, which morphed into lust and somehow blossomed into love.

You didn't leave for you.

That reminder—that righteous thorn in my side—gave me strength.

I can do this.

For him.

Inhaling hard, I strode onward.

* * * * *

Late afternoon, and I still hadn't left the limbo of heartache.

I hadn't come up with a plan. I hadn't done anything but mope.

The hungrier and more tired I became, the more the crowds caused cold sweat to trickle down my spine. Sunshine burned me as if I was an ant under a magnifying glass. Every pair of eyes was malevolent.

The streets slithered this way and that, deeper into chaos.

I had no idea where I was going. I had no clue how I would find money to return to England or how I would track down my mother.

With every step, I hunkered down a little more, curling around the emptiness inside.

However, as hunger pains took precedent, my mind stopped torturing me with images of Elder and focused on survival. I needed money. For food, shelter, and transport. I needed a passport to cross the borders. I needed a miracle to achieve such things.

Or the sticky fingers Elder had taught me to wield.

The thought of stealing wasn't new. I'd deliberated all night, looking, despite myself, for easy opportunities. But now another day was here, and my throat was dry, and a headache pinched my eyes, and I finally had no choice. The luxury of being above such necessities had faded, and I sagged against a building, trying to stay out of the way of bustling pedestrians.

I didn't want to loiter like a criminal, but I also couldn't keep walking with no direction.

I needed to be smart.

It was time to steal.

Self-disgust filled me even as I settled in to study potential victims and find the rhythm of the city. I eyed laughing tourists and assessed sharp chinned businessmen. I did my best to recall everything Elder had taught me about pickpocketing.

My fingers fanned out by my sides, willing to pilfer a wallet or purse but still so unskilled at being unseen.

As much as I didn't want to do this, I had two choices: steal enough to get home or put myself at the mercy of others. I would have to blindly trust that the police weren't corrupt, good Samaritans weren't evil, and whoever came next into my life wouldn't abuse me.

No.

I couldn't.

I was too fragile. My confidence still so new. I couldn't turn to another and trust. I had *one* person I trusted, and I'd run from him. The second best was me, myself, and I.

And No One.

No One...*damn*.

The crippling in my chest was all thanks to Elder and his story about being called No One by his family.

My journal would forever be linked to him.

He'd ruined the only sanctuary I had.

I missed him more than I could stand.

What was he doing? Had he decided to hell with me and left? Had he stayed and tried to find me?

Where I stood deep in the city surrounded by buildings and strangers, I couldn't see the ocean. I couldn't see the Phantom or the balcony where we'd stood side by side and faced the storm out to sea.

I can't see if he's gone...

Four girls walked past, two with gaping-open handbags and brightly coloured purses just begging to be looted.

It was as if fate had given me direction and told me to stop mauling painful thoughts. If Elder had gone, so be it. If he was still here, that wasn't my concern.

I'd left because I loved him.

And I would steal because I needed to take responsibility for myself again.

Clutching my conviction, I pushed off from my resting place and followed.

For the first few steps, I felt nothing. Then, the longer I committed to doing this, the more adrenaline drenched my veins. I turned jumpy and edgy and paranoid.

I guessed the girls were in their early twenties, and judging by their tired faces from late nights and immaculate new clothing they were here to do some serious partying with unlimited shopping budgets.

Lucky for me, passers-by didn't peg me as too out of place. I might not be wearing the latest catwalk fashion like my chosen hunted, but apart from a little toil from spending the night outside, my sundress was still appropriate; my hair still acceptable.

I was merely the fifth wheel to this quad of happy spenders, and no one noticed me lurking behind them.

My ears rang with their plastic laughter as they regaled tales of flirting with men last night only to drink their gifted cocktails before telling them they were too ugly for their tastes.

The more I listened, the less I liked them. Although, one girl didn't say a thing, merely nodded and smiled when her friends were looking and cringed and rolled her eyes when they weren't.

I liked her but not the others. I didn't know why not liking them helped my resolve, but I continued to follow, eager now for an opportunity to rob rather than dreading it.

Finally, they stopped outside a café to read the menu, and my opportunity was handed to me.

I slammed to a stop. Two of the obnoxious girl's handbags remained slung carelessly over their shoulders, one silver purse and one turquoise begging me to take them.

So I did.

Without looking around, my two hands vanished into two handbags and stole two purses.

A split second later, I turned and walked the other way.

The moment I marched away, the shakes started. A drenching of anxiety. A rush of sick excitement. A drowning of self-disgust.

Oh, my *God*.

I'd stolen for my own gain.

I hadn't left a note apologising.

I'd judged those girls on their moronic conversation and bitchiness.

But I was the one in the wrong, not them.

Holy hell, I stole from them.

My heart couldn't believe I'd become a criminal while yet more adrenaline spiked, making me drunk on such a scam.

I didn't look where I was going as I tucked one purse beneath my arm and unzipped the silver one. Inside was a wad of hundred-dollar bills with more credit cards than I'd ever seen.

I didn't know the first thing about credit card fraud, so I only took the cash and zipped up the wallet again. Passing by a café with its sunshine-bathing clientele, I left it on an outdoor table, hoping a nice waiter would find it and drop it at the nearest police station.

At least the girls would have a chance to have their cards and other mementos returned. I'd just take their cash. I'd use it wisely and gratefully and get myself home where I'd never have to steal again.

"Hey, you!" a screech whipped my head around.

The blonde girl who'd regaled and cackled about leading men on last night pointed at me. "Stop her. She's a thief!" Her gaze went to the turquoise purse in my hands.

Her brunette friend yelled, "That's my wallet! See!"

Pedestrians frowned, not willing to get involved just yet, giving me a few seconds to panic before everything exploded.

For a moment, I froze.

I couldn't deny their accusations as they were entirely true. I was the one at fault, and all I wanted to do was apologise and beg for forgiveness while returning their property.

But if I did…I'd be arrested, and my previous imprisonment would begin all over again as a ward of the Monaco state rather than free at home with my mother.

No.

I couldn't be locked up again.

By anyone.

"Stop, you little bitch!" Seeing as onlookers weren't tackling me to the ground, the girls took matters into their own hands. "Get your thieving little ass back here!"

They charged.

I bolted.

I didn't think. Instinct took over.

I ran as fast as I could through congested streets beneath hot sunshine. I weaved and parried. I didn't look back. My lungs burst, my bones screamed, my eyes darted for a safe haven.

I might've run for two hours or two minutes—fear turned it into an unwinnable race. Gasping for air, I careened down a side street, hoping that by being off the main road, it would help me disappear.

I hoped wrong.

Oh, no...

Swallowing my terror, I came upon a dead end.

No, no, no.

Spinning around, I took three steps back the way I came only to slam to a stop as the slap of expensive sandals heralded the appearance of my victims.

They skidded into the alley, breathing hard, sweat dancing upon their perfect brows. They were all so pretty with styled hair, immaculate makeup, and top-of-the-line moisturised skin, but for three of them, no beauty could hide the ugliness inside them.

The blonde wearing a polka dot dress sneered. "Trapped now, aren't ya, you little thief?"

I huddled in the shadows, wishing to God I hadn't done what I did, desperate to make amends. My voice deserted me. Silence became my old friend and enemy.

The girls didn't care.

They pressed forward. "Give us back our stuff, bitch."

I tossed the turquoise wallet to them, watching it skid in a dirty puddle.

"And mine," the blonde demanded, her gaze locked on the cash in my hands.

I opened my mouth to tell her I didn't have it. That I'd left it on a café table and would gladly take her there to make amends, but a black-haired girl who looked more in control and cruelly intelligent than her fellow holiday goers pulled out her phone.

"Ladies, don't stress yourself." With a cold smile, she said, "Let's call Harold and have him sort this matter out, shall we?"

The girl who hadn't spoken, who stood a little away from her friends and hadn't joined in the spiteful retelling of hurting men's feelings, cringed. "Miranda...I don't think—"

The black-haired girl shot her a look.

She shut up.

Glancing back at me, Miranda pressed a few buttons on her phone. Her smile was beastly. "You really shouldn't have taken what wasn't yours. Now Harold and his friends will have to teach you a lesson."

Her brunette friend in grey shorts and white polo held up her hands. "Whoa, wait. We don't need to get the men involved."

I hoped she'd stand with her quiet friend and stop whatever was about to happen. Instead, her lips spread over sharp teeth. "Don't let them have all the fun. We could do it." She put up her fists with a mad laugh. "Just rough her up a little."

Blondie wrinkled her nose. "Eww, I'm not hitting someone. I might break a nail." She flashed vibrantly pink-glitter fingernails. "They're gels, Monique. I spent hours at the salon yesterday getting them done."

"No one is breaking a nail or resorting to D.I.Y," Black-haired Witch snapped. "We are ladies, and ladies do not brawl." Her chin came up. "Ladies deliver vengeance without getting their hands dirty. Therefore, Harold will take care of her. I have no doubt he'll have a lot of fun teaching her how it feels to have things taken without consent."

My knees buckled at the darkness in her tone. At the way her eyes glittered at the innuendos barely hidden in such a terrible sentence string.

I didn't need to be taught.

I already knew.

Knew how it felt over and over again to have personal things taken without consent.

How my body had been used as entertainment for others.

How I'd had no say in it.

The betrayal.

The horrible knowledge I was worthless to the person hurting me.

Oh, my God, what have I done?

They were right.

I'd taken something of theirs without consent. I was just as bad as the assholes who'd hurt me. They had every right to be hurt and angry. *I* was hurt and angry. I'd been hurt and angry for years.

I wanted to open my mouth and apologise. To assure them that I would *never* steal again as I knew all too well what it was like to be on the receiving end of such theft.

But once again, my throat closed up, hiding my words, silencing my pleas. I wished I'd never used muteness as protection. I wished I could break such a curse and *scream.*

Then Miranda stabbed me with yet more horror as she murmured, "Harold is ingenious with his punishments. I imagine he'll come up with something quite unique to remind you that stealing is not okay—" She narrowed her eyes, looking like a serpent ready for her next meal. "—*Especially* stealing from us."

The mental images she painted.

The memory of ropes

and chains

and whips

and classical music
and blow jobs
and rapes
and pain.
No!

Falling to gristly knees long since ruined from doing such a thing, I collapsed into submission before them. Clasping my hands together, I fought every safety mechanism and willed my tongue to move.

In jilted begs, I whispered, "I'm s-so sorry. I didn't mean…I have no excuse. I know what it's like. I don't need a lesson. I've had too many lessons." Tears drenched my face without me crying as if my eyes evicted every droplet in preparation for the beating I knew was coming.

I never screamed with Alrik.

I never cried with Alrik.

I wouldn't do that with this new punishment.

Old habits would never die.

"Please…" I hissed. "*Please*, don't do this."

Blondie and the girl who wasn't like her friends stumbled back, alarm painting their pretty features.

Blondie switched from cursing me to rationality. "Hey, Miranda…know what? No harm done. We've got the cash back. I can cancel my cards. It's fine…"

"I agree." The nice girl tugged the black-haired one. "Come on, let's just go."

But Miranda shook her off, the same glint in her eye that Alrik used to get glowing brighter. "Nope. What's done is done. She needs a little payback." Moving forward, she held her phone to her ear and smiled as whoever she'd rung answered. "Harold, baby? Yeah, it's me. Look, I need you to come here. A chick just tried to rob us." Her smile turned from beastly to downright fatal. "Yep, that's what I said. I knew you'd understand." She nodded. "Yep. I've told her that you'll come *'talk'* to her. Make sure she doesn't do it again."

Laughing at something he said, she tossed her hair over

her shoulder. "Okay, baby. See you in five." Hanging up, she pointed a finger in my face. "And now, we wait. Get ready, bitch. You're in for a world of pain."

ELDER

THE OCEAN HAD a power over me that could circumnavigate the mess in my brain better than anything. It was one of the many reasons I'd chosen the sea as my home.

Normally, the chaos from land slipped from my shoulders the moment I stepped on board. Normally, I could breathe a little easier, focus a little better, and pretend to be normal after fighting addictive tendencies.

Normally was the key word.

It wasn't occasionally or infrequently; it was *normally*: as in usually, consistently, reliably.

Damn Pimlico had changed that.

Yesterday had been one of the hardest days of my life, and that was saying something after the fuck-ups I'd caused.

Selix had arrived at the hotel. I'd had a joint. And I'd paced until my heart galloped as if I'd jogged for miles trying to decide what to do.

Stay or go?

Accept or deny?

Chase or sail?

She'd left out of some stupid courtesy to help me.

But what if I didn't want to be helped?

What if I should man the fuck up and help myself, instead of making it her responsibility to enter a world where she had nothing and no one? Why did I have to accept that she'd given me her love and then taken it right out the goddamn door with her?

Selix hadn't swayed me in either direction. He'd sat flicking through a hotel magazine for hours while I willed the pot in my system to help make a better decision.

And the decisions I came to was...I couldn't let her do this.

I couldn't let her put herself in harm's way for me. It wasn't right. It wasn't fair. I wasn't the only one with a screwed-up brain. Others had what I did, and they lived a normal life. They weren't fucking pussies, untrusting of doctors or unwilling to try new things.

I would be more like them. I would get my life together. I'd find Pimlico, take her to England without touching her, and by the time we arrived, I would've calmed down and be able to be around her without fucking her. Then, once I had her back in my life and knew she was safe, I'd see someone and discuss a regime or pill that could help me. I would take control of my mind so I could deserve everything Pim gave me so purely and selflessly.

It was a plan I could live with.

So, I'd marched from the hotel with Selix in tow and patrolled the streets for hours. Side alleys and main arteries, shops, and restaurants. I kept my eyes searching for a flash of chocolate hair or a glimpse of sensual limbs.

But I couldn't find her.

Anywhere.

It didn't matter.

She couldn't have gone far. She had to be in Monte Carlo. And as the sun set on our first day apart, I settled in for the challenge of tracking her down—confident in the knowledge that I would find her because I wouldn't fucking stop until I did.

But then my phone had rung.

And the call I'd been dreading finally arrived.

The Chinmoku had found where my mother was living with her brother. They'd followed her from my house on the hill and raided her brother's home late last night. They'd managed to murder a second cousin I'd never met before the security detail I had watching my estranged family stepped in to defend anymore from being executed.

Another member of my blood killed all because of me.

But at least my men had slaughtered the two Chinmoku who'd attacked.

Only two.

It was a motherfucking insult by the leader of the faction I used to fight for. Did they think they'd only need two to take out my entire dynasty? There were countless of them and only one of me, yet I planned on painting my hands in blood until they were all extinct.

They'd made the first move in this long, overdue war.

It was my turn.

As per my request, if and when the Chinmoku ever found where my mother had hidden, my men were to get everyone out. They'd tried. They'd used negotiations and threats, but my mother had stuck in her heels.

My men had saved her life, and the lives of my cousins and whoever else was related to me. *My* men being the bane of her life.

She didn't care that she would be dead without me watching over her.

All she cared about was that my father and brother were dead, and that sin could never be absolved.

The security team called to discuss potentially drugging my family so they could be moved to safety while fast asleep.

I was about to agree when I'd looked up at congested streets, watched shopkeepers and children and happy men with loving wives, and I couldn't do it.

They had free will just like Pimlico.

Who the fuck was I to do something without their consent?

So I'd hung up and made the hardest decision of my life: to return to my family and face what I'd done. To finally talk to them and beg their forgiveness so I might keep them alive until I'd done what needed to be done.

Pimlico was not family, no matter how much my heart disagreed.

I had to make a choice then and there, and it motherfucking broke me in half.

Pim would survive without me.

But my family would die because of me.

I *never* had a choice.

At two in the morning, I'd stepped on board the Phantom, hoping to find that reliable magic where problems were halved and worries were muted but this time...nothing.

The rocking of the tide didn't calm me, the tang of salt didn't soothe me, and the open-skied horizon mocked me because there was no such thing as freedom.

It was a sadistic joke; utter make-believe to think I had the freedom to love a woman and remain living in a world where I hadn't resolved my past transgressions.

I had to put things right before I deserved anything more.

As the engines kicked in and my home sliced through the harbour out to sea, I did my best to ignore the paralyzing pain of leaving Pim behind.

My family had to come first. I owed them too big a debt to forget that. Even though all I wanted to do was find the woman who'd stolen my heart and get on my knees before her.

To tell her I might never be able to have a normal relationship, but I *needed* her. I wanted to be selfish and keep her even though I knew she didn't belong to me.

My arms were empty without her, my heart useless, my honour nothing more than scum.

That was yesterday.

This new day was just as painful.

"Morning, sir." Jolfer smiled, not knowing the torment I lived with as I marched onto the bridge.

I nodded but didn't greet him back.

I'd come for one thing only. To check he'd changed course from England to America.

Glancing at the instruments and the large nautical map pinned down with heavy magnetics on the centre table, I inhaled deep, doing my best to shed the debilitating guilt at leaving Pim behind.

Jolfer stroked the old-fashioned marine schematic he preferred. He hadn't evolved to computer screens and technology plotted directions. He preferred his sextant, tidal currents, and other seafaring tricks to get from point A to B.

If I was honest, I preferred his way, too. It was a nod to our past as men on the sea. Besides, if the Phantom ever lost power or we were stranded on a lifeboat with no Siri to tell us which direction to sail, he could look at the stars and find our way home.

Then again, so could I.

Before I met Pimlico, I spent most of my time on the bridge. It was my favourite place apart from playing cello on the deck or swimming in the sea.

Now I hated everything and everybody as each wave roll and engine purr took me farther away from her.

"All set?" I swallowed my mouthful of disgust.

She'd left to protect me.

I was leaving to protect my family.

We were both doing things for other people when all I wanted was to be with her.

Goddammit, what am I doing?

I couldn't leave her behind. I couldn't be so damn cruel.

You don't have a choice.

You have to go.

Jolfer grinned. "New course is all plotted. I was about to open her up now that we're far enough away from Monaco and her shallows."

I cleared my throat around the ball lodged there. "Fine."

Turning to his second-in-command, Jolfer said, "Let her

free, Martin."

"Roger, cap." Martin pressed a button, relayed orders to crew on the stern via the intercom, and turned a heavy key.

The whirring of motors grew louder as the colossal blades of the propellers turned from chewing the water to downright devouring it.

Painted with shame, I left the bridge and barely made it to the balustrade before I curled my fists and shot profanities at the sky.

There, in the far away distance was Monaco, growing smaller by the second.

Soon there would be no more mountains oppressing me, no more car fumes suffocating me, no more population surrounding me.

Soon Monaco would just be a bad memory left in my wake.

Pimlico would continue living without me.

I would continue living without her.

Our love was over before it ever began.

Pimlico

"SO YOU'RE THE thief, huh?"

Don't look.

Don't look.

Don't look.

I tried to obey my frantic commands, but my eyes had a mind of their own. Trading dirty concrete, I followed the baby blue shoes to navy slacks to cream chequered shirt with the Ralph Lauren polo pony logo on the breast pocket.

My gaze stopped there.

It didn't want to study the pretty rich white boy with sandy blond hair and a matching goatee. It didn't want to have yet another pain-deliverer staring in my nightmares once this was all over.

But I couldn't stop myself from cataloguing him, just as I'd catalogued so many others.

I noted his languid pose—relaxed and eager to begin.

I registered his sneer—stuck-up and confident.

I tabulated his manicured appearance—endless money and ego.

It seemed wealth had the power to rot certain people into unscrupulous citizens.

He hummed with boredom and malice. He grinned with self-righteousness and resentment. He was the younger version of Alrik.

A sob dug talons into my throat, making me choke. I lowered my head again, allowing brown tangled hair to screen me as I remained bowed on my knees on the painful dirt beneath.

"Don't want to admit your guilt, huh?" He chuckled, glancing at the three women surrounding him. His black-haired girlfriend, Miranda, smirked. "She begged for us to let her go but hasn't said a word since."

The quiet friend stood off to the side with her lips thinned and arms crossed as if she could deny what was happening. Her mousy brown hair was natural whereas her friends were bottled and bleached. Her face only had lip gloss and mascara instead of stain and rouge and her eyes...they were kind.

And terribly apologetic.

I ripped my attention from her as Harold stepped toward me. My heart started whirring while at the same time slammed to a stop. The conundrum of muscle turning supersonic as well as playing dead made me rub my chest where it lay.

"Ready for your lesson?" He cocked his head.

The nice girl shot forward, wringing her hands. "Look, this has gone on long enough. We've kept her in this alley for over half an hour. She's been nothing but apologetic. I fully believe this was a first offense, and I doubt she'll do it again."

My eyes swooped to the kind reluctance of the girl fighting my battles for me even when I'd been at fault. She gave me a nervous smile, warming to her crusade. Moving toward her friend, she said, "Let her go, Miranda. We have better things to do than—"

"*Better* things than reminding this thief not to take what isn't hers?" Miranda hissed. "I'm not going to be taken advantage of, Simone. *No one* takes what is mine." She moved forward and stroked her boyfriend's arm, looping her fingers with his. "Isn't that right, baby?"

Her boyfriend, Alrik's younger doppelganger, nodded importantly. "That's right. Just 'cause we look like easy, rich pickings for the likes of her doesn't mean we have to put up with being robbed."

"But we weren't robbed—" Simone sighed impatiently. "We got back what was ours, minus Callie who's already cancelled her credit cards while we were waiting for you. Please, Harold, let's just go. Monique? Callie?" She glanced at her other friends who watched the battle play out.

Amazingly, Callie returned Simone's smile. "I'm okay to go. Like you say, I have my cash, and my cards are cancelled. The bank is couriering new ones to me as we speak. I'm okay to call bygones, bygones."

"Great!" Simone clapped her hands, backing toward the sunshine of the busy street where rich and middle class mingled in relaxing holiday vibes. "Let's go swimming before the Versace party tonight."

"Not so fast." Miranda held up her finger. "I might consider forgetting this...."

"You will! Great." Simone beamed. "That's so nice of you, Miranda."

"*If*," Miranda continued. "That little thief stands in front of me and apologises."

I flinched as she directed her wrath at me. "Stand up, come here, tell me you're sorry and you'll never do it again, and I *might* consider telling Harold not to teach you a lesson."

I didn't move.

I didn't take her up on her offer as I was an expert in these games.

Her friends didn't know.

But I did.

Alrik toyed with me far too much for me to forget the sound of an empty invitation. He'd promise me clothes—dangling them in front of me, waiting for me to trust that this time, *this time*, he would finally let me touch and claim them.

Only for him to beat me stupid when I did.

He'd offer me fresh food, allowing the fragrances to make me drool after starving me for two days, coaxing me to hope that maybe, *maybe*, this was the time he showed mercy.

Only to dump the contents into a toilet when I reached out.

Miranda had the same cat-like meanness in her eyes.

The one that said...*come here...I want to torment you*, *little mouse.*

That nickname shot my thoughts to Elder where I suffered yet more agony.

Poor Simone with her heart as warm as the sunshine outside our dark alley brushed past Miranda with her hand outstretched to me. "Come on. You heard what she said. You're free to go if you just say sorry. And I know you're sorry. You're white as a ghost." She squatted in front of me, offering her hand, being so damn kind even after I'd inconvenienced her holiday by robbing them so callously. "I don't know why you stole, but if you don't have any money for food or if you're lost or alone, I'll gladly give you funds for whatever you need."

Oh, my God.

No one had given me such a beautiful offer before. Even Elder's generosity had come with a payment plan.

This girl...

A tear of utmost gratitude escaped my iron clad control. Unlike Miranda and her games, Simone was genuine in her proposition.

My voice shrugged off its self-imposed muteness. "You're the kindest person I've ever met."

She blushed self-consciously. "No, I'm not. Believe me. I just...there's something about you. Come on. Say you're sorry and then we can leave. I'll go with you if you'd like. Oh, I know...you can come back to my hotel for lunch. My daddy will make sure you're taken care of."

I glanced behind her at Miranda and Harold who stood snickering, watching this show as a pre-dinner snack before the main course of my pain.

I wanted to speak to Simone for as long as I was able. I would tell her anything. I would fib and lie and spin about a happier life if it meant I could avoid the impending fists and kicks.

I would even go as far as telling her the truth and accepting any charity she gave me so I could return home and never have to steal again. I would somehow get a job and repay her magnanimity then start working on stitching up the holes in my soul from leaving Elder.

"You can speak to me..." Simone coaxed. "I won't bite. I meant what I said. If you need money or help, I'll gladly give it to you."

My shoulders rolled as a flush of thankfulness filled me. Even if I suffered a beating today, I had another guardian angel willing to help me. I didn't know what I'd done to deserve it, but if all it cost were a few bruises, then I would pay it proudly.

Sitting taller, I clasped my hands in my lap and looked over her head at Miranda. If she was half as kind as Simone, I would do as she asked and apologise—for the second time.

But she wasn't.

And nothing I said would help me.

"I'm truly sorry." I forced my voice to be calm and collected. "And I want to make this right. But I could stand in front of you. I could bow before you. I could kiss your hands and apologise for days, but it wouldn't make a shred of difference."

Simone stiffened, a small gasp falling from her lips. "What are you doing?"

Something I should've done years ago.

Standing up for myself.

I was done being taunted with. There was nothing I could do to avoid what would happen, but I could say something that would hopefully haunt them when they were older and wiser and less cocky and cruel. "Want to know why it won't make a difference?" I bared my teeth. "It's because I've known people like you. I've lived with people like you. I was *sold* to people like you. Every day, I was played with, and every day, I learned to fall less and less for his tricks. Unlike you, I never hurt another person until yesterday when I walked away from the one man I've ever loved. So perhaps this is punishment for hurting him, and I'll accept it because what I did was wrong. I take full responsibility for that and for stealing. But I also know that even if I could somehow convince you of how sincere I am...I'm still going to end up bleeding."

I tensed and glowered at Miranda. "So tell your little lap dog there to do his worst. He won't break me. *No one* can break me even though plenty have tried."

Silence fell in the alley.

Tears filled Simone's eyes. "Oh, wow. You were *sold?*" She reached for my hands, but I flinched backward out of habit. She stilled, dropping her head. "I'm so sorry."

I couldn't stomach her understanding even after I'd wronged her. I opened my mouth to assure her I wasn't after her sympathy. I just had to stand up for myself for the first time in my life, but the cackle of disbelief from Miranda and Harold rang in my ears so familiar.

I was used to such a response.

I was used to being ridiculed and abused.

"Seriously, Simone!" Miranda giggled. "You believe that shit? What a little liar."

Simone lashed out and grabbed my hand. With a burst of surprising strength, she pulled me unwillingly to my aching feet. My ankles screamed from being sat on for so long, my knees indented and red from dirty gravel.

Tugging me toward her evil friend, she clutched my fingers tight. "I do believe her, and I'm going to help her. I'm taking her to see my daddy right now. He'll know what to do."

I stumbled from shock at how such a wondrous creature could be friends with such a monster as Miranda. Was she just naïve to the wily ways of maliciousness, or did she think she could change Miranda by drowning her in goodness?

Either way, I was at both their mercies as Simone brought me to stand in front of her friend. "I'm leaving with her." Looking at me, Simone ordered, "Say you're sorry, and then we can be done with this."

I lowered my eyes to the baby blue loafers of Harold and the sparkly silver sandals of Miranda. It physically pained me to talk to such beasts, but I did it for Simone, not them.

If she believed they'd stop, then perhaps I would trust her judgement over mine. I might be clouded from past experiences. I would take that first step into normalcy and treat each occurrence as separate not joined.

I tilted my chin and spoke with a bravery I didn't own. "I'm sorry for taking what wasn't mine. Rest assured, I'll never—"

Miranda's palm connected with a short sharp, slap on my cheek. "You're right, you'll never steal again 'cause you're going to remember this lesson for a lifetime, bitch!"

Heat instantly bloomed, dousing me in quick-fire pain.

I stumbled backward.

Simone cried out.

I shut down.

Pain...my old friend.

I focused on it, welcomed it. I knew it. I *was* it. I knew nothing else because of it.

"Miranda, wait!" Simone's voice sounded as if she was underwater as her fingers were ripped from mine and I was shoved heinously against the wall.

"Ready to enjoy that lesson?" Harold's face appeared, slamming my skull into the brick behind me, his breath a sour mix of alcohol and seafood.

I looked over his shoulder to a crying, begging Simone; a laughing, pleased Miranda; and the other two girls who looked petrified at how suddenly this had escalated.

They all gasped as Harold's fist connected with my belly.

Not me.

I doubled over silently.

Not one gasp.

Not one grunt.

Mute.

Like I'd always been.

Simone screamed, Miranda cheered, and the blonde girl spun around and charged out of the alley.

I couldn't blame her. Being beaten was an awful task to endure. Watching it be done with no power to stop it might even be worse.

Simone should run, too. This would scar her for life. It would ruin her goodness. It would change her too much.

Go.

After all, unlike my previous broken bones and ill healed injuries, I did deserve this. No one had told me to steal their wallets; I'd done that all on my own.

Harold's fist connected once again with my stomach. This time to the side where my appendix lived. I buckled in his hold, slithering down the wall where his leg cocked back, and his foot buried itself in my ribcage.

The pain wasn't really describable.

I'd lived with it for so long; it was like trying to describe how I breathed or pumped blood through my veins. It was a part of me and happened without conscious thought.

I huddled up, protecting my head and drawing my legs up, locking everything else out.

I no longer heard Simone screaming. I didn't listen to Miranda's goading or Harold's stream of '*Take that, bitch. Does that feel good?*'

It was silent inside and out.

My thoughts drifted to Elder. Where was he right now? Had he kept my letter? Had I hurt him all over again by telling him how I felt only to run because I didn't want to be the one to break him further?

Another kick, this one winding me until my lips parted like an ocean creature turfed from the sea.

Time lost all meaning.

Another fist landed on top of my arms as they cradled my head. My spine scraped against the wall as Harold kicked me hard enough to send me scooting forward from the blow.

Knuckles kissed my cheek, sending instant pressure into a very familiar black eye.

I wondered briefly how long he would abuse me and how ruthless he would become the more he warmed to his task.

Another strike, this time somewhere on my leg. The agony-blossom seeped instantly into my bones; a tuning fork settling fire to old injuries like a door knock to a new friend.

I didn't try to get up.

I hadn't learned how to run while being beaten.

All my instincts said to shut up, lock down, curl tight.

Another kick.

A gob of spit on my arm.

And then a new noise. Something that didn't belong.

"Stop!" the shout vaguely rippled its way into my consciousness.

"Hey!" another shout, male and authoritative.

My heart reached out with eager arms. Imaginings of Elder arriving at the perfect time. My villainous knight with his dragon ink. Had he come? Did I dare let hope surface?

I tensed for another punishment, but the looming figure of Harold suddenly vanished. Removing his oppressive shadow left me with open skies. I dared peer up through the forest of legs.

Two things slammed into me.

One, gratefulness that someone had come to my rescue.

Two, utter wretchedness that it wasn't Elder.

Miranda screeched as two men grabbed her boyfriend.

Harold cursed and swung, doing his best to get free.

But the two saviours never let go, quickly grabbing Harold's flailing arms and wrenching them behind his back. Their uniforms filled my vision with legal domination, a gold shield stitched on the sleeve, and an array of weapons, badges, and tools.

In my painful haze, I witnessed them slap handcuffs on Harold and stand squarely in resplendent livery. "Anything you do and say can be used against you. I would calm down, buddy, before you do something you regret." Their French accents were thick and commanding.

Harold spat at one of them. He missed. "Fuck you."

Before the cop could retaliate, Simone wrung her hands. "Thank goodness you're here!" She danced out of the way as the two cops nodded curtly and manhandled a very uncooperative Harold forward.

Harold kicked out, connecting with an officer's knee. "Unhand me, you son of a bitch!"

Not showing any sign of being injured, the older cop with greying hair growled. "Refusing a direct order will result in nasty consequences, sir. Kick me again, and you're in trouble." Shoving Harold against the same wall I'd been beaten against, he added, "Stand up. As I said, you're under arrest."

"Bullshit, I am!" Harold fought harder against the cuffs. "Don't you know who I am? Who my father is? You've just lost your jobs, you cunt."

"No need for profanity, sir," the younger cop muttered. He stepped back a little, eyeing his trussed-up prisoner. "You're the one who committed the crime of assaulting this young woman, not us."

"Why you fucking—" Harold's face twisted with such fury, I blanched. His mask of acrimony granted a flashback to the white mansion and Alrik slicing my tongue.

I closed my eyes, doing my best to dispel such terrible memories. When I opened them again, I noticed Callie—the blonde girl who'd run off—lurking behind the cops. She waved at Simone for her to join her.

Simone obeyed, moving toward her and smiling in thanks. However, her eyes never left mine as she said to the cops, "We need to help this poor girl. She said she was sold. That she was tormented. My family will pay if she needs to see a doctor or anything like that."

Once again, my chest swelled with gratitude.

I flinched as a cop came toward me, ducking down on his haunches. "That true, miss?"

I didn't answer.

After a few seconds of frowning at my silence, he looked back at Simone. "Don't worry. We'll take it from here and provide excellent care for her."

Ice cubes settled in my belly.

What does that mean?

"What do you mean?" Simone asked on my behalf. "I want to help."

Ignoring Simone, the younger cop with kind hazel eyes and a mop of brown hair stood from his crouch and captured my elbow.

My skin crawled beneath his touch, but I forced myself to focus on his uniform and the goodness on his face and find some element of trust to help him brace my bruised weight to stand.

"Come along, miss. We'll have someone look at you and listen to what you have to say."

I grimaced as my muscles pounded from Harold's kicks and my kneecaps seized. My ribs hurt, my eye had swollen, and my cheek still burned from Miranda's slap. Even though the cop said the right things, it was the things he *didn't* say that churned my blood into rancid butter.

There was something else. Something he hadn't said yet.

"What the fuck?" Miranda planted her hands on her hips, reminding me that her conquest to make me suffer hadn't been fulfilled. "She *robbed* us. She deserves to go to jail, not treated like some fragile flower." Stomping her foot, she demanded, "Let my boyfriend go. He was only teaching this stupid thief a lesson. This is all *her* fault."

The older cop narrowed his eyes, using the words of his colleague but in an entirely different tone. "Is that true? Did you steal from these girls?"

I waited for Miranda to condemn me, but strangely, it was the blonde this time. Now that there was no threat of bloodshed, she returned to her prissy ways. "We caught her red-handed stealing purses from our bags."

The young cop's hold on my elbow tightened, becoming more shackle than support. "Time to speak, miss. Tell us the truth."

I bowed my head. My voice became a frightened passenger, slipping down my throat to hide.

Simone answered for me. "Can't you see she has issues? What if she was stealing 'cause she has nothing? Maybe she just escaped from the men who bought her and needs our help instead of our judgment?"

"Ugh, what a crock of shit!" Miranda threw her hands up. "She's lying to you, Simone. There is no way anything she said is true."

I didn't open my mouth to defend myself. There was no point.

Harold stood taller, seeing yet another opportunity to make me pay, even if it wasn't by his fists. He became a chameleon—shedding his fierce brutality, replacing it with concerned chivalry. "I was just protecting my woman, officer. That girl is a thief and a liar. She put my girlfriend in danger. She *robbed* them. If anyone deserves to be arrested, it's her."

The young cop pulled me away from the wall, disgust replacing his compassion. "Speak now if you want to deny those accusations, miss. Otherwise, you're coming with us."

I shrivelled.

Rusty blood tainted my tongue.

My mind swam from being struck in the head.

I wanted to deny it so much. I wanted to lie, but I'd already committed one crime. I wouldn't add another to that tally.

Simone darted forward, taking my other elbow. I didn't owe this girl a thing, yet she continued to fight for me. Under normal circumstances, I would thank her profusely and beg to be her friend. I'd never met a girl like her—not in my past and not since Elder found me.

It would be so nice to have a female friend. Someone who would listen and sympathise what I'd lived through. I could talk to her about Elder and ask her opinion. She could tell me if I did the right thing by leaving, or if I'd been ridiculously stupid to walk away from the man who'd not only rescued me but given me back the will to live.

You did it for him.

I kept forgetting that part. I kept forgetting the agony I nursed was to protect him not me.

My silence irritated the officers.

Their patience ran out.

"Right, seeing as one of you is sprouting nonsense and another refuses to say a word, I guess we'll have to bring both of you in." The older policeman yanked Harold toward the busy road where rubberneckers tried to ease their rampant curiosity. "Let's go."

The young cop dragged me forward. "You, too."

I went willingly, offering no refusal. A few stumbles and limps but I didn't fight. Not that I could with the new aches and pains Harold had granted me.

Simone cried, "Wait, where are you taking her?"

"To be processed and questioned." The young cop dragged me forward. At some point in my beating, I'd lost a shoe, and I winced as pebbles bruised my sole.

The older cop placed a pair of aviator sunglasses on as he left the alley and entered the sunny street. Pedestrians changed their direction and speed as we disrupted foot traffic, cutting in front of nosy tourists all eyeing me and Harold in the grip of law enforcers.

A small sedan with the police logo sat skewed on the curb as if Simone's friend had hailed them down as they were driving down the road.

The blonde had done me a favour and stopped the beating, but now she'd taken away the chance of possibly being loaned some money and being free to find my way home.

I looked over my shoulder at Simone who stood with her arms crossed and worry on her innocent face. She waved hesitantly as I was marched away.

Would she come see me in jail? Would her father let her? Or would she forget about the poor little prisoner who tried to rob her the moment I climbed into that squad car?

Either way, it didn't matter as my head turned and my eyes kissed the beautiful ocean no longer hidden behind buildings.

The horizon glittered with sunshine glory, but I wasn't interested in the prettiness of this place. I didn't care about the schooners and spinnakers and sunbakers.

I cared about one thing.

One thing that I searched frantically for even as I tried to look away.

I shouldn't look.

I should forget—

Too late.

I couldn't stop my tattered moan as I found the spot where the Phantom had moored, floating just out of harbour congestion, a beacon for home.

Only, there was no yacht.

There was no home.

Only an empty turquoise spot like a lost tooth in a jaw of bejewelled vessels.

Elder had read my letter and agreed with me.

He'd boarded the Phantom, taken one last look at Monaco, and left.

Something fissured inside me.

Something akin to a blade filleting my heart from my ribcage. Short, intense, *blistering* in its viciousness.

I keeled over as the young cop stuffed me into the back of their vehicle.

I fought my tears, straining to keep my eyes on the horizon, begging for it to be a mistake. That I'd been looking in the wrong spot. That the Phantom was still there, and by some miracle, Elder had ignored my need to leave and was this very moment searching for me.

Please...

But as the door slammed shut and the sounds of city life and traffic were muted, I couldn't hold back the tears anymore.

This hurt more than any fist.

Worse than any kick.

This was the worst agony I'd ever endured.

The agony of a broken heart.

The pain of a sailed away lover.

ELDER

TWO OF THE worst fucking days I'd ever had.

Instead of my heart pain fading, it only grew worse.

Hour by hour, missing Pim tightened like a garrotte around my chest, just waiting for that perfect pressure to slice me clean through.

It took everything inside to stay the course and not turn around. To stop myself from wrenching the controls from Jolfer and reversing the moment Monaco vanished in our wake.

I gave up hoping for any resemblance of relief. If anything, this time sailing from society filled me with nausea at the thought of Pim out there...alone—surrounded by strangers and doing who knew what to survive.

What the *fuck* was I thinking leaving her?

I couldn't sleep.

I could barely eat.

I rarely left my position on deck—staring at the horizon, desperate to find something to heal the parts of me that Pimlico had broken.

But nothing could stop the jangling discord in my brain. The unfathomable knowledge that I'd left something priceless behind. The awful swelling in my heart that I'd done something un-fucking-forgivable.

I hated myself.

And her.

I despised both of us for letting emotions ruin a perfectly acceptable arrangement.

She should be here with me instead of by herself where I couldn't touch, talk, or guard.

Needing to keep myself focused on *why* she'd left and why I'd sailed away, I spent most of my time on the phone with the leader of the mercenaries who stood guard, unwanted by my family.

He gave me hourly reports and increased his team's size to spread out and protect even the furthest blood relatives. People I'd never even heard about, let alone owed any kind of allegiance to.

I knew that, once again, my addiction had taken something pure and sullied it.

My duty was to my mother, uncles, and aunties and approximately six to seven cousins.

That was all.

In reality, the Chinmoku probably didn't even care about the third cousins and in-laws who'd become one of us over the years.

But I did.

Not because I had a sudden craving to keep strangers alive but because of the goddamn obsession in my head.

They were mine—regardless if we had anything in common or a connection. They were linked to the web of my kin, and my brain switched from protection into something bordering old-world possession over tribe and pedigree.

I tried to stop it.

I did my best to order the leader to pull back from scouting outside homes of people who didn't even know my name.

But I couldn't.

If I wasn't allowed Pimlico, then I would do whatever was in my power to watch over everyone—regardless if it was an addiction, obligation, or appropriate.

I stood on the deck staring at the pink horizon and rubbed at the spot where my heart used to be. No seagull squawk or midnight swim could fix what I feared would forever be broken.

I should be sick with worry at the thought of my mother in danger and riddled with nerves at the impending family reunion where no one wanted me.

But all I could think about was Pim.

Pim.

Pim.

I clutched the phone, willing it to ring, so I had a distraction from the way my heart thumped lifeless and accusing, hanging itself on a gristly rib.

Every beat made me growl with guilt. Every palpitation a reminder of no more dinners or pickpocketing lessons. No more falling in love.

Where was she now?

Had she found someone to help?

Was she on her way to England?

Was she already there?

I liked that most of me hoped she'd already found her way home and was back where she belonged. However, I hated myself because another part of me—a dark, disturbed jealous part—hoped she hadn't.

That she needed me even after walking away.

That she hurt just as much because we were apart with no way of contact. No cell phone. No email. No physical way of tracking the other down.

You sailed away.

You chose blood over heart.

And for what?

To be cursed all over again and ordered to leave? To be kicked out and called No One? To remain lonely for the rest of my days?

Shit!

My free hand curled around the banister, wanting to wring the wood and brass for its hypocrisy. For *my* hypocrisy. The awful conclusion that I'd sailed away under the guise of doing the right thing...when really, I'd done the fucking opposite.

She. Left. Me.

She'd decided that in order for us both to survive, we had to end whatever was building between us. She was the courageous warrior in this scenario, and I was the spineless wretch who would never forgive himself for taking the easy way out just because he was scared fucking shitless of hurting her.

Goddammit, what have I done?

The phone rang in my hand as the emotional landslide slammed into me.

I owed Pim just as much as my family.

If not more.

She'd given me love when all the others had taken it away.

And what had I done? I'd allowed her to take that love away under pretence of saving me from myself.

Fuck that.

And fuck her.

I shook with rage as my heart finally started doing its job and woke me up after three and a half days of grief-stricken listlessness.

Selix's voice ripped into my thoughts, echoing through the phone. "Ready for our sparring session?"

I blinked, slamming back into my body. Seeing the waves and clouds and glinting yacht around me. We'd arranged to fight until we either passed out or someone was seriously injured.

Last night, when we'd made the appointment, nothing had sounded better because even my cello couldn't stop my thoughts from returning to Pim.

I'd hoped pain would do the trick.

But now, I knew better.

There was only one way that pain would go away, and it

wasn't through fighting or killing or being the perfect son to a mother who'd cursed me.

It was by being the perfect man to a woman who loved me regardless of who I was. A woman who said yes when everyone else had said no—including myself.

I was done feeling guilty for everything that I was.

I was through giving myself excuses.

I couldn't pretend anymore.

I couldn't do it.

Any of it.

Unless I have her.

Squeezing the phone, I marched into my room. "Our fight has been postponed."

"Oh?" Selix grumbled. "Why exactly?"

Shrugging out of the clothing I hadn't changed since leaving Monaco, I grabbed a handful of fresh items and stormed to the bathroom. "Because I said so."

"That's some reason, Prest. Never took you for a cryptic son of a bitch."

Wrenching on the shower, I ignored him and said the words I'd been desperate to say ever since I made the worst mistake of my life. "Ready the helicopter. I'm going back to Monaco. Immediately."

Pimlico

I'D NEVER BEEN so nervous in my life.

Sure, I'd been in situations that made me scared, petrified, and wishing for death. But I'd never been in one where I jittered with nerves rather than outright terror.

I knew the police wouldn't physically abuse me—*or at least, I hope.* They weren't criminals—*or at least, not all of them.* I would be safe here as long as I cooperated—*or at least, until I'm sentenced.*

Fear came on the back of that thought, becoming equal hitchhikers on my spine.

Get it together. Stop thinking. Just stay quiet and get through this.

Taking my own advice, I kept my chin high as the police car pulled to a stop and I was helped from the vehicle. I didn't look at Harold who cursed and kept commanding them to release him. I remained docile as they escorted us into a large building full of bustling officers, the sounds of printers and phones, and the rich scent of metal handcuffs and pungent coffee.

The policemen who'd arrested us waved over two fellow crime fighters from their current tasks. They nodded and came to collect us.

The rapid-fire questions and answers were delivered in

French. I'd become used to the sounds of French accents while exploring Monaco with Elder, but this was the first time I wished I spoke the language so I knew what I was about to face.

I stood silently as Harold entered into his own tirade, forcing another officer to come over and try to keep the peace.

As quickly as the conversation began, it was over.

Hands from a new male officer took my elbow and nodded at his colleague while another took Harold.

With a livid expression at me, Harold growled. "This isn't over, cow. When my father hears about this—"

The officer holding him jerked him into silence. He was carted off while I did my best to ignore his threat and was guided to a different area of the station to be processed.

No one spoke to me as I was shuffled through a barricade only opened by a swipe of my escort's badge and keypad press. I tripped as my one sandal stuck to the scuffed linoleum, and the officer's grip tightened to help me balance, activating a new bruise I'd forgotten about.

My vision only half worked—thanks to Harold giving me a black eye, and in some morbid way, I was glad I'd endured pain worse than this because it allowed me to forget about the hot swelling in my joints and thundering discomfort in my muscles.

All I wanted to focus on was this corridor and this moment, so I could understand better just how much trouble I was in.

Turning left at the bottom of the hallway, my uniformed guide opened another door and pushed me through. Marching me to a high-top desk where a female officer stood shuffling paperwork, he muttered in French then pushed me forward.

She nodded but didn't come to grab me. Instead, I was left standing alone with my wrists cuffed, waiting until she'd finished her task while the man who brought me here disappeared out the door.

Finally, she looked up, scanned me from head to toe, and

motioned me to follow her into yet another room. This was one smaller but very bright and clean.

She was younger than the rest of the officers—no doubt fairly new to this career and not yet jaded by thugs and thieves.

She didn't bother asking any questions, just nodded kindly and pointed at the wall where a height graph had been painted. "Please stand there. Don't smile."

I did as I was told and blinked as the flash from a camera blinded the rest of my wonky vision.

"Great. Now come here, please."

Blinking a few times, I moved toward a computer station with a multitude of wires and equipment linked to it. She pushed a chair toward me.

For the next few minutes, I sat still and didn't make a sound as she took my hands and pressed each finger against a pad that somehow scanned my prints and appeared instantly on the screen.

Tapping away on the keyboard, she entered my height and whatever other information had come to her about my circumstances, slowly taking me from unknown citizen to catalogued felon.

My eyes prickled as my mug-shot was dragged onto the file and attached in place. Pressing the printer icon, she smiled then headed over to retrieve the warm freshly inked paper. A lot of areas for details such as my name, personal description, and other things remained blank.

She hadn't asked a single question. Almost as if—

The door opened, and another officer appeared.

—she'd been doing the paperwork for another person to do the questioning.

The new arrival was a woman dressed in a black suit with an A-line skirt, crisp white blouse, and a gold shield sewn over her breast pocket.

The woman who'd processed me said something in French, handed over my newly created file, and returned to her post at the desk.

Turning in my chair, I faced yet another stranger and tensed, ready for the interrogation that all good movies showed. Only, her eyes fell to my handcuffed wrists, and she tutted. "They should've been off by now, don't you agree?"

I didn't know what to agree with.

This was all so bizarre to my realm of comfort.

Not that I had a normal range of comfort anymore.

Pulling a key from her pocket, she motioned for me to stand then quickly unlocked the metal. She smiled as the shackles fell away and placed them on the desk. "Better?"

My eyes widened—or as much as they could with bruising swelling them.

These women treated me as a human being rather than a lowlife member of society who'd broken the rules. I kept waiting for the strike to my head or the disdained quips about how I'd screwed up my life.

Not this civil processing.

The older woman ran a hand over her cheek, touching up her immaculate makeup that'd been artfully applied to look as if she wore none at all. As if the pretty shadows over her eyes and pinky hue on her lips were natural.

She was handsome with a no-fuss brown bob and simple gold chain with a medallion and some saint dangling from it.

Clutching my file to her chest, she opened her arm in invitation. "Shall we?"

Shall we what?

When I didn't reply, she moved in no-nonsense heels and opened the door to the corridor. "Let's go have a little chat and get the basic stuff out of the way then I'll summon the doctor, okay? My name is Carlyn Grey, and I'll be in charge of your case from now on." She pursed her lips sympathetically. "You're not looking so good, you poor thing. And you've lost a shoe, too. Oh dear. I'll make sure to find something in the meantime."

I froze, once again gobsmacked at the kindness in her tone. Had I lumped all humans, male and female, into an unfriendly light because of my past?

Was that a product of Alrik's lessons or my mother's upbringing?

Either way, this woman reminded me of a kindly aunt inviting me to unload my woes rather than the upholder of the law whose job it was to take away my freedom.

Even though I wished upon a thousand wishes that I could rewind time and never *think* about stealing—I had to face the consequences.

Elder...

I'd successfully kept him out of my thoughts, but his gorgeous face appeared with such vibrancy, I gasped at agonising memories and a bone-crushing desire to be with him.

I *needed* him.

Not just for this terrible situation but because I couldn't breathe without having him near.

When I didn't reply, Carlyn Grey leaned forward. "Do you need some water? I can't give you any painkillers for your injuries until the doctor has assessed you, but if you're feeling faint, I can order some food."

Food?

That did sound good. I managed a small nod and drifted toward her.

With yet another kind smile, she marched ahead and guided me down the nondescript corridor to another door—this one with a label stating it was Interview Room Four. "Right this way."

She held open the entrance and waited until I'd passed her before closing it and taking a seat in the black plastic chair. A large table separated her from a spare seat which I hesitantly took and winced as my bones took on the agonising job of realigning to sit and not stand.

She watched me. "You're not looking so good." Using a walkie-talkie resting on the table, she commanded, "Bring some water and a sandwich into IR Four, please."

A crackled response managed to overshadow the sudden

growling in my stomach.

A sandwich had never sounded so great.

Smoothing the paperwork before her, she looked at me intently. "These questions are just a formality. The moment we're done, I'll call for the doctor and get you sorted. If at any point you're not feeling well, tell me." She narrowed her eyes with the first hint of warning. "If you cooperate, tell the truth, and help me get this done, it will only take a few minutes."

Swallowing, sending a message to my voice not to hide this time, I nodded.

"Great." Pulling a pen from her breast pocket, she pressed the nib against the first empty box. "Are you ready to begin?"

She'd asked so softly it painted a scenario as if I was a child lost in a busy supermarket and she was merely trying to find out who I was to return me to a loved one.

I hung my head, my fingers dirt covered and scraped from clawing at the pavement while Harold kicked me.

I wished talking was easier. I wished it was first nature to answer when spoken to. But it took such effort to trust a stranger enough to give them my voice.

Carlyn Grey didn't lose her temper, though—waiting patiently as I glanced up from my tangled hair and sighed deeply. I had to get over this. Sitting straighter, I winced as my side throbbed. "Yes, I'm ready."

"Good." She smiled encouragingly. Glancing at the page, she asked, "Name?"

This was it.

The moment where I ceased to be Pimlico and returned to my previous existence. I wasn't quite ready to embrace my full name. I wasn't quite strong enough to be a normal citizen with work worries and tax obligations. But ready or not...my journey back into the light had begun.

"Tasmin Blythe."

The officer acted as if my name was given out freely every second of every day. And why shouldn't she? A name was the most common thing shared. But to me...she was the first in so very long to hear it.

I should've told Elder.

I shouldn't have held so much of myself back from him. All he'd asked in return for my safety was to know who I was. Why didn't I share the name of my favourite stuffed rabbit when I was a child? Why didn't I tell him how I'd read epic fantasies by torchlight of warrior fae and princesses, secretly wishing for my own magical fairytale?

I wanted to tell him now.

The urge was overwhelming to the point of bursting with the desire to sit him down, open up, and spill years upon years of hiding.

My heart stole all the bruises on my limbs and centred them in one location. I needed a bandage for the agony.

"Nationality?" Carolyn looked up expectantly.

"English."

"Address?"

"Apartment Three, Century Building, Pollyworth Road, London."

Just saying that brought back the taste of butter chicken from my local Indian takeaway and the scent of pink roses from my neighbour's window boxes. The sound of my mother's disapproval as I flew up the stairs rather than walked like a lady, and the heaviness of my backpack filled with textbooks from school.

"Age?"

I paused. How old was I? *I was eighteen when I was stolen….*

"Twenty."

I shuddered to think I'd spent the rest of my teenage life—the years of innocence and reckless fun—locked up being sexually abused. I'd never get those years back. I'd never find that innocence again.

My breath turned raspy.

I hugged myself as a nefarious chill descended.

Carlyn noticed, her brown bob swinging around her jaw. Her hazel eyes warmed in pity. "Know what? I've got enough for now. Let's get that doctor's visit sorted, shall we?"

I didn't look up, too swamped with old memories.

* * * * *

The rest of the day was a blur.

Officer Grey guided me into another room—this one with a medical gurney covered in pale blue sheets and a simple workstation for a doctor to dispense their advice. Waiting until I'd winced my way onto the bed, Carlyn fastened a small handcuff around my wrist to the silver frame.

I stiffened at the cold bite on my skin.

"Policy, I'm afraid." She shrugged apologetically. "I'm going to leave you alone for a bit while I arrange for the doctor. I can't leave you unattended and not be restrained."

The fact she explained and acted as if she regretted cuffing me spoke volumes about her nice nature.

I forced a smile. "I understand."

She left me to my heartache, reappearing a little while later with another female in tow. Carlyn left the moment she'd given instructions to perform an overall check-up, granting me privacy.

The exam started off fine.

The doctor—after telling me her name was Michelle Annaz—asked questions on where I'd been hit and kicked. She politely asked to inspect me and pulled up my dress to reveal the fresh contusions rapidly blooming over my hips and thighs. She ran her hands over my joints and ligaments, and while I locked my jaw to prevent squirming away from her unwanted touch, her face slowly fell from polite professionalism to concern.

She eyed my many scars.

She traced my many abuse-given imperfections.

Unlike Carlyn Grey, her eyes held deeper laugh lines, and silver threads decorated her dark hair. Her tanned skin spoke of an island life on this party destination, but the shrewd calculation in her gaze said she missed nothing.

She certainly didn't miss anything regarding me.

Oh, no...

Removing her rubber gloves, Dr Annaz stepped back. For a moment, she didn't speak, but then with a thread of unquestionable authority, she said calmly, "You've been hurt a lot in your past."

It wasn't a question, so I didn't respond.

Not that I needed to.

My body told the truth.

Crossing her arms, she murmured, "What you tell me can remain off the record and be protected by client-doctor confidentiality, but it can also be used to help your case. The officer said you were beaten by the boyfriend of the girl you tried to rob, is that correct?"

I looped my fingers together and squeezed, ignoring the gravel abrasions on my palm. "Yes."

"And before that? Do you want to tell me how you have bones nodules that are self-healed breaks without the aid of a cast or other medical supervision?"

No, I don't want to tell you.

Yes, I do want to tell you.

God, I don't know.

I was *sick* of hiding.

Perhaps if I'd given more of myself to Elder when he'd asked, he would've gotten what he needed to tolerate my presence for longer.

Maybe questions weren't something to be feared anymore but a tool to somehow get better.

Rubbing my face with one hand while the other remained cuffed to the bed, I sighed heavily. "If I tell you, what will happen to me?"

Would I be sent to a psychiatric ward instead of jail?

Would my mother be told in explicit detail? Details I never wanted her hearing?

Dr Annaz softened. Moving forward, she perched on the bed beside me. She didn't touch me, but her presence was comforting. "You get to decide. If you tell me in strictest confidence, I can provide advice that comes from years of study and experience, and we can leave it there. Or, if you feel you're ready to take back whatever was stolen from you, then I'd probably suggest including Officer Grey and letting us help you."

"Help me by putting me in prison?"

She shook her head. "Sometimes, we endure single events, and each event must be dealt with as such—either earning forgiveness or consequences. And other times, the things we survive aren't single events at all but are joined in sequence that give an explanation to things that before had no answer." She sighed before saying, "I won't tell you what to do and I can't tell you what will happen if you make either choice, but at some point, you need to trust that not everyone is out to hurt you."

I didn't know what part of her wise paragraph broke me.

Only that it did.

One moment, I sat stiff and stoic.

The next, I crumpled into silent sobs.

Forgiveness or consequence.

Single events or linked by sequence.

At some point...you need to trust.

I wanted so badly to trust.

Perhaps, it's time to start...

Speaking around my tears, I admitted, "I was imprisoned for two years after being sold into sexual slavery."

That sentence.

That confession.

It was the final blockade in the dam of agony.

Michelle Annaz took my hand and squeezed. That was all. She squeezed and stayed silent as I trembled with the knowledge that more people than just Elder knew now.

My ugly truth was out, and this woman treated me as if I was so, so strong for surviving it.

Dr Annaz asked her first question: "How?"

And I answered.

The rest of her questions turned into bees buzzing in my

skull.

How long?

Where?

Who?

Why?

What was done to me?

My answers were the nectar those bees fed upon, slowly sweeping up the pollen that'd suffocated me for so long, flying away to churn into honey.

I was brutally honest and held nothing back, doing my best to stop the memories from having power over me.

And by the time I'd finished, I had no idea how much of the day had passed.

My head ached from the emotional purging, and my stomach had skipped past hunger into vacant emptiness.

"I have one last question for you, Tasmin. And I need you to think about your answer very carefully."

I looked at Dr Annaz and the strictness on her weathered face. I waited for her to finish.

"Do you wish this to stay between us? Or are you happy for me to include Officer Grey?"

Once again, a question with two very different outcomes.

If my tale remained in this room, then my thievery and slavery would forever remain two separate events with no explanation about how or why I'd done what I did. But if I let others know, then their scolding would most likely turn to sympathy. They would have a deeper understanding that this wasn't a separate event but part of a sequence—a sequence Elder had been a part of, and now these two women who'd taken the time to talk to me.

I didn't do it for sympathy.

I did it for truth.

"Tell her. I want her to know."

Without a word, Dr Annaz stood and disappeared out the door.

Ten minutes later, she returned with Carlyn Grey.

Both women gave me a gentle smile as Carlyn unlocked the cuff around my wrist and nodded at Dr Annaz. "I'll escort you to the hospital and remain there while the tests are done."

"Tests?" My eyes bugged. "What tests?"

Dr Annaz patted my shoulder. "I came here to treat a few scratches and bruises, Tasmin, but you need much better care than that."

"I do?"

She sighed sadly. "You do."

* * * * *

The tests were invasive.

They brought back terrible memories and broke some of the glued pieces of me.

Elder's doctor, Michaels, had been the one who'd sewn up my tongue and put me back together again. He'd been gentle and patient and understanding.

These new doctors, with a multitude of accents and machinery, asked probing questions about my periods, internal organs, and other terribly private things.

A gynaecologist was enlisted to see if I had permanent damage after I admitted what Alrik used on me. Multiple x-rays were used to determine if I had any broken bones.

Blood was taken.

ECGs were recorded.

Hours went by between answering yet more questions, submitting to whirring machines, and waiting, shivering with nerves on starched sheets, for yet another consultation.

By the time Carlyn Grey approached me with a tired smile and an air of completion, the sky was black with night, and she held out a third cup of coffee.

Between the first and second cup, she'd told me I'd dealt with everything better than she could've hoped, and she was in awe of what a human body could withstand. I didn't think she enjoyed hearing my tales of the tortures I'd endured, but the evidence was plain upon my skin.

"Well, we're done." She sat heavily in the chair by my bed

with a long sigh.

It'd been a long day…for both of us.

"The results of your blood work will be back tomorrow, and Dr Annaz is getting a second opinion on your internal examination."

I wanted to ask why they needed a second opinion…*what's wrong?*

But she continued, "For now, you're patched up from your recent injuries, and another officer has interrogated the culprit who hurt you. His girlfriend is pressing charges, but as there are two other witnesses who aren't, we'll hold off writing you up for another twenty-four hours until we have confirmed reports and know where to go from here."

Taking a sip of her coffee, she added, "Seeing as you're still in my custody and by your own admittance have nowhere to go, you'll spend the night here. Rest, have some dinner, and I'll come get you first thing in the morning." Her eyes met mine. "A guard will be posted outside your door so you don't run."

"I won't run."

She smiled. "I know. You're a good girl, Tasmin. We'll get this mess straightened out."

No matter how many times I'd been called Tasmin today, it still sounded wrong.

I was Pimlico…for better or for worse.

Carlyn finished her coffee. "Once we get your results back tomorrow, and know where we stand with the case, it might be time to start tracking down a family member, don't you? Find a way to get you home—if we can just chalk this incident up to a misdemeanour."

Home.

Free.

Safe.

Even though it was bittersweet.

Even though I wished it was Elder taking me the final way.

Even though there were so many unknowns.
I burst into tears of gratitude.

ELDER

I COULDN'T FIND her.

Out of all the cities in all the countries in the world, I preferred Monaco the best and not because of the tax haven and rich safety surrounding the French Rivera. I loved it for its air of individualism and respect. No one had to bow to anyone.

Now, the place was on my shit list.

How could Pimlico vanish so spectacularly?

Not one café worker had seen the girl I described.

Not one shopkeeper admitted to seeing her loiter on the streets.

I travelled to train stations and ferry terminals and the airport.

Between Selix and I, we covered most areas I could think of...and *nothing*.

Darkness had fallen, and I finally had to admit that my body needed sustenance and my mind needed sleep.

This missing her devoured me from the inside out, and if I didn't start being smart, I'd lose her for good.

My phone buzzed.

Selix: *In the business district. A security guard said he saw a girl matching Pim's description being shoved into a police car.*

Christ!

I was an imbecile.

Why hadn't I thought to check the police stations around town? It should've been as obvious as checking the points of exit in this damn country.

Clutching my phone, I prepared to charge back into the night and ransack every precinct I could. Only...

Why do the leg-work when I had a better way?

Pimlico

THE NEXT DAY brought the results of my medical tests.

It was not a good day.

Dr Annaz was the one to deliver the news.

At the start, I listened remotely, as if she reeled off bodily complications about another person and not me. She repeated what I already knew: that I had early onset arthritis, a minor hearing problem from being cuffed around the head, and vision that would most likely need glasses thanks to all the tricks he'd played.

That was nothing.

That was livable.

The last thing she told me was not.

By the time she finished, I wrapped arms around my womb and fought the rageful tears threatening to flow.

I thought I was done hearing things that could hurt me.

I was wrong.

So wrong.

Alrik, it seemed, had scarred me so bad internally, he'd ruined any chances of me conceiving. The items he'd used, the incorrect lubrications he'd smeared, had turned me infertile.

I can never get pregnant.

I didn't need those terrible injections he gave me. I didn't need to ever worry about contraception again.

I was barren. Useless. *Empty.*

I'd never even thought about children until the moment I was told I could never have any.

It was as if a dream I'd never dreamt turned out to be a reality I wanted more than anything. Only to be told I had to remain in this nightmare.

It was surreal.

It was unthinkable.

It was as if Alrik had reached from the grave and stolen yet more from me.

I was left alone for a time to process yet another tragedy, and by the time I was escorted back to the police station, I had vowed an oath never to think about it.

To forget how it felt to be told I could never have something I suddenly desperately wanted and get used to the idea without having a panic attack. Who cared if my femininity had been ripped to shreds by a monster I wanted to murder all over again?

I was still alive.

Still here.

Still *winning.*

Luckily, the interrogation kept my mind on other things.

Just like yesterday, my treatment was unlike any of the police shows I'd seen. There was no good cop, bad cop. No slamming hands on metal tables or being peppered with hardnosed questions. Just the same courteous kindness and respect that I still couldn't get used to.

My sundress wasn't warm enough against the station's vapid air-conditioning, and somewhere along the line, someone had given me a cosy knitted cream jumper that acted as a hug as I huddled deeper and deeper into my chair.

I'd been fed, showered, given a new pair of shoes, and the bruises on my skin had darkened to a nice mosaic that even Alrik would've been proud of.

The first part of the day's questioning hadn't been easy

because I honestly had no answers.

Where had I been kept?

How had I been taken there?

Where was the place where I was sold?

All I could tell them was my cell had been a white mansion on a hill, I'd been taken by private plane, and I'd been sold to men with paper mache masks at an event called the QMB.

Other questions were dangerously personal.

Who had saved me and where had they gone?

Why hadn't I contacted my mother the moment I was free?

Who had sewed up my tongue after what had happened to me?

Those, I hedged.

I refused to answer with the truth and instead gave half-starts and nonsense-rambles.

I didn't mention Elder's name once.

There was no way I would get him into trouble—especially after everything he'd done for me. I merely told them a good Samaritan with money had found me, taken me from my master, and paid for my medical upkeep.

I definitely didn't tell them about pulling the trigger and shooting Alrik or the god-awful sound of Darryl's neck snapping in Elder's strong hands.

Those were secrets for a reason, and I protected them with all my might.

Just like the unmentionable that I was no longer able to have a son or daughter.

Other questions I threw myself wholeheartedly into.

What was my mother's name?

Her date of birth?

Anything I could give them to find her faster?

By afternoon, a Caesar salad was delivered, and I was left alone to eat while my answers were undoubtedly processed in their system.

I expected more of the same after eating, but Carlyn

arrived, sombre and strained. The usual sweetness on her face had been replaced with stark tension.

Wait…what's happened?

I shifted in my chair, pulling my jumper tight around me.

Her eyes pinched as she sat in the chair in front of me, resting the file she carried on the table. "Hello, Tasmin."

I jolted.

Partly from that name still not belonging to me and mostly because her tone filled me with dread. "What is it? What's wrong?"

For an insane moment, I wished she'd call me Pim.

I hated the name Pimlico for so many reasons, but I felt more in tune with that girl than this new imposter pretending to be Tasmin. I needed to find some courage even if it came from false places. "Why are you looking at me like that?"

Officer Grey spread slightly trembling fingers over the file. "I have some news."

I couldn't tear my eyes away from the logo on the top of the paperwork followed by a grainy photo of a woman I didn't think I'd ever see again.

My mother.

Shakes took hold of me with a cruelty I couldn't deny. I wanted to demand she tell me everything, but once again, muteness became my shield.

My throat closed up.

My eyes blurred.

My heart galloped.

What is it?

Tell me!

She patted the file. "Do you know anything about your mother? Since you last saw her the night of her charity gala?"

I shook my head, unable to unglue my eyes from that tiny grainy photograph.

Mum…

Carlyn's shoulders slouched a little, condolences already filling her gaze.

I stiffened.

I couldn't hold back the question. "Is…is she dead?" Numbness followed on the syllable of that awful, awful question, already protecting me from the answer.

If she was dead, I was truly alone. If she was dead…how did that make me feel? I loved her because she was my mother. But I didn't necessarily like her. But at the same time, she represented my future, my past, and my one chance at finding somewhere safe to recover without relying on Elder or his magical floating palace called the Phantom.

Carlyn gave me half a smile. "No, she's not dead."

My lungs stopped working. Wasn't that good news? Why did she sit there almost afraid to tell me the rest? When neither of us spoke, she murmured, "Something…happened when you were taken."

My mind raced ahead, trying to figure out what she was about to say.

What happened? What could my mother have been capable of—

A blizzard howled down my spine.

I sucked in a harsh breath.

No.

It's not possible.

All this time, I'd hoped my snatching was an opportunist deviant who spied a naïve little girl and saw dollar signs instead of a human life. But what if my mother—in all her studies and work with paedophiles and criminals—had somehow embraced the darker part of her psyche?

What if she'd sold me as an experiment?

What if she'd given me up to a monster to study my survival from afar?

The idea was preposterous and far too farfetched, but it didn't stop the concept from morphing into a terrible nightmare of her using me as a guinea pig on how a white girl with a middle-class upbringing could survive rape and torture and mind games.

How much I could endure before I broke...

"...I'm so sorry, Tasmin."

I looked up, shocked to find Carlyn had spoken—had delivered the truth—and I hadn't paid attention. Fear that she wouldn't repeat the news had me throwing myself forward, grabbing her hands with mine. "*What* did you say?"

She frowned at where I touched her but didn't reprimand. "I said I'm sorry that you'll be alone. That your family apartment was sold, your furniture auctioned off, and your childhood dismantled because of what your mother did."

The shakes were back a thousand times worse. "And what did my mother do?"

She blanched a little before pushing the paperwork toward me. "See for yourself." She lowered her voice. "A crime is a crime, and I will never be sympathetic to those paying for what they've done, but the woman in me understands why your mother did what she did. After meeting you, I can see why."

See why what?

My fingers scrambled at the paper, tugging it close and smoothing out the curled-up corners. My mother's photo was over-exposed and pixelated, but one proper look showed me everything I needed to.

It was a mug shot.

The board in front of her stated the date of her arrest, her height, weight, and date of birth.

Her face, so similar to mine with its button nose, high cheekbones, and wide eyes, was harsh and almost proud. She didn't stare into the camera as a criminal—hunched with remorse and pissed at what her future held.

Hell, no.

She stared victorious and vindictive as if daring the photographer to take away her accomplishments.

Why was she arrested?

What did she do?

In no universe could I understand my mother throwing away her career. She worked in the prisons out of sick professional curiosity on what made rapists and murderers tick, but she always returned home at night. She'd go stir-crazy locked up with the same people she studied like rats in an experiment.

My eyes reluctantly left her photo, my fingers drifting to her face as if needing to keep contact even while I read the brief report.

Prisoner: 890776E

Name: Sonya Blythe

Summary of crime as follows:

Sonya Blythe filed a report on the 3rd of November 2014 stating her daughter, Tasmin Blythe, had been kidnapped from her popular charity ball held at the Baglioni Hotel near the suburb of Pimlico, London. An investigation was on-going but to no success. After the initial interviewing of all the guests at the charity ball, no new leads were forthcoming, and the case stalled.

I glanced at Carlyn. It wasn't news to her that I was that girl. That my slave name was Pimlico after where I'd been stolen and that the missing person file on me could be closed thanks to my reappearance.

She knew that because she'd already uncovered the file on my disappearance. It was yet another reason she was on my side instead of persecuting me for stealing. She knew I was telling the truth.

I kept reading.

The case for Tasmin Blythe's whereabouts is still on-going. Due to her own impatience in this matter, Sonya Blythe admitted in her confession that she felt let down by the police and took justice into her own hands.

Oh, my God.

My hands shook as I read faster.

After two months of research, which she willingly handed over to authorities, Sonya Blythe uncovered the man responsible for her daughter's kidnapping was a Mr. Keith Kewet. A man who had a reputation for under-aged girls and a flashy lifestyle that couldn't be maintained by his regular city planning job. Instead of alerting the task force in charge of her daughter's disappearance, Sonya Blythe took it upon herself to subdue and imprison Keith Kewet in order to extract answers.

I slapped a hand over my mouth.

Sonya Blythe kept Keith Kewet alive for four days using her own techniques to extract the truth. She used a lie detector test from her contacts at work and enlisted other unsatisfactory methods disclosed during her confession. During this time, she managed to gather the truth that he was the culprit for her daughter's disappearance, where he had taken her, and recorded all interactions as evidence.

As part of the video log Sonya Blythe recorded, she said she would turn him over to authorities in the morning, and hopefully, the London police could find her daughter and bring her home.

How had she done this?

Why had she done this?

I didn't think she cared about me...yet, she'd hunted down my killer. She'd found him. She'd done something the police hadn't been able to do.

Unfortunately, later that evening, Keith Kewet managed to escape the apartment in which he was being imprisoned, and Sonya Blythe chased after him.

She struck him with a well-aimed bookend to the back of his head, and he fell down the apartment steps. Neighbours heard the commotion and man's screams and left their homes to investigate. There are multiple reports that Sonya Blythe then bludgeoned Keith Kewet to death, all while cursing him for taking her daughter. Despite his breaking a leg when he fell down the stairs and being unable to run, she didn't stop hitting him until he was dead.

My eyes glassed with tears.

She'd killed...for me.

Instead of turning herself in to authorities, Sonja Blythe grabbed her passport, gave the video-tape of his confession to a neighbour, and jumped on a plane to Germany where a sex trafficking ring called the QMB, Quarterly Market of Beauties, was supposedly where her daughter was sent to be sold.

A few hours after her crime was reported, Sonya Blythe's passport was frozen, and German authorities tracked her down upon her arrival into Munich. She was expatriated to England and found guilty by her own admission and sentenced to seventeen years with no parole for the manslaughter of Keith Kewet.

Authorities, both English and German, did their best to track down the QMB but to no avail. Both the trafficking ring and Tasmin Blythe are still yet to be found.

Tears plopped onto the file, turning the paper translucent and the ink glowing with every hardship my mother endured.

How could I think so terribly of her?

How could I ever believe she didn't love me?

She'd committed *murder* for me.

She threw away her life, her career, her future all because she couldn't let me go.

My heart, that'd somehow retained some of its childish whimsy—even buried beneath the hate I'd had for her and the survival I'd armoured myself with—howled in despair.

Carlyn reached over and patted my fingers still tracing my mother's photo. "It's okay. At least we know where she is and that she's alive."

A tangled laugh fell from my lips. "Like mother, like daughter. She's in prison, and I'm about to be." I looked up. "Could we at least share a cell? Could I be sent to England to serve my sentence?"

She smiled in pity. "Your mother is in a maximum security for murderers. Your petty theft isn't enough to make you join her."

How strange that I was both relieved and disappointed.

Sniffing back my jumbled emotions, I said, "Thank you for finding her for me." Looking once more at my mother's mug-shot, I slid the file back to Carlyn even though I wanted nothing more than to keep it and break her out of jail. "What will happen next? Am I officially under arrest? Seeing as I have no home or mother to go back to, I suppose I'd better start planning my future."

Carlyn gave me a crooked smile as she slipped the paperwork neatly into a folder beside her.

And just like that, my mother was gone again.

The moment I was free and back in England, I would visit her. I would hold her hands and kiss her cheeks and thank her on my knees for doing her best to find me. I would beg her forgiveness for the awful, *awful* things I'd thought about her. And I would wait until she'd served her time and then find us somewhere to live, just us...together and far away from the life that had been so cruel in splitting our family apart.

And Elder?

I would continue to nurse a broken heart and hope to God he was happy...wherever he was.

Carlyn cleared her throat. "Well, I have a question for you before we go down that path."

My head snapped up. "What question?" And why did her voice turn coy with suspicion?

"The man you said who rescued you. You said he was wealthy."

I nodded slowly, my hackles rising, ready to defend Elder. "I did."

"And you still refuse to say his name?"

"I do."

"Is he a member of the law?"

I frowned. "What?"

"Is he in any way associated with a police force, FBI, or member of overseas law enforcement?"

I shook my head. "There are many things I don't know about him. I don't believe so, but he might...why?"

She cocked her head, studying me for lies.

She wouldn't find any answers because I was as blind as her on this topic.

"Could the men who took you have ways to hack into the police servers?"

I froze. "*What?* What does that mean?" I hunched, looking into the empty corners of the room. "You think someone is *tracking* me?"

She tried to soothe me unsuccessfully. "No. However...something strange happened overnight."

I didn't like strange. I *hated* strange. "Strange how?"

"Well, your file was accessed by two different sources. Illegally, I might add, outside our servers and through a crack in our firewall."

The knitted jumper I'd been given couldn't ward off the ice spider legging its way down my spine. "What does that mean?"

"It means someone hacked into our data-base and instead of ransacking our files or looking at anything they wanted, they merely stole an electronic copy of your information and left, patching up the code as they did. Our technology crime divisions are already searching for the culprits but without much hope. The only thing they've been able to confirm is your file was accessed by two different people within hours of each other." She narrowed her gaze. "No explanation or answers on who could've done that?"

I huddled in the chair, suspecting everything and everyone. "None."

Elder was great at many things, so hacking might be one of them. That would explain one invasion, but why two? Who was the other person?

I didn't know how these things worked or what could be done to find the infiltrators. "What were they searching for?"

Carlyn rolled her neck as if she'd had a tough night and only expected more where I was concerned. "We don't know, but it seems as though one hack was thanks to an alert on the name QMB and another was a red flag on your name."

She sighed full of frustration, repeating as if she couldn't quite believe it. "Both entered, copied, and left without a trace."

Stupidly, I'd believed while in the curiosity of the police that I was safe. That no matter what evilness lived out there, while in here, I could relax.

Was that not true?

Who was searching for me?

Who knew about the QMB apart from the men who

bought and sold women illegally?
Was Elder trying to find me?
Was someone else?
Good and bad.
Right and wrong.
Friend or foe?
Who would find me first?

ELDER

* The Night Before *

WHAT WAS THE point of having skills if I didn't use them?

I knew how to create magic with computers.

I barely used those talents anymore unless hacking into a client's bank account to ensure he had the funds before agreeing to do business with him.

But Pim...shit, I'd do anything to find her—including illegal things.

In the time it took for me to stalk back to the hotel, crack open my laptop, and log onto the secure server so my IP and other activity would be hidden, I'd already formulated a code that would work.

The Monaco police firewall wasn't nearly as impenetrable as a lot of the high-level criminals I designed yachts for, and I found it a simple matter of cracking open a back door, creating a patch, and firing off the search alert under the name I had never used but belonged to the woman I'd come back for.

Tasmin Blythe.

While I waited, I opened as many news sites and historical

links attached to Pim's disappearance as I could find. I skimmed the headlines all over again of what her mother had done, the murder she'd committed, the unapologetic way she confessed, and the pride in which she served time.

I could understand Sonya Blythe.

She'd done the right thing when others had failed. She would rot in jail, but at least her conscience would be clear.

I subscribed to the same rule of thinking.

I might be doing illegal shit to find Pimlico, but at least I could fix the wrongs I'd done. I could continue my promise to keep her safe. And that was all I cared about.

I didn't have a Facebook account but quickly created a fake profile in order to track her down and stalk the sporadic and uninteresting posts Tasmin had shared before she was sold.

There were a few tags with her barely smiling with bitchy looking girls and another with her fists curled as a boy draped his arm over her shoulders.

She was younger.

Less damaged.

She'd had a life before me, but it didn't look like a happy one.

Not that the life with me had been happy, either.

I would do everything in my power to change that when I found her.

Twenty minutes after I cast out my fishing line, dangling her name as bait, something latched on, and my computer pinged.

Closing my web browser, I scanned the code that gave me everything I needed to know.

Pim had been caught for thievery. She wasn't stealthy enough, quick enough, corrupt enough. She'd stolen before she was ready, and whose fucking fault was that?

Mine.

All goddamn mine.

My heart cramped at the thought of her in captivity yet again. Shackled behind bars. Interrogated and ridiculed.

Alone.

Goddammit, Pim.

At least, I knew where she was now.

And I wouldn't fucking stop until she was mine again.

Pimlico

I'D BEEN MOVED to a room just off reception and left alone for the past hour.

After delivering the terrifying news that not one but two people had hacked into the police system all because of me, Carlyn had guided me to this new waiting area, complete with a metal barred window and large one-way mirror, and mumbled something about getting the rest of this mess sorted out as soon as possible.

A few minutes upon arrival, a male officer popped his head into the room and asked to see Carlyn privately.

Reluctantly, she secured a cuff to my wrist and the table and left. It took all I had to remain calm and not let my thoughts slither back to another time when I'd been restrained against my will.

I'd never been a bored person. Too many things went on in my mind to ever let me get fidgety and impatient, but that hour seemed to drag for days.

I was in limbo.

I hadn't been booked for my crime nor had I been told I was free to go. They'd given me free medical treatment and tests, and all for what? So I was healthy in prison, or so I was strong enough to survive if I was released?

Until I knew an outcome, I couldn't mentally prepare for

jail or concoct a new plan.

I had no mother to go to.

No lover to return to.

No womb to create life—

You said you wouldn't think about it.

Resting my head in my hand, I pressed my fingers against the bruising on my eye. Luckily, the night in the hospital meant the swelling had gone down considerably, and only the discolouration and the odd twinge remained. My other bumps and scrapes were nothing I couldn't handle.

Harold had been fiendish, but he was a baby shark after the great whites I'd swam with for two years.

Thinking of Harold and the girls, I wondered what Simone was doing. Hopefully, she was back with her family and second-guessing her relationship with such violent friends.

Would I see her again?

Or had she decided I wasn't worth the hassle, after all?

Can't say I blame her.

The door finally opened, and Carlyn returned. She gave me a bright smile, and I jangled the metal around my wrist in a silent request.

"I have news." She came around to my side of the table and released the cuff.

I rolled my arm, rubbing where the cold metallic kiss had turned warm over the hour of waiting. "I'm going to jail?"

She laughed softly. "No."

My head whipped up to look at her. "No?"

Her bob swung as she beamed. "We were able to make a bargain."

"A bargain?"

What sort of bargain?

"Yes." Moving to take her seat, she added, "My team has discussed different scenarios that would work for both Harold and you and have luckily reached a happy median."

I sat taller in the chair, doing my best to understand cop speak. "So what does that mean?"

"It means the two women you stole from have agreed not to press charges if *you* agree not to press charges against Harold." She waved her hand as if this hiccup was nothing. Which compared to a lot of the crimes she dealt with was probably true. "If you agree, it would mean the entire thing is null and void. There won't be any crime from either party."

How was that possible? Last time I saw the girls, the black-haired one had been out for my blood. Could people change their minds like that? Could time cool tempers?

If it could...did it mean Elder's addiction toward sex could be cooled given time, too?

That new thought sprang like a leak, gushing with possibility.

What if I—

Leaning over the table, Carlyn's face became stern but encouraging. "We're a small city, Tasmin, and like to make friends rather than enemies. If you can live with that, then you're free to go."

I scowled, forgetting for a moment that I was the thief here and the one who'd started this mess. I couldn't ignore the fact that Harold wouldn't be punished for hitting me. But then again, hadn't my past taught me that most men got away with hurting a girl—*especially* if they had money and connections.

That's why she's done this...

I narrowed my eyes, reading between the lines. "Even if I pressed charges, he wouldn't serve time, would he? He probably wouldn't even get community service."

Carlyn scowled with displeasure but nodded. "You're right. Money talks and good lawyers are expensive, but they usually get the job done." She lowered her voice. "Meanwhile, you would be the one paying as he would ensure to come after you with every tool available."

His creative lawyers would spin a good tale while I rotted in a cell with no hope of appealing.

It burned my throat at the injustice, but I nodded slowly. "Fine, I won't press charges." My side, where his fist had imbedded itself, twinged as if in argument, but I pressed my elbow into the throb and said with more conviction. "I accept the deal."

Carlyn smiled sadly. "I know what this means, and I don't like it, just like you. But at least you'll be free. Your momentary lapse of judgement won't be punished, and you'll live a life without a record. I'll contact the English embassy and start the process of arranging a new passport for you, so you can go ho—"

"Where the fuck is she?" A roar tumbled through the station, cutting Carlyn off mid word. Our heads whipped to the heavy door cracked open and leading toward the reception area.

Adrenaline whizzed through my veins, panic rearing up, ready to run from such ferocity.

Carlyn marched to the door, her hand flat and ready to slam it shut to block out the domestics of criminals, but she wasn't fast enough to stop another shout.

"Sir, you can't just barge in here and—"

"Tasmin Blythe. I expect answers. Now."

The world stood still.

I recognised that timbre.

I recognised that anger.

That *voice*...

It was deep and dark and dangerous, thicker than what I was used to, yet...my ears tingled with besotted memory.

My heart scrambled out of its lovesick bandages and cartwheeled.

Elder...

He found me.

Carlyn turned with her hand plastered on the door. Her eyebrow rose as rageful footsteps sounded outside. "Expecting someone?"

My heart stopped its cartwheeling and became a bobble-head, nodding in eager happiness.

Elder had come back for me.

He'd ignored my letter.

He'd been one of the hackers to access my file.

Whoever else had searched for me no longer mattered.

He's here.

I'm safe.

A scuffle sounded outside, followed by a loud thump. "I know she's here. Hand her over." A flutter of paperwork as if someone had swept it off a table. "Now!"

"Sir. Unless you wish to be placed under arrest for abusing a police officer in his own establishment, I suggest you calm down and—"

"She's here because of me. Get a manager, a captain. Anyone who can fix my mistakes." The sound of boots stomping painted a mental image of him prowling the reception, glowering like a caged beast.

Carlyn closed the door, locking it quickly. "Tasmin, I need an answer from you. Is that a friend of yours or someone I need to arrest?"

My smile was so wide it hurt it. "You don't need to arrest him."

A small injection of worry pricked me. Elder was a murderer and a thief. There was no way he should be in a hundred-mile radius of a cop.

He'd put his own safety and freedom at risk to come and fight for mine.

How the hell did I walk away from him before?

And how the hell would I ever keep my hands off him now?

"So...he's a friend?" Carlyn crossed her arms. "Sounds pretty aggressive."

"He's also gentle."

My dreamy voice tipped her off. She stiffened, eyeing me closely. "That's the man who recused you?"

My instincts immediately smothered my joy, and I painted a blank look on my face. "No." I couldn't under *any* circumstance tell them Elder's name. As much as I liked and respected Carlyn, I would never tell her. If she had his details, who knew if she could pin Alrik and Darryl's murder to him.

He'd be taken away.

He wouldn't be mine anymore.

I cocked my chin, daring her to argue with me. "He's someone else."

She didn't buy it. "Someone else, huh?"

"Someone else."

She rolled her eyes. "And you want to see this *someone else?*"

Quietness reigned over the station, but the vibrations of Elder's temper continued to seep through the walls.

How did he return?

Why did he return?

"Am I *allowed* to see him?" I glanced at the door, wishing I had x-ray vision.

Carlyn planted her hands on her hips. "You're free to go, Tasmin. Just sign a statement saying you won't press charges against Harold Medessa, and I'll give you a copy of his testimony stating the same thing." She shrugged. "Then you're free to walk out the front door with whoever you please and do whatever you want." She shook her head with a small smile. "Within reason, of course. No more purse snatching or illegal business."

With a short sigh, her face turned serious. "If you go with whoever is out there, then you should arrange to have your medical files sent to your chosen doctor. When you get home, you might want a third opinion on your arthritis and infertility issues—"

"I understand." I flinched, hating the quick-lash of wetness to my eyes. "I don't need a third opinion."

I gritted my teeth, doing my best to forget the tests, the questions, the doctors, and ultimately, the conclusions about my black and blue body.

This was supposed to be a happy moment.

I didn't need to ruin it by mourning things I never wanted in the first place.

Carlyn softened, sympathy glowing in her hazel eyes. "Is there anything else you need? Anything at all? Money? Food? A change of clothes?"

I smiled gratefully. "That's very kind of you. But along with being aggressive and gentle, that man out there is also extremely generous. Too generous most of the time." I shivered with anticipation. "He'll give me everything I need. He's far too good to me."

"No one can be too good to another." Motioning for me to stand, she tugged her suit jacket into a more military precision. "How will you return to England without a passport or identification? I know you're not a minor, but I need to know you're going to be okay on your own."

Her brusque question didn't hide the affection in her tone. These past couple of days had been hard, but somehow, I'd made a friend in this detective.

I wanted to assure her I was no longer her problem, but I couldn't give away too much. The safe road of information was narrow with cliffs of secrecy on either side.

"My friend will get me home. He err—" *has a yacht and staff and has no problem breaking the law to get what he wants.* "—he'll help me apply for a new passport at the embassy, I'm sure."

My body tingled at the thought of seeing Elder, touching him, embarking on the Phantom with him.

Unless...

My shoulders fell.

Unless he wasn't here to take me the rest of the way.

Unless this was just a courtesy to break me out of jail and then dump me back on the streets.

Just because he was here to free me didn't mean he was any better equipped to have me infiltrate his space again, sharing his bed...wrecking his mind.

My heart wept at being so close yet so eternally far from what I wanted.

Suck it up.

Self-pity is not becoming.

Sniffing up my fears, I smiled brightly. "He'll find a way. You don't need to worry."

Carlyn frowned but finally conceded. "Well, I'll give you a copy of your paperwork and fingerprints. Perhaps that will help get some form of identification."

I dramatized a shiver, doing my best to seem normal and able to joke now that the horror of jail had passed. "Rocking up to an airport with a police file for stealing? I can't see that going very well."

She laughed, relaxing just like I intended. "Glad to see you haven't lost your sense of humour through all this."

"I have my moments."

She chuckled.

A companionable but awkward silence fell.

Our time together had come to an end.

She'd finished her job.

Elder had come to continue it.

I was ready to pass from her custody into his.

She stood taller and in a stage-whisper said, "I guess it's time to see what that man out there is screaming about."

Finally.

Yes.

Let's go.

I couldn't fight my happy shakes as I moved toward the door. "I guess you're right."

ELDER

"NO, *YOU* DON'T understand." I pointed a finger in the face of a pubescent cop who thought he had the right to keep me from Pim when he was just a glorified receptionist. "Tasmin Blythe, as I told you before. I want to see her. Immediately."

"And like I told you before, we don't work on demands." He puffed up his very breakable body. "Take a seat, and I'll look for any updates on her case."

All I wanted to do was grab the computer and smash it over his goddamn head.

Didn't he understand that she was incarcerated because of me?

If I hadn't taught her to pickpocket. If I hadn't forced her to steal to pay me back for nonsensical debts, she wouldn't be in this place.

Christ!

My entire body shook as I slammed my fist onto the desk again. "There *is* no case. She's innocent. I don't care what the charges are. Let her go."

"That isn't possi—"

"Carter, it's okay."

I spun around as a female officer in an ironed skirt, crisp

blazer, and shiny gold buckles appeared from a room to the right.

I opened my mouth to tell her nothing was okay. Nothing would be okay again unless I could get Pim's crime revoked. Shit, I'd give myself up if they needed a perpetrator to prosecute.

But then my eyes fell onto the woman beside her.

And the rest of the world no longer mattered.

I stumbled at the sight.

My heart burst into flames.

A black eye painted her beautiful face. She moved stiffer than her usual liquid grace, reminding me all over again of the beaten creature I'd stolen months ago.

The fact she stood next to an officer made my rage fucking explode. How *dare* these assholes trap her against her will. How *dare* they take away her freedom when she'd fought tooth and fucking nail to earn it.

Couldn't they see the trials she'd endured?

The horror she'd survived?

So fucking what she'd stolen from some pretentious, self-absorbed mark? If anyone deserved the right to bend the law for her own gains, it was her.

Her.

Her green eyes met mine, her shoulders tight. "El—"

I didn't let her finish.

Launching forward, I grabbed her in a possessive embrace as if she'd be snatched away at any moment.

She was so fragile in my arms. So warm and small and *right.*

I groaned as her breasts pressed against my chest. I needed her closer. Touching her wasn't enough. *Nothing* would be enough.

Plucking her from the floor, I relished in her light weight, squeezing her as tight as I dared. Far tighter than I should.

I squeezed her in protection, affection, and most of all, aggression for what she'd done to me. The *agony* she'd injected into my heart. The poison she'd infected my brain with. The knowledge I now carried that she was selfless in trying to shield me from myself, and I was selfish in letting her try.

Never again.

She's mine.

It'd taken a separation to understand that, but now I did.

Good luck to the rest of the world and anyone else who wanted her because they couldn't fucking have her.

Even if it meant tying myself up for the rest of the trip to England. Even if it meant I could never say goodbye when we arrived. Even if it meant I lived the rest of my life in a fog of marijuana just to be able to talk to her without the incessant need to be inside her. Even if it meant my mind finally cracked, and I became so helplessly tangled I might never be normal again.

Even then.

She would remain mine.

I should've seen this coming. I should've sensed the warning signs: the first time my heart tap danced when she smiled. The moment when my gut clenched because her happiness affected my future rather than just my present. The second my entire body drenched in sensitivity whenever she came near.

All those warning signs I'd ignored or misread.

But now I understood the message.

I was dead without her.

I was alive with her.

Simple.

Her breath escaped into my ear as I clutched closer—doing my best to crawl inside her. Her arms wrapped around my shoulders, hesitantly at first then braver as I buried my face into her neck and inhaled.

Christ, she smelled amazing beneath the stench of police and stupid laws. Laws I'd spent most of my life breaking and had the smallest amount of tolerance for.

Did she still mean what she'd said in that hotel room?

That she loved me?

Did she love me as a friend or something more?

The question stained the tip of my tongue, ready to demand an answer.

Because just like the other two epiphanies, I had another one.

I loved her.

I was *in* love with her.

There was nothing platonic or grateful about my love. It was cruel and wicked and unwanted because love almost destroyed me once, and it would destroy me again if I did what I was hardwired to do and hurt her.

And I *would* hurt her.

Eventually.

By loving her, I not only doomed myself but her too. She would be a part of my world—a world she still knew so little about. A world where war was coming, death was hunting, and curses were sure to rule.

"Elder…" Her whisper kissed my cheek, grounding me and sending me into a tailspin all at once. I shouldn't have come here clear-headed. I should've smoked every joint on the Phantom and been numb before attempting to see her.

Someone patted me firmly on the arm, clearing an authoritative throat. "Put her down. Immediately."

"Do as she says, Elder," Pim breathed. "I'm okay. Truly."

It hurt right down to my bones to obey, but slowly, I unlatched my death grip and released my hug—not that it could be called a hug…more like an embrace of apology, of acknowledgment, of soul-crushing fear of what I'd just signed my life to.

Backing away, I pinched the bridge of my nose and forced myself to get it together. At least standing with a precinct of police for an audience kept my twisted thoughts on Pim's incarceration and her needs, not mine.

I didn't get hard or drown in all the ways I needed to fuck her.

The past few days had done what my past tricks used to achieve and gave me enough mental distance to ignore sex.

Plus…I loved her, and because of that awful, terrible fact, I was now celibate as a fucking monk.

"She's coming with me." I glowered at the officer in her unattractive suit. "No discussion. Whatever you've booked her for. Unbook it."

The woman nodded, a smirk planted firmly on her lips. "Shouldn't you ask Tasmin if that's what she wants?"

I froze.

Tasmin.

To hear it outside my head. To have it become real.

I'd fallen in love with Pimlico, not Tasmin. I had enough on my damn plate to worry about switching her name. The stupid tic I lived with refused to acknowledge the new address.

"I know what she wants. Her freedom. And you're trying to take it from her."

"Oh, I am, am I?" The officer crossed her arms. "Do you see her in cuffs?"

I scowled.

I didn't know what this woman's game was but no dice. I'd come here with the purpose of a jail break, not to speak in riddles. "You arrested her. You still have her in custody. I've come to rectify that."

"So you thought you'd storm the station and throw some threats around, did you?" She rolled her eyes. "You think that would work?"

Who is this bitch?

"Listen." I drew myself up to my full height. The black t-shirt I'd thrown on acted like an eclipse next to the sunshine that was Pim. "I don't care what your angle is. I'll hire a thousand lawyers. I'll pull in favours with the prince. I'll do whatever it damn well takes."

Her eyes widened at the mention of his Royal Highness.

It was my turn to smirk. "That wasn't an empty threat. I know the prince. We had a business arrangement, and I'm sure

I still have his personal number on my phone." Pulling my cell from my pocket, I made a show of unlocking the screen. "Want me to call him or will you do what I ask?"

Pimlico shot me a look then glanced at the officer, "Carlyn...it's okay."

Carlyn held up her hand to silence her, frowning. "You have it all wrong, Mr..."

"My name is not important. What *is* important is you releasing Pim. She's coming with me."

"This is highly entertaining. Not only do you think you can overthrow the law, but you also continue to speak for Tasmin while using a name I highly doubt she has a tolerance for. I don't care who you're friends with. I don't care why you call her Pim instead of her correct address. I would've thought someone who obviously cares about my prisoner would want to know her opinion on the matter."

I saw fucking red. "She's *not* your prisoner."

"You don't know that." Carlyn sniffed. "I have a good mind to lock you up for disturbing the peace."

My blood ran cold. "You want me? Fine. Arrest me and let her go." I pointed at Pim. "I'll take the rap for her theft. I've stolen—"

"Whoa, whoa, okay...that's enough." Pim jumped in front of me, her small hand landing on my stomach. "I think you should calm down."

"Calm down?" I snorted. "I'll be calm when they do what I ask and release you." Clamping my hands on her shoulders, I snapped, "What's your bail? I'll pay it. Right now."

Whatever trial they thought Pim would face, she wouldn't.

The moment I had her on the Phantom and sailing in international waters, she was out of their jurisdiction.

She smiled softly. "There is no bail."

"What does that mean?"

"It means I'm free to go." Steel threaded her words. "So stop being so grouchy and be polite."

My eyes shot wide. "*Excuse* me?" I'd flown here to bust

her out of prison. To be her protector and liberator. Yet instead of a frightened inmate, I found a freshly bruised goddess just as regal, just as fearless as I remembered.

She was in control of herself and the situation.

I was...unneeded.

That thorn lodged deep in my heart, deflating my anger. I blinked past the red in my vision, ready to listen to whatever the hell was going on.

Pim's fingers fluttered against my stomach, reminding me I could make an oath of celibacy as easy as breathing, but keeping it would be a fucking disaster.

Glancing at the officer then back to me, Pim smiled. "We've come to an arrangement. I won't press charges if they won't."

"What charges?" I growled.

Pim rolled her shoulders, letting her hand trail down my belly and fall away. "I'll tell you later." With a shared look with the woman she'd called Carlyn, they moved toward the desk where I'd bellowed at the receptionist.

I wanted to bark that I needed to know now.

That reading the bare essentials of her file wasn't enough for my information starving brain. I needed to know what she stole, from whom, and why the hell she was covered, yet again, in bruises.

Whoever had done that to her...they were motherfucking dead.

She shot me a look as my fists clenched. It took every ounce of control I had left, but I kept my lips tightly glued.

I *behaved*.

Moving closer to her, I remained stiff and alert—a guardian with weapons ready.

Carlyn spoke to the receptionist who eyed me warily. Passing over a manila folder, she opened it and pointed at two pages for Pim to sign.

Pinching a pen from the desk, Pim skim read whatever the statement said then scribbled a signature that looked suspiciously like Pimlico and not Tasmin.

Perhaps, just like me, she hadn't traded one name for another yet—even though others had.

Nodding in approval, Carlyn headed to a large floor printer and scanned a duplicate. Passing those to Pim, she waited for yet another signature beside an already messy one at the bottom.

"And just like that...it's like it never happened." She smiled conspiratorially at Pim.

I knew what the damn cop was doing—doing her best to make me snap and give her a reason to lasso cuffs over my wrists and take Pim away from me all over again.

I was angry.

But I wasn't stupid.

I let her have her moment because in exactly two minutes, we'd be gone, and Pim would be far, far away from her.

"It's done?" Pim stroked the pages. "Just like that?"

"Just like that." Carlyn beamed. "No more stealing, though. You hear me?"

Pim shot me a look beneath her lashes. A look that said *'tell that to him. He's the one who taught me.'* Then she lowered her gaze and nodded demurely. "No more stealing."

"In that case, Mr. I Don't Need To Know Your Name..." Carlyn skirted around the desk, throwing a judgmental look my way before clipping to the exit in high heels. "If Tasmin, or as you like to call her, Pim, wishes to go with you...she's free to leave."

Tasmin.

That damn name again.

All this time, I'd wanted to know her true identity.

But now that I did, it didn't suit her.

She was *Pim*.

Would I have to start calling her Tasmin? Would everything have to change all because I sailed away when I should've fucking stayed?

Crossing my arms to hold my thundering heart in place, I

glowered at Pim and asked the unthinkable. "Do you *want* to go with me?"

It was a question I hadn't even considered. A question I should've asked myself before storming in here as if I was once again her knight in dinged-up armour when really, she'd helped herself better than I ever could.

The question hung between us, unanswered and lonely.

Pim slowly folded the paperwork and tucked it into her palm. Coming toward me, her eyes softened, searching mine with a silent intensity that made my skin crawl under her scrutiny and my cock harden under her sexuality.

How had I not seen how stunning a creature she'd evolved into? No wonder I broke under her will. No wonder I didn't stand a chance.

Look at her.

She was no longer a prisoner—she was my jailer, and I would happily remain sentenced to her for the rest of my godforsaken life.

Her feet stopped in front of me. Biting her lip, her face turned sad as she reached with delicate fingers to cup my cheek.

My knees almost buckled beneath her touch.

Locking my jaw, I fought every lust and addiction and instead focused on how warm she was, how sweet, how delicate, how beautiful.

Her fingers kissed my skin then fell away.

I lashed out, catching her wrist with a hand that wanted to squeeze not caress.

She sucked in a breath at my possession, her eyes heating with the same mixture of forbidden lust I felt.

Her voice wobbled. "That isn't the right question."

I struggled to remember what I'd asked.

All I could remember was her and me and *us*.

"The question isn't if I want to go with you, Elder." Her eyelashes hooded over molten eyes.

I swallowed the thick wash of desire. "It isn't?" I forgot we stood in a police station. I forgot we had an audience. I forgot about everything—the Chinmoku, my family…every stupid, inconsequential thing and hyper focused on her.

Her.

Pim.

Tasmin.

The woman I needed to prove I was worthy of because, *fuck*, she was ten times the person I could ever be.

My lips tingled to touch hers.

My tongue ached to dance with hers.

Every inch of me burned to possess and taste but for *connection* rather than empty satisfaction. I needed to be inside her to feel her, not to rip into her only to finish quickly and start all over again.

That mindless addiction was overshadowed for a moment. A moment where I wanted the best for her above all things—no matter the cost.

"What *is* the right question?" I murmured as she slotted herself against me and kissed right over my heart as if I was something to be worshiped and not the other way around.

I couldn't win with this woman.

I didn't stand a fucking chance.

I was completely, utterly, undeniably hers until time stopped ticking or the world stopped spinning—whatever came first.

I'd never felt that before.

Never wanted to be so irrevocably tied to another that I was willing to do anything to make it possible.

"The right question is…do *you* want *me*?" Her eyes glistened with memories of the hotel room, her letter, and my subsequent reply by leaving.

I swallowed the sudden hand grenade in my throat. "Do you even need to ask, Pimlico?"

She smiled. "You didn't call me Tasmin."

"Do you *want* me to call you Tasmin?"

She paused, thinking it over with a seriousness I hadn't expected. "I think…one day I might. But not today."

I didn't need any more clarification. I understood better than she knew. Not letting her change the subject, I breathed, "Do you honestly think I don't want you?"

She blushed. "It's not that you don't want me. It's if you can survive me."

I shuddered at how perceptive she was. "I can't."

She froze, doing her best to seem okay with the truth but crushed regardless. "That's okay…"

It was my turn to cup her face, wincing as my fingers burned from her softness. I choked beneath the weight of confession. "I can't survive you, Pim. That's the problem."

Her bottom lip quivered. "I-I underst—"

"But I can't survive without you, either. And I know now which of those I choose."

Tears glittered in her gaze. "I'm sorry."

"I'm not." I bent to kiss her.

I didn't bother looking at the officer or receptionist. I didn't care we'd brought a damn soap opera to them. All I cared about was kissing her, convincing her, showing her that no matter what happened…we were already bound and doomed.

We'd started this path the moment Alrik emailed me to arrange a meeting. We'd given into this direction the moment I'd draped my jacket over her shoulders and felt something inside my loveless heart that I should've bolted from.

And now look where we were.

Fucked.

Well and truly fucked.

But I wouldn't change a thing.

I wouldn't stop.

I *couldn't.*

My neck ached with tension as I lowered myself the rest of the way and dared kiss her.

Dared to activate the curse in my blood all over again.

Dared to lose myself to her where I could never be free.

But as her lips touched mine and her tongue flickered into

my mouth, I knew I would fight myself tooth and nail to deserve her.

As quickly as I'd bestowed the kiss, I pushed her away, curling my fists against the sudden roar for more, more, *more*.

I would not take more.

I would take that single pleasure and control myself.

Trembling, I held out my hand. "Please, Pim. Come home."

With an unsteady breath, she slotted her fingers into mine. "I'm already home. I'm with you."

Pimlico

SO MUCH HAD changed yet nothing had changed at all.

The way Elder glared at me was still the same, yet there was a new layer to his glower that not only activated my tummy to heat and prickle but my heart and soul, too. The weight of his stare held so many familiar and unfamiliar things.

He didn't touch me again as he escorted me from the police station and held open the door to an unknown white sedan.

I gave him a curious look and scooted in, mindful of my tender spots and bruises.

Selix sat in the front seat with a driver. He turned to face me; his long hair twirled in a top knot.

I almost asked where the usual black Town Car was that travelled on the Phantom, but Elder landed beside me with his fists tightly curled by his thighs as if forbidding himself to reach for me.

"Hello, Pimlico." Selix smiled, eyeing us and noting the tension resonating like bad karaoke.

I didn't know if that was the first time he'd called me by name—even if it was a false one—but it was as if some ice thawed between us. I'd never felt entirely welcome in Selix's presence, and I could understand why. His loyalties were to

Elder, not to me, and rightfully so.

I respected him for protecting his friend. But at the same time, I was glad that chilliness had melted into an extension of friendship. I could guess why. By leaving, I'd shown I would put Elder's welfare above my own.

Returning Selix's smile, I said, "Nice to see you again."

The driver glanced at me in the rear-view. Selix noticed, shrugging. "This is a temporary measure. Our car is still on the Phantom."

Why was that any different? The Phantom was moored back in its spot in the harbour...*isn't it?*

"Elder here" —Selix cocked his head at the man sitting rigidly beside me—"didn't give us time to sail back. He said it was urgent."

"It was urgent. She was in jail, for Christ's sake." Elder's gaze turned tortured as he looked at me. "The thought of you spending time in a cell damn well butchers me." He took my hand, squeezing it hard. "I'm so sorry, Pim."

I clenched my fingers around his. "Don't be. I actually spent most of that time at the hospital, so I was looked after in style."

His eyes narrowed. "Hospital?" His gaze dropped over me, calculating, assessing. "I see your black eye and the stiff way you move. How badly are you hurt? What bastard did this to you?" His nostrils flared, filling the car with an aggressive vengeance. "I'll gut him."

Selix turned to face the front, giving quiet instructions to the driver to depart. As the car slid into motion, I shook my head. "It's nothing."

"It's not *nothing*."

Looking out the window, I said far too blasély, "I've had much worse."

Whoops.

Elder turned arctic with fury. His thighs clenched as every muscle stiffened in a mixture that shot way past anger and turned wild with the need to kill. "I positively *hate* that that is true." His face turned dark with torment. "I'd do anything so you never knew the feeling of a fucking bee sting, let alone such abuse."

Shifting in the fabric seat, I rushed to delete such thoughts from him.

He had to stop taking the blame.

And I had to stop reminding him of my past.

"The police were very understanding. I was—"

His eyes turned blacker than normal. "Understanding how?"

"Well, I told them about…me and other things. They took me to the hospital to do tests."

He went deathly still. "And these tests…were the results good or bad?"

My chest turned hollow with the newfound emptiness that I would never be a mother. Never carry that magic. I had no intention of telling him such a thing. Ever.

Ensuring calmness decorated my face and not pain, I nodded. "The results were fine. I'm well on the mend—thanks to you. I'm healthy." Touching my cheek where the swelling of injury remained, I shrugged. "This will fade in a few days and then no more. I'm done being someone's punching bag."

Elder locked his jaw, glaring out the window at downtown Monte Carlo. "I suppose it's a good thing they checked you over. Saves the appointments I'd booked in. We don't need to worry about them now."

I sucked in a breath, grateful that I'd seen a gynaecologist who wasn't a member of his team and would stand by their confidentially clause.

My barrenness was my own hollowness to bear—not his.

Taking a deep breath, Elder asked a short, painful question—almost as if he hadn't meant to ask it, but his mouth betrayed him. "Did you tell them about me? Give them my name?"

My head whipped to face him. "Of course not." Misery barbed my heart that he assumed I'd expose him like that.

"You saved my life, El. Why would I deliberately try to ruin yours in return?"

He instantly chagrined, rubbing his face with his hand as his shoulders slouched. "Fuck, of course, you didn't." He massaged his forehead. "I'm losing my mind." His heavy palm landed on my knee, warm, powerful, apologetic.

"It's right for you to be nervous." I patted his knuckles.

His body shifted as he shook his head. "I trust you. Trust implies that I don't need to ask such things."

Silence cloaked the car for a few seconds, both of us trying to figure out what to say next. When Elder spoke again, it was as if his question bypassed his lips and entered my mind before he'd even uttered it.

I knew exactly what he would ask.

And I answered before he could phrase it. "No, I didn't."

His eyebrow rose, his lips tight even as curiosity shoved aside some of his anger. "You don't know my question."

"I do." I twisted closer to him. "You were going to ask if I gave them Alrik's name. And the answer is no, I didn't."

He shrugged, his illusion of calm not convincing. "Why not? Don't you want justice…didn't they want proof?"

My heart suffered a crestfallen beat. We'd been so connected before. Now, we were this odd stumbling thing, stuck between incorrect comprehensions and rotten confusion.

His question once again was hurtful. "You gave me all the justice I needed, and they didn't need any more proof than what my body provided. My missing person's file, I assume, is now closed. I had more than enough evidence that I was sold—"

"Fuck." Slouching into the seat, he covered his eyes. "What a bastard thing to say." His fingers clenched around my knee. "Forgive me, Pim. It's been a long few days."

He didn't need my forgiveness. He already had my understanding.

Reclining to match him, I rested my head on his shoulder, granting comfort to both of us. The matching tension in our spines trickled away breath by breath until we were able to step out of the misunderstanding and discomfort and find our way back to each other.

We sighed in sync as I murmured, "I didn't give them Alrik's name as you helped deliver the justice he deserved. I also didn't give them his name as I didn't want any ties of them finding you." I snuggled closer. "I might have walked away from you, Elder, but I did it because I care. You hurt when you're around me. Just because I couldn't physically hurt you anymore doesn't mean I'd blab to anyone about you, destroy your business, your life, or wish anything bad for you."

My voice lowered to barely a whisper. "You're the most important person in the world to me. My mother and father might have given me life, but you returned it to me when I no longer wanted it. For that you have my undying loyalty—no matter if we're together or apart."

His body turned stiff as if he fought the desire to clutch me close and drag me into his lap. His steely gaze remained steadfast on the back of Selix's head, breathing deeply through his nose. Closing his eyes for a moment, he spoke in the same hushed but heavy tones I'd used. "You were wrong about you physically hurting me."

I looked at his powerful jaw, three-day-old shadow, and black endless eyes.

He wet his lips with a flash of his tongue. "You emotionally *crippled* me, Pim. You've reached inside and wrapped around everything vital keeping me alive." He smirked at nothing, not dropping his gaze to see me. "You should never have left because now I know what it feels like to no longer have you, and I have no fucking idea how I'll ever let you go."

His pain became a visible thing, a heavy scarlet wave seeping from his chest into mine. I knew what he felt because I felt it, too. I knew the emptiness he feared because the same emptiness resided in me at the very thought of being apart again.

Words danced on my tongue.

Promises I could never keep.

It wasn't up to me to tell him what to do. If he couldn't live with me as friends, just like he couldn't live with me as lovers, then I must be prepared to leave again.

I sucked in a sharp breath and layered my silence with another.

I didn't utter any oaths.

I didn't make any vows.

Because I didn't want to be condemned if I broke them.

Selix saved our awkwardness, turning to face us as the car rolled to a stop. "Ready?"

His voice shattered the moment.

Thank goodness.

Elder rolled his shoulders, granting me a fleeting smile as he sat taller. "Come on, Pim. Let's go home."

I didn't speak as he slid out of the car, giving me his hand to help me climb from cushion to airfield.

I did a double take.

Selix had mentioned they'd had no time to sail, but I hadn't expected a helicopter in lieu of the behemoth yacht.

Not giving me time to get used to the idea, Elder clutched me close and guided me toward the hulking rotary machine as if afraid I'd reassess my desire to return with him. As if I'd suddenly turn contrary.

Nothing was further from the truth.

I'd always been a serious girl, thanks to my mother's strict rules and discipline.

Now, I was morbid in my convictions. When I spoke a promise, it was a blood oath. It was better than any contract and deeper than any vow.

And that was why, as Elder helped me climb into the small helicopter and strapped me into the five-point harness, as Selix jumped into the pilot seat and Elder commandeered the co-pilots, I whispered softly what I never dared breathe in the car.

I really shouldn't. I definitely shouldn't.

I couldn't help it.

"As long as you want me, Elder Prest, I'm not going anywhere. I'm yours until you decide otherwise."

He didn't hear me as the rotors slowly wound, louder and louder.

He didn't look back as I wrapped my arms around myself and smiled.

My promise was my life.

And I'd just given it to Elder, wrapped in a bow, gifted in a box, willingly donated with my heart.

ELDER

ARRIVING BACK ON the Phantom, I unbuckled and leapt from the helicopter before the blades finished spooling.

The entire flight, I couldn't stop berating myself for what I'd done to Pim.

How I'd left Pim.

How I'd interrogated Pim.

How she'd been poked and prodded by doctors and interrogated by police about circumstances I wished I could rip from her memory and incinerate—or better yet, prevent from ever happening.

Something about her felt different.

Something not quite right but not exactly wrong, either. Something secretive? Something accepting?

I didn't know what it was, but as I held out my hand for her to balance herself while jumping from cabin to helipad, she gave me the softest, kindest smile I'd ever seen. A smile that somehow basked me in forgiveness while making me stupidly hope everything could work out, no matter that I had a ticking time bomb inside my skull.

Her fingers tightened in mine as I went to tug away, preventing me from leaving. Having her clutch me did strange but wonderful things to my heart. Her smile turned sweet as chocolate and just as dark.

My cock instantly reacted. I jerked her close only for Selix to clear his throat, raising his eyebrow in my direction.

I stepped back, managing to extract my hand from Pim's.

She gave me yet another smile—this one slightly self-conscious and apologetic—then dropped her arm.

How could a smile have so many different dialects and conversations? How could I understand the nuisances behind different shaped lips?

The intricacies of human interaction filled my mind before I could calm my overactive thoughts. I wanted to know how evolution had turned a warning signal of baring teeth into what Pim wielded—the perfect beauty of conveying everything she thought but would never say.

Selix moved off toward the bridge as trained staff members came to tether and look after the chopper.

Clearing my throat, I made the mistake of making eye contact with Pim and having my heart suffocate with crushing desire to grab her, kiss her, drag her back to my room, and never let her leave my bed.

Marching away, I didn't wait for her to fall into step. "Come, I'll take you back to your room."

Her smile fell, but she pushed off into a quick stride to keep up. We didn't speak as we traversed the deck. We didn't look at the horizon and flocking seabirds, we didn't pay attention to the milling staff, and we definitely didn't look at each other as I pressed the elevator button and stepped inside the mirrored box to ascend to her level.

I kept my eyes resolutely on the doors as they closed in front of us.

Pim knew better than to interact.

She sensed everything I was battling, and I was grateful she understood enough to stay quiet and let me get a hold on having her back in my domain.

My skin hummed having her so close.

My hands opened and closed with the need to touch her.

It was a blessed relief when the doors slid open. I bolted into the wide corridors of her deck. Inhaling deep, I tried to delete the sickening lust quickly building into unavoidable.

Pim padded beside me, close but not too close, her presence slowly forming a mushroom cloud of tangles inside me. By the time we stopped by her door, my muscles seized and minor tremors quaked down my legs.

She was back on my yacht.

She was back in my *life*.

I wanted to fucking celebrate and jump overboard in equal measure.

Turning the handle to her room, I stopped on the threshold then moved to the side for her to enter.

She carried forward then turned sharply as I said, "Well, goodnight then."

"*Goodnight?* It's not even evening."

"Well, I, eh, I have work to do." I wasn't lying. I had a shit load of replanning to do regarding my family. No way in hell would I take Pim anywhere near my family if there was a chance she could get messed up with the Chinmoku. New plans were needed. Better ones.

"Oh." She rocked on the carpet. "Will you...at least come in?" She glanced beneath thick alluring eyelashes, wrapping her magic around my cock, my heart, and practically yanking me into the room.

Gritting my teeth, fighting her power, I shook my head. "Too much to do. Besides, you need to rest. How long since you've slept, showered...ate?"

"They have showers and beds in the hospital, you know. I'm not going to fall into a dirty coma from lack of care." Taking a breath, she softened. "Please, El. I'd love some company. If only for a little while."

Company.

Right.

I swallowed a dark chuckle. She expected me to willingly enter a room with her—with lockable doors and utmost privacy after what happened in Monte Carlo?

Silly girl.

Couldn't she see I liked her way too much to do that to her again? And I liked myself too much to slip into addiction.

Like her?

My conscience rolled its eyes.

Like wasn't the right word for what I felt for her.

I'd already admitted it was love.

Yet for some reason, that word fucking petrified me.

"You need your rest." I pointed at the bed. Fresh sheets and fluffed pillows invited sleep and other activities I couldn't think about. "I'll send someone to bring you a meal."

She glanced at the floor then back to me. "You're welcome to join me for dinner. That is…if you'd like?"

I would like.

But I shook my head again, fighting a building headache from denying myself everything I hungered for. "Maybe tomorrow. In the dining room." *Where we will have an audience, and you're not in danger of being molested.*

"Oh."

That tiny but destroying word again.

She frowned, her gaze drifting from my eyes to the door handle that I held in a death grip. Her gaze darkened; her body tightened. "That's new."

Shit.

Just as she was far too observant when it came to my moods, she'd noticed a change in decorating.

Playing dumb, I asked, "What's new?" Removing my hand from the handle, I scowled as if it was same old, same old. "I don't know what you're talking about."

"Yes, you do."

Shit, I do.

There, in very noticeable glory, was a brand-new deadbolt.

It glinted with accusation—straight out of the box and installed by yours truly a few minutes before I boarded my helicopter to find Pim and bring her home.

Precautions were necessary.

She has to understand that.

"It's just a lock, little mouse."

Her lips parted at the nickname even as her forehead furrowed. "Liar. It's *so* much more than that."

It was as if she'd already investigated and found it was completely inaccessible from the outside—no key insert, no quick hack, no way to unlock it.

Only the occupant from inside the room could grant access.

With hands balled, she strode straight for me.

I backed away as she tapped the polished silver hardware. "Why did you put a lock on my door?"

I shrugged as if it was no big deal. "There wasn't one before. I thought you might feel safer."

"Safer?" She rolled the word around, tainting it with suspicion. "Why wouldn't I feel safe on your yacht? Why would I need a barrier between us when you're the only one I trust?"

I rubbed the back of my neck.

Lots of reasons.

Me being the main one.

Allowing a trace of anger to thicken my voice, I replied, "You've been through a lot. Excuse me for trying to ensure you continue healing by giving you a safe place that only you can open."

She crossed her arms—in no way intimidated by my temper or ready to back down. "You expect me to believe that?"

"You don't have to believe it to be real."

"But it's *not* real."

I pointed at the lock. "What isn't real about that? You can touch it, turn it, and once you've slid the latch from the inside, nothing and no one is getting through there." I used the memories of our first night at Alrik's together, hurting her like a jackass. "I seem to remember your previous accommodations didn't have locks. It didn't even have doors. I had to fetch one

---

123

from the garage before we were able to be alone. I would've thought this was a much better alternative."

Her face froze.

Her breathing stalled.

She stared as if she couldn't quite believe I'd gone there.

I couldn't believe it, either, but that was what happened when I was pushed. When I was trying to do the right thing, only for temptation to roar until I gave in.

I won't give in.

We glowered at each other before a tight smile tilted her lips and she came forward to rest her fingertips on my forearm. "Okay." Her touch was infinitely gentle but it held the power to decimate me.

I shivered as she shook her head gently. "We both know why there's a lock on my door when there wasn't one before."

"Look, you've had a long day. Instead of standing around talking about things that are of no consequence, do as I ask and relax. We're at sea for the next—"

"It's so you can't come in."

Her interruption stole any understandable language, giving her the perfect stage to unman me.

"You don't trust yourself. You've *never* trusted yourself." Her eyes turned sad. "And that's the true problem, isn't it? It's not the fact that you have a mind that fixates on things but the fact you don't trust yourself to be able to fight it."

I crossed my arms, chilled to the bone and furious. Deciding to strip her, just like she'd done to me, I muttered, "Your mother was the psychologist, Pim. Not you. Don't speak about things you don't understand."

"*I* don't understand?" She cocked her head. "I don't understand that you would rather leave me than face yourself? That you would rather place locks between us than enjoy a meal together? That you would rather *blame* me for tempting you than believing you have the self-control to stop?" Placing her hands on her hips, her voice lowered to sympathy rather than argument. "I'm not saying what you live with isn't hard.

I've seen how you struggle. I've been with you. I've watched you. I've *felt* you—"

"Stop, Pimlico."

"No." She held up her hand. "Let me finish." Inhaling hard, she continued, "I may not be trained like my mother, but she coached me enough to see between the lines, and you...well, your problem isn't that you have the capacity to lose yourself to a sensation. Your problem is you don't trust that you can have what you want and keep it within reason. You can—"

"I can't! That's the whole fucking point. You don't understand. What I want most is *you*. And when I get what I want, nothing else matters." Stalking toward her, I pressed my body against hers.

She didn't back away. Instead, she held her ground, chest to chest, hips to hips.

And *fuck* it was the best thing I'd ever felt.

"I want you, Pimlico. I'm about two seconds from taking you, and even now you look at me as if my needs aren't something to be feared but challenged."

My jaw clenched at the delicious sensation of her soft curves against my hard edges. I'd give anything to grab her, toss her on the bed, and stop *fighting*.

It was exhausting living this way.

Didn't she think I'd give anything to stop battling myself? To give in?

I swallowed my groan. Christ, I'd do whatever it took.

But it wasn't that simple.

"If I kissed you now..." My eyes dropped to her lips where her teeth indented the plump flesh. "If I touched you now..." My fingers grazed her hips where she swayed on the spot. "If I fucked you now..." I pulled her forward where my hard cock wept for freedom. "I wouldn't be myself. It wouldn't be me kissing you, touching you, fucking you. It would be something unhealthy. Something that doesn't deserve you."

She sucked in a tattered breath, her eyes molten, nipples

peaked. "But it *would* be you, and you *do* deserve me."

"No—" It took every drop of willpower I possessed, but I pushed her away and stepped back. "I don't."

The sexual fog that'd slowly wisped around us was so dense I could barely breathe. My skin was on fire. My body in torture. And she'd pissed me off thinking she could psychoanalyse me. That she could stand before me and write a medical script of bullshit, providing me with a cure that meant nothing.

She wasn't a doctor who could snap her fingers and fix me. And she definitely couldn't stand there, dangling herself as bait, persuading me to *try*. To trust.

Trust what?

That I wouldn't screw everything up again?

"El—" Pim stumbled forward, her fingers micro-beats away from touching me.

If she touched me, it was all over.

Unleashing my temper to full gale, my arm shot up and my hand wrapped quickly around her throat.

Pim switched from turned-on to petrified.

Night and day.

Black and white.

She'd tried to manipulate my flaws to get what she wanted. Well, now I'd do the same to her.

Panic swirled in her fascinating eyes as her fingers looped over my wrists, the hint of nails digging in warning.

My hand shook, my stomach queasy at deliberately making her fear, but she had to listen, had to hear, had to behave. My fingers tightened around the delicate column, feeling the gushing of her blood and rapid heartbeat. "I'm done talking about this, little mouse. It's off-limits. Do you understand?"

I waited for the panic to evolve into a full-blown attack. For her to associate my imprisonment with whatever torture she'd lived through. I cursed myself for doing such a thing even as I condemned myself for not letting go.

She stopped breathing as my fingers tightened, but her

terror never escalated—if anything, it receded—slowly switching the whiteness of her face to flushed bravery. Her eyes remained steady on mine, daring me to go further. Her temper billowed, shoving aside whatever weakness she might've felt and facing me head on.

Christ, this woman.

Swallowing hard, I was the one who backed down. Loosening my fingers, I caressed her throat with my thumb in homage and utmost respect. Her pulse hammered, but it wasn't from horror anymore, it was anger.

Her skin broke out in goosebumps as my fingers continued to pet. I didn't give them permission. I simply couldn't survive if I didn't touch her.

Lust leapt back into my body—a terrible toilsome passenger, twining its limbs through mine, doing its best to turn me into a puppet and obey its mastery to fuck this woman and damn the consequences.

My mouth watered to kiss her. To lick her.

I was so close to giving in.

So, *so* close.

But I didn't.

Because I love her.

Dropping my touch, I backed up a step. "I'm sorry."

"You should be."

My eyes snapped to hers. I didn't know what I'd expected, but dripping fury wasn't one of them. "Excuse me?"

She stood with her hands balled and a wildness in her gaze I hadn't seen before. Something damning and provoking, something that punched me in the gut and had way too much power over me.

It made me want to bow at her feet and do whatever she commanded.

"You heard me." Her chin tilted with defiance. "You *should* be sorry. Not for trying to scare me with your hand on my throat—I've learned to control it. Wait." She held up her hand. "If I'm going to be honest, that's a lie. I haven't learned to control it. You're the one who helped me because you've shown I can trust you not to hurt me. That touch from you—on any part of my body—is not only wanted but *invited*."

"Pim…"

"If you were looking for a trigger to put me in my place, too bad. That trigger is gone. If I can do that…who's to say you can't work on yours?"

Coming toward me, she licked her lips, her eyes dancing over my mouth with a flash of liquid need. "I won't fight you on the lock. If you had it installed for your own peace of mind, then fine. I can live with that. But don't expect me to use it."

"You will use it." My voice came out harsh—a barbarous demand. "I want to know you're safe."

She shook her head, irritation bright on her face. "I *am* safe. I'm safe around you. Why don't you believe that? When you next let me into your bed, Elder, I'll show you."

"There won't be a next time."

"Ha." Walking around me, she paused by the door, tapping her foot impatiently. She cocked her head toward the empty corridor. "Leave."

What the hell?

First, she'd invited me into her room, and now, she'd *banished* me?

I moved stiffly over the threshold. "You're telling me you've rescinded your dinner invitation?"

"You did that, not me."

"And now you don't want my company, at all?"

"That was you, too." Running a hand through her hair, the arching of her body made me goddamn insane. "If it was up to me, you would spend the night. Here. With me. We'd be completely honest with each other. I'd tell you everything you're dying to learn about me, and you'd tell me everything that made you so afraid of your intelligence and perfectionism. We'd fall madly in—"

"Hold up. Intelligence and perfectionism?" I laughed coldly. "*That's* what you think this is? Some glamorous, *romantic* condition that makes me smart because I have to repeat and repeat until I'm a master at something? That I'm in love with perfectionism just because I crave the best of the best and not because I can't accept anything less?" I rolled my eyes, another dark chuckle escaping. "Once again, you're being completely naïve, Pimlico."

I didn't ask this time if I should keep using that name. That *was* her name. Especially when she was acting like this...this crazy.

I was trying to be good.

Why the fuck did she want me to be bad?

"You think if we lived together, side by side in one room, we would survive each other?" I laughed. "That we'd fall madly in love—that *was* what you were going to say, wasn't it?"

Pain lashed through her gaze before she tipped her nose arrogantly. "You'll never know what I was going to say because you cut me off. Love—that silly word. I don't think I know the meaning of it anymore. I thought you deserved my love." She tutted condescendingly. "However, you're quickly proving I might be wrong in the matter."

My fists pounded to hit something.

How *dare* she give me something I held so highly, only to rip it away in our first fight.

I wanted to maul her in anger and desire.

A sick, twisted combination that would only lead us further into hell.

I was losing control.

I need to leave.

Pointing a trembling finger in her face, I snarled, "You're the one messing this up."

"Oh?" She smiled cavity sweet. "How exactly? How does my understanding and forgiveness screw up your already screwed-up existence?"

My brain misfired as I fought the sudden wash of acrimony. She was pure vexation. "You could stop believing in fairytales for one."

"I haven't believed in fairytales for a long time, Elder. I think you're mistaking me for someone who hasn't lived with evil. Who doesn't know true darkness. And someone who isn't afraid of a little greyness inside you when you're trying to convince me it's the end of the world." She leaned toward me, baring white teeth. "Newsflash, it's not."

I almost lost it.

Almost.

It was the challenge and provocation on her face that tipped me off and kept me human rather than a monster.

She was *trying* to make me angry.

She was trying to make me to snap.

I stumbled backward. "I'm done listening to this."

"Good." She crossed her arms. If I wasn't watching her so closely, I might've missed the tremor hidden beneath the airs and graces of indifference. "Leave, then."

Retorts were hot on my tongue, but I swallowed them back like razor blades. I wouldn't listen to her half-cocked theories anymore. And I wouldn't play this game.

My voice thickened with gravel as I straightened, seeking some resemblance of calmness. "Stop thinking the flaws in my brain are something to be embraced rather than run from, Pim. Stop tempting me and making it seem as if I gave in and fucked you—if I shoved you against the wall and stopped fighting myself—that it wouldn't be the end but only the beginning."

I invaded her space, inhaling her soft fragrance, our noses close to touching. "It would be a beginning but not one either of us could survive."

Her gaze glowed with fire. "El—"

"I put a lock on your door for a reason. Use it. If I come by in the night because of some misstep in judgment, I hope to fucking God you obeyed me and locked me out because if you don't, Pim—if you don't do this one thing for me, then whatever happens is on you. I carry too much guilt for things I've done to carry any more. Especially when I've done my best to prevent them."

Raking a hand over my face, I backed into the corridor and bowed stiffly. "I know my limitations. I suggest you learn yours. Goodnight, Pimlico. It's a pleasure to have you back on board. Don't make me regret coming back for you."

She clutched the door, her body calm despite my cruelty.

She looked me up and down slowly as if assessing me and finding me wanting. Finally, she sighed, pushing the door inch by inch to block me from her. "You say it's a pleasure, yet you look at me like it's a curse." Angry tears glittered in her brilliant eyes. "You've been honest with me, so I'll be honest with you. You came back for me, not out of gentlemanly behaviour or guilt, but because there was no other way for us. Whatever exists between us, Elder—it won't allow separation—whether physical, emotional, or sexual. And until we either acknowledge that or agree to never see each other again, no locks can stop what will happen. No rules or negotiations will prevent it. I've accepted that...I wonder how long it will be until you do the same."

With just a fraction of space between the door clicking home, and only half her face visible, she murmured, "I suggest you get some rest or play your cello or do whatever it is you do to find peace because until you give in, until you *trust*, until you allow yourself to live rather than stay chained up the way you have been, you're not going to be happy."

Her final words as the door closed were, "And I want you to be happy. With me."

Pimlico

I DIDN'T LOCK the door.

I probably should have.

Just like I probably shouldn't have antagonised him, especially after he'd come back and been fully prepared to break me out of jail.

I didn't mean to make it harder for him...he just made it so hard to love him.

He'd coped with having me around the first time because I was recovering and lost—not to mention mute. The scraps of his affection had been as unique and beautiful as stars.

But now, I was awake and ready to feel *everything*. And those scraps and stars weren't enough anymore. I wanted planets. I wanted galaxies.

I wanted his heart.

He couldn't blame me.

He was the one who brought me back. I'd walked away to prevent this from happening.

Currently, my very presence hurt him...so what did he hope to achieve? Did he expect to keep me close but never see me? To know I was safe but never touch or speak to me—as if I were a priceless figurine polished and shatter free on his mantle?

I don't think so.

If that was the case, then whatever this was would never work.

I knew what I wanted now, and after a lifetime of being someone else's, I was ready to bravely go after it.

Besides, Elder had acquiesced to my hunting him the moment he'd marched into that police station. I wouldn't let the guilt at picking a fight with him make me forget that part.

Yes, he was off somewhere, no doubt livid and cursing my name. But wasn't that better than being apart? Hadn't the past few days shown us that pain had many layers and pain apart was unbearable compared to pain together?

Ugh! Men.

Pacing in my lovely room, I didn't reacquaint myself with the furniture or balcony. I merely kept moving, allowing my brain to sort through this mess so I could stop thinking about it.

Slowly, my anger subsided and remorse settled instead.

Damn...

I'd pushed Elder too far, too fast.

I'd embraced confrontation instead of diplomacy.

What I should've done was hugged him and thanked him profusely for being so generous.

What the hell was I thinking?

For someone to take me on was a *massive* responsibility. I came with baggage and not just the slavery-suitcases that were full to the brim, but also the empty parcels just begging to be filled with new experiences.

It was those reasons that made me a hard to care for lover.

I'd been denied so many enjoyments and luxuries, it had made me greedy. I wanted to grab each life morsel and indulge in every activity. I wanted to eat delicious food instead of leftovers in a dog bowl. I wanted to kiss every sunrise after being locked inside for years. And I wanted to be loved and to love after only knowing hate.

There was nothing wrong with that. In fact, if I had to

guess my mother would say that was healthy. Only, Elder was in the unfortunate place of being the one I'd chosen and not able to give me what I needed.

I was frustrated and annoyed at him.

He was frustrated and annoyed with me.

We'd skipped happy courtship, sprinted through contented marriage, and headed straight for a bitter divorce.

I came to a stop in the middle of the room.

I didn't want to think about this anymore.

I can't see a way forward.

On the one hand, I could return to my old life, finish my degree, seek out friends I never cared about, and leave. On the other, I could play by his rules for a time and see if there was some way to, perhaps not break them, but bend them just enough so we could both be happy.

It wasn't late, but exhaustion fell over me. My feet guided me toward the bed, my hands tugging at my clothing in preparation of warm sheets and hopefully healing dreams.

As I climbed into bed, I wished I could apologise.

To whisper that I hadn't meant to be such a problem.

I only wished he could see how much I cared for him. How much I wanted to curl into his lap and watch TV, to wipe away ice-cream from his bottom lip after sharing a dessert, to wrap a towel around his waist after indulging in a shared shower.

There was so much I hadn't experienced, and Elder didn't want to do any of it with me.

Elder had said he knew his limitations and expected me to learn mine.

Well, I already knew.

Love.

Love was my limitation and flaw combined.

I needed to love as much as I needed to be loved.

It wasn't a whimsical thing—it went deeper than that.

If I was to put myself on the couch, if I (heaven forbid) ever asked my mother for advice on romance, she'd probably say that need was a by-product of what'd happened to me.

For so long, I'd hated humans.

Despised men.

Cursed life in general to such a point I craved death.

But now, I was obsessed with living.

Of living to the maximum of my capacity.

Of giving my heart wholeheartedly.

Of falling in love chaotically.

Of soaking up every wonderful moment of togetherness that I could.

That was my flaw.

And it meant I would struggle every second of every day to stop my flaw from playing havoc on Elder's.

But I knew something he didn't.

Beneath his fixating mind and horror at causing more pain, he carried the same flaw I did. In the beginning, I hadn't seen it. Now I understood because his aches and bruises were the same as mine, and just like mine, they couldn't be tended to with bandages and pills.

He craved love, same as me.

He gasped for connection, same as me.

He needed physical touch so much it stole his humanity and turned him into someone he couldn't control.

That was the true problem between us.

Not OCD.

Not abuse.

Love.

And the one issue we might not overcome.

* * * * *

Two things: I didn't sleep well, and Elder didn't visit—despite my door remaining unlocked all night.

After living a few days on terra firma, the sensation of rolling water wasn't as comforting as it once had been. The slight queasiness of sea-sickness kept me company, even in sleep, prodding me awake to stare at the door, begging it to open.

All night, fantasies had tormented me: of Elder creeping in, me opening my eyes, all hooded and hazy, to see him standing over me with such a depthless adoring look, I instantly became wet. I'd open the covers, beckon him to join me, and sigh in relief as he cuddled me into his body.

The rest of that fantasy had become so X-rated that bubbles and dustings of untended to desire kept me hyper-sensitive for the rest of the night.

With my mind full of him, I showered and dressed in a simple black shift to begin my day.

I didn't know where Elder was and I tried not to seek him out. I made a promise to let him be and focused on everything else to keep my loneliness at bay.

I breakfasted on my own, thanks to visiting the kitchen and being gifted two warm freshly-baked croissants, smoked ham, and cheddar cheese with a bottle of squeezed apple juice. I took my stash to the top deck and had a picnic—sitting cross-legged on one of the canvas-wrapped lifeboats.

By the time I'd finished, I was dopey from the sunshine and turning pink.

Deciding I needed some sun protection and to walk off my breakfast, I explored the decks I'd never been to.

There was no one to tell me no and no Elder to warn me otherwise. Entering the lift, I went to the bottom and worked my way up.

For hours, I investigated engine bays, staff quarters, engineering offices, store rooms, and spare bedrooms. Somehow, I managed to focus on how wondrous the Phantom was and not torture myself about its elusive owner.

I became entranced with a small but well-stocked library. I allowed fascination over crates with enough food for an army to keep me occupied. But then I explored the centre deck and my resolve not to think about Elder fell apart.

This place...

I trailed down the same wide corridors and thick carpeting as all the other levels, yet for some reason, this one had an air of abandoned desolation.

Everything was pristine: the painted walls smudge free, the skirting boards unblemished. It seemed as if everything had been decorated and then forgotten about—locked up and left with its original purpose no longer required.

Goosebumps sprang over my arms as I passed bedroom after bedroom, slowly growing more and more chilled.

A large suite with Japanese screens and a dressing table adorned with cherry blossom artwork reminded me all too well of Elder's mother and the cherry blossom blouse she wore while screaming that she wished her son was dead.

This room couldn't be for her...could it?

Hugging myself, I carried on.

Next was another suite—complete with cracked leather wingback and masculine décor—aimed for an elderly man but completely unlived in.

This place couldn't be for his uncle...could it?

Trepidation tiptoed down my spine.

I'm not meant to see this.

I didn't know how I knew, but this area was private.

Painfully private.

I should leave...

Even as I scolded myself, my bare toes sank into the carpet, propelling me forward. My eyes caught the next door— a splash of colour inviting me to peek.

Holding my breath, I inched farther and slammed to a halt in the doorway.

A child's room.

A cute ruffle bedspread complete with carrousel floor lamp and shelving with Christmas in every cubby. Brand new toys sat in perfect packaging, waiting to be played with. A cream rocking horse, complete with silver mane and tail and baby blue saddle with reins waited to be ridden.

I backed away, my hand clamping over my mouth.

Oh, no...

Behind me was another room.

This one was taffy and butterscotch with a princess bed, child-size dollhouse, and a tower of bow-tied unopened boxes of Legos.

My heart literally broke.

Into pieces.

Into fractured tinkling pieces.

Wedging balled hands against my chest, I did my best to stop those pieces clinking together and giving away my trespass.

What did this mean?

What *was* this place?

Had Elder painstakingly designed each space for his cousins and aunts and uncles? Had he sent out invitations for them to join him, begging them to turn him from No One into someone again? Into an uncle...a *son*...?

Oh God, had he stood here, night after night, day after day with only shadows for company? How long had he sailed the seas with this agonising reminder that love had been stolen and never given back?

No wonder he fought me so hard on the subject.

No wonder he was so difficult, so prickly.

I choked on the blasphemy of family. I suffocated on the acidity of affection.

How did he survive it?

The relentless wishing for something he would never earn?

This was a secret I shouldn't have seen. I collapsed into repentance.

All I wanted to do was embrace him. Kiss him. Show him his family might have forgotten him but I never would.

I would chase away the silence; I would scatter away the shadows. I would spend my life making sure he was never lonely again.

I have to get out of here.

What would he do if he knew I'd been down here? How would I look at him without seeing these empty unwanted rooms?

Inhaling hard, I tiptoed back the way I came.

It was late afternoon, and I still hadn't heard from him. Where was he?

What is he doing?

Pressing the button for the elevator, I fully intended to return to my room, shower away this terrible secret, and compartmentalize so Elder would never know. However, that was before a loud shout ripped my head up, directing my attention to the opposite way I'd explored.

A masculine shout.

A growl.

Followed by something smashing against a wall.

What on earth?

The lift arrived with a soft chime, but I drifted toward the raucous, jumping when another angry grunt shattered the quietness.

I didn't want to see any more of Elder's private pain, but I couldn't stop myself.

Another shout followed by a male reply.

Elder and Selix?

I thought Elder's office was on the upper levels, closer to his living quarters.

What's he doing down here?

My toes ghosted over the off-white carpet, my black dress floating around my calves. I stepped lighter, wishing I could float so my breach of personal space would remain unheard.

I'd become a master at eavesdropping—thanks to doing my best to pre-empt what Alrik and his bastard friends would do next—but this time, I felt dirty trying to listen.

This conversation had nothing to do with me...

I should leave.

I didn't.

Coming to a stop, the muffled shouts enunciated clearer through a closed door to my left. With my heart scrabbling up my throat, I pressed my ear against the wall.

"Not gonna happen, Selix. For fuck's sake."

Elder.

My tummy clenched just hearing his gorgeous timbre.

I really shouldn't be doing this.

I battled with right and wrong. I even pulled back a little and glanced at the waiting elevator. But then one word made me slam my ear back into position, and I gave up any guilt at listening.

Chinmoku.

"They've found you. You realise that, right?" Selix asked.

"I've been well aware since my mother decided to stay in my home without telling me. Or have you not noticed the number of times I've been on the phone, arranging a human fortress to protect my family?"

"Of course, I've noticed. You're not the only one running this shit show. All I'm saying is, I think we should turn back— head to the warehouse. If you're going to do this, we need more ammunition on the Phantom."

"There's enough armament on this boat to sink ten Titanics," Elder growled. "If they attack us on the ocean, we'll win. I don't care about that."

"Then what the hell is your problem? You've been sour for days."

"My problem is I don't know what to do anymore. Sail home and fight the Chinmoku's underling dogs who are toying with my family, or hold my ground and hunt the head of the pack from where I have the best advantage."

"You already have your family protected better than you ever could on your own. It's not just you who gets updates, Prest. I help juggle those security guys, and they've been telling you all along not to bother coming. The Chin's are relying on you falling for their bait and being easier to kill on land."

A small pause before Selix added, "I get that you're torn. That not going home feels like betrayal, but you're doing the right thing. Stay the course. Fight the head. Ignore the fucking tail because you've got men to do that for you. Focus on getting *your* head on straight and—"

"My head *is* on straight."

"Could've fooled me." Selix snorted. "The mood you're in? It's fucking getting on my nerves."

A warning grumble came through the wall followed by Elder's retort, "Well, that makes two of us."

"What's up your ass?"

"I'm fucked off because I don't understand how they knew she was with me."

"What?"

My forehead furrowed with the same confusion as Selix.

Elder said, "When I hacked into the Monaco police records, I wasn't the only one who'd infiltrated her record. Someone else deliberately looked up her file." A slight pause. "They didn't use her name, though…"

"What did they use?"

"QMB."

"QMB?" Selix asked.

"Quarterly Market of Beauties." Elder's voice turned dark. "The place where Pim was sold."

No one spoke for a moment; my heart roared so loud it threatened to overshadow my ability to listen.

"Oh, shit," Selix said. "You don't think…?"

When Elder didn't reply, my mind ran rampant with questions.

Think what?

What did the QMB have to do with the Chinmoku?

Why had someone else accessed my file?

Was it Monty?

Was someone still hunting me?

Was whoever in charge of the slavery auction hunting me down to silence me?

What?

Elder finally muttered, "What if the Chinmoku are the directors of the QMB?"

The question hung heavy and unanswered, winding around my heart.

Selix didn't reply.

Elder answered his own pondering. "I always knew they were into trafficking. I was too young to fully understand how deep their ring went, but what if they know Pim was sold? What if they were the ones who sold her? What if they're not only chasing me for breaking my oath but also chasing her to take her back?"

I stumbled away from the wall as a sudden vicious, *vicious* panic attack hit from nowhere.

The thought of unknown strangers.

A faction filled with heartless slavers.

Ripping me from Elder's safety.

Selling me to yet another life of misery.

I almost passed out from sick, icy fear.

My heart stopped beating.

My throat closed up.

Elder and Selix continued to speak, but I couldn't listen anymore.

I was seconds away from collapsing to my knees and having a full-blown relapse.

Using the wall as support, I half-stumbled, half-bolted toward the elevator. There, I punched the button while clawing at my throat for air as the silver doors slid open and I threw myself in.

Please, please, please.

Breathless, careless, I barely managed to press the floor number before my knees gave out and I landed on them with a painful crunch.

I didn't know if the lift moved or if the doors closed or if I was still alone.

All I knew was Alrik

and classical music

and whips

and chains

and blood

and agony

and begs

and the knowledge that if anyone, *anyone,* tried to do that to me again, I wouldn't hesitate to see how bad my fate would be.

I would slit my wrists, eat a bullet, jump into the vast, vast ocean and be done with it.

I would say no.

No to the Chinmoku.

No to evil.

No!

My lungs struggled to convert air into oxygen, granting a much needed gulp, mixing with suffocation. My back rounded as I landed on all fours, gulping for more, noticing tears dripped down my cheeks, landing on the floor. My recent bruises from Harold's kicks and fists swelled into an orchestra of old injuries—reminding me all over again that just because I ignored the pain didn't mean it wasn't there…haunting me.

The elevator opened, revealing the rose-gold accents of my corridor, beckoning sanctuary.

Hauling myself to my feet, I swiped at the tears, opened my mouth wide for scraps of oxygen, and hugged myself as tremors and shivers added to the quick attack.

I thought I was through with them.

That every day away from such events patched up the final holes in my damaged psyche.

I hated that I was so weak the very thought of going back to where I'd come from was enough to shove me straight into suicide all over again.

I entered my room, closed the door, and collapsed on the floor against it. I gave into the sobs and allowed the rest of my attack to take me.

I wasn't weak knowing I would rather die than survive that again. I was selfish because I understood what life and love *should* be like. I was grateful to have a comparison.

It wasn't weak to know my limits.

It was strength because now I knew where the lines were

drawn. How far I could be pushed and how far I could bend before I broke.

If what Elder suspected was true, I wanted every last Chinmoku to die the most horrific, agonising death. In a way, I wanted Elder to pay for the small part he'd played as their errand boy, no matter how young and naïve he was.

Guilt infected me at the thought.

The Chinmoku had stolen his life just the way they'd stolen mine. They'd taken his brother and father and banished him from his family. They'd taken my mother and made me vanish from girl to toy.

If what Elder said was true, we both had a reason to fight.

One thing was for certain, I wouldn't let him go to battle on his own, and I wouldn't waste any more time pining for something he wasn't ready to give.

Worst things still existed out there.

Leaning against the door, my eyes climbed upward until I stared at the new lock above my head.

I would never use it to lock Elder out.

I would never treat him with suspicion or coldness.

But for now…I reached up and turned it.

The soft click of the barrier helped eradicate the rest of my panic attack, and I inhaled a shaky breath.

The lock was both symbol and real.

I didn't lock out Elder.

I didn't lock out bad memories or future perils or any other nightmare the world had to offer.

I locked out my fear.

I locked out my panic attacks.

I finally managed to say…no more.

I'd had enough.

If the Chinmoku were hunting us…let them come.

They would be the ones dying, not us.

ELDER

SHE DID AS I asked.

Locked.

Sighing, I pressed my forehead against her door. My fingers trailed from the unturnable handle and up the lacquered wood, wishing it was Pim I touched.

What did I expect?

Three a.m. and I hadn't been to see her all day. After hours of strategizing with Selix, I wasn't good company. It was out of chivalry that I kept my distance. She didn't deserve my strung-out temper.

Were the Chimmoku involved in her selling or had my mind finally cracked—running around a maze with no answers, bumping into theories, ricocheting off dead ends.

I honestly didn't know anymore.

It didn't mean I wasn't desperate to see her, though.

The wood of her door was smooth beneath my fingers as I rested my forehead against it and breathed for the first time all day.

I let go of my stress and worry and guilt and stood outside her room, finding a scrap of peace just by being near her.

Ever since my brain decided to figure out who had accessed her police record, I couldn't think about anything else.

I couldn't stop searching with binoculars to see if the Chinmoku sailed behind us. I couldn't stop checking the weapons cache, ensuring guns and other firepower were in good working order in case of an ocean siege.

I was fucking exhausted from patrolling the Phantom and seeking out any weaknesses. The hull was enforced with carbon fibre. The framework with titanium. Bullet-proof armoured plating encased each of the bedrooms, and the missile defense system was top of the line. If it was a war they wanted, my yacht would stand up to whatever weaponry they had. But if it was Pim they wanted, then I would rip them limb from fucking limb.

I would turn savage and not just shoot them as I'd planned.

They'd taken my family.

There's no way in hell they're taking her, too.

For the second time in days, I came face to face with the thought of not having Pim in my life. Leaving her in Monaco showed me the agony I would endure knowing she lived in the same world as me, talking to others, smiling at others, falling *in love* with others.

That was brutal enough.

But the thought of the Chinmoku taking her, selling her, hurting her….It showed me a horror I couldn't even contemplate, let alone survive. I raged at the thought of them killing her, of her *not* talking to others, smiling at others, falling in love with others.

Of not falling in love with me.

Of blank eyes and lost soul.

Of death.

And that unhappy train of thought was how I'd found myself outside her door at three in the morning when I should've numbed myself with a joint and fallen into a fitful sleep.

I wasn't here to force myself on her. I wasn't here for sex period. The images of her dead and broken did not turn me on in the slightest.

I wasn't here for any of the reasons why I'd installed the lock in the first place.

I was here to stare at her while she slept—to remind myself she was still alive and safe. That she was here with me and not lost in Monte Carlo. I was here to lie silently beside her, to breathe her in, to hold her close, to bury my face in her hair and try to find some sanity.

I'd turned to her and not the weed in my bedside drawer for comfort.

And what had she done?

She'd locked me out.

On my orders.

Fuck.

I could knock.

I could punch the door and wake her up. I could grab her the moment she opened it, all sleep warm and dream fuzzy, and carry her back to bed. I had no doubt she would welcome me with open arms. She'd run her fingers through my hair and be both lover and mother for however long I needed. She would let me hold her until I could breathe again.

But I couldn't ask her to do that.

I was supposed to be the protector in this world, not her. She was supposed to trust me to stay strong and know what the hell I was doing. I wouldn't tell her I'd been lying to her all along.

Lying that I had no fucking clue about any of it anymore and needed guidance. That I was willing to try whatever she wanted if it meant I could finally be normal.

Drawing away from her door, I balled my hands.

Earlier today, I'd made the agonising decision not to sail to America—to trust the men I'd put in charge to handle the mess over there and focus on life on this side of the globe.

My business didn't stop running just because I was having a crisis of identity and loyalty. Pim didn't stop existing just because I couldn't get my head on straight.

Life moved on.

I had work to attend to.

Therefore, I'd commanded Jolfer to change our course back to the original one.

We had a few days before we arrived in England. Not only would Pim be my plus one at the Hawk's Masquerade but she'd also accompany me on a few other visits around town.

But before we docked, I had every intention of finding my way back to being kind and generous. I *missed* her.

I'd missed her when I left her behind, and I missed her now that she was back in my life.

It's ridiculous.

Why keep myself from the one person I wanted to spend time with?

Why believe in delusions that the more distance I put between us, the less I'd fall in love with her? That there was some possible way of revoking the fall and returning to stable ground where my heart belonged to me and not a woman who had the utmost power to shatter it?

Stalking down the corridor and back to my quarters, I finally admitted to myself.

No distance or avoidance could cure me.

Because I was no longer falling.

I'd crashed and burned and had no possible way of getting up.

Pimlico

"GOOD MORNING."

I glanced up, squinting against the bright sunshine. Elder's silhouette was black and sharp against the glowing fireball behind him.

Bringing my hand up, I did my best to block the over-saturation of light and focus.

To study his face.

To see if any remnants of his awful overheard epiphany yesterday still lurked on his features.

He gave me a sad half smile. An apologetic warmth in his gaze. He stood in an open neck muslin shirt with light coloured jeans. His hair glistened with shower-droplets and the way his jaw clenched as he studied me made my heart race to eradicate the distance between us.

To clamber off the canvas-covered lifeboat and leap into his arms.

To tell him I'd eavesdropped on his conversation and knew everything.

To promise him I wasn't afraid, and I would do whatever it took to keep him safe.

But before I could return the greeting or move from my perched spot, he moved closer and sat beside me. His thighs tensed as if ready to spring back up, his body coiled tighter than anyone should be at this time in the morning.

"Mind if I join you?" He glanced at me; his eyes narrowed against the sun.

His hair glittered blue-black while his skin seemed to glow. The sun wasn't an enemy to him, painting him in warmth and sincerity while, at the same time, revealing fine lines around his mouth and stress that shouldn't be there.

"Of course." I scooted sideways to give him more room so the rigging wouldn't dig into his thigh.

He scowled, seeming hurt that I'd moved away from him.

Worry bubbled. Patting the canvas next to me, I murmured, "Come closer. I don't want you uncomfortable."

"Why would I be uncomfortable?"

"The rope." I pointed at his leg where the giant salt-frosted rope pressed against his jeans. "I'm making you squish onto the end."

He shook his head, his lips curling into a smirk. "I'm not uncomfortable."

"Okay." I glanced away, unable to hold the intensity in his gaze for more than a few seconds. He'd replaced the sunshine with his onyx stare, and it was just as blinding.

Despite his assurances that he wasn't uncomfortable, he shifted toward me. His hands flexed on the canvas, hoisting his weight closer. I couldn't look away from his perfect fingers, square nails, or the veins running along the ridges of his knuckles.

Those hands had been on my skin.

Those fingers had been inside my body.

This man had touched me, loved me, and I hadn't run away screaming.

So why did everything with Elder now feel as if we'd reverted back to strangers? Why couldn't I figure out what to say? How to act? Why was self-consciousness ruining this sweet, simple moment of sitting quietly in the new sun?

Elder must've felt the same way as he moved restlessly,

making the pulleys groan a little. He cleared his throat as he looked at the sky, a staff member buffing a banister, a seagull soaring past—anything but me. Anywhere but where I truly wanted him to look.

The silence was no longer a visible thing; it was a wall between us—thick and soundproof.

This couldn't be allowed to continue.

Turning a little to face him, I placed my hand on his.

He jolted, his fingers curling around the edge of the lifeboat as if having me touch him was physically painful. Which could entirely be the case seeing as he fought more complicated desires than me. A simple touch for me might be a lewd promise to him and one he'd sworn never to break.

My heart hurt as I quickly removed my hand. "Sorry."

He swallowed a gruff groan. "I'm the one who's sorry."

I didn't know how to respond to that. My mind sifted through too many things he might be apologising for. But I couldn't see anything that was his direct fault and not a combined effort on both our parts.

"You've nothing to be sor—"

"I do." Jumping off the lifeboat, he spun in front of me. His large hands landed on my knees and without thinking, he pushed my legs apart.

Today was the first day I'd braved a different wardrobe item other than a baggy dress. I no longer suffered claustrophobia and rather liked the idea of mixing up my style choices. Today, I'd opted for an over-size t-shirt in the softest blue coupled with a pair of grey shorts with a pleat ironed down the front.

It'd taken some getting used to having the waistband tight around my belly, but I was ridiculously thankful I'd worn them as Elder spread my legs and stepped into the gap.

He didn't seem to notice I'd battled my hatred for clothing and won. He didn't notice his thumbs circled my naked knees or that his touch tightened on my thighs to jerk me closer.

It all happened too fast to micro-analyse, yet that was

exactly what my brain did.

It hyper focused on how warm and hard he was between my legs. How his hands drifted over my thighs and wedged themselves under my ass, squeezing me with a thread of violence. I no longer sat on the lifeboat. I sat on him, and God, the *thrill* that gave me, the knowledge he'd gathered me close without me fighting for it...

It turned me to stone and jelly all at the same time.

My heart wobbled like some ridiculous raspberry dessert while my limbs locked into granite. I wanted to melt. To throw my arms over his shoulders, cup the back of his head, and bring his lips to mine.

Instead, I waited. I studied. I paused until he blinked hard and his nostrils flared, slowly realising how he'd gone from sitting beside me to wedged as tight against me as he could.

"Ah, shit." He exhaled heavily, his fingers loosening around my ass.

"Wait," I murmured as he went to pull away.

He stopped, his eyes meeting mine in a silent plea to tell him what to do.

That look of uncertainty when Elder had been everything but uncertain dove into my chest and took a pitchfork to my heart.

"I don't want you to leave." Holding my breath, I reached up and cupped his cheek with a shaking palm. "I've wanted you to touch me since I saw you at the police station."

"I've wanted to kiss you since I saw you at the police station." His eyes burned into mine. "The kiss I gave you wasn't enough. I doubt any would be enough where you're concerned."

His brutal honesty tripped me up.

"You can kiss me again...if you want."

"I can't."

My head swam with gooey desire. "What's stopping you?"

"You know what's stopping me."

"It's just a kiss."

He licked his lips as his body gave in, all the while fighting it with words. "We both know it's not just a kiss."

My hand crept up his cheek to his temple.

He shuddered as I ran my fingers through his hair, caressing him. I had to sit higher to direct my hand around to the back of his neck. My back arched, pushing my breasts out, my position giving him all the signals he needed.

"Kiss me." Applying a touch of nail, I pulled his head downward.

The strength of his neck fought me, not budging. His eyes danced over my face as if deciding how to thwart me without hurting my feelings.

Then…it was as if something cracked inside him…as if a tiny box he kept padlocked and protected smashed beneath a sledgehammer.

And then he collapsed forward.

And his mouth crashed against mine.

And his lips were so warm and wet and welcoming.

And he *kissed* me.

I'd asked for the kiss, but he wholeheartedly donated it.

His lips kissed soft and hard. His tongue flicked over my mouth, not asking, not begging, but demanding entry to taste me.

I let the stress-granite leave me and the lust-melting happen. I shivered as his arms wrapped around me, clutching me close as our lips fused and the kiss turned primal in its intensity.

The warmth of the morning sun beat down on us as my breathy moan met his tattered groan—fuelling us ever harder into something that should be so tender but was so utterly violent.

I matched his ferocity with my own. My fingers clutched at his hair, tugging for more, *more*.

I forgot myself. I forgot we were in open view of the staff. I forgot about the past few days and the fear of what was coming. I forgot about everything but him.

But Elder didn't forget.

He tore himself away, backing up and rubbing his mouth as if desperate for another kiss but determined to only take one. "Pim…"

His voice bordered on a reproach. As if that kiss was my fault.

Was it my fault?

I would take responsibility for some of it, but he was too strong for me to manhandle if he didn't want it.

Leaping off the lifeboat, I stood with my hands on my hips. "If you say something like that was a mistake, or it won't happen again or any other stupid cliché, I'm going to…to…"

A slight smirk twisted his lips. "You're going to what?"

"I don't know. Throw you overboard."

"The captain would stop." He crossed his arms, enjoying my temper.

"Fine, I'd—I'd hit you on the head with an oar."

His gaze went to the lifeboat oars resting neatly in their brackets. "Those weigh a ton. Even I wouldn't be able to use it as a weapon."

"You're taking all the fun out of my hypothetically harming you." I hid my smile even as one brewed. "Let a girl have some fantasies."

He cocked his head. "You have fantasies about me?"

And just like that, we were back to the dilemma of sparking attraction, high-octane lust, and the unbearable need to touch, thrust, and consume.

Goosebumps prickled as said fantasies that included nakedness and no weapons filled my mind.

Elder's lips parted, picking up on the way my chest rose and my fingers fluttered to touch him again. "Well?"

Stepping toward him, I nodded. "I can't stop having fantasies about you. If you know of a cure, then please…tell me."

Any hint of joking and games vanished as his shoulders slouched and he rubbed his face with one hand. "If I knew that cure, I'd take it myself."

I schooled myself not to be hurt. He hadn't meant he wanted to be cured of me, just like I hadn't meant I wanted to be cured of him. We both just wanted to find a way through this minefield of my past and his obsession and learn how to be together without an airport of unclaimed baggage following us around.

"Ah, sir?" A staff member appeared, carrying a small tray with two coffee cups. "As you requested."

Elder nodded respectfully as he claimed both drinks. "Thank you. Please tell the chef we're ready for breakfast if that suits."

"Right away." The man bowed, gave me a smile, then returned the way he'd come with his now empty tray.

I eyed Elder's new possessions. "Didn't sleep last night?"

He spun to face me, suspicion written all over his face. "What makes you say that?"

For some reason, I got the distinct impression he hadn't slept. That my blasé comment had hit a nerve. What did he get up to yesterday after I overhead his conversation? I hadn't heard his cello, but that didn't mean he didn't play.

After I'd locked my door, I'd slept surprisingly well. I didn't know what that said about my state of mind, but for the first time, I wasn't on high alert waiting for someone—friend or foe—to come through the door uninvited.

"Double coffee." I pointed at the two cups.

He shook his head, dispelling whatever he'd been thinking. "One of them is for you." Coming toward me, he held out the cup.

I took it gently, careful not to spill the creamy flower design made from the milk on top. "You knew I'd be here?"

"I saw you from the bridge." He pointed at the highest point of the yacht where the shadows of staff and captain hinted that just because we weren't looking where we were sailing didn't mean countless other people weren't.

Taking a sip of his coffee, he added, "I went to see Jolfer

this morning. Wanted to confirm the route to England. I spotted you sitting on the lifeboat and figured I owed you an apology."

"Back to the apology."

He nodded. "Back to that." He took another sip. "I'm sorry for abandoning you the past two days, and I'm sorry if I made you feel anything but welcome. I...I love having you here with me and haven't done a very good job of showing that."

I didn't want to tell him I'd been reading between the lines long enough that I understood more than I should. That he loved me being here but cursed himself for not being able to take advantage. That he loved spending time with me but didn't trust himself to keep it purely platonic.

If that kiss was anything to go by, I'd say his worries were founded upon fact. Not that I would tell him that as I didn't want such boundaries or fears to remain between us.

I joined him in drinking the perfectly brewed caffeine. "What way did you tell him?"

"Hmm?" He licked his lips free from frothy coffee, making my stomach twitch with a carnal hunger I'd only just begun to understand.

"With your captain? How many ways are there to sail to England from here?"

His face lit up, grateful for a neutral topic where innuendoes and sexual undercurrents couldn't dwell. "Two technically."

When I continued to drink, waiting for him to elaborate, he said, "Basically, we can go through the Strait of Gibraltar or down past the Cape of Good Hope."

"Which is better?"

He shrugged. "Both are great journeys, but one is approximately six to seven days, and the other is over a month."

"Oh, wow."

He smiled. "I'm guessing you'd like to get home faster than a month, and we have a function to attend, so I have no choice but to go the shorter route."

I didn't mention that returning home wasn't a draw card anymore. In fact, England was rather the opposite. I didn't want to go back. My mother was locked up and untouchable while bad memories were free and rampant. If Elder hadn't just mentioned a function, I would suggest turning around and going somewhere else.

Curiosity built inside me. "We have a function? What is it?"

He scowled. "A masquerade in a drab English estate called Hawksridge."

Hawksridge…that name sounded familiar, but I didn't know why.

Elder noticed my kernel of enlightenment. "The Hawk family deal in diamonds. They supply most of the jewellers in London and far beyond. You might've heard of them."

"I've heard of Hawk diamonds. Yes."

"There you go." He finished his coffee with a disgusted look. "We're to attend because their clientele are often my clientele. The rich demographic normally likes the same things. Yachts, horses, diamonds…"

"So…this is a business meeting?"

"Something like that."

"Why do I have to attend?"

His eyes narrowed. "You're my plus one. However, if you'd rather not go…"

I held up my hand. "No, I'm honoured to accompany you." Even as I said it, I wondered if I would be up to mingling in a crowd. The last time I'd been at a function with finely dressed gentleman and prettily gowned women, I'd been strangled and abducted.

This might be even worse because everyone would be wearing masks.

Just like the auction at the QMB.

Oh, God.

My heart kicked into a canter, but I hid my trepidation.

I wouldn't give Elder any reason to suspect I couldn't handle whatever it was he needed me to handle—including him.

"We'll only be there an hour. Two at the most." He finished his coffee. "I'm reluctant to go, but I have an oath to keep, and that oath means earning money until I reach my target."

I hid my surprised laugh. "You have a target to amass *more* money?"

He cringed a little as if noticing how it sounded. How the idea of Elder—who had wealth far beyond what I could conceive—admitted he had the drive for more.

What could he possibly need that he couldn't afford with his current financial position?

I shook my head a little, trying to understand. He didn't come across as superficial or someone who spent a great deal on things just for flash and recognition. Sure, the Phantom was beyond luxurious, and he owned helicopters and Maybachs and whatever other expensive brands the rich and famous had, but he still retained an aura of someone who wasn't used to wealth.

Someone who had somehow stumbled into it and still wasn't comfortable spending unless it was to lavish a lifestyle on his family.

A family who never shows up to enjoy his generosity.

"It's hot today. Perhaps we should go inside out of the sun." Taking my empty cup, Elder kept his voice level, but something ate at him—something relating to money and secrets and reasons why he was the way he was.

I desperately wanted to know those reasons and was finally ready to give him any part of my past for a tiny fraction of his.

"El…" I moved toward him, placing my hand on his forearm.

He jolted at my touch but didn't jerk away. His gaze locked with mine, and everything I was about to suggest flew out of my head. I'd had envisions of inviting him to my suite.

Ordering a quiet breakfast and doing something we'd never done before.

Talk.

Truly talk like two strangers who didn't know a thing about each other but had one thing in common: a sexual attraction—a mutual fascination and hearts that'd whispered the same message the moment we'd met.

I liked Elder far too much. I loved Elder far too deep for logical reasoning. And I still knew nothing about him.

My tongue slid over my bottom lip while I did my best to coerce my thoughts into orderly sentences and not the tumbling acrobats they'd become.

Only, an excited voice rang on the warm sea breeze, breaking the heavy spell and snapping our eyes to the bow of the ship.

"What on earth is she pointing at?" I asked as a staff member with blonde pigtails bounced up and down. Her face was luminous with excitement. Her finger pointed at the water below.

Elder smiled. "Dolphins probably. I don't know why staff continue to get so excited. It's not like they're a rare occurrence." He said it so matter-of-factly, as if dolphins were as common as house flies.

My eyes widened. "They surf the wake?"

"Exactly. They're just using us for their own enjoyment."

"Can I see?"

He chuckled as I drifted toward the girl, becoming intoxicated by her joy. I hadn't seen a dolphin since my friend had her eighth birthday party at SeaWorld and the dolphins leapt and frolicked with big red balls. At the time, I'd been mesmerised. Now, the place had been shut down for animal welfare.

I couldn't stop my feet moving, but I didn't want to leave Elder. "Come with me?" I held out my hand, glancing over my shoulder as I continued to step toward the bow.

His face fell just for a moment.

My throat tightened with questions. I wanted to know what pained him. I needed to know how to fix it.

But then he smiled, shoving aside any hint of melancholy. "I have a better idea."

I stopped, totally unconvinced. "Better than watching dolphins?"

"Better." Crooking a finger, he murmured, "Come with me."

ELDER

I DIDN'T KNOW what the fuck I was doing.

Pim would no doubt laugh in my face or, worse, roll her eyes at such a stupid extravagance, or even worse, look at me differently for spending ridiculous sums of money on something no normal person should own.

But as we stepped into the elevator and I pressed the bottom level where the storage rooms, kitchen cold stores, and a motorbike rested, I told myself this was a good decision.

I'd bought it for times like this.

Originally, I thought it would be for my family with young cousins to impress, but that would never happen, and besides…this was even better.

Pim was better.

Pim was everything.

As the elevator doors opened, Pim looked up. Instead of the expected question of 'why did you bring me to the working part of the ship', she seemed at ease—as if she'd been down here before.

I frowned.

She had full run of the place—nothing was out of bounds. Well, the level where I argued with Selix yesterday I'd prefer she didn't see (or anyone else for that matter). I didn't know how I felt having her snoop, learning pieces about me without me telling her.

"Have you been here before?" I kept my voice light when really my question was heavy. If she had explored, what had she discovered? She wouldn't have seen what I was about to show her as it was behind a locked door and only I had the key, but still...my privacy had been tiptoed through.

She rubbed her arm, her gaze lighting on the wooden grates with a multitude of languages spray-painted on the front to the strapped and chocked motorbike. "Um, I might've explored a little."

"When?" My nostrils flared trying to taste her truth.

"Yesterday."

"Did you go anywhere else yesterday?" My back prickled. "Any other levels?"

She shrugged, laughing awkwardly with a guilty ring. "Only a couple. I got hungry and went to the kitchen for lunch then back to my room." Flashing me a look, she strode ahead, weaving around the strapping holding everything secure. "What did you want to show me down here?" Tossing over her shoulder, deliberately changing the subject, she pouted. "I can't believe I'm missing dolphins for this."

I had a good mind to force her back to my interrogation, but after being at odds for days, I wanted to find that happy place again.

I *needed* it.

The kiss on the deck had been the only good thing in my life, and the craving to continue had blended with the addiction for sex and the comfort of connection.

I wanted to touch her.

I just didn't want it getting out of control.

"You won't be missing out for long." Guiding her around a row of heavy-duty freezers and a huge walk-in fridge, I fumbled for the key chain in my pocket. "You'll see."

Pim followed, her face bright and quizzical. "You know...this isn't the prettiest level, but I find it fascinating."

She trailed her fingers over a crate labelled *fragile*.

I had no idea what was inside, but I paid my staff enough to figure it out. They had carte blanche to order more, purchase whatever, and stay on top of usage versus expenditure.

"This way."

She nodded with a soft smile as I marched ahead down the long corridor made up of stacked parcels, boxes, and containers. This level had no individual rooms apart from the area I was about to show her.

In my profession—the career of making toys for the mega rich and constantly having to come up with new and unique additions to best some other wealthy bastard's plaything—I experimented on the Phantom.

This yacht was the first to have it. It had been the showpiece to earn more business than I could handle. And a luxury I hadn't seen since I built the fucking thing.

"Oh, cool." Pim pointed at a jet ski that I'd completely forgotten, resting beneath a clear tarpaulin.

Unwanted millionaire toys all gathering dust.

What if this other toy didn't start? What if dragging her down here was an utter mistake and she missed out on the dolphins while I screwed around with something I should never have purchased in the first place?

My heart sped up with worry as we reached the end of the long yacht and paused. My hand landed on the doorknob of a special airlock. The large circular dial operated hundreds of little seals and locking mechanisms, completely unneeded unless someone tried to creep aboard this way or we sprung a leak.

"Ready?"

Pim joined me, her body so small beside mine. "What's in there?"

"You're about to find out."

She crossed her arms as if hugging herself would offer some form of protection. "Okay…"

Forcing myself to look away and ignore my own self-consciousness, I unwound the dial, unlocked the final seal with my key, and pushed the thick barricade open.

The sound of air rushing into the sealed chamber made a noise like a thundering tornado, only to end a fraction of a second later.

Pim shook her head in awe. "My ears just popped."

"That's because this place has its own circulation. It's completely cut off from the rest of the ship."

"Why?"

"For safety."

She pursed her lips as I stepped aside, letting her pass.

The room we stood in was cylindrical and held hooks and shelves for fresh towels, dressing gowns, and an array of bright swimming gear. Snorkels and masks, dive equipment, bikinis and shorts.

No expense was spared.

And nothing had been touched.

I hoped she wouldn't notice the child-size swimming gear or the still-in-their boxes inflatable lilos and rubber rings.

The silver walls held no windows or portals. The only way in and out were two doors—the one we came through and another at the end of the tube-like room.

"What is this place?" Pim moved forward in awe.

I turned and closed the door, wincing a little as the seals clicked into place, cutting us off from the rest of the yacht.

The new air pressure pushed down on us—warm and muggy, inviting us to explore the world where such a breeze came from.

"It's a changing room."

"If it's just a changing room why the bombproof door?" She turned to face me, eyebrows high.

"The room we're about to enter is special. It's secure, but in the case of an emergency, it could flood. The door is to prevent us from sinking if that happens."

She gulped. "Having a room that floods doesn't sound like the brightest idea when you live on the ocean."

I chuckled. "You might change your mind when you see what's in there."

"What *is* in there?"

"So impatient." Flashing her a smile, I moved toward the racks of bikinis and selected an emerald satin criss-cross thing. I tossed it to her. "Here, put this on."

She caught it mid-air. "Why?"

"Stop asking so many questions. Do you want to see the dolphins or not?"

"Yes."

"Well, then. Obey me and put the bikini on."

"But..." She fingered the brightly coloured Lycra. "There aren't any curtains or doors."

I swallowed my laugh. "You're saying you're shy all of a sudden? The girl who is more comfortable naked than clothed?"

She threw me a dirty look, her fingers straying to the slouchy t-shirt barely clinging to her shoulders. "I'm saying I'm trying to make this easier on you."

"On me?" I stabbed my chest with my finger. "How is a changing room going to help me?"

She rolled her eyes as if I was being deliberately obtuse. Which I couldn't deny, I was.

I hadn't come here with the intention of perving at her while she changed in front of me. But now, faced with the opportunity of seeing her naked and being allowed to stare but not touch made me rock fucking hard and utterly unable to stop.

I really should've thought this through.

I should've ordered her to change before coming into this tight chamber.

I should've commanded her to wear a parka and ski boots instead of throwing scraps of material at her and telling her to strip.

Fuck, just the thought of her stripping made my cock leap for attention.

Her attention.

Bad, bad idea.

I wouldn't be able to look without touching. I'd need to feel her so much, my heart would probably stop if I didn't.

"Shit." I gulped, backing up a step. "I'll—I'll turn around." Grabbing a pair of black swimming shorts, I went as far as I could and faced away.

It didn't help.

My mind took over, providing a private strip show where Pim shrugged out of her t-shirt and wriggled out of her shorts.

I groaned, digging my fingers into my eyes.

Turn around.

Touch her.

Kiss her.

I locked my knees and ripped my shirt off, giving my hands something to do.

She didn't move for a moment, but then the softest sounds of her t-shirt and shorts cascading to the floor echoed in my ears as loud as Big Ben. Her breath hitched and the damn silver walls reflected a wavy, distorted figure all skin tones and willowy bending down to step into green bikini briefs.

Goddammit, even looking like a Salvador Dali painting, she was still stunning. I couldn't tear my eyes away as her reflection reached up and wound her hair into a temporary bun at the base of her skull before tying two triangles over her breasts.

Just knowing how beautiful she was naked made denying myself all that much harder.

She was right.

She wasn't the one with nakedness issues. It was me. And it wasn't an issue but an obsession. I could turn and stare at her. I could move and touch her. I could undo the tiny bows and turn her naked all over again. I could sit in the middle of this tunnel, pull her onto my lap, and be inside her within seconds.

We could be joined, connected, instead of on opposite

ends of this godforsaken chamber.

I wanted her so much it *hurt*.

But I didn't move.

I won over the rampant desire and somehow managed to extract my hands from the twisted swimming shorts that I'd brutalised until I lost circulation.

Staying away from her was getting harder every day.

A few moments ticked past before Pim asked quietly, "Everything okay?"

I nodded curtly. "Fine."

Her voice broke the spell, and I quickly unbuttoned and unzipped my jeans then shoved them down with my boxers in one go. I was barefoot and kicked the offending material away as if it burned.

The most erotic moan met my ears.

Did Pim find me as attractive as I found her? Did she stare at my naked ass and not deplore my male flesh but actually want me as much as I wanted her?

My throat went dry as my cock—now free and no longer restrained in denim—stood to full mast.

The exhibitionist part of myself wanted to turn to face her. To show her the state she put me in. But if I did that—if she looked at me with the same heat from our kiss, if she came toward me and, heaven forbid, grabbed my length and squeezed...

Fuuuck, I almost came just thinking about it.

Trembling, I stepped into the board shorts. I struggled to shove my over-eager erection into the bathers and fasten the Velcro. There would be no hiding my reaction, but it served her right.

She knew the way I thought about her. She understood how much I wanted her. She'd tried to make this easier on me, yet it had made it that much fucking harder.

Kicking my discarded clothes into one of the small partitions, I muttered, "Come on. I need to get out of here."

She padded closer, looking far too gorgeous and bruised in

the strappy green bikini. Acres of delectable flesh painted in a multitude of colours from the asshole who'd caught her stealing. The globes of her breasts sat above ribs darkened by a boot, the swell of her ass creamy apart from a fading mark.

I wanted to commit murder as well as worship her for never complaining, never being less than invincible.

My fists curled as I did my best to curb my temper. No one would hurt her again.

No one.

Drinking in her beauty rather than her injuries, I cursed that everything I wanted to see was kept secret by emerald Lycra and tightly knotted bows.

Her cheeks pinked as I struggled to tug my gaze away.

Her voice turned breathy. "I agree. I'm suddenly feeling rather claustrophobic."

She was feeling claustrophobic? Try being in my skin when all I wanted to do was attack her. Having her in such a small room—utterly soundproof, completely people proof—made my instincts to climb inside her go berserk.

Spinning the dial on the opposite door, I focused on the sounds of multiple locks slipping from their casings to break the seal and grant us entry into the most surreal place imaginable.

"Oh, my God, Elder." Pim bowled past me.

I let her, moving aside and closing the door after me.

This room was nothing but extravagance.

Canaletto walnut and polished rosewoods added depth and warmth to eggshell walls. A sprawling couch with a palate of cushions ranging from earth to magenta begged to be lounged upon. A white bar glittered beneath spotlights holding bottles of expensive liquor.

An elevator rested next to the door we'd come through—non-operational but available for when I stopped being so paranoid about infiltrators or flooding. It wasn't fair for such an incredible space to have access only through the storage area.

Eventually, guests would be able to sail down in the lift, but for now…this place was a private jewel, hidden deep inside my home.

"I don't know what to say." Pim spun on the spot, taking in the splashes of artwork and the expensive toy sitting pride of place in a large sunken rectangle next to the couch. It took up most of the space, proudly ready to be the main attraction to any party.

"This is incredible." Her hands covered her mouth as a purely innocent squeal escaped. "I can't believe you have a submarine!"

Tension siphoned from my spine at the untamed rapture on her face. When she spun to look at me, her eyes held an unfiltered joy that I'd never hoped to earn.

I'd never seen something so guileless or angelic in my life. She was *happy*. For the first time, the hardship she carried had been eradicated. Whatever nasty wisdom previously chiselled into her turned into a mischievous charm, allowing her to be juvenile.

Today, right here, I glimpsed what she might've looked like as a child. A gorgeous trickster with spun chocolate for hair and new leaves for eyes.

If that was the magic of revealing the three-person cab submarine, then it was worth the expensive price tag a thousand times over.

The large bubble-headed aquatic adventurer looked out of proportion and almost comical out of the water. Large bolts and portals granted rigidity along with as many viewing angles as possible.

"Wait until you're inside." I prowled toward the control panel that operated the secret of this place. I'd had a week tutorial on how to use everything required, including driving the sub, but that was years ago.

I should probably have bought Jolfer or someone down to help, but the sub represented too many things I'd given up hoping for. My heart barely tolerated having Pim here, let alone insensitive staff who didn't know my soul ache.

"Are we going to watch the dolphins in this?"

I nodded, pressing a button. Instantly, the colossal noise of ocean water spilling inside deafened us. Pim jumped as large pumps spurted twenty thousand litres of sea into the space.

"Holy..." She backed up, coming toward me. "That's why you said it could flood."

"The hydraulic jets are meant to keep water out when it's not required, but I'll never trust anything one hundred percent." I nudged her shoulder with mine. "Three minutes to fill that pool to the brim. If it can submerge so quickly, imagine what it could do to the rest of the yacht."

She shivered as the dry-docked submarine that'd been tucked into bed with protective pads on either side slowly began to float.

We didn't speak as the eight metre long holding tank went from dry to soaking. Finally, the pool reached capacity and the gushing-noise silenced, leaving us in a sparkling new world. The walls glittered with threads of water. Blue and silver and navy and turquoise all rippled over the ceiling and furniture— including us.

Pim held out her hand, twirling her fingers as water reflections danced over her.

Her beauty transformed from stunning to something that reached into my chest and ripped out my useless heart.

Clearing my throat, I grabbed the intercom. I waited for someone to respond on the bridge, then said, "Stop all engines until further notice."

"Right away, sir."

Hanging up the receiver, I waited for the constant power whir to dwindle and the forward momentum to be replaced with stationary rocking.

Only then did I press the second button.

A loud click and hissing sounded, slowly transforming the room we stood in.

"Oh, my God, it's a garage," Pim murmured as the side of

the Phantom opened like any other garage door—ready for us to reverse the submarine then sink into the depths below.

It had to be done with no speed applied; otherwise, the door wouldn't open due to pressuring currents. It was a risk to cease creating the wake—the dolphins might swim off—but if we hurried, Pim would get to see something extraordinary.

"Come on." I headed toward the small terrace where loungers and tables were set up.

The submarine hovered, perfectly level and buoyant. I'd bought this thing on a stupid whim thanks to the inventor setting up shop in Monte Carlo and holding an expo right beside my warehouse. It was an idiotic thing to buy, but I hadn't suffered buyer's remorse even when I'd had to task my engineers to come up with the floating garage.

Pim spun to face me. "You know? I'm having a moment where this all feels so familiar."

"Familiar?" My eyebrows rose. "You mean you've been in a situation like this before?"

Shit, I owned the bloody thing and hadn't played with it yet. This was as new to me as it was to her. I couldn't deny the small rush of jealousy at the thought that I wasn't the only one with flashy things to impress her with.

Such a superficial want but where Pim was concerned, I no longer held rational thought.

She laughed, shaking her head. "No, not me personally but one of my favourite movies growing up as a child was *The Abyss*."

I froze, my bare feet digging into the kwila deck beneath me. "*The Abyss*?" I did my best to hide my sharp interest.

Finally.

Finally, a tiny glimpse into who she'd been before me and what affections she harboured.

She nodded all bright eyed and happy. "Yes. I loved the water aliens and the way they had those exploring robots." She laughed, shaking her head. "Not that I'm saying this gorgeous place is anything like the sterile white lab they had."

I couldn't move.

Should I tell her?

Should I admit that after weeks of spending time together, of desperately wanting to know more about her, she'd finally given me a scrap of what I ultimately desired? That she'd successfully struck me dumb, given me a pill, and allowed some addictive part of me to relax.

What would she say if I admitted that her favourite movie was one of mine, too?

That as a kid—before all the shit I put my family through—my mother called me a water sprite. She had a hard time getting me out of the bath, the ocean, a pool. Any movie beneath the sea was my ultimate. And *The Abyss* was every good plotline in one.

Pim continued toward the submarine, a wistful smile on her face. "The romance between those two main characters...Bud and...I can't remember his wife's name. They were divorced, but you could tell they still loved each other." She glanced back at me. "I always loved the bits when they were arguing. In my mind, those fights were saying they still cared. They just didn't know how to work past everything keeping them apart."

I cleared my throat again at the overwhelming need in her gaze. The way she threw her words across the water and pushed them into my ears. As if every hidden message and veiled insinuation decided to leap from behind their mask and pummel me over the goddamn head.

She'd told me she loved me. She'd written it in a letter. She'd told me I'd *earned* that love, but she'd never told me if that love was out of obligation or because her heart mimicked mine and couldn't imagine a future without each other.

She loved me, but was she *in love* with me?

I had a throbbing need to put aside the bullshit and ask one question.

The question.

The most important question that negated every other.

Do you want me the way I want you?

Clearing my throat yet again, I did my best to prevent such a soul-destroying query from climbing free. Instead, I grumbled, "His wife's name was Lindsey." Moving closer, I leaned over her to push the button on the sub that opened a small waterproof cubby for the handle. Cranking it, the thick Perspex bubble cracked open.

Pim froze.

She stopped breathing.

My arm remained over her shoulder, my half naked body a fraction away from hers.

Stupid idea.

I should've asked her to move instead of reaching over...

Sparkling water spangles decorated her body. My mouth went dry as cotton.

Her eyelashes fluttered as she dropped her gaze to my dragon tattooed chest. "You know, when you move, sometimes I think you can fly. That this—" She reached out, stroking the inked scales and horned mythical lizard protecting me. "Lends its wings to you."

I shivered as her fingertips became fingers then flattened to her palm. The heat of her touch undid me. My back arched, pressing myself into her. My arm fell around her shoulders, jerking her close.

She gasped as I buried my nose in the crook of her neck, breathing her in, using her scent as my new drug to try to remain calm.

Once again, she'd given me access to a small part of her thoughts.

She had no fucking clue what it did to me, how it made me feel, and how fucking desperate it made me for more.

Her arms wrapped around me, hugging me hard.

And I let her.

I didn't pull away or try to climb on top of her. I fought every instinct and stood ramrod straight, indulging in a simple embrace, all the while quaking beneath so much shit in my life that I could no longer differentiate good or bad, right or wrong, sane or crazy.

Pim nuzzled my chest, pressing fluttering kisses on my dragon's snout. "I love any dessert that has raspberry. I'm a sucker for romantic comedies, no matter how cheesy. I used to read by torchlight when my mother thought I was in bed. I would do my homework at the last minute as I much preferred to people watch out my window and make up stories about where they were going than do silly arithmetic."

Her lips glided toward my nipple, making me lock down with lust while shivering with shame that this woman who had been through so much was comforting me.

Comforting me in the best possible way she could. By sharing herself. Not just her body. *Her.* Every little thing that other people took for granted, I would hoard until my dying breath.

"When I first saw you, I knew you were different. I knew you were stronger, braver, more man than Alrik could ever be. When you first touched me, I hated you because you showed me I wasn't as dead as I'd hoped. When you first saved me, I feared you because you placed me in a debt that I could never repay. When you first kissed me, I cursed you because I knew you'd be the one to destroy me. Not him. Not anyone. *You.*"

She shook as badly as I did; her fingernails digging into my back. "Elder, I know this is so hard for you. I know I push you. But I need you to know…I just *need* you. If we never have sex again, I'm fine with that. If you only want my friendship, I'm ecstatic with that. I just…need to be around you. I'll tell you anything you want to know. I'll reveal every stupid fact about how I hate milk on cereal and how toast is the most boring food I can imagine. How some days I prefer rain to sun, and some nights, I prefer clouds to stars. I'll share myself completely with you, not because I owe you for everything that you've done, but because I *want* to. You're the only one I want to know all of me."

I very nearly collapsed.

Tenderness threaded with the constant violence in my veins. Words flew into my head and were discarded. Thank yous and appreciations all faded in the beauty of what she'd just done.

Sentences could never do justice to what she'd just given me.

But she had to know. Had to understand how much I fucking loved her for trusting me to share. Pulling away just enough, I used my knuckle to tip up her chin.

Her eyes danced over mine, wary and wishful.

She was so beautiful.

I sucked in a breath just before my lips kissed hers.

This was totally different to anything else we'd shared.

This was soft and sweet and gentle.

This was everything I'd been wanting and everything I could never hope to find.

This was pure fucking love, and I sank to the bottom of it and didn't care if I drowned.

Pim's tongue flicked out to taste me. I met her with the tip of mine, sweetly, sedately. For once, the rush in my blood was absent. My brain was quiet...satisfied.

My arms wrapped tighter in gratitude, crushing her far too close. Her breasts pressed against my chest. Her hipbones dug into me, reminding me she was so much smaller and fragile than I was. Another wash of tenderness crippled me, and I gasped into the kiss. I was shocked by the beauty of it—the *simplicity* of it.

Her hand landed over my heart as if she wanted to make sure the beating muscle was hers, doing her best to tame it.

Pulling away, I nuzzled my nose against hers. "What you're touching used to be my least vulnerable spot. I swore off feeling anything for anyone. I couldn't stomach being hurt again."

She kissed me fleetingly, stealing my voice. "El—"

"But then you came along. A better thief than I could ever be."

Her eyes widened, the hazel and emerald breathtakingly pretty this close. She laughed softly. "But I was arrested. I suck as a thief."

"You're the best thief." I kissed her nose, her eyelids, her cheeks, and finally her ear where I whispered, "You've done what no one else ever could.

"You've stolen my heart."

Pimlico

SITTING IN A submarine ought to have been the highlight of my day—no my *life*.

Having Elder sit beside me in a matching bucket seat with his dragon chest on display ought to have been something I imprinted for eternity. Watching him pull levers and press buttons to glide us backward out of the Phantom ought to have filled me with giddy excitement at the thought of sinking into the depths on an intrepid excursion.

Just him and me and a vastness of water that honestly terrified me a little.

Feeling the small submarine, with its pretty lights and large bubble, leaving the shallowness of its pool and revealing a blue-black void below us ought to turn me squirming with impatience to chase the dolphins.

But I wasn't.

Because nothing, *absolutely nothing*—no matter how stupendous or extraordinary—could overshadow the words ringing in my head.

'*You stole my heart…*'

He said it woundedly. Bruised and damaged and wary.

But he'd *said* it.

And, *God*, the overwhelming love in my chest…I couldn't contain it.

Who cared about the crystal clarity of the water world below us? Who cared how the sea slowly crept higher up the bubble the more buttons he pressed to descend us?

The moment he'd told me I'd stolen his heart, he'd *ruined* me.

He'd turned me useless and legless as he'd scooped me up, folded me reverently into the submarine, then climbed in after me. He didn't say another word as he sealed the portal, buckled me in, then cracked a pained smile as his long legs and big bulk struggled to find a comfortable position in the pilot seat.

Had that moment truly happened?

Did he truly kiss me that softly? Whisper that ardently?

Was that all it took to make him fall for me? To share a few inconsequential titbits of my past? Did I hold the magic all along to make him weak-kneed and besotted just by telling him I didn't like traditional breakfast foods?

For the hundredth time, I shook my head in a mixture of awe and obsession. How stupid was I to think I loved this man? How naïve to believe someone could fall with barely any information. If Elder kept revealing different sides of himself, showing the chivalry behind the warrior and compassion behind the thief, I was utterly destroyed.

I would trade my life for his.

I would never again think of suicide no matter how bad things got because ultimately, I no longer lived for me...

I lived for him.

The bucket seat's moulded plastic stuck to my naked skin uncomfortably. Why had he made us wear swimming gear in this dry machine? Had he planned ahead in case it leaked? Would we drown in here?

My thoughts finally left romanticism and focused on the new world we entered.

The sky vanished, the garage door sealing back into position as down and down we floated.

Elder grabbed the radio. "This is Viperfish clear from the Phantom. Door is closed. Resume engines at slow speed."

"Right you are." The crackled response filled the pressurised cabin.

I didn't speak as Elder fiddled with levers and switches, activating different whirring sounds and propulsion. Once we sank low enough to make me feel crushed by the amount of liquid, he shot me a smile. "Look up."

I gasped as the entire length of the Phantom floated above us.

Slowly, as the captain resumed speed, the rudders and propellers woke from their nap and turned into ginormous sickles, slicing the ocean into pieces, pushing the majestic floating home toward a new destination without us.

Elder kept his eyes pinned on his yacht's belly, his face in shadow from the ship blocking what little sunrays managed to make it this far. "It's hard to believe we sleep and eat and go about our lives believing the Phantom is so sturdy and strong, yet from here, it looks so fragile."

My brain heard him but my heart still heard '*you stole my heart.*' I never wanted to forget the power and shock that small sentence delivered.

'*You stole my heart.*'

But you, Elder Prest...you stole my everything.

Everywhere I looked, crystal blue water cushioned us. From our vantage point, the ocean had no bottom—just a deeper blue that stretched eternally downward. Large schools of fish swam too far away to distinguish.

It wasn't like any snorkelling I'd done. There were no coral or anemones; no clown fish or angelfish. Just us...suspended in aqua.

I jolted as his hand touched mine, sending fiery need straight to my core. I'd told him I would be his friend, sailing partner, and cello confidant. And I *would* be all those things. I'd tell him anything he wanted to know; I'd go wherever he set course. I'd even suffer through classical music and terrible memories—all for him.

But if I believed I could keep my promise that I didn't

need him touching me, kissing me, loving me, or if I thought I could survive without having sex with this man again, I would end up combusting in utter agony.

Pushing down such desires, I curled my fingers around his only for him to pull away. "Dolphins?"

I nodded slowly. "Dolphins." The one thing I'd been beyond excited to see had now paled in the repetition of *'you stole my heart.'*

His brow dropped over heated eyes resembling burnings pieces of coal. He heard everything I'd tried to keep hidden. Biting his lower lip, he fed some speed to the sub. "Dolphins and then we'll talk. Deal?"

I let out a huge sigh—I didn't know if it was relief, frustration, or gratefulness. "Talk?" How could I tell him talking would only make me fall harder and falling for him meant my awakened sexuality became harder to deny?

The answer was, I couldn't. I already made his life a living hell.

He nodded gently. "Talk. Like two people. A date."

I blushed. "You want to go on a date with me?"

It was his turn to sigh heavily. "More than anything."

What untainted air remained in the sub quickly switched to lust-drenched fog. We might as well have been trapped in a bubble of sexual thirst. The small cab throbbed with it, threatening to burst the waterproof seals and let gallons of cool seawater gush in to put out the fire.

Doing my best to change the subject so I didn't throw myself into his lap, I laughed quietly. "So far, this is the best date I've ever been on."

Recognising my smile for what it was—a gateway out of this intensely dangerous, unknown territory—he returned my light-heartedness—or as much as he could for such a serious thief. "I aim to please."

"And you do please."

His eyes turned from charcoal to blazing black flames. Tearing his gaze away, he focused on the controls. A small buzzing filled the bulbous cabin, sending us forward. I sat taller, my attention fighting to remain on Elder but finally succumbing to the incredible view outside.

We climbed upward, chasing the Phantom as it speared through the sea, causing white froth to spill behind it.

And there, at the front of the missile-shaped yacht, were the dolphins.

Leaping and lolling, swimming and sojourning. Having a great old time riding the Phantom's wake. Their grey, streamline bodies effortless and quick.

"They're still here," I said.

"If they're having fun, it's hard to get them to leave." He added a touch of speed. "They're like dogs...just wanting to play."

"We should teach them to fetch."

He chuckled.

The closer we got to the pod, the more my heart burst with joy. This day. Oh, my God, this day was the best day I'd ever had, and it wasn't even afternoon yet.

"There are so many of them." I tried to count, but they moved too fast and in a flipper-cloud. One twist of their powerful bodies and a flash of dorsal fins later, they appeared twenty feet from where they'd been two seconds ago.

"Twenty? Thirty?" Elder squinted at the twining, threading creatures. "Not the biggest pod."

"How many have you seen?" Curiosity rose along with a mild case of jealousy that Elder had sailed the seas with dolphins without me.

My jealousy made no sense. Our lives had been separate just like any other couple before they met. Maybe it was because while he was free, I'd been locked up. Or maybe it was because I'd begun hoarding every moment with him and was jealous of time itself. Of not being able to go back and claim those minutes and hours when we didn't know each other.

I'm being ridiculous.

If this was what love did to people, I didn't know how

they functioned normally. No wonder people needed psychologists—everyone turned crazy when they fell.

"Probably the biggest was off the coast of Australia. Easily in the hundreds, maybe more."

"That must've been amazing."

"It was." His eyes glazed, remembering. "It was lacking, though."

"Lacking how? I can't imagine something as extraordinary as—"

He pinned me with a brutal stare that told me to stop playing games. "You weren't there."

"Oh."

"Everything in my past suddenly feels lacklustre without you."

I had no other reply but the truth. "Me too."

Once again, tension built. How much longer could we dance around this third wheel? How much more could we take?

"We'll get closer." As he guided us from spectator to participant, the juveniles of the pack spotted a new toy and came to investigate.

One moment we were the audience, the next we were enveloped by grey blubber, perfect flukes, and intelligent glossy eyes peering into our bubble.

I swore one looked directly into me—right *through* me. He didn't care what'd been done to me or where I'd come from. All he cared about was I was alive. He was alive. And that was something to celebrate.

I was warmer, happier, wiser than I'd ever been.

Reaching up, I placed my hand against the cool Perspex. The dolphin who'd striped me bare pressed his long nose to nudge against me as if saying *'I see you. I accept you. Now come and play.'*

Another wash of goosebumps scuttled down my spine.

Could this day get any better?

The prickle of Elder's gaze whipped my head to face him. I quickly removed my hand from the dolphin's snout. I didn't know why but guilt filled my chest along with self-consciousness. "Sorry."

His expression switched from awed besottment to a nasty scowl. "Why are you apologising?"

Why *was* I apologising?

I shrugged. "For being silly? For saying hello to a dolphin?"

His perfect lips tugged into half a smile. "Never apologise for that." He didn't elaborate, but his features darkened and lightened all at once. "I confess, you're not wearing that bikini purely for me to stare at you."

My skin heated as his eyes dropped to the green triangles hiding me from view. I had the insane urge to pull aside the material and show him just what his stare did to my nipples. How hard they'd become. How achy every inch of me was.

"Do you want to do more than just say hello?"

"What do you mean?" I looked at the dolphins looping around us.

"I mean...let's go swimming."

My heart nodded in glee already dressed in flippers and a snorkel. "Are—are you sure it's safe?"

"Is anything truly safe?"

He has a point.

"If we stayed in here until they vanished or we returned to the Phantom, would you regret not swimming with them or be relieved you hadn't been so reckless?" He raised an eyebrow.

Regret. The answer was immediate. There was no other reply I could give. "Let's go swimming."

"I thought you'd say that." With a grin, Elder called the Phantom to tell them to cut engines and hold position. Once the yacht slowed and the whitewash diminished, he pressed yet another button and propelled us upward.

Up and up, brighter and brighter as turquoise gloom gave way to glittering sun.

My stomach flipped a little as we popped like a corkscrew and came crashing down on the surface. Considering the submarine was shaped like an egg, we didn't roll out of balance or sink back down. The constant hum of engines and ballast kept us the right way up.

I unbuckled my seatbelt, flinching a little as a dorsal fin swam past, imagining for a moment it was a shark and not the friendly dolphins we'd seen beneath.

Elder copied me, tugging off his harness and twisting uncomfortably to undo another portal above our heads. "We have to go out the top. The side is still underwater." He pushed it wide, making me blink from the brightness, then placed his hands on the top and hoisted himself up effortlessly.

Once again, my mind painted a fantasy of his dragon making him fly. How did such a big man come across so graceful and weightless?

Scrambling to stand, I assessed how to climb out. My bones were useless; my muscles an embarrassment after two years of no exercise and lots of pain. But a hand appeared, followed by Elder's gorgeous face as he blocked the sun. "Take it."

My heart transformed into a butterfly as I clutched his forearm and his fingers wrapped tight around me. He yanked me upright, through the porthole, and straight to my feet with one powerful jerk.

I wobbled as my toes landed on the slippery outer shell of the submarine. Back on the Phantom, the vessel had looked silver. Out here, beneath the sun, it glittered with the coolest luminescent blue—so light and reflective it almost became invisible amongst the waves.

The Phantom loomed above us with its gleaming brass rigging and immaculate balconies. Images of me tethering myself to one while the thunder and rain did its best to kill me brought back yet more heart squeezing memories of Elder being there with me. Of Elder protecting me even when I didn't want to be protected. Of Elder understanding and standing beside me as an equal rather than my saviour.

I wanted all my memories to include him.

I wanted all my experiences to be with him.

"After you." He bowed, releasing my arm as he turned to face the sea. Dolphins lolled on their backs with flippers out of the water while others swam on their sides, their intelligent eyes tracking us.

Could dolphins turn aggressive? I didn't know the correct etiquette for swimming with these mammals, but Elder didn't give me a choice. "Go on. Stop thinking. That ruins all the fun."

"*Worry* is what ruins all the fun...not thinking."

His eyebrow rose as if to say sometimes circumstances wanted worry, but this was not one of them. "Suit yourself." With a smile, he spread his arms then back-flipped off the submarine.

"El—" I darted to the side; my feet slipped and gravity took hold.

Oh, no!

I made the split-second decision to leap rather than tumble.

My tummy flipped as I shed standing for flight, then held my breath as the smack of cool ocean sucked me into its embrace.

Something alive shot by my foot, followed by a quick nudge of something not quite skin and not quite slimy.

Holy hell.

I kicked for the surface only to have Elder wrap me in his arms and haul me from the deep. Water streamed over my eyes as I hung in his arms, extremely aware of how slippery our bodies were now wet and glued to each other.

Memories of swimming beneath the moon with him made my insides clench. My eyes latched onto his mouth, desperate for a kiss.

I'd gone from normal to frenzied in two seconds flat.

My legs wrapped around his hips, partly for buoyancy, but mostly because of the pounding instinctual need to join. He groaned as his legs continued to kick, keeping us afloat. My fingers threaded through his soaking hair.

I need...

His right arm let me go, circling in the water for balance. His left arm tightened around me, his fingers digging into my waist. "Pimlico...what are you doing?"

My eyes turned heavy. My voice thick. "I-I'm...just, let me...once."

I kissed him before he could argue.

The surge of affection made me breathless as his cool, salty lips yielded to mine.

He let me kiss him. Before...he didn't.

In a breath, I went from kissing him to being kissed by him. Spinning me with a powerful kick, he slammed me against the submarine and pressed himself against me skin to skin.

His cock seared my core. Lightning bolts sizzled. I rubbed against him, using his body as a climbing frame.

We went from swimming to attacking all in a fraction of a moment.

I forgot how to do anything—all I knew was if I didn't have *something*, I would die. I would combust. I would explode from the pressure.

With a savage bite, his teeth captured my bottom lip as he wedged a thigh between my legs. His fingers latched onto the rivets and small ladder of the submarine, somehow holding us afloat.

His kiss turned violent as his thigh rocked up, deliberately rocking against my clit. Tearing his mouth from mine, he growled in my ear. "You want to play this game, little mouse? *Fine.*" He reared up, wedging his cock against me as his thigh thrust harder between my legs. "Come."

Come?

No way could I come. Not with dolphins and oceans and submarines and—

My head fell back as he yanked my wet strands, giving him access to my throat. He bit me, but it didn't activate bad memories; instead, it made my body gush with heat and liquid, the desperation inside me reached lava levels.

My hips thrust under someone else's command: Elder's, some sea god, who knew? But definitely not mine because I didn't know this person. Why was I suddenly so *hungry*, so reckless, so selfish to use Elder for my own gain?

I gasped as his voice turned filthy—hot and thick against my ear. "That's it. You know I can't fuck you, Pim. But *fuck*, I want to. I want to stick my cock in you so fucking bad you have no idea. Feeling your heat on my thigh…it's taking everything I have not to spread you wide and sink inside you. *Christ*, I want you."

My heart relocated into my clit, thundering with each visualization. My hips rocked faster, harder, braver.

"That's it. Use me. Come for me. Imagine I'm fucking you. That you're not empty, and I'm not insane, and we can do something like fuck like rabbits wherever and whenever we damn well please." His tongue licked around my ear, pressing a kiss to my hairline. "Come, little mouse. Come. *Come*. Goddammit, come before I run out of self-control."

His thigh thrust again, and I rode him.

My brain forgot about right and wrong, and dolphins and depths, and just…let go.

The bikini couldn't stop it.

Dolphins watching us couldn't stop it.

I came.

The rippling fantasia was different to what he'd given me in the hotel in Monte Carlo. This was a crackling hair-trigger release. Formed from intensity and released with ferocity.

Fast, wild, and crazy.

The second the last clench left me spinning, his hands landed on the submarine with a wet smack. With a grunt, he pushed himself far away from me. His eyes weren't that of a man anymore; they were savage and primordial and reached inside me to ravage my heart and make me *crave* to be filled.

I was so empty, so achy, so wanting.

More…I need more.

"Don't." His voice was a murder weapon to my libido.

I shook my head, tears springing to my eyes for hurting him this way. For thinking only of myself while he suffered under epic self-restraint. Rubbing my mouth, fighting to stay afloat, I dropped my eyes submissively. "I'm so sorry, Elder."

"Don't ever apologise for showing me who you are, Pim." He chuckled, raw and torn open. "You're waking up. You're finding what you want."

"What I want is you." My whisper barely made it across the tide.

"I know." His voice turned grim. "And I want you. And that's what makes this so fucking hard."

I dared look up. "I can't apologise for wanting you, but I can apologise for kissing you. I-I won't do that again."

A dolphin swam behind him, the dorsal fin coming close. He glanced at the swimming missile only for it to parry off at the last minute, leaving him to sigh and rub his face with a dripping wet hand. "This is all screwed up."

Looking at the sky with a tormented growl, he shook his head. "I don't want you to stop kissing me. I don't want to stop kissing you. But back in the garage when you told me pieces of yourself...that gave me something I needed. It gave me peace even while you stress me the hell out."

He smiled sadly, still treading water out of reaching distance. "My mind was...quiet." He shrugged as if struggling to verbalize what was different now. "It's noisy again. I need some distance from you. Please." The fact he'd tacked on a plea rather than leaving it as a command unravelled me. It wasn't a simple word. It'd been infused with every matching ache he held.

This sucked.

This hurt.

This was all my fault.

"Consider it done." Forcing the biggest smile on my face, I made it my life mission to prove I was the master of my desires. That I could control myself around him. That I wouldn't make this any harder.

It didn't matter it was all a lie.

It didn't matter we both knew something would have to break and soon.

All that mattered was spending the day together, swimming with dolphins, believing in magic, and forgetting that love could cause the worst pain of all.

ELDER

FOUR THINGS HAPPENED that night.

First, I somehow managed to keep my dick in my pants while Pim and I finished swimming with the damn dolphins and returned the Viperfish to its garage. I had the self-control of a monk as I invited her to a quiet dinner beneath the stars as Jolfer set us back on course. We hardly said a word, but that wasn't the point. The point was proving to myself that I could be in her presence—even sex-infused and addiction-infested—and not give in.

It was the hardest thing I'd ever done, and I enlisted every trick imaginable, but I managed to come across sane... *I think.*

One, two, three taps of my knife.

One, two, three scrunches of my napkin.

One, two, three breaths before answering any of her softly murmured questions.

Second thing that happened that night—after a strained but survived dinner—I created her a dolphin out of a hundred dollar bill, quickly bringing the total of origami animals closer to a thousand in cash value. She watched me silently as my fingers creased and folded, accepting my gift with a heart-pounding smile.

Third, I walked her back to her room after dessert of raspberry cheesecake, keeping my hands, lips, and cock to myself as we traversed the deck beneath the Milky Way and entered the elevator side by side. I almost broke every finger from clenching my fists so hard with self-restraint, but I managed to escort her to her door and bow respectfully as she entered her room.

I didn't try to kiss her.

I didn't try to spend the night with her.

I managed to remain in control.

And fourth, when I entered my lonely quarters, and all I could think about was returning to Pim, I rolled a joint and pulled my cello from its home in the cupboard. With smoke stinging my eyes and drug-fake peace circulating through my blood, I placed my fingers on the frets and played.

I played soft.

I played loud.

I alternated between traditional classical and self-composed metal.

I created music until my joint was nothing but ash and my fingers bordered on splitting. My bow once again was shredded. And my eyes strained from staring at the door, begging for a midnight visitor.

Pim might have a lock on her door, but I didn't. And instead of hoping she'd stay away, I spent the night begging her to come find me. In the midst of the song, I imagined her walking in dressed in a nightgown which fell from her body the moment she saw me. I hung onto the fantasy of her crossing the room, unperturbed by my music to sit on my lap, kiss me, and beg me to make love to her.

But she never came.

And I never went to see if her lock was engaged.

By the time I fell asleep and woke to dawn, I had a few emails to attend to from the warehouse and a couple of new enquiries requesting a consultation at the Hawk Masquerade. Turned out my attending that inconvenient affair had already circulated and the unwanted night's entertainment would be profitable indeed.

Which I was thankful for as it was my six month mark. My next payment to my debt was due, and I had every intention of paying it. Even though the man I paid didn't know me. Even though he had no clue how or why the money mysteriously entered his bank account.

Watching from afar, I'd witnessed my first righteous human when that initial instalment appeared in his account. Instead of staying quiet like greed demanded and claiming it as his own without knowing if it was true, he contacted the police to inform them of an incorrect deposit.

A deposit from an encrypted account in Monte Carlo valued at thirty million dollars.

I'd ensured his name, address, and phone number were listed on the transfer, so no one could doubt it was meant for him. For the reference number, all I'd put was...*'from someone who owes you more than you know.'*

The first instalment had been the smallest but the hardest. If it had been up to me, that amount would've had an extra zero attached. But Selix had forbidden it. He'd spoken sense at the time, so I'd settled with thirty instead of three hundred—hoping to buy off my never-ending guilt one repayment at a time.

Every six months since then, I paid another sum—always bigger than the first, steadily multiplying—forever working to the final tally I owed.

"Phone call for you." My intercom buzzed, allowing Selix's voice to interrupt my thoughts.

It was almost noon, and I'd been sketching a few amendments on Alrik's (now Pim's) yacht to ensure the build team got it perfect. I'd also been poring over nautical maps, both digital and paper, to figure out if and when the Chinmoku would make their stand.

Would they dare take me on in the middle of the sea? Would they have the right armada to become pirates as well as slavers? Or would they wait until I reached shore again? Would the Hawk Masquerade be too dangerous to take Pim?

Tossing down my pencil, I growled. "I'm not expecting any calls."

Oh, wait.

I was. A sneaky, low-handed secret I'd done behind Pim's back the night she'd returned to the Phantom. "Shit, she called back."

"She did. You'll want to talk to her."

"Your bossy replies aren't wanted this morning, Selix."

"Your argumentative, stubborn ass isn't wanted, either." He chuckled. "Get up here." He hung up before I could berate him.

Leaving my touch-ups on the desk, I stormed down the corridor from suite to office. Selix looked up as I slammed the door closed. I didn't know where Pim was, but I didn't want her to know what I was up to.

Not yet, anyway.

He held out the phone. "I had to accept the charges, and you only have five minutes according to the terms and conditions relayed before you got your ass here."

Shoving the phone into my hand, he practically pranced to the exit. "Oh, and Pim has been asking about you. I told her you were working, but that excuse expires in a few hours. I'll tell the chef to expect two for dinner."

I gave him the one finger salute as I raised the phone to my ear.

A crackly voice came down the line. "Prest? Mr. Elder Prest?"

The air in my lungs evacuated in a rush. I knew that voice. That same voice turned me mad with fantasies and wishes and needs far beyond my control. However, it was harder, older, less loving, and more accusing than Pimlico's.

Or should I say Tasmin's?

Would Pim kill me for this or thank me?

Sucking up the oxygen I'd just expelled, I clutched the phone tighter. "Hello, Mrs Blythe. What a pleasure to finally talk to you."

Pimlico

DINNER STARTED OFF strained.

Elder acted differently.

As I reached for a helping of roasted vegetables, his eyes tracked me. Yet when I picked up my knife and fork and looked at him, he glanced away as if his own cutlery was far more interesting.

He seemed almost guilty of something.

But what?

Most of the day, I'd spent relaxing on my own and learning what it was like to be bored. I'd never known the concept before or after such an unusual fate. But now, as I hung on the Phantom wishing Elder would find me and put me out of my misery, and learning I could stare at the horizon for only so many hours before my thoughts annoyed me, I was ready for a task.

Any task.

I wanted to get back to work, and because my mind was now healthier and happier than it'd ever been, I turned to the last thing that'd stretched and formed it.

My university degree.

Psychology.

I found myself going over Elder's body language without

thinking. Finding hidden snippets of understanding in the way he touched me, looked at me, and up until now, had successfully hidden things from me.

I analysed our time in the hotel, going over sleeping with him, recalling the way he'd forced me to bind him and reading between the lines.

He wasn't lying when he said he would've hurt both of us because he couldn't stop. He wasn't dramatizing his OCD to keep me at a distance or to earn sympathy from those who knew him.

Everything he said and did was the truth.

With one exception.

And now that I'd seen it, I couldn't *unsee* it.

It was so obvious I wanted to cuff myself around the head for being so blind.

Three.

Elder might have a brain bordering on genius perfectionism, but even he had safe-guards in place. Life had rules and everything—humans, flora, fauna, and every microbe followed those specially specified rules—always staying within their species boundary, forever moving forward.

Elder just moved forward at a faster rate than most.

Tonight, he'd ladled three roast potatoes, three sprigs of asparagus, and three salmon medallions onto his plate.

Meanwhile, I had two potatoes, one piece of salmon, and no asparagus.

I was chaos.

He was uniform.

He thought he was chaos.

He was wrong.

To prove my quickly evolving theory, I watched him eat. Three sips of water followed by three taps of his fork against his plate. Three chews before swallowing followed by three cuts of his knife.

Did he know himself?

Did he feel himself doing it, or was it so ingrained, he

didn't even notice?

I became mesmerised watching him. He was no longer just Elder eating dinner. He was a musician creating a dance.

One, two, three.

One, two, three.

A waltz.

Forever moving forward, just like life intended, but in threes not ones like the rest of us.

My heart stopped.

Oh, my God.

Was that the key?

Was that all it would take?

Don't be stupid, Pim…it can't be that easy.

But then, in a long ago memory, my mother's voice came back to me. About how textbooks and pharmaceuticals and so-called professionals often gave long-winded diagnoses and even more complicated treatments to hold the allure that they knew how to help when others didn't. How paid therapy was upheld with regulations when true therapy—*real* therapy that worked—was sometimes the simplest of things.

There wasn't one perfect fix for everyone. Each person was different. Some needed chemical help. Others just needed to talk. Some needed a new environment to heal. Others just needed loved ones around them.

My mother, despite her flaws, was good at her job, and her motto was simple:

Literally S.I.M.P.L.E.

Sometimes

Impossible

Mostly

Probable

Largely

Explainable.

She meant that the impossible cases normally came with probable reasoning and those explanations could be used—if not to find a cure, then definitely to grant an easier way of life for the suffering.

She studied all walks of life to understand and focus on her clients' strengths and not their weaknesses—even if those weaknesses included crime.

Elder had a weakness; there was no denying that.

But he also had so many, many strengths.

And those strengths might be the key to sleeping with me without trying to kill us with an obsession that could never end.

One, two, three...

Repetition was his strength.

Could it work in the bedroom?

Was it conscious or unconscious?

Deciding to test my theory, I raised my glass of water and toasted him. "To my gracious host and for everything he's done for me."

His cheeks darkened in a suspicious masculine blush as he copied me and held his glass aloft. With a regal smile, he clinked with mine then held it to his lips.

I sipped once.

One time.

Like a normal person would in a toast.

Then put my glass back onto the table.

Elder, on the other hand, took another sip, followed by another before placing it down.

That could've been a coincidence. He could've been thirsty.

Needing another experiment, I pulled out what I'd been able to scrounge up this afternoon. I'd felt terrible asking, but boredom made me look for other ways to entertain myself. When a girl I'd become friendly with came to clean my room, I'd asked with flaming red cheeks if she had any one dollar bills.

She'd raised an eyebrow but hadn't asked why. It wasn't like a dollar could buy me freedom if that was my intention. Instead of giving me the single I'd asked for, she'd passed over a small handful and smiled. She'd given them as a gift even when I told her I'd pay her back...even if it meant dismantling my upcoming origami creations and ironing the bills to return to her.

 I'd intended to teach myself from unfolding one of Elder's. I had visions of creating a perfect crane and giving it to him like he gave currency animals to me, hopefully making him as happy as he made me.

But no matter how many hours I'd tried…I couldn't do it. The folds didn't work, the creases didn't compute in my brain. I'd become far too frustrated and ready to tear up the money rather than create art with it.

This was Elder's expertise, and if I was to learn, I needed the master to teach me directly. It didn't matter that this lesson came with other intentions as well—veiled and secret research into him as a person.

Smoothing out the creases from my failed attempts, I deliberately placed four notes on the table and pushed them toward him.

His shoulders stiffened. His hands unwrapped from around his knife and fork. "What's this?"

"I want you to teach me origami."

"Now?"

"I'm not really hungry."

He looked up. Our eyes glued together, and once again, that nasty tingly tension sprang into awareness.

Please let this work.

I needed a kernel of hope if I was ever going to attempt seducing Elder again.

Seduce?

That word…what a foreign word.

What a strange concept that I could even *think* about seducing someone.

Pride immediately followed my surprise. How far I'd come from deploring sex to scheming ways in which to earn it. How quickly I'd braved my past to clutch onto the passion Elder made me feel.

I ought to be embarrassed for orgasming on his leg

yesterday; instead, I found myself sitting taller. He'd given me that release, but if I hadn't wanted it, no way could I have achieved it.

I wanted sex.

I want sex.

My jaw slackened as I finally came to terms with such a strange epiphany.

I was a woman, and Elder was a man, and I loved him and lusted for him.

I needed to know everything there was to know about the way his mind worked before I did something that put us in danger.

We were a recipe for gunpowder…with our fuse growing ever shorter and more volatile.

Besides, all of this was because of him. My world was in an upheaval thanks to falling in love. And I liked to think his life was in an upheaval because of me, too. I would take responsibility for ruining his peace, but it didn't mean I wouldn't do my damnedest to find a cure that would work for both of us.

"All right…" He pushed his plate away and fisted the notes. If I wasn't watching for a purpose; if I wasn't peering at him like he was an experiment, I might've missed it.

But sure enough, as he counted the bills and found four and not his welcome three, his lips twisted in disgust. His body twitched as if the extra note was abhorrent. But then his disapproval was gone, and he placed the notes on the table before peeling one off the top and snapping it between his fingers. "Origami takes patience."

"I have patience."

"It takes a steady hand."

"I'm steady."

I sat on my shaking hands, doing my best to hide my lie. I didn't have concrete evidence that three was the magic number with Elder, nor should my mind be awash with scenarios of pouncing on him and forcing him to make love to me purely to see if he'd end after taking me three times.

But the more I studied him, the more my belly liquefied and the more I craved. It was past rational at this point. I'd walked away from him to stop this behaviour. I'd left him to protect him from the awakening inside me.

But I couldn't ignore my female to his male anymore. The lust to his desire.

"You need to come closer if I'm going to show you." His voice turned dark with a hint of soot.

Scooting my chair closer, the hairs on the back of my neck rose as Elder bent toward me then discarded the dollar on the table. Arching sideways, he pulled his wallet from his back trouser pocket. "We'll do this on a different note, okay?"

I expected him to pull out worthless paper—after all, why waste money when I was a beginner. Instead, he yanked free a ten-pound note. The currency of my home. The colours and details just as I remembered.

"Pounds from England?"

He nodded. "We'll be there in a few days. It's appropriate."

I'd started this purely to find some way into his lap, but now he'd pulled out a tenner and his eyes glittered with harsh intelligence, I found myself wanting the fake lesson.

His hair slipped over his forehead as he bent and smoothed the bill on the tablecloth. "It's not square, so that's your first challenge. Most origami—or at least the easier designs—are with perfect squares."

"I want to do what you do."

He smiled sadly. "Believe me...you don't."

Believe me...I do.

Silence thickened my heartbeat, and Elder somehow pulled away from me. Not physically but something mental and internal captured his attention, stealing him from the dining room, from the Phantom, from this moment.

Regret shadowed his features, followed by a cringe of denial and shame. Such thick, thick shame.

He fingered the money as if it wasn't his but something he'd stolen. It wasn't just an innate piece of paper with the value stamped on the face—it was a reminder to him...a reminder of what?

What could he be thinking to justify such self-hatred?

I placed my hand over his, cupping the ten-pound note. "What is it?"

Shaking himself, he blinked. "Nothing."

"It's something."

"Nothing you need to know."

"Everything I want to know."

His lips pursed, his eyes dancing from my mouth to my nose to my gaze. "If I tell you, you'll once again think differently of me."

"I've never once thought differently of you—no matter what you've told me."

His fingers flinched under mine as if trying to deny the truth. Not once had I feared his honesty, nor had I made him regret showing me what he hid deep inside. I hadn't asked questions about his father and brother's death even though his mother blamed him. I didn't demand to know if he was a good guy or bad because my heart had made its choice.

"Tell me..."

He sighed heavily, crushing the note beneath his palm. "You might as well know."

"Know what?"

"How big a fraud I am."

ELDER

* Ten Years Ago *

LIFE HADN'T ALWAYS been this way for me.

I hadn't always been respected for my wealth or shunned because of my unsavoury background. That was entirely new.

Three weeks to be exact.

Twenty-one days ago, I was invisible. I got by with pickpocketing the rich who now knocked on my fucking door to be friends. My fingers that'd been taught to be nimble at snatching a wallet after being a maestro with a cello were now imprisoned with more money than I could ever spend.

What the fuck am I supposed to do with that?

And why did people care what existed in my damn bank account when deciding if I was a good or bad?

I was bad.

Through and through.

I'd stolen this life, not earned it. It wasn't luck or karma or any other happy circumstances. Only Selix knew the truth, and the truth ate me up inside until I was riddled with more holes than I could bear.

I already had far too much guilt to carry. This? It just added another world of hurt.

I'd wanted to give it back.

All of it...every penny.

But that was before Selix took thievery and twisted it into a more acceptable concept.

A loan. A helping hand. Borrowing from someone to fix my past, absolve my sins, and ensure my family was never in danger again because of me.

So here I fucking was.

Swallowing my shame, going by a new name, and doing my best to keep the truth locked deep down tight and lie to everyone. I lied to the station producer. I lied to the news anchor. I lied to every useless person watching this program.

It was a goddamn shit-show. And I was angry. So damn angry.

These ingrates wanted to know me. They pretended to like me so they might stand a chance at stealing what was now mine. But they would never know me. I would never let them get close to knowing me. My value of the human race had been low before this had started. Now it was in the fucking gutter.

"Mr. Prest."

I pulled at the collar of my shirt, hating the tight confines of expensive blazers and ties. Before, I'd lived in hoodies and jeans—things I could move fast in, run quick in, and vanish into crowds without being caught.

Now, I was adorned in appropriate rich-man's wardrobe, and it suffocated me.

These people wanted to know me? Well, tough shit. I'd never tell them about my days on the streets, the worry of not being able to afford healthcare for myself or my mother, and the god-awful truth that I was the reason we were homeless.

Not that those circumstances had mattered when I'd stolen the one thing that'd changed my life faster than a fairy fucking godmother and ensured I'd never be alone again if I didn't want to be. I could buy affection, bribe friends, and pay for anything I wanted.

I had money, and people loved money even if you were a liar, a cheater, and a con-artist.

Turned out, the only thing it couldn't buy was family.

And I knew...I'd tried.

After I grew used to the idea of borrowing the money instead of outright stealing it, I decided to give most of it to my mother. I envisioned her welcoming me back, letting me resume my place, and forgiving me.

She'd merely spat on me and told me never to call her Mother again.

"Uh, Mr. Prest?"

I jerked as some idiot tapped me on the shoulder.

"Are you ready?" *she asked with beady, jealous eyes. Jealous that I'd won and not her. Jealous that I got to live the life everyone dreamed.*

Having money meant my entire world had changed. Including who I was, my name, and every other identifying piece of me. I needed to learn my new address before I got caught and the sham came tumbling down.

Clearing my throat, I nodded. "Yes…fine."

"Right this way, please."

Swiping a hand through my hair, I tried to tame the thick black strands courtesy of my heritage and reluctantly followed the organiser hugging her clipboard.

She moved briskly but with a sexy sway. No doubt for my benefit. Not because she wanted me but because she wanted the pennies and dollars that'd magically appeared in my life.

"Right through there. You're on in three minutes."

Not replying, I marched onto the set, fighting the urge to tuck my hands into my pockets. My hands were my prized possessions. Every thief knew that if his fingers were hurt, there went his livelihood and any chance at surviving. I had another reason…my fingers were priceless because they gave me music to calm my chaotic thoughts and somehow connected me to my dead father, keeping his kindness alive.

I missed him.

I missed Kade.

I missed a simpler life where lies weren't the only things keeping me from going to prison for a very long time.

Christ, why am I doing this again?

Because it was the rule.

Win this big, and you were subjected to a televised interview. Mostly for the public's benefit, so they could see the system wasn't a scam, and everyone would keep playing, keep spending, keep stupidly dreaming.

One day, if they were lucky, they could be here…in my shoes.

Not my torn and dirty Adidas from my days on the streets, but the expensive, pretentious loafers by some prick called Givenchy.

"Take a seat, Mr. Prest." *The interviewer smiled, pointing at a red velvet chair next to him. It would just be us on that stark white space with the backdrop of the lotto logo bearing its celebratory colours and floating dollar bills.*

I sat, fighting every instinct to run. A pickpocket never showed their face. That was why we never hit the same place on consecutive days. We followed the tourists, careful never to be pegged by an overzealous local or donut-loving cop.

A cameraman stepped into the harsh lights with a snap board showing my name and the episode number.

How many idiots had done this before me? How many of them still had the money? No matter that I already had grand plans for my stolen winnings, I refused to be a dick with it. I would use it to make more. I would formulate everything I needed to have my revenge.

And then it would be all over.

I would beg for forgiveness and ensure I paid every penny back.

"On air in three, two, one." *The cameraman mouthed, snapped the board, and vanished into the darkness past the recording lights.*

Fuck, this was truly happening.

My host didn't look at me, staring with a bright, idiotic smile down the lens at an audience I didn't want to see. "Welcome, ladies and gentlemen, to the weekly interview of our lotto millionaires. Let's begin by welcoming Elder Prest and giving him a warm congratulations on his recent win."

I wanted to rip the cameras apart. To tell everyone in their homes to stop watching. They didn't need to know who I was. They didn't need to see a shame-riddled liar.

The presenter, with his over-hair-sprayed brown pompadour—and holy shit, is he wearing mascara?—*smiled in my direction.* "First, tell us, Elder, how it feels to have won such a large amount?"

I balled my hands. What was I supposed to say? It's amazing, and it's changed my life, and I'm ever so fucking grateful?

Those were lies, and I'd had enough of them.

I wouldn't bow to these assholes. If I was a pickpocket, then they were involved in a larger theft. The lottery was a Ponzi scheme, and somehow, I'd become the head of it.

When I didn't answer, the presenter prompted. "Eh, how about you tell our viewers your first thought when you were informed that the lotto ticket you'd purchased was worth seven hundred and ninety-eight million dollars?"

Shit, those numbers didn't seem real. They still didn't—even though they'd appeared in the hastily created bank account under my new false name. Getting the forgeries to do such a thing had been yet another headache-inducing story.

I muttered, "It took a lot of getting used to."

And I didn't buy the ticket, you asshole, I stole it from some poor guy's wallet.

The win had a sour taste because it was destined for someone else. Did they need the money? Did they even know what they'd had?

The poor schmuck's license sat in my pocket even now. Ever since I walked into that convenience store with his stolen wallet, wanting to buy a bottle of water to slake my day-old thirst, I'd carried the license around as a good luck charm and a reminder of what a bastard I was.

I'd paid for the drink with a five-dollar bill from his wallet. Along with the bill popped out a scrunched-up lottery ticket. The perky attendant had snatched it up before I could stuff it back into the well-used leather and squealed as she scanned it for me. Bells rang, lights flashed, she bounced up and down like a moron.

I almost fled the scene, thinking I'd been set up and the cops were on the way. Only for her to shove the monitor in my face and reveal all those terrifying numbers.

I was the winner.

Of the biggest jackpot in years.

I'd won.

No, he'd won.

And I, the thief, had stolen it.

I'd torn away any chance he had of quitting his job, spoiling his wife, and giving his children the kind of future only a select few could dream of.

I'd not only stolen his wallet.

I'd stolen his life.

And shit, that guilt? It was just as bad as killing my father and brother because I'd killed an alternative life for my victim—a life he would never know thanks to me.

That night, I'd become blind drunk and spilled the news to Selix. If it wasn't for him, I would've ripped up the winning ticket instead of officially lodging it the next day. Only because we'd fought as enemies for so long did I listen to his friendship and sage advice.

He was the reason I was dressed like a fucking peacock and accepting false congratulations. And the bastard refused to take half. Hell, I'd even slurred around the cheap vodka that he could have it all. That my karma was too sullied to accept another false achievement.

But he'd flatly refused.

Some noble reason he never told me and still to this day kept secret. He preferred to be second, not first, but without him...I doubted I'd still be alive to even think about accepting almost one billion dollars.

After that fateful night, my life had been a whirlwind of executive meetings, form signings, and limelight interviews that I cursed to the depths of hell.

I'd never had money. I'd been happy in my family of lower means with my beaten up cello, annoying little brother, and strict but doting parents.

Everything I ever loved was gone.

And who was to blame?

The Chinmoku.

The TV interview suddenly went from fakery to full of purpose.

I'd been burning with the need to extract revenge and honour the deaths of my family for years. Now, I had a way to bring that revenge to fruition.

In a fit of rage, I decided to use this fleeting fame to my benefit. Glowering down the camera lens, I answered the questions the presenter asked. I preened for the suckers at home wishing they were in my shoes and dreaming of the day they'd have such a stroke of luck.

Meanwhile, I placed gauntlet after gauntlet on the Chinmoku.

I'd changed my name but not my face.

If they were watching, they'd know I wouldn't give up. It was them or me. And eventually, they'd hunt me down. I'd buy every weapon I could and learn every skill there was so I could murder them one by one when they finally did.

Revenge and payback—two things I'd dedicate my life to.

One of death and one of debts.

After that night, I kept Oliver Gold's license in my wallet, and paid an private investigator to hunt down his address, social security, and bank account details, and sent him thirty million dollars.

The rest of the money had a job to do—earn itself three times over so I had funds for my revenge, my family, and to pay back my debt.

A few weeks later, after extensive research into what fields would pay best dividends, I decided to purchase a super yacht business. The numbers thrown around by billionaires for flashy toys was obscene.

I'd invest the first five hundred million into making the best yacht I could. I'd sell it for profit. I'd earn a reputation. I'd do it again and again until everything was back to rights.

The moment I decided Monte Carlo was the place to reinvent myself and plot my enemy's demise, I turned my back on America and boarded a plane to Monaco.

"Elder? El...you're scaring me."

I blinked.

Pim slowly came back into view. Her eyes strained; mouth pinched in pain. Looking down, I snatched my hand from hers. I'd squeezed her so hard her fingertips were white from blood loss. "Shit, I'm sorry."

"It's okay." She rubbed her fingers, half-smiling, half-grimacing. "You disappeared on me there. Are you all right?"

Was I all right?

I'd thought I was. It'd been years since I fully relived where the money had come from. I'd even managed to live with the guilt—justifying it because I paid Oliver Gold and still managed to build my yachts to earn more.

Touching the money to give Pim the origami lesson had somehow shot me down bitter memory lane.

Why? What was on my mind?

Fuck, everything is on my mind.

Perhaps, it was because I was sick of waiting for the

Chinmoku to make the first move. Perhaps, I was over begging for a fresh start with my family. Perhaps, I was done trying to hold myself back where Pim was concerned.

Selix had told me once to go easier on myself. To accept the good as well as the bad. I'd been fighting Pim since the day my heart first took notice of her. She was the opposite of me. She was everything good, and the more I fell for her, the worst I dragged her into my world and made her bad.

Goddammit, I'm exhausted.

Jamming my elbows onto the table, I held my head in my hands. My mind formulated lies and discarded them. Only the truth tasted decent on my tongue. "Everything you see? Everything you know…it's all a lie."

She froze. "What do you mean?"

"I mean the Phantom, the submarine, the warehouse in Monaco…it's all fake."

"What do you mean fake?"

"I mean I stole it."

Pim fell silent for a moment before she lowered her voice. "How do you mean *stole* it?" She shook her head. "That can't be possible. I saw your logo on the wall in that warehouse. I saw how the staff loved you. I saw your house on the hill where your mother stayed. I saw—"

"You saw nothing. It's all stolen."

"How can you say that? I can feel your sweat and blood in everything around us, Elder. I know how hard you work. How meticulous your designs are. How many clients you've delivered product to. Something like that can't be faked or stolen."

Sitting taller, I forced myself to be rational and start at the beginning. "The warehouse, the company…you're right, those are real. I created those from nothing, and they generate incredible wealth. I am the reason that company exists."

"Then what do you mean—?"

"I mean I could never have afforded to buy that house or the warehouse or the lumber and staff and machinery required to build such vessels without first stealing the money from someone else."

Taking her hand again, I begged her with my eyes to let me touch her. She didn't shy away—if anything, she leaned forward with no judgement or criticism on her face.

If I didn't already love her, I'd love her for that alone.

Her gaze turned forest green with earnest acceptance. "Tell me."

The only way to do it was to spit it all out. "I stole a man's wallet in New York. Inside was a lottery ticket. It turned out to be a jackpot of over half a billion dollars." My head hung. "I kept it when I should've given it back."

She fell utterly silent. She stared gobsmacked, her head shaking slightly.

My heart died, believing this was the point where it was all too much for her. Where she finally said...'*thanks but no thanks.*'

Instead, she blinked as things shifted over her face, solidified in her mind, and were once again accepted with no questions asked.

Who the hell was this girl? How could she be so kind and generous with her boundaries of right and wrong? How could I ever repay her?

Squeezing my fingers, she murmured, "This makes so much sense."

"What do you mean?"

"The guilt you carry. The shame I don't understand. You've never accepted the crime, so you pay for it constantly."

I didn't admit she was right on every level or tell her that in another few years, I would've paid off the man I robbed in full. I'd turned his winnings into double the amount. Soon, my debt would be clear, and I could finally admit I used him as an interest-free loan to get ahead, provide for my family—even if they didn't want to be provided for—and right the sins of my past.

I inhaled deeply, ready to deliver my final confession. Weren't revealing truths you'd harboured for years supposed to leave you light-hearted?

Somehow, I felt heavier, more tired than I'd ever been.

Bringing her hand to my lips, I whispered against her knuckles, "The man who saved you is a fraud doing his goddamn best to make up for all the shit he's done. But…it's never enough."

Tears sparkled in her eyes. She opened her mouth to speak, but I cut in, needing to finish, needing to end this. "Even my name is a lie."

She gasped.

"You are Tasmin Blythe. That is your true name even if you don't want it. I understand that more than you know. Ever since I met you, I've done my utmost to steal your letters, rob your past, and learn everything about you. Yet, I'm a fucking hypocrite."

"El—"

"No. Listen, Pim. I get that you're not ready to use your old name. Just like I'll probably never use mine. I'm no longer that boy. And good fucking riddance."

Cupping her cheek, I couldn't tear my gaze from her lips. I wanted so badly to kiss her but after this confession—this completely unplanned and shockingly stupid confession—I had no willpower anymore.

All it would take was for her to lean forward and press her mouth to mine.

And it would be all over.

The dishes would be on the floor, Pim would be on the table, and we'd have an entirely different dinner than the one we'd come here for.

My voice tore with a growl as I fought myself yet again. "I demand to know everything about you. Every scrap of thought and fragment of memory I want to hoard. I *need* to make it mine. But to balance such a demand, I should be willing to share myself. But I'm not ready. I might never be. I have so much I wish I could erase. So many things I never want you to know. And because of that, whatever we have will forever be unequal. I'll always demand more from you than I can give, and that is yet another debt I'm struggling to bear."

I needed to leave before I told her anymore incriminating failures.

Letting her go, I stood and kissed the top of her head, lingering over the soft scent of vanilla and sea salt. "I need to be alone, Pimlico. Don't come find me."

I left before I could change my mind.

Before I could drag her into my lap, beg her for forgiveness, and bury myself inside her.

I left before I could create any new mistakes when I was trying so fucking hard to rectify my old ones.

Pimlico

FOR FORTY-EIGHT HOURS, I did my best to give Elder some space.

I'd found him in his office the next day, but after a stilted, distracted conversation about the weather, I'd left him to drown himself in work.

The rest of the day, I'd relaxed on my balcony and watched the horizon blur into one magical line where tide met sky and sizzled with sunshine.

The next afternoon, I headed up on deck only to find Elder at the bow with binoculars pressed to his eyes, his back rigid, and the faintest outline of another vessel on the horizon.

When I tiptoed beside him and stared at the faraway vessel, my skin prickled from the crackle of energy he gave off. His whole persona was tense and brittle, ready to shatter at any moment. Only, when he shattered, I had an awful feeling he'd take out entire cities with his rage and regret rather than just implode.

I stood beside him for twenty minutes before I got up the nerve to ask if he knew who manned the boat behind us.

He ripped the binoculars away and gave me a look so black and bleak, I struggled to catch a breath.

A moment later, he returned to looking through the magnifying glass only to mumble something about an urgent meeting with his captain then vanish to the bridge.

Something nasty gnawed at him. Something that had nothing to do with me and everything to do with his past.

Chinmoku.

Did he expect them to find us here? Was his worry over going to war or their involvement in the QMB and my fate?

My questions sank to the depths of my belly and made me nauseous.

That night, I ate alone even though he sat beside me. We exchanged salt and pepper, we commented on how fragrant the chicken laksa was, and once again, we shared awkward pleasantries on the weather.

Ever since the botched origami lesson, he barely made eye contact with me. I knew in his mind it was out of respect...to give me time to get used to the idea that his entire wealthy existence was based on a lie, but his lack of friendship left me stranded and chilly.

I was lonely even as I shared dinner with him.

The questions in my stomach curdled until all I wanted to do was hug him and say I didn't care if his name was fake and his wealth was stolen. All I cared about was *him*. The man I knew right here, right now. The man who could have nothing and no one and I would still love because I recognised his soul as one that I valued and respected.

When dinner was over and I'd burned more calories in stress than I'd consumed, I tried to ask why the presence of another boat unsettled him so much. His eyes once again blackened with protection and temper, delivering a harsh chuckle designed to sound light-hearted and carefree but was the heaviest blood-icing laugh I'd ever heard.

For the first time, I didn't find comfort in his presence; I only found frustration from not being allowed to share his burdens.

I stood and said a quiet goodnight, only for him to escort me wordlessly to my room.

And then, after we parted painfully outside my door, I

locked the handle for the second time.

I willingly accepted what Elder told me to do and withdrew a little. I locked the door because he told me to. Because he wanted that barrier between us. Well, he'd successfully erected one by cutting me out of his problems.

With my heart raging, I padded onto my balcony and stared at the starry sky. No signs of another boat. No lights on the horizon or billowing sails.

We'd travelled past other yachts and schooners before, especially when we left Morocco. Therefore, I couldn't understand why Elder had gone from exchanging friendly horn blows to glowering at them through binoculars.

If he truly believed the Chinmoku would attack at sea, why was he worried? He said so himself that the Phantom had more weaponry than it needed.

That night, I didn't sleep well. Dreams of pirates and kidnapping and men in black masks kept me company. By the time morning came, I was relieved to open my curtains to a bright sun and empty horizon.

Once again, I had breakfast on my own.

My mind returned to the secret Elder had told me. His biggest secret perhaps. If it wasn't, I didn't know how I would endure yet more heart felt revelations. If I was any other person, I might judge him for taking a life of financial security from one man and claiming it for himself. If I hadn't seen how pure he was beneath his temper, I might've pulled away.

But I didn't.

And then Selix found me and told me the parts Elder hadn't.

After finishing a simple breakfast of muesli and yoghurt, I strolled the deck looking for something to keep me entertained. Looking over the railing, I spotted Elder as he swam in the ocean below, cutting through the tide like a great white shark.

Resting my elbows on the balustrade, I settled to watch the man I loved pummel his frustration and anger out on unsuspecting waves. Selix found me mulling over rights and wrongs and how I could accept some but not others.

He mimicked my position, watching companionly as Elder did his best to outswim his demons. For a few minutes, I tensed, still mildly uncomfortable where Selix was concerned.

What did he want?

I doubted he wanted to talk. He was too loyal to Elder for that. However, it didn't mean I had to obey such rules.

"You know, don't you?" I twisted to face him. "Where the money came from?"

His eyebrow rose as he kept his eyes on Elder. "Do you?"

I looked back to the sea where small splashes from Elder's arms and feet ruined the otherwise marble appearance of the ocean. "He told me."

"Did he also tell you that crime made him reassess everything? That he went from being a brilliant thief to reformed overnight?"

"Not in so many words."

Selix fell quiet.

I didn't know if I should ask what other skeletons rested in Elder's closet, but Selix gave me a snippet of information that released my heart from the anchor Elder had attached to it.

His voice was low—barely audible over the sea breeze. "Do you also know he's almost paid back what he stole?"

"What?" My jaw fell open.

"He would never have accepted it if I hadn't convinced him to look at the money as a loan rather than a heist. He's referred to his success as a debt ever since."

"A debt?"

He shrugged. "The crime."

My eyes widened as his words sank in. "You mean…Elder found the guy and paid him back?" The concept that anyone would do that, and could somehow take one wealth and turn it into double blew my mind.

"He wanted to give it all back, but I talked sense into him." Selix smirked. "Then he wanted to give most of it and keep a few million for his family. I told him life had given him this break. He could borrow it without issue if he couldn't outright steal it."

"I don't know what to say."

So *that* was why Elder worked so hard. Why he sailed the world dealing with ruffians and criminals and created such beautiful floating pieces of art. Not because he had a need to be in the underground world but because he knew that crime paid and he needed pay checks to service a debt.

"I know he's told you about the Chinmoku, so I'm going to give you a word of advice." Selix turned to me, looking over his shoulder to make sure Elder was still power swimming around the yacht. "Over the years, he's built up a fearsome reputation, pissed off people, befriended others, and lied through his goddamn teeth. All he wanted was to go home and live in peace, but that isn't how revenge works. He's playing a long game, and the big match is coming."

Moving away from the rail, he paused as his shoulder brushed mine. "They're coming. He knows that. I know that. You might as well know that because when they come for him, he'll need all the fucking help he can get."

My hand shot out as he moved away, latching around his forearm.

He looked down with a quizzical look as if shocked I'd touched him.

Before he could request I unhand him, I asked, "What can I do? How do I help him?"

"Not for me to say." He shrugged, his face aloof and slightly cold. "You left because you thought it was the right thing for him. That makes you a good person, and I won't try to stop him from being with you. But you need to find a way to stop hurting him. He needs to have a clear head when they come. Because they are coming, Tasmin Blythe. Mark my words. And if he's not ready, he'll die. And then his family will die. And you will die. And everything he's fucking created from nothing? It was all *be* for nothing—he might as well have burned with his father and brother just like his family wanted."

Removing my hand, he muttered, "He's lying to you. Don't take his bullshit and you'll help him far more than by giving him what he wants."

My heart grasped at his advice, soaking it in with desperate knowledge-thirst. "Is that what you do?"

"That's what friends do. And I'm many things, but first and foremost, I'm his friend."

He strolled away, jamming his hands into his pockets as if we'd never spoken. As if he'd not given me clues on how to seduce the very same man who'd painted himself in the blood of my old master and claimed me.

A gust rose from the sea below, revealing Elder as he completed yet another lap. I wrapped arms around myself as a shiver worked down my spine.

Selix had used my real name.

It hadn't been comforting or inspiring.

It had been ominous and unsettling and done exactly what his words had failed to do.

The Chinmoku weren't going to let Elder get away with what he'd done.

And I wouldn't leave Elder.

Eventually they would enter my life, and I no longer had umpteen time to figure out if Elder could sleep with me safely and finally find a place of peace.

A stopwatch had started.

Ticking fast.

Running toward a finish line that I didn't know would end in victory or bloodshed.

* * * * *

That night, I woke to calamity.

One moment I was curled beneath warm blankets, the next the door slammed wide, footsteps pounded to my bed, sheets were ripped off, and I was jerked into powerful arms.

My eyes flew wide.

My mind shut down.

Horror and panic drenched me.

I hadn't locked the door.

I really should have.

My voice did two things at once: it tried to hide and become mute. It tried to scream and become noise.

I settled on a combination. A stuttering caterwaul full of sleep and horror. "Put m-me *down!*" I screeched and kicked, doing my best to attack my assailant. "No! Stop! Let me *go!*"

"Pim…it's me."

I blinked back terror, latching onto the voice that'd been whispering sweet nothings in my dreams. "Elder?"

What the hell is he doing?

"I'm not going to hurt you."

Could've fooled me.

I bounced painfully over his shoulder as he rushed from my room, down the corridor, and flew down the stairs instead of waiting for the lift. The Phantom was a blur of carpet and sconces, making me sick. "Where are you taking me?"

What the hell had gotten into him? Why was he flying around the Phantom at God knew what time in the morning?

"Almost there. The majority of staff are in position." Selix appeared from a floor above, chasing us down another flight. "Machine gun ready at your command."

"What?" I squeaked as Elder shoved his free shoulder through the door blocking a level I'd explored but found boring and discounted, jogging with me slung over him like a sack of sugar.

He ignored Selix entirely.

At the end of the corridor, he slammed to a stop, swung me from horizontal to vertical, and dropped me to my feet. I stumbled in place as my brain sloshed with dizziness.

I swallowed a thick mouthful of nausea.

With a clenched jaw, Elder yanked open the façade of a simple cupboard, revealing a thick bombproof door behind it.

My eyes popped wide as he pummelled the barrier with his fist. "Open up."

It opened instantly by a girl I recognised from the kitchen

staff. Her blonde hair fuzzy like a halo around her head from rubbing on a pillow in sleep. "Roster has been counted. All accounted for minus the staff manning the bridge."

Elder swiped a hand over the sweat glistening on his forehead. "Keep them here until the all-clear is given." Shoving me forward, he didn't touch me, kiss me, or whisper anything kind to me. I was nothing more to him than someone to protect while his mind was in a battle elsewhere. "Keep her with you. Don't let her out. Do you hear me?"

I bristled. I didn't appreciate being talked about as if I wasn't there or had any brain cells to understand simple commands. The head cleaner—an elderly woman with curlers in her hair—took my bicep, tugging me unwillingly into the room. "We'll take good care of her, sir."

Elder grunted in acknowledgement, already focusing on another task.

Instead of seeing me as an ally and someone who could help fight with him, he saw me as a liability to remove so he didn't have to worry.

How *dare* he?

I knew I'd been weak when we first met. I knew I still had fading bruises from Harold, and I knew I still had other issues to overcome, but how dare he not trust me enough to lean on me?

After everything.

Whatever was happening, I wanted to be with him—not stuffed in some closet and forgotten about.

I grabbed his hand. "El, let me come with you. I need—"

His fingers wrapped around my wrist, tugging my grip away. "I need you to stay here, Pimlico. Got it?"

I eyed the door. Or rather the fortress entrance—it wasn't lacquered wood like the rest of the Phantom's entrances. This was utterly bullet-proof with thick hinges, dead bolts, and metal encasing front and back.

Shoving me once again into the hold of the cleaner, he barked, "Keep her here. Understand?"

The woman nodded. "Understood." Grabbing my elbow again, she pulled me away from Elder.

I yanked my arm against her tugging, locking my knees. "Elder, wait. What's going on?"

The air of apprehension and concern infected me. Every staff member on the Phantom stood worried behind me.

That could only mean one thing.

Oh, my God, they're here.

Elder's black eyes met mine, glowing with remorse, brutal with violence. "Nothing. And for the love of Christ, Pimlico, stay here and do as I say." With a sharp shake of his head as if fighting the same need I had to touch him and find some sanity in this crazy wake-up scare, he stormed off down the corridor, leaving me entrapped with staff members.

The moment he vanished into the stair-well, the girl with blonde hair shut the door, and I whirled on the woman holding me. "Let me go."

She unwound her fingers, backing into the room. "Just keeping you safe."

"Well, don't. My safety is not your concern." My eyes followed her. My temper fizzled out as I took in the space. Just like the door wasn't just a door, this wasn't just a room. The walls had no windows, there were couches around the perimeter but narrow and uninviting compared to the luxury of other Phantom furniture. A long table to the side with buckled down crates held hundreds of water bottles and packet food ready for a famine, but it was the centre piece that caught my attention.

In the middle of the large space, hidden behind multiple milling people, sat a boat. Not just any boat but one Fort Knoxed with guns and canopies, big enough to hold everyone in the room.

What on earth?

My gaze shot to the back wall where a small slope in the floor disappeared into nowhere. There weren't windows, but the wall wasn't just a wall. It was a door—a large exit ramp for the lifeboat.

"What *is* this place?" I blinked at staff members—some wired and awake, others blurry-eyed and napping on the uncomfortable couches.

A guy I'd seen tending to the helicopter said, "It's the safe room."

"Safe from what?"

"Pirates, of course."

My mouth hung open. "There's no such thing."

"Not the typical ones in storybooks, no. But there are many rogue ships that board, rob, rape, and kill. It's a maritime requirement to have a safe room with enough food and water for all souls on board. Normally, the protocol is to call for help and wait it out, or the pirates take what they want and leave. But Mr. Prest went one step further and ensured we had a way off the yacht in case something catastrophic happens."

My heart was what turned catastrophic. Bombs detonated inside me, sending shrapnel ripping through my blood.

Why was Elder out there and not in here? Who would protect him and the men on the bridge?

The longer I stood in safety with food and escape at my fingertips, the more I couldn't stand it. Elder. The captain. They were out there...fighting for us.

What the hell are we doing?

Why were our lives worth more than theirs? Why should we be out of danger when they faced it head on?

I-I can't stay here.

I needed to be with him. If the Chinmoku were paying a visit, I couldn't let him face them on his own.

I wouldn't.

I didn't care it was stupid to put myself in danger. I didn't care that Elder would be livid at me for getting in the way.

I literally couldn't stand here while he was out there facing who knew what.

A loud foghorn shattered the tense murmurings in the room, dragging our eyes to the ceiling. A loudhailer sounded, but the words were warbled and hard to hear.

"Oh, God. We're being boarded," the head cleaner said, pacing by the lifeboat.

Staff members forgot about me as another horn sounded—this time vibrating and echoing through the Phantom. The captain had replied with his own thundering call.

Was it a call to war or surrender?

Elder will never surrender.

I still didn't know all his secrets, but if it *was* the Chinmoku, then he would kill or be killed. There were only two scenarios available, and I refused to stand here and let him face such terrible choices alone.

Pretending to keep my eyes on the ceiling like everyone else—waiting for another boom of gunfire or horn of retaliation, I inched toward the door. No one paid attention as I fumbled with the locking mechanism and unhooked multiple deadbolts.

Safety did that to people. The knowledge they were untouchable in their special bunker allowed them to focus on the way life had split. Them versus us. The soon-to-be extinct and the ones who would survive.

My hands worked faster at the thought of Elder being hurt.

Please let him be okay...

Another loudhailer bellowed, chopped and incomprehensible. Whatever they were telling Elder and his crew to do, I didn't think he'd obey. My skin prickled for the first round of gunshots, already picturing carnage and hoping to God my over-active imagination never came true.

With shaking fingers, I finally managed to unlock the door. The damn thing weighed a ton. I struggled to pull it wide enough to slip through. Pushing my leg through first, I angled my hips and slinked past the gap.

At the last second, a young maid spotted me. She opened her mouth to say something, but I shook my head, pressing my fingers to my lips.

This was my decision. Not hers.

If I wanted to risk my life, it was my choice. I'd had far too many choices taken away to let her take that away from me, too.

She scowled but nodded, watching me wriggle my way through the gap.

The staff had to stay here. Their loyalty to their employer worked with service in exchange for money—nothing more, nothing less. My loyalty to Elder was something completely different. I offered my love hopefully in exchange for his. He would never make me face something horrific on my own. Therefore, I wouldn't let him.

I'll never forgive myself if I'm not there when—

I cut off those thoughts.

Slipping the final way to freedom, I swallowed my huff of frustration at being so slow and leaned on the massive blockade to slide it back into position.

I knew it was secure when the sound of deadbolts clicking into place echoed in the corridor.

I had no regrets. No second-guesses.

Hoisting up my pale pink nightgown, I took one last look at the safe room then flew down the corridor.

Hair flying.

Heart winging.

I soared up the stairs—up, up, up toward Elder and the Chinmoku.

ELDER

ALL I WANTED to do was tell these bastards to get the fuck off my yacht.

But I wouldn't because that would earn me a one-way ticket to jail.

I stood facing the man in charge—boss to boss—eyeing up his uniform, hating his arrogant airs, and scowling at the patches on his arms. Patches celebrating his rank as if I gave a flying fuck.

Jolfer stood on my right with fists clenched, and Selix stood on my left—his face mimicking my unreadable mask.

My night had turned from bad to worse, and now I waited to see what other new hell they'd bring.

Goddammit, couldn't they have waved us on? Did they have to board after giving me a goddamn heart attack thinking it was the Chinmoku about to terrorize my entire crew?

Swallowing my temper, I growled. "Look, you know us. You don't need—"

"Wait!" Something pink and fast and suicidal bowled through the bridge's door and careened straight toward me.

"Oof." I stumbled as Pim barrelled into my side, knocking me off balance.

She shied away with an apologetic look then pinned her

gaze on the uniformed interlopers. "I don't care who you are, but if you hurt anyone on this boat, I'll ensure you all pay."

What.

The.

Ever.

Loving.

Fuck?

Her pure, perfect voice ripped my balls off. Her strength and ferocity bulldozed through my knees and spine.

I couldn't bloody move.

What the *hell* was she doing? What the hell was she *thinking*?

She could've gotten herself killed with a stunt like that. I was in charge of her protection, not the other way around.

Christ, this woman!

My heart froze even as it gushed with bone-deep affection for the calamity she almost caused. All because she would rather die to keep me alive than permit me to do the same.

I didn't have the luxury of figuring out how twisted up that made me feel.

How awed I was. How annoyed I was. How amazed and pissed and happy and *furious* I was.

Lucky for us, tonight wasn't what I thought it was. I'd locked everyone in the safe room for nothing. In fact, they'd all have to slink from hiding and meet these ship visitors. Questions would be asked and answers would be given just as ocean law commanded.

I blamed my overreaction on my paranoia, insomnia, and chaotic mess of a brain.

I'd studied the horizon with too much suspicion, seeing Chinmoku instead of other travellers and happy-go-lucky seafarers. I'd painted the maritime police as the bad guys.

Grabbing Pim's upper arm, I jerked her to me. "Keep your mouth closed."

Even though the safe room drill was a false alarm, I would've still hidden Pim because technically, she wasn't cleared to be on the Phantom. No one would be murdered tonight but someone—mainly me—would be in for a world of interrogation and rule book berating.

As if I don't have enough on my mind.

"A guest of yours, Mr. Prest?" The man in charge looked Pim up and down, his beady eyes not permitted on her. My fists curled as his look of suspicion slipped to appreciation. The pink nightgown didn't exactly hide much of her slim, tempting figure, especially with the bright lights in the bridge highlighting her curves.

My hands curled, but I kept my face professional. "She's not important."

Pim sucked in a breath. I tightened my fingers around her arm.

I'd never said a more heinous thing. She was important. Far too fucking important. And that was why she'd utterly ruined me by disobeying a direct order and coming to fight my battles.

My heart literally shot itself at the thought of what would've happened had it been the Chinmoku and not the coastguard.

She needed disciplining. She needed to be taught the repercussions of not listening to me.

"Everyone, regardless of importance, must be logged and cleared for travel. You know that," the M.O.—maritime officer—in command muttered. "Don't tell me you need a refresher on sea etiquette, Mr. Prest?"

A growl percolated in my belly.

I prepared to lie, but if I bullshitted she was staff, they'd know instantly. I couldn't fib thanks to the meticulous records and employee passports we had to lodge.

My teeth wanted to stay locked together, but I clipped, "She's a guest."

"Ah, so you just lied when you said there was no one new on board?"

I stuck my chin in the air, daring him to come closer to

that line. The line where I'd snap and throw everyone off my boat—consequences be damned. "Momentary lapse of judgment."

Pim glanced between me and the coastguard captain. Her beautiful face contorted with confusion, doing her best to catch up and understand.

It was a simple enough mistake. I thought we were under attack and called for a routine shutdown and call to arms. I hadn't seen the coastguard logo, and Jolfer failed to tell me they'd radioed ahead for the request to board and perform a common inspection.

I'd been on edge ever since finding out someone else had accessed Pim's file. No boat could sail close without me instantly going on the defence and believing it was fucking war.

"Ma'am?" The chief inspector pulled out a notebook. "Can you tell me your name?"

Pim narrowed her eyes; her throat working as she swallowed. She didn't answer, and once again, I was reminded how silence was her friend when she was uncertain or afraid.

If I was to get out of this without an arrest or a serious fine, she had to do what they asked—including giving up her true name. Nodding gently, I encouraged, "It's okay. Answer him."

She frowned as she looked from me to him, trying to see a trap. Finally, she straightened her spine and said with ringing steel, "My name is Tasmin Blythe."

"And how long have you been a guest on the Phantom?"

Ah, Christ, I'd get a fine tonight no matter what she said. Another rule I'd broken: I'd refused to lodge any of her details. No mention of embarkation or places visited. I hadn't logged a single thing or notarized what country she was from for ports and immigration.

Why did I do that?

Was it because Pim technically didn't exist? That if anyone knew I had her, they could link me back to sex trafficking and the QMB? Maybe it was because even when I first rescued her,

I knew I wanted her far more than I should, and a woman like Pim would be missed. She would be searched for.

I'd deliberately kept her presence a secret for my benefit.

"Umm," Pim hedged, her bare toes turning white as she dug them into the hardwood floor. "Not sure...." Turning to me, she searched my face for guidance.

She was too obvious.

The officer rolled his eyes, telling me what I already knew—that I was an idiot for not following protocol. This could've been a simple board, cross check, walk around, and departure.

Now, with Pim's arrival and the extra weapons on board, it would mean a full-on snoop fest.

"Answer me, girl," the officer pushed.

I nodded for her to continue, not giving any hints on how she needed to reply. This was on her. I'd tried to prevent her from being in this mess, yet she'd ignored me.

You're on your own, Pimlico.

And then, when we're alone...you and I are going to have a serious chat.

Tearing her gaze from mine, Pim cleared her throat. "I'm not sure exactly. A few weeks. A few months? Time seems to pass differently on the ocean."

"And do you have a passport? Visas?"

She stiffened. "I wasn't aware I needed them."

"Anyone sailing on international waters must be prepared for immigration."

"Oh." She looked at her feet then back to the man in question with rebellion in her gaze. "I might not have a passport, but I do have a police file with my fingerprints and who I am. Is that enough?"

I swallowed my groan, doing my best not to slap myself in the face.

Fucking great. She just admitted she'd been processed for a crime.

The M.O. gave me a snide look. "Aiding and abetting

criminals now, Mr. Prest? This just gets better and better." He strolled forward, his notebook clutched self-importantly. "What else are you hiding around here?"

"Nothing to concern you with." I crossed my arms. "Look, just book me and—"

"He's only trying to protect me," Pim offered, stepping forward to meet the officer in the middle of the bridge. Buttons and monitors flashed from the control panel, painting her nightgown in an array of colours. "He saved me and is taking me back to my mother in England." She threw me a quick glance as if to reiterate privately that she had no intention of being left behind in the UK while I sailed away.

I was glad because just the thought of her leaving buckled my knees—even while I was fucking *furious* with her.

"Well, isn't that noble of him?" the officer asked even though he looked at Pim as if she'd told a silly bedtime story. "How about you give me your mother's name, address, and that police record you mentioned, and we'll see if that's enough to clear you for passage."

"And if it isn't?" she asked, crossing her arms like a brave, stupid girl.

The guy narrowed his eyes, looking over her head to me. "If it isn't, someone might be arrested or worse—his boat confiscated."

Oh, hell no.

I'd pay any fine—shit, I'd even spend a couple of days in the slammer. But take my boat? I wouldn't survive.

My body turned brittle with aggression. Images of throwing these men off the stern and chopping them into sushi with the propellers filled my head. "She's telling the truth. I'm taking her home. Nothing more. Nothing less." I glanced from the M.O. to Pim, glowering at her spitefully, doing my best to put her in her place.

All of this was her fault.

If she'd stayed where I'd told her, this wouldn't be an issue. She'd disobeyed me, and goddammit, she'd pay once we were no longer under inspection.

Crossing my arms, I took back my power as ruler of this yacht. "Does the coastguard make it their duty to board at four in the morning?"

"The world never sleeps, Mr. Prest. You know that."

"I do, but a simple radio call would've sufficed."

"We did. Can't blame us if that message was never passed on."

I glared at Jolfer who shrugged with a tight nod. I might be the ruler of this vessel, but he was the captain. I trusted him to deal with things like radio conversations without micromanaging. Besides, at four a.m., I should've been asleep and not peering at the horizon waiting for an attack.

I sighed, accepting defeat. "I'd say this was a pleasure, but I'd be lying again. I'll ensure to log Ms. Blythe correctly. Anything else?" I repressed the urge to tap my foot one, two, three. Or wring his puny neck.

"Yes, there is something else. I think a routine inspection is in order, don't you?"

I swallowed my groan. "Nothing new to see."

"Oh, I beg to differ." He smiled coldly. "I never like to miss out on an opportunity to inspect yachts as nice as this under the call of duty." Discounting me, he pointed at Pim. "Relay your details to my colleague over there, Miss." With a pompous smile on his weather-beaten face, he rubbed his hands together. "Now, captain. Pass me the logs and unlock all the doors. Let's see what you guys have been up to since our last visit."

* * * * *

Three hours.

Three long, interminable hours for the coastguard to finally satisfy their curiosity.

Staff members returned from the safe room and confirmed their right to sail against the log we'd supplied each port we frequented. Maritime officers ticked their names off a register and verified their passports and visas were still up to date.

I stayed with Pimlico as she handed over her release from the Monaco Police and the signed statement proving no crime was lodged.

Jolfer showed our previous itineraries and activities while yet another team of inconsiderate men all puffed up on fake power thanks to their uniforms invaded every room on the Phantom.

Meanwhile, I waited for the accusations.

Sure enough, around dawn, I was summoned to a meeting with the head M.O. as he listed the extra weapons I'd installed and hadn't advised.

The fine was substantial. The slap on the wrist fairly painful.

Throughout the inspection, I managed to keep my body still and straight—belying the twitching rage in my gut. My fingers, however, weren't so easily tamed, and to anyone watching, they would've seen the musical notes and cello strings I practised to keep my brain focused and not spin into directions I couldn't control.

Around seven a.m., Pim noticed my forever moving hands. Her lips pursed, her forehead furrowed—not just watching me strum out a chord but studying me as if trying to crack the answers to tricky questions she burned with.

I still couldn't talk to her without wanting to throttle her, so I jammed my fingers into my pockets and strode to the other side of the bridge where a rookie guard was trying to tabulate the crew lifeboats ratios and determine if it was up to code.

By the time we'd been well and truly trespassed over, Pimlico was issued a temporary pass to enter England with the proviso that she speak with immigration the moment she disembarked and applied for a passport replacement.

She agreed, but I had no intention of marching her to a stuffed-up shirt in an office and wasting yet another day of our life waiting for forms to be filled out.

We had things to do. Places to go. People to visit. There wasn't time for any deviations to my plan.

Already, my stomach roiled at the thought of our first appointment when we arrived on Great Britain soil. I still hadn't told Pim I'd spoken to her mother. And now, I didn't know if I would be apologetic if she was mad or glad because if she gave me attitude, I would finally be able to let loose the anger caused from her being so damn reckless.

My nostrils flared as my temper fired hotter. It was probably a blessing this rigmarole had taken three hours. It should've given me plenty of time to cool down and see her valiant arrival as idiotic but good hearted. Instead, it only made me worse because I wasn't able to yell at her in company.

All I knew was she'd put herself in harm's way. What if it *had* been the Chinmoku? What if she'd run directly into a bullet meant for me? What if they'd fucking killed her right in front of me? Didn't she see I put her somewhere safe so I could be who I needed to be? She made me weak, and that could never be tolerated where my past was concerned.

Ever.

My temper vibrated thicker and crazier the longer the coastguard took. When they finally signed off, nodded their approval, and got the fuck off my yacht, I was a goddamn mess.

Standing on the bow, I kept my fists tight against my thighs as the police boat pulled away in a wash of froth. The Phantom towered over their piddly excuse for a craft, casting them in a shadow from the new sun.

Pim sidled up beside me, shielding her eyes with her hand from the new day's glare.

The second, the very fucking *second*, the coastguard was far enough away from my territory, I snatched her wrist and dragged her across the deck.

"El—" She tugged, tripping and skipping at my pace. "What—"

"Not one word, Pimlico." I managed to bite. "Not. One.

Word."

Staff saw us coming and veered in a different direction. Jolfer spotted us and held his tongue. Selix narrowed his eyes but gave a firm nod.

Everyone knew Pim was in deep trouble.

Even her.

She fell quiet as I dragged her past lifeboats and rigging and on-deck spas. I didn't stop until I reached my bedroom. Stony silence was our method of communication as I yanked open the sliders and tossed her inside. Spinning around, I slammed the doors closed, engaged the lock, pressed the button to turn the glass opaque, then stalked her. "You crossed the line, Pim."

She backed up, her bare feet scrambling. Green fire burned in her gaze, trying to deny her sin but knowing full well what she'd done. "I-I don't know what you're talking about."

"You know *exactly* what I'm talking about."

Her toes did their best to glue into the thick carpeting, refusing to run from me, but her body continued swaying backward as if my temper buffeted her like wind. "I was worried about you—"

"And I was worried about you. That's why I put you in the safe room."

"But you were in danger. If those men had come to hurt you…I couldn't have hidden in a room while they kill—"

"You think so little of me that I'd be the one to die and not them?"

She froze, her mouth parted. "No…but it's dangerous. I can't stomach the thought of you being hurt."

"Exactly!" I roared. "Don't you think it's the same for me? To know I'm putting you in danger just by having you in my life? That I can't offer you a safe future until I'm done with my past?" I paced, doing my best not to grab her and shake her hard. "This isn't your battle, Pimlico."

"It is, though, because I'm with you now, and I won't let you face things alone."

"Never say that." My eyes turned to snipers. "The mistakes I've made are not yours. Got it?"

"But—"

"No buts! You disobeyed me. I put you somewhere safe, yet you scampered off as if you could protect me. That's *my* job, Pim. Not yours. You *obey* me. You do as I say."

"My safety is not your job, Elder." She huffed condescendingly. "And if you believe I'm going to obey you on everything...well—"

"Goddammit, you test me." I fisted my hair, taking my violence out on myself and not her. "If you were my staff, I'd fire you for being insubordinate."

"Good job I'm not your staff." Her chin cocked, baring her teeth. "I wouldn't work for a man like you."

"Good job," I copied her, lowering my jaw, already cursing myself for this. For letting myself get so wound up, my control was seconds away from snapping. For letting myself get so obsessed with obedience, I was about to break every fucking rule and go past scolding her as a naughty child to punishing her entirely as a woman.

Like a woman I was in love with.

A woman I wanted to sleep with.

A woman I tried to deny myself over and over only to break because I couldn't fight her influence anymore. I couldn't stomach her infection on my carefully structured life.

"Good job what?" She scowled, her throat working, belying her fight with the truth. The truth that she was scared of me. As she should be.

"Good job you aren't my staff." My voice was thick molasses with an edge of razor blades. "Otherwise, you could sue me for what I'm about to do."

Her breath came quick and shallow. "What *are* you about to do?"

"I think it would be called employee sexual harassment." I stalked her, coming to a stop before her locked limbs and bristling uncertainty. Her cheeks pinked with a mixture of defiance and terror. She swayed toward me even while leaning away; a strange light lit her from within.

Incredibly, her fight and fear morphed into recognition, melted into acceptance, and solidified into determination.

Her entire body went from fight to invitation in a matter of seconds.

The fact she could stand me down while my temper threatened to do what other yelling abusive males had done, then somehow switch to crackling lust and utmost trust broke the rest of my control.

I launched myself at her.

She didn't run.

She was weightless as I crushed her to me.

She was eager as my mouth slammed on hers and every last thought exploded into nothingness.

There was nothing else but me and her.

No coastguard or Chinmoku or staff or dawn or dusk or *anything*.

Just her.

Just Pim.

The noise in my brain gave up a million things at once, zeroing in on the one thing it wanted above everything else but had been so vehemently denied.

The chains on my fingers fell away as I cupped her breast. The ropes around my tongue fell away as I kissed her deep. The padlocks around my cock didn't stand a chance as I turned rock fucking hard and ground myself against her soft, warm belly.

She gasped as I manhandled her to the bed.

Her legs twined with mine.

We stumbled.

We kissed.

We groped.

I grabbed her from the floor and toppled onto the mattress.

We fell together. Her beneath. Me on top. Collapsing in a pile of messy, desperate limbs. Everything was on fire.

Everything was in pain. Aches and bruises—torturing desire crippling every inch as my lips dominated hers, and her hands skated down my back.

Passion I'd never let myself indulge in set us alight and made us *burn*. Blaze. Cremate beneath the mastership of longing.

Her legs parted, allowing me to slot against her. Her back bowed as my hips arched into her, pressing everything I wanted to give her into the one place I couldn't stop craving.

Her fingernails sliced over my spine, making my skin char beneath the white t-shirt I'd thrown on at the first sign of the coastguard. My track pants did nothing to stop the heat in my balls or restrain the need swiftly spiralling out of control.

I was past common sense or rationality.

I had no impulse supremacy or dominion over my unbreakable rules—they'd all turned to useless dust.

"You disobeyed me." I bit her bottom lip. "You deliberately put yourself at risk."

She wriggled beneath me. "I did it because I care."

Care?

Fuck, that word was pathetic compared to the wealth of emotion she caused.

I needed her. I couldn't breathe if I didn't have her.

Somehow, she knew that without me telling her. Her legs opened wider, her fingernails digging deeper into my back with commands this time and not just reaction. She rocked against my length, moaning softly, sweetly, entirely seductively.

If she was any other woman, I'd guess it was a coy way of saying *'take me...now'* but with her background, it could be a cry for help. Even in my current lawlessness, I wouldn't accept her invitation unless I knew for certain...

Through the red haze in my brain, I did my best to look at her and not see sex, sex, sex but rather a woman who'd stolen my heart and therefore was owed civility even when I had none.

Instead of seeing the wide eyes of someone desperate to

run away or the white skin of someone petrified, she looked back soft and calm and ready—the exact opposite of how I felt.

Her hand came up to cup my cheek—shocking me stupid with the tenderness of it. "Elder…you have me. Do whatever you need."

I swallowed some filthy reply. Some terrible sentence accepting her gift even knowing how wrong I was to do it but then her eyes filled with pure love, bathing me in redemption and approval.

She fucking *slaughtered* me.

I fell on her, clawing, clinging, mauling, thrusting.

My lips sought hers again as I ripped at my waistband and shoved my track pants out of the way. I didn't want to do this so fast, but I had no choice. I had to be inside her.

Now!

Tearing her mouth from mine, she wriggled beneath me, hitching her nightgown up over her hips.

Bare skin touched bare skin.

I shuddered, my balls clenched in eagerness, and the softest of whispers fell onto my ears as I lined up my erection with her entrance. Her voice entered my skull like spun sugar. "I trust you…"

And that was it.

The three little words most men kill to hear. More than '*I love you*' or '*I adore you.*'

I *trust* you.

Because that one untouchable, highly tangible notion was priceless and so often undeserved.

Trust was the epitome of what a woman could give.

Trust was Pim giving me carte blanche to do whatever I wanted because she *trusted* me to keep her safe. I could kiss her, fuck her, do all manner of debasement to her, and she'd let me because she *trusted* me. I could take her swimming at midnight in the big wide ocean with predators beneath the waves, and she would go because she *trusted* me.

She would let me lose myself in her and use her

mercilessly again and again because she trusted that eventually, I could stop. That I wouldn't hurt her. That I wouldn't cross certain boundaries.

I trust you…

Christ.

The furious fire in my blood suddenly clogged my lungs with choking smoke. I coughed with horror, crawling back onto the precipice I'd almost leapt from and collapsed on top of her.

It wasn't enough.

I could still feel every swell of her breasts and every hitch of her breath. I was too close to the warmth and wetness of her pussy.

Grabbing my waistband, I hoisted my pants up as I rolled off her, landing with my arm over my eyes, breathing tormentedly on my back.

She didn't move.

She didn't speak.

The bed rocked as she hesitantly sat up and faced me. "What—what happened?"

You happened.

You and your perfect trust happened.

I couldn't have her here any longer. The need to discipline and my rage were gone.

I'm done.

I sat up in one quick jack knife then leapt off the bed. "Go to your room, Pimlico."

She scooted her legs up, sitting on her knees—so similar to the time when I'd first demanded a night with her and spent most of it prying into her brain. Her hands wedged like a bowling ball against her stomach. "Just like that?"

I looked at the ceiling and not her. "Just like that."

"But why?"

"Because I can't have you near me right now."

Her gaze flew to the wardrobe where I kept my cello. "Are you going to play?"

The thought of frets and bows did nothing to quiet the chaos in my head. Raking fingernails over my scalp, I shook my head. "No."

What would I have to do to tame the rioting need in my blood? How would I exterminate the acidic guilt in my veins?

"You could play me." Her soft voice wavered as if her offer wasn't given entirely willingly. As if her trust made her say it and not her lust. Pain and confusion once again lived in her gaze.

I'd done that.

I'd taken her trust and twisted it into doubt.

I whirled on her, pointing at the door. "Get out."

"But—"

"But nothing. Get out. Now." I couldn't look at her without snapping. I couldn't touch her without breaking. I needed her so goddamn much, but I couldn't have her. She trusted me to keep her safe. This was me honouring that trust even while she begged me to break it.

She was the worst kind of creature.

Never trust me, Pim.

I don't trust me.

My family doesn't trust me.

Never fucking trust me.

Slowly, she climbed off the bed and came toward me.

I turned around, keeping my back to her, doing my best to keep up the barricade and icy request for her to leave.

She sighed softly. "I don't want to go. And I think you don't want me to go, either."

"It doesn't matter what I want."

"It matters, El." Her touch landed on my shoulder blade making me shudder with supernovaing desire. My gut twisted into knots as I shrugged her off. "Everything matters."

The aggression in my spine turned to barbwire as her palm returned, heating my muscles, delivering love even while I was cruel.

Please, Pim…leave.

Pressing her forehead against my back, she murmured, "I want to tell you something." Her voice remained low like a lullaby as if she could somehow convince me to return to bed and prove she was right to give me her trust.

I didn't buy her convincing.

I didn't relax even though it killed me not to turn around and take her in my arms. I wanted to apologise and explain, but I couldn't, because how could I tell her that earning her trust was the one thing I never wanted to hold? That I needed her to treat me with suspicion. I wanted her constantly aware of me, so I never let down my guard.

I could fall in love with her, but I could never trust her because I could never trust myself.

Before I could command again for her to leave, she whispered into my taut rigidity, "I have a theory."

My ears pricked despite myself. "A theory?"

Her lips landed on my spine, twin warm cushions slightly damp and trembling. She spoke into my back. "It's only a theory, and like all theories, it needs to be tested. But...I want to test it."

Kissing her way around my ribcage to the slightly ticklish sides, she moved around to my front where my dragon hissed. I stood frozen to the carpet as her eyes entreated mine. "I need you as much as you need me. I don't want to leave. I want to stay. And I want to kiss you and touch you and lie down with you on top of me. I want to have sex with you. I think you want that too, and my theory is that if you let go—"

Her touch had pulled me under her spell only for it to shatter the second she said '*let go.*'

I rose to my full height, taking a step back and breaking her hold on me. "You expect me to let go?" I chuckled with disbelief. "Just like that. I'll snap my fingers and...*let go.*"

"Yes." She nodded. "Let whatever desires inside your mind loose. Don't try to fight them. Don't try to control them. Just...be with me. Give me everything."

I laughed icily, pinching the bridge of my nose to try to

combat the headache caused by her insanity. "We'd never leave this room again."

Her hands clenched. "I don't believe that."

"You don't believe I wouldn't be able to stop? That I wouldn't ruin you? That I wouldn't take utter advantage of you?" I chuckled again with every self-hatred I felt. "I know what would happen, Pim, and I'm not willing to be your little experiment to prove me right and you wrong."

She pursed her lips, a touch of anger highlighting her cherub cheeks. Her hair glistened from the skylight above, sunlight pooling around her as if she was some guileless goddess trying to tempt me into damnation. "That's what you believe. What about what *I* believe?"

"What *you* believe?"

The only thing I could believe was how senseless this woman was. She needed to leave. Instead, she stood there, daring to debate me on a condition I knew inside out. Trying to school me on my own bloody theories when she had no clue what she was talking about.

My forehead furrowed, deepening my stress headache. "Tell me, seeing as you've known me all of a few months. Tell me how wrong I am and over-dramatizing this condition after living with it for my entire useless life." I waved my hand patronizingly. "Please, go right ahead."

She clutched her fingers together as if gathering fortitude from herself. "You think you'll slip into obsession. You think you'll—"

"Wrong already. I don't think. I *know*. And obsession is too light a word."

"What would you use then?"

I barked a laugh at the ceiling. "I don't know. Life-consuming addiction? Common-sense abdication?"

"Whatever it is—" Pim growled. "You said so yourself that you've found ways to master it. I don't see you obsessively cleaning or folding or tiny tics and twitches you can't stop."

"That's because you don't look hard enough." Even now,

my fingers twitched in a chord from A minor to B flat, splitting my brain into two halves so it couldn't form one concise thought and overpower me. That was a tool I'd always used—even as a kid.

Her lips thinned in frustration as she glanced at my constantly moving fingers. "I look harder than you think." She eyed me up and down almost in pity. Goddamn pity. "I've been watching you, Elder, and I have my own theories about you."

"And so far those theories have been entirely based on fantasy and not fact."

She shook her head sadly. "I don't think they are. And I'm willing to test them. To use myself as the experiment if it means helping you."

"Helping me?" I snarled. "I told you, I don't need helping." The longer this conversation continued, the weaker I became. I was a fraud already—I'd admitted as much. For her to hack at my knees and make me fall even further wasn't just cruel, it was barbaric.

Pointing at the door, I cursed the shake in my arm. "Leave. Now."

"I'll go. This time." Her cheeks heated. "But next time? I'm not letting you say no."

"Next time?" I laughed. "There won't *be* a next time. This was all a mistake caused by you disobeying me."

She headed toward the door, glancing over her shoulder. "And like I said before…if you think I'll obey you on everything…well." She smiled sadly. "I respect you, Elder. I care for you, and I'm willing to trust you to see if we could work together and have another element to this connection between us. But if you think I won't disobey you again? If you think I won't run to your aide when you try to banish me, or that I won't speak my mind when you're being an idiot, then you might as well charge full steam to England and say goodbye because I guarantee this is only the beginning. I've found my voice, and under no circumstances will I shut up just because you don't want to hear the truth."

"Fuck." I stormed toward her. "I don't have the patience to beat sense into—"

She held up her hand, back stepping over the threshold as if I was a raging bull and she was the bright crimson flag I wanted to rip to smithereens. "You don't need patience. Mine has run out anyway, so I'm leaving. But I have a theory. I'll say it as many times as required. This *theory* is based on fact and body language and other tools my mother taught me—not fantasy or whimsy. You might not like it. You can argue against it until you're passed out on the floor. But one day I *will* find out if that theory is correct." Her eyes glittered with tenacity. "I'll put it to the test, and then one of us will owe the other a huge apology."

I crossed my arms to prevent wrapping my fingers around her neck.

Who was this self-assured minx sent to undermine me? How did she make me so hard and achy my bones were brittle and body totally foreign and alive?

I forced out, "We'll see about that."

"Yes, we will." With her chin held high, she gave me a little wave. "Goodnight, Elder. I hope for both our sakes we sleep well tonight."

"I can safely say I won't."

"Me, either."

"Good."

"Fine!"

We stood glowering. More juvenile arguments burned my tongue. I wanted to grab her arm and drag her back into my room. I wanted to snag her hair and kiss her stupid.

But with a condescending sniff, she glanced once more at the pounding erection extremely visible in my track pants, tossed her hair over her shoulder, and padded down the corridor without a backward look.

I slammed the door.

And didn't sleep a fucking wink.

Pimlico

ENGLAND.

The land of my birth.

The land of my parents—one dead, one in jail.

The land of my death and slavery.

Sailing into South Hampton filled me with dread rather than homecoming. Why was I back here when my childhood apartment had been sold, my mother was locked up for twenty-plus years, and I had not one friend to stay with?

Elder joined me on deck as the Phantom slowly traded open seas for the gloomy shore of an industrial city. A light drizzle fell from the grey clouds above; a perfect memory of the mercurial moods of England. I already missed the gentle swell of the ocean and the unhindered sunshine dappling the yacht with sunbeams.

Ever since our argument two days ago, Elder had studiously avoided me. I'd caught him smoking a joint outside his room the night after. We'd shared a very stilted dinner, and I half expected him to find me on a lifeboat and star-gaze once he'd finished smoking and was mellow enough to be near me without wanting to yell at me.

But he hadn't.

I'd star-gazed on my own.

And my anger and hurt grew from an annoying pinprick to a throbbing bruise.

We'd had our first argument, and neither one of us had apologised or moved to end the residual feud.

I wasn't above being the first to admit defeat and withdrawing my threat to test my inconclusive theory. That was—if Elder stopped avoiding me or, when he was in my presence, stopped filling up the awkwardness with mundane comments about seagulls, yacht maintenance, and upcoming shore endeavours.

He'd said he was exhausted living the way he did. Well, I was exhausted begging him to lean on me a little and forgive me for wanting to be beside him when danger called. I wouldn't apologise for disobeying him, and I definitely wouldn't apologise for running to his side.

It should make him feel loved, not smothered.

My blood iced over again with annoyance, coaxing me to give him the cold shoulder, but England spread before us. Conversation would have to be indulged in and token sightseeing endured.

Whatever happened in the future, today had to be the moment where we ripped off the Band-Aids from our mutual wounds and cleared the air.

Something would snap if we didn't.

Something was already fraying.

I couldn't continue to wave the white flag without moving forward because we couldn't continue to coexist this way. The barricades and distance had only worked when I was still healing mentally, physically, and sexually. Elder could endure me on his boat because I hadn't healed enough to tell him who I truly was.

Hell, until recently, I'd *forgotten* who I was. Or perhaps I'd been stolen too young to ever fully develop into who I should've become.

I might never know who Tasmin might've been. Now, I'd been shaped by those experiences that'd fractured the old me.

I'd persevered and matured and found I had a temper to revile his. I had dreams to challenge his. I had needs that ran parallel to his if only he trusted that I could cope with whatever it was he gave me.

Stealing a glance at him, my heart swooned a little as the sea breeze tangled in his blue-ebony hair, and grey drizzle added severity to his already severe face. His nose, his cheeks, his stubble-covered chin—all of it screamed the same message as his eyes: tread in my stead and don't deviate. Do not make my life any harder than it is even if it could be made great if I actually gave in and tried.

Just tried.

If he was so terrified of sleeping with me with no end barrier, then tell Selix to stand by with a tranquilizer gun. Have safeguards in place to experiment with different methods because the one he was currently using. . . .It wasn't working.

For either of us.

I'd healed enough that his distance was no longer welcome, and pity for him, I'd learned how to read him and knew he didn't want to be estranged from me either.

For a girl who'd begged for a life of no physical connection after rape, I'd changed my mind quickly where he was concerned. My adaptability surprised even me. My tenacity to keep forging ahead, leaving the darkness behind where it had no power over my future was my true strength.

I might not have muscles to overpower evil, but I did have a strength of mind that ensured I wasn't beaten. I no longer wanted to be Pimlico, the mouse. The girl who might have teeth but was still happiest not using them.

I wanted more than that.

My teeth had grown to fangs.

And although I was free from my past, I was still trapped. Elder was now my master, and I was still in a cage.

I want out of that cage.

I didn't know how we'd taken on the roles we'd been custom designed for, now that I'd opened my eyes, it was painfully obvious.

I might be in a cage of his doing, but he was in a cage of his own making. A cage he was born into just from the way his brain had formed from the womb. It wasn't his fault, and I had to remind myself not to take his surliness or pig-headedness personally.

My theory that he thought in threes—my concept based on watching his fingers dancing and the common waltz whenever he did something…was dying to be tested.

If he'd just heard me out, I would've given him my hypothesis. I would've listed all the reasons why I thought it would work. I would point out that whatever he was doing was discounted easily the moment he hit that magic number.

Obsession had laws too.

I just needed to learn more about his to convince him.

"Over two years and you're finally home," Elder murmured, his shoulders rounding as he sank deeper into the moleskin jacket he'd thrown on. The tan material turned darker with little circles as the mist steadily turned to rain.

I'd also dressed in a jacket—mine down to my thighs with a large wraparound belt and oversized buckle. Clothing was no longer optional but wanted—especially to ward off the familiar chill in England.

"Yet it doesn't feel as if I've been away a day." I kept staring at the horizon, refusing to look at him. My heart hiccupped at the truth. Everything that'd happened and the reason I'd been away for so long was suddenly nothing more than a single paragraph on a long letter of my life.

Two years was nothing.

It could be scribbled out or erased or torn from the page and burned.

England meant nothing to me because it had taken everything I'd cared about and cast me out. The only thing I wanted here was locked away out of reach.

You couldn't scribble him out, though.

Looking at Elder, I didn't think I could ever erase him or

scratch off the letters he'd written on my heart. No matter how much or how little time we spent together.

He was permanent. Inked. Tattooed.

And if he didn't start trusting me to share his life and *help* him, he would also be thrown overboard.

His lips locked tight as he peered at the harbour and the other vessels moored along the shore. There were no steam-propelled boats or coal-powered cargo ships these days, but the haze of working-class toil painted South Hampton in a dreary light, no matter the new glitz and glamour of restaurants and cafes intermixed with warehouses that'd stood tall for centuries.

A massive clock, housed in its coal-blanketed brick tower, chimed the time at two p.m.

Elder quickly glanced at his watch, a scowl painting his face. "Shit, we're late."

"Late?"

"The Hawks ball is tonight."

My heart raced. "Tonight, tonight?" I looked down at the black pea coat I wore, hiding the simple long-sleeve navy dress beneath. I looked the part of sleek heiress arriving on her floating expensive island, but beneath the rich fabric and heavy wool, I wore no underwear.

I was still a little wild. Still a heathen at heart. Wilder than I should probably be and slowly relearning who I was. I might not be Tasmin and might be growing out of Pimlico, but I still didn't know who I wanted to be.

I had opinions. I wanted to voice them.

I had dreams. I wanted to live them.

I had desires. I wanted to enjoy them.

I had fears. I wanted to slay them.

Was I so different from everybody else, or was I normal? Was I sane in my desire to put my safety on the line to prove a point with Elder? Would any woman in love do the same for a chance to fix the one she wanted? Were there other girls who hated the restriction of elastic and lace? Who never finished university? Who'd been initiated into sex in the worst possible way, only to find that on her own terms, she was a hot-blooded female who needed sex in her life? Who needed to be touched and kissed and to feel a man filling her?

Am I so different?

And if I'm exactly alike what makes me custom designed for Elder?

Why did I think I had the right to fix him? Why did I believe I could test a silly theory? Would another woman do such a thing?

How does anyone find a soul mate if we are all the same?

"What are you thinking about?" Elder turned to face me, his eyebrow raised and lips half tilted. The smile didn't reach his eyes as if he'd placed himself behind prison bars and reached out to me behind them instead of giving me a key to join him.

I shook myself free from such runaway, unanswerable questions. "Nothing."

"It was something."

"Nothing important."

"Your face looked as if you were trying to solve the world's hunger issues."

I shrugged, self-conscious that my mind had twisted into a tangent. "Nothing as important as that."

He paused, his gaze searching mine, doing his best to pry apart my secrets. Slowly, his jaw clenched, and he placed his hand over mine on the balustrade. Licking his bottom lip, he whispered, "Are you happy?"

The question wasn't something I expected. My eyes shot to his, wary, guarded, but beseeching him to let *me* steal *his* secrets. What had made him so uncertain that he had to ask? I was the happiest I'd ever been, and it was all thanks to him. My voice matched his in decibel. "Why do you ask?"

"Because I need to know."

I should've put him out of his misery, but I answered his question with another. "What about what *I* need to know? What of that?"

His teeth ground together, understanding instantly what I

hinted at. "Your theory?"

"Yes."

Removing his hand from mine, he wrapped his fingers tight on the banister as if wishing it was my neck he wrung. He looked back at the port. His tall height gave him the advantage, blocking me from his eyes and deciphering his blustery moods.

He came across so forceful and unmovable—a true disaster in human form waiting to wreak havoc on anything and everyone, but now that I'd started looking... *truly* looking, I saw bone-deep pain beneath that rage. I tasted the soul-crushing hurt beneath his temper. And I felt the burning lust, not for bodily pleasure, but for the beauty of letting go entirely and falling.

Falling in love.

Falling in lust.

I understood more than he knew.

Perhaps that was what made me perfect for Elder where any other woman would pale? I'd been through my own trauma. I'd learned the darkest facets of myself and the lowest of lows. I knew what sort of human I was when faced with the purest of poison, and I knew how much I fought to survive.

Not many people knew the answers to those lessons— through luck of an easy life or lack of broadening horizons— but *I* knew.

I understood who I was in the worst of times.

I only needed to know who I was in the best of them.

Elder was like me. He knew how wrong he could be. How his flaws turned him from perfect to dangerous and just what happened when he let go.

He could never be normal, but unlike me, he didn't catalogue everything he knew of himself as a strength. He looked at them as downfalls. He didn't understand himself; therefore, he could never know how *he* could be in the best of times.

I want to show him.

I wanted a life where I grew into someone well-rounded

and sexual and able to laugh at a stranger and not cower in the shadows. I wanted a dream where I held the hand of a man who others might call broken and kiss him without fear of his mind snapping or our trust breaking.

"I won't push you, Elder. But I will know those answers...soon."

"Not if I leave you here."

My heart coughed. "Do you *want* to leave me here?"

My question was a pit full of sharp spikes ready to impale him. If he answered truthfully, he would be skewered with the knowledge I wouldn't let him keep the walls up between us. And if he lied, he'd be lanced because I already knew he didn't want to leave me.

He knew as well as I did the pain of being apart and the overwhelming feeling of wrongness when we weren't by each other's sides. Anything was better than that. Including being pushed by the one you didn't want to push away.

He swallowed hard, glaring at the grey horizon. "You know I don't want that.'"

The resounding agony in his tone restarted my heart into a rhythm entirely orchestrated by him. He might play the cello, but in that moment, he strummed my soul and sent the chords vibrating through me.

Pressing against him, I placed my hand over his, once again taking the initiative to touch and interact and speak. So long I'd been silent, and now I was a natural at conversing with him.

Him.

This man I wanted to be mine more than anything. "You know I won't stop. If that makes me selfish and cruel...so be it. I'm doing it for other reasons than my own."

His head hung. "I know."

"And you know I'm strong enough."

He squeezed his eyes closed. "That's the part that terrifies me."

"All things worth having are terrifying."

He snorted under his breath, glancing at me with blue-black hair dancing over his forehead. "Then you must be the greatest thing on earth, Pimlico, because you fucking petrify me."

My belly danced, clawing at me to release the fluttering of moths and winged things and take flight. To soar up his tall body and claim his mouth. To whisper against his lips all manner of promises—some I had the strength to keep and others I was still too fragile to grant.

But I couldn't do any of those things as Jolfer stepped into our passion, popping it as surely as a pin would a bubble. "Sir, we'll be docked in fifteen minutes. The car is serviced and ready to go. Selix already has your itinerary, and the appointments you asked the staff to make are all arranged."

Elder jerked back, returning me from the midnight depths of his eyes to the dreary English drizzle. "Thank you, Jolfer."

Jolfer, with his kind, weathered face, nodded politely, tapped his temple at me in respect, and then carried about his duties to bring the Phantom home for her well-earned rest.

Unable to return to the deeply raw place we'd been before, I asked, "Appointments?"

Elder rolled his neck as if doing his best to shed what'd happened and realign himself in the now. "Dress fitting for you. Tux fitting for me. Then hair and makeup before the masquerade at Hawksridge."

"Why does it have to be a masque?"

I hated not being able to see people's faces...to see their plotting.

"I'm of the same opinion. If it wasn't for work, I'd cancel."

Far off memories of paper mache masks and faceless men bidding on me at auction trickled like tar. I clamped down on such things. Tonight would be different. Tonight, I would be with Elder and safe.

Forcing myself into brightness, I nudged his shoulder with mine. "I'm getting a new dress?" I smiled as if I was superficial enough to only care about a wardrobe.

He didn't buy it. "Next time you feign excitement, try to do it over something I know you don't hate."

I laughed softly. "I didn't hate it when you made me wear that lingerie." I blushed and flushed and glanced at the polished deck beneath our feet. "The way you looked at me…it made the claustrophobia worth it."

Elder sucked in a breath, tattered and heavy and so full of regret—it pierced my heart like countless arrows, their feathered shafts quivering painfully.

"I…" He squeezed the back of his neck as his shoulders slouched. "Goddammit, Pim."

For some reason, tears prickled my eyes. It wasn't tears of sadness but more of frustration. I had the power to relieve him of his stress, if only he trusted me as I trusted him.

Instinct told me to pull away, but I fought it and swayed into him instead.

He froze as I wrapped my arms around him, wriggling between him and the banister to lay my head against his chest. I stiffened as his heartbeat filled my ears. It wasn't the steady thunder I expected but a lightning storm. Fast and fleeting as if being touched by me made his heart work triple time to keep him standing.

He rested his chin on my hair as his arms hesitatingly came around me.

We stood there like that for I didn't know how long. Breathing each other in. Listening to the havoc we played on each other's bodies. Unable to say what we truly wanted but knowing anyway.

Finally, he kissed my hair, murmuring, "There is one appointment that isn't so superficial. It doesn't include clothes or makeup or glitzy ridiculous balls. Will you go with me?"

"I'd go anywhere with you."

"In that case…let's go."

* * * * *

I stood outside a nondescript entrance overshadowed by

turrets and towers. Barbwire and soaring chain-link glittered in the clearing rain, surrounded by brick walls and whitewashed window frames.

It could've been any number of corporate buildings: a hospital, a no-frills university—somewhere where wire and spikes were required to keep its inhabitants safe, not for locking them in.

I preferred to think of it that way: a school. A school where my mother taught and studied her favourite criminal patients, diving into the minds of psychopaths before walking from such a depressing place and going home to a warm apartment filled with comfy familiarity.

But it wasn't a school, and this wasn't a fantasy.

I'd never understood my mother's love of delving deep into what made a criminal tick, and now...*she is one*.

I baulked as Selix slammed the car door behind me and Elder held out his arm. I didn't know the name of the prison or even what suburb we'd driven to.

All Elder had told me was it was important and to trust him.

Most of the drive through congested English motorways and then quaint village roads, I'd pondered on the hypocrisy of such a request.

When I'd given him my trust the night the coastguard came, he'd shut down on me and refused to sleep with me. He acted as if giving him my trust was an abomination.

Yet here he was asking for the very same gift he'd thrown in my face.

"Pim?" His gentle voice interrupted my thoughts.

I blinked, bringing him into focus, standing with his arm empty and requesting my hand, his gaze imploring me to *trust*.

I shivered as an icy gale whipped around the harsh corners of the jail. My mother was in there. She was in there because of something she'd done for me. I was so close to seeing her, yet the vinegary guilt made me step back. "I...why did you bring me here?"

He didn't need to tell me who we were here to see or how he'd arranged this. I'd known the moment I'd set eyes on this place. This place housing my murderess mother.

I didn't need to know *how*. I needed to know *why*.

Why?

Especially as he'd read my notes to No One. He saw how much I blamed her for what'd happened to me. He would've witnessed the misplaced hate I'd carried for her in the way my pencil scribbled harder whenever I wrote her name.

I'd thrown around the fantasy of visiting her but in reality...I wasn't ready.

I doubted I would ever be ready.

"Because she asked to see you," Elder murmured. "And more importantly, you need to see her."

"She asked about me?" I shook my head, my hair coiling around my cheeks as if protecting me from the breach of his tampering in my life. "When? How?"

He winced, dropping his arm uncomfortably. "I called her. I left a message telling her who I was and that you were safe. I didn't think she'd call me back."

"But she did?"

"She did."

"And?" I snapped. "What did you tell her?"

*Oh, God...*imagine if he told her everything? How he'd found me at Alrik's days away from committing suicide. How my tongue was half severed. How my panic attacks made me so weak.

She was in prison. She didn't need such terrible thoughts when she already lived in a terrible place.

Elder stepped slowly toward me, remorse painting his handsome face. "I'm sorry I didn't tell you. I know now how that must feel." He shook his head with a harsh cough. "If anyone spoke to my mother on my behalf...I'd be fucking livid." Rage burned in his gaze, directed at himself. "I'm truly sorry, Pimlico, but you have my word, not once did I tell her how we met, where you came from, or what we've done since finding each other."

His hand crept out, touching mine with a barely there coax. "She doesn't know anything more than you're alive. The rest is up to you to tell her...if and when you're ready."

I snatched my fingers back from his. "But the things I thought about her...the hate I held while those things were done to—"

Elder lurched forward, stealing my hand and squeezing it hard. "Stop. You didn't know. You were alone. You were abandoned to that bastard's whims. You didn't know you were loved and searched for. Just like she didn't know how much she loved you until you were gone. She didn't show it, and it made you doubt." He cupped my cheek, beseeching me to understand. His face harsh and wind-bitten but still just as lovely. "You didn't do anything wrong."

I swallowed the ball in my throat. "I did. I blamed her...for all of it."

I still do even when I shouldn't.

"Blame is good. You needed someone to blame."

"I blamed him, too."

"He deserved it. He deserves to rot on his kitchen floor for eternity."

"But how can I look at her knowing what she did for me, all while I harboured suspicions that she might've been the one to set it up? That I concocted ideas that I was merely an experiment for her to see how her child would react with the same monsters she studied?"

Elder gathered me close, tucking me against his warm moleskin jacket. "Fuck, Pim."

I trembled, spilling my darkest confessions—even the ones I daren't write in my notes to No One. "I hated her for not hugging me like other mothers. I despised her for making it feel wrong that I wanted to be a little girl playing with dolls. I told myself I was lucky to be treated as an equal and an adult even when I was young enough to be afraid of the dark. Instead of rocking me back to sleep, she'd give me textbooks to read about the psychology of why children fixate on things that can't hurt them. That phobias for irrational things can be over-come if one just grows up and faces what they're truly afraid of."

Elder's jacket was warm and heady like the incense flavour he carried on his skin. Its rich scent siphoned up my nose, doing its best to soothe me when I didn't deserve to be soothed.

My voice turned small. "All I wanted was some small sign she loved me, and a lot of those childish insecurities would've gone away."

"We all love in our own ways, Pim." His voice was deep and rich, entirely mollifying while, at the same time, not doing anything to mollify my nerves. "You need to forgive yourself for thinking such things, just like you need to forgive her for making you feel that way."

Pushing me out of his embrace, he nudged my chin with his knuckles. "I'll come with you. If you want me."

My eyes trailed to the squat, bristling-in-barbwire building behind him. How was I supposed to go in there? How was I supposed to speak to her after so much had happened to both of us?

"Pim..."

Forcing myself to look at him, I waited for whatever he wanted to say.

His eyes tightened, the stress lines around his mouth deepening. "When she called me back, and I told her about you..." He trailed off, tucking wind-whipped hair behind my ear and smiling with love born from being denied his own mother's affection. "She broke. I've never heard someone's voice turn from guarded to distraught so quickly. All she wanted to know was if you were okay. She didn't ask anything else. Just *were you okay*. And then she begged me to bring you to her. I couldn't refuse."

I wanted so much to believe this would be easy. That she would forgive me and I'd forgive her, and we'd somehow fall into a relationship we'd never had, but all I could visualize was her lack of cuddles and abundance of coldness, and once again, I was flooded with fear that I was broken. That I was only capable of hating her when all I'd ever wanted was to love and be loved by her.

I'm a horrible, horrible person.

Even now, even knowing what she'd done, I still couldn't let go of the pain of my childhood.

Something nasty entered my brain. Something totally out of character but I had to spit it out to prevent it from corroding me. "You couldn't refuse. But I can. I don't have to go in there if I don't want to. I don't have to do anything I don't want to again."

"That's true. You've been made to do enough bad things." His commiseration turned to scolding. "But could you be that person? After everything you know? Now you know the truth about how she searched and killed for you?" He shook his head proudly and sadly. "I still have so much to learn about you, Pimlico, but I already know you aren't capable of doing that. You're too pure."

I shot him a sharp look.

In one moment, he made me sound like an angel and the next, an ungrateful brat—something my mother had called me many times in my past. If anything, that reminder helped me stand taller; to shoulder my responsibility while figuring out hers.

If I didn't visit, I would be proving her right by calling me an ungrateful brat. If I didn't see her, I would forever hate myself for being so weak and heartless.

I was eternally grateful to her even though we'd never been mother and daughter. Her love had come from a complicated place and landed her in hell.

Even though it tangled me up inside, Elder was right.

I couldn't refuse because I wasn't that person.

I wasn't selfish.

I wasn't cruel.

I'm better than this.

My mother was my mother.
I was her daughter.
For better or for worse.
I was a Blythe.

ELDER

IF SOMEONE HAD asked me what my ultimate dream was, I would've said a reunion.

A forgiveness.

A ceremony turning me from No One into someone again and being welcomed back into my family.

I knew that would never happen for me, but to be lucky enough to witness such a reunion and not have it be my own was bittersweet. But then again, it was somehow even better as it was for someone I loved more than myself.

It was someone who deserved it more than I did.

And someone I would stand beside for as long as she wanted me.

For the past twenty minutes, I'd remained steadfast by Pim, helping fill in the visitor forms, answering guards when she turned mute, and touching the small of her back as we were guided from entrance to belly of such a dismal place.

I'd meant what I said outside. I was eternally sorry that I'd gone behind her back and spoken to Sonja Blythe.

At the time, I thought I was doing something courageous and romantic. Tampering with her future, I set in motion a reunion I wanted more than anything but overstepped boundaries.

I hadn't asked what Pim wanted...

I hadn't thought to include her in my sweeping gesture of meddling in her relationships.

Perhaps too much water and time had passed under that bridge to rebuild it.

I hadn't stopped to ask.

Just like I hadn't stopped to think about her when I'd made other phones calls while at sea. In some way or another, each of my conversations would affect her—just in different ways.

The first had been to her mother.

The second was to Jethro Hawk—our host at tonight's masquerade. It was a well-known fact he dealt in diamonds—exquisite gemstones that sometimes had a cheap buy price while others were so rare they were utterly priceless.

I wanted to give Pim something better than origami dollar animals. I wanted to show her the depth of my affection. I'd emailed Hawk the design I'd sketched and hoped to God he had time to create it.

The third was to my uncle Raymond. As usual, he filtered his phone calls through his answering machine, so I was forced to leave a terse message, warning him and my family that the security guards surrounding them were for their protection. That the cousins murdered by the Chinmoku last week were only the beginning and not to be stupid by listening to my mother's hatred for me. He needed to stay alert even though I'd increased security. He had to guard the children even though I'd added around-the-clock care for the smaller members as they tottered off to school.

I did my best for everyone, and it still wasn't enough.

Even now, as I sat beside Pim in a private room waiting for her mother, I wished I could've done more.

The exclusive use of this space had only been granted after hours of arguing on the phone with the warden and providing a hefty donation to the educational program to ensure Pim and her mother's first encounter in years would be behind closed doors and not with bars barricading them or other inmates around to hear.

Once again, I rubbed my neck from the prickles of tension and awareness running over my flesh. I'd offered to stand outside. I'd wanted to give Pim privacy. But as we'd traipsed through the drab, depressing prison, cutting through locked gates and being buzzed into sections of the establishment by our escort, Pim had taken my hand even while standing rigid and regal.

She had her own power, yet she wasn't too proud to borrow a piece of mine.

That made me tumble even harder. To know she had the strength to do this after so many terrible things had been done to her. My feelings toward her weren't of obligation and a desire to protect her because I found her weak.

Shit, no.

My feelings were enamoured because she used her healing as a ladder.

One rung at a time.

Each one climbing higher and higher from her past and hardship, slowly growing bolder and more beautiful each height she scaled.

I knew without a shadow of fucking doubt she would've achieved this without me. She would've found a way to kill Alrik. She would've found a way to come home. And she would've found a way to continue living.

She wasn't alive because of me.

I was living because of *her.*

If there was any debt where we were concerned, it was me to her. Not the other way around.

We'd sat at this table in deathly silence for five minutes before the door opened and in walked a stiff guard followed by an older, sadder, crueller version of Pimlico.

Pim froze.

My eyes narrowed, drinking in the mother of the woman I loved more than myself.

Sonja Blythe wasn't like the photos I'd studied online. She

no longer had access to makeup and hairdressers. She neither wore business suits nor had airs and graces. The almost snobbish look she'd perfected—the smugness of knowing what others were thinking and that no secret was safe around her—was buried beneath a harsh dare to provoke her.

I'd never admit it, but Pim looked a lot like her—not in appearances so much—but in the way they took on the world and won.

Even though Sonja Blythe no longer wore suits or makeup, I preferred this version—the skinnier, harder version—because it was honest. Her arms were ripped from whatever pastimes she kept herself busy with. Her body thin beneath grey overalls but not sickly.

If she picked a fight, I'd put my money on her to win.

Her hazel green eyes, so like the daughter I was in love with, locked onto me in recognition of our phone call then immediately discounted me for Pim.

Pim didn't move an inch, her fingers turning white on the table.

The officer tapped his prisoner on the shoulder, breaking the connection for a second while he removed the handcuffs. When Sonja Blythe was untethered, he said, "Fifteen minutes. Everything you say and do will be recorded for future use."

Part of the prison's policy was an officer remained in the room for the safety of the visitor. After I'd lost my temper and pointed out the visitor would be the daughter the inmate killed for and paid an extra bonus to yet another in-house inmate program, I'd managed to secure utter privacy—minus the eavesdropping video and audio recorder.

The officer glanced at me then Pim and finally nodded reluctantly and stepped from the room. The clang of the closing door reverberated around us.

A few endless seconds ticked by as Sonja Blythe moved toward us and sat on the opposite side of the table.

There were no explosive hugs.

No watery tears.

Nothing to signal these two women had any foundation of physical affection.

The only sign of history was a gloss in Pim's gaze and a tremble in her hands.

Sonja Blythe absentmindedly rubbed her wrists where the cuffs had been, never taking her eyes off her daughter.

Pim vibrated beside me, but it wasn't from fear or sadness. I couldn't put my finger on it. Rage perhaps? Forgiveness?

I had no idea what I was doing here or how to shatter the sudden unbearable tension in the room.

Her mother half-smiled as if—just like me—she didn't know the correct etiquette on how to begin.

Finally, she whispered, "Tasmin, Min, Minnie Mouse." Tears welled in her eyes only to retreat as she cleared her throat. "My how I've missed you."

Pim's breath hitched then she nodded frantically as if she lost control of her ability to respond in half-measures. She stopped herself just as quick, clearing her throat just like her mother. "I-I heard what you did." Her voice was stilted and impersonal as if she struggled to return to an era of child after hating her mother for so long. "I owe you the greatest apology."

Neither woman looked at me.

As it should be.

I was here for Pim, but in terms of input, I wanted to remain invisible.

Crossing my arms, I leaned back in the chair, further extracting myself from the conversation. I had no fucking clue how this would go. I would be there if Pim needed me but I wouldn't dishonour her by stepping in before she asked.

"You owe me nothing." Her mother curled her upper lip with disdain. "It was me. *All* me."

Pim stiffened, toxic questions spilling from her lips. "You mean...you *did* have something to do with my abduction?"

Sonja Blythe's eyes widened in horror. "No! *What?* No, not at all. I only meant I wasn't a mother to you." Her voice lowered. "Min, you have no idea how often I wish I could go back and do it all over again. Be a better mother. When I thought you were gone…well, I wanted to kill everyone I'd ever put before you. Every appointment I took when I should've taken you to school. Every session I booked when I should've taken you to dance practice."

Her shoulders caved as her face turned haggard with confession. "I was a teacher, coach, and headmistress when I should've just been your mum. I dragged you out to functions and forced you to act as my eyes and ears and tell me what you saw. You didn't want to be there—not for the long hours I commanded. I knew that. I knew keeping you out late ruined your concentration at school the next day. I knew teaching you how to see things people wanted to keep hidden would make you an outcast at school, yet I did it anyway."

Pim's posture softened a little, still unable to accept. "So you killed to make up for your mistakes? You did it to ease your conscience?"

Her mother's eyes glassed again. "You know…I've asked myself that same question. I really studied myself. I searched and searched to see if I was as heartless as I felt. But I can safely say, on my life and yours, I killed because that bastard stole you. I killed because no one else had a right to you but me. I killed because you were all I had left of your father, and I screwed up. I killed because he hurt my baby almost as much as I'd hurt her and stolen any chance for me to make it right."

Silence fell like rain, sizzling on the table-top while wounds were licked and truths were accepted.

"You didn't screw up," Pim finally muttered. "We were just different people."

"Other daughters are different from their mothers, and they didn't get sold or hurt." Sonja swiped at her eyes, smearing tears over thin cheeks. "Other mothers are different, but at least they put their child's well-being first."

Pim smiled sadly. "You did, though. You never stopped hunting for me. You *killed* for me."

"I would've burned the entire world to the ground for you." She growled, sounding every bit a feral inmate.

I could understand why Pim struggled to see the caring parent in her mother. She spoke of avenging her daughter's disappearance but with a righteousness born from an egotistical pompousness of getting her own back. She killed for her daughter—no denying that sacrifice—but she did it for her own satisfaction, too.

She did it to shout that no one could take what was hers and not suffer the consequences.

She was ruthless.

She was coldblooded as well as hot.

But there was also no denying she loved Pimlico with everything born of tragedy and regret, and now it shone brighter than the other parts of her.

She'd redeemed herself. And now it was up to Pim to recognise and judge if it was enough.

Pim leaned back a little, studying her mother. I had the strangest sensation that our thoughts were in sync—that she'd come to the same conclusion I had and mulled over such things.

Slowly, she leaned forward and placed her hands on the table, waiting for her mother to link fingers. The moment they touched, Pim spilled, "I'm going to tell you the truth because you deserve that. I'm going to be honest because that's what you always demanded from me. And I'm going to be indifferent because that's what you said a good psychologist must be to truly see the truth."

My heart stopped beating, my eyes snapping onto her.

Was I prepared to be privy to this? What if Pim had forgotten that I might not be contributing but I still had ears—still heard things she might not want me to know?

But before I could stand and excuse myself, she sucked in a breath, looked at the ceiling for fortification, and visibly shuddered. When she spoke again, her voice was cool but passionate, lecturing but fragile. "He killed me only metres away from you, mother. He asked me to dance, and I went with him. Do you know why? Because you were the one to tell me not to judge others on appearances. That first impressions were often wrong and to grant him a piece of myself even though my instincts were screaming at me to run. He took me outside. He stole my Minnie Mouse watch. He wrapped his hands around my throat."

My legs bunched with fury.

I wanted to fucking *gut* him.

Pim continued in her colourless narration. "I don't know why he did what he did, and I won't guess. Was it purely for money? Was it because of your need to crack open the minds of murderers and rapists? Was it because I liked to dawdle on the way to school and attracted the attention of someone I shouldn't? We'll never know, and no one is to blame.

"When he revived me—brought me back from the dead with his lips on mine and his rancid breath in my lungs and told me of my fate—I *hated* you. When he dangled Daddy's watch and told me he'd keep it for safe keeping, I cursed you. When I was imprisoned in a hotel waiting to be sold, I screamed for you. And when I was auctioned off like a piece of meat and that bastard Alrik flew me to his home and stole my virginity, I cried for you. I cried for me. I cried for everything that'd been stolen because I knew no matter what happened from that point on, we could never be the same."

Tears spilled down Pim's face, but she didn't cry. It was as if her soul purged everything in that moment but didn't affect her outwardly. She was stronger than I'd ever seen and more broken than I could stand.

My heart thundered to see her torn between so many different things.

I wanted to slay every memory and erase every pain.

I struggled to stay in my chair and not scoop her into my arms and kiss her, make love to her, do whatever it took to take her thoughts somewhere else.

Anywhere but here.

This wasn't what I had in mind when I arranged for her to see her mother.

I hadn't meant her to slice deep and carve out the blackness still suffocating inside.

Fuck!

Pim bowed her head for a long moment, her breathing harsh and tortured; when she looked back to her mother, she whispered, "For two very long years, I will admit I cast a lot of my hurt and pain onto you. I wrote letters. So many letters. I purged my thoughts and fears—just like you taught me in one of our many lessons about being the master over our emotions. I made the choice that no matter how much he hurt me, I would never speak a word to him. I lived in silence, Mother. I endured every one of his beatings and rapes. I let him break me, brutalise me, all the while screaming at me to speak to him. And not once did I do what he asked."

Her jaw clenched as her chin came up. "Do you know why?" She flicked a glance at me, flinching as if only now remembering I was here.

Her voice wavered a little, but she repeated her question to her mother. "Do you know why I stayed silent? Why I refused to give him my voice? Why I locked that part of myself away and preferred to die than speak to that *fucking bastard*?" She snarled the last words with more vehemence than I thought capable.

All this time, Pim came across as stoic, making me believe that with him being dead she'd found a degree of closure.

Yet with those two words, I knew how wrong I'd been. How much she still had to work through. How the stages of grief were tracking through her without my input. Anger was this stage. Despair, disbelief, denial.

What would be next, and how could I help her through it without her being in this much agony?

Her mother shook her head, her own tears spilling faster as her teeth lodged deep in her bottom lip. She barely managed to say, "Oh, Minnie Mouse..." She clutched Pim's fingers, dragging her closer to kiss her knuckles, begging for forgiveness. "No wonder you hate me."

I didn't understand.

What did her mother understand that I didn't?

What family connection just flew over my head?

She wasn't just referring to Pim's accusation of her upbringing. It was something worse than that.

Pim sighed heavily, squeezing her mother's hands, relieved that she understood even if I didn't. "I remained your daughter even though I cursed you. I chose death over speech because, thanks to you, I knew what he ultimately wanted from me."

Sonja wailed. "I know. I know. I'm so, so sorry, Min. Please...I'm so sorry."

"It wasn't my body, my pain, my pleas he wanted...was it, Mum?" Pim choked, her own sadness switching to sobs.

The fact she'd flipped from mother to mum released the last of the barriers, and her mother collapsed over Pim's hands, falling to the floor on her knees. Her chair toppled backward as Pim remained sitting like a queen with a tormented smile on her face.

She didn't wait for her mother to answer her, delivering her question as vicious as a blade, stabbing me right through the heart. "It was my mind. He wanted my mind. He wanted to know how it felt to be raped by him. He wanted me to tell him how his fists bruised, how his chains bit, how every little thing he did changed me from my past to his future. He wanted to take my thoughts and hoard them, chipping them away, slowly stomping them to dust. He wanted to take my memories and taint them with his possession, so I had nothing left. He wanted every single scrap that made me mine and ruin me until I became nothing but his.

"And thanks to you, Mum, I understood that even when I didn't. I stayed silent to spite him. I remained mute to protect the pieces of me I thought were long-lost dead and gone. But now I understand I was doing it for another reason. A reason that perhaps trumped all of that." Her voice strangled, hanging itself from her lips. "I was still obeying you...even then."

Her mother cried harder.

Another wracking sob clawed through Pim's throat. "Are you proud of me? Did I do the right thing? If I was on your couch right now, would you wrinkle your nose like you did at the weaker or would you stare with pride at the stronger? Am I strong in your eyes? Did I do well? *What*, Mother? Tell me so I know if I've finally earned your admiration."

My heart motherfucking broke.

That was what Pim carried?

That was what chewed her inside?

The need for her mother's approval? A mother who had twisted her up long before she'd ever been stolen?

The fact she'd survived more abuse than anyone and instead of needing to be hospitalized for a broken mind sat there demanding parental admiration *undid* me.

Who the fuck cared if her mother approved?

I'd never been so goddamn proud. So humbled. So traumatized by another's cravings.

Fuck me.

I couldn't...*I can't*...

Fuck, fuck, fuck.

My mind exploded with noise and shame and humiliation and utter self-disgust.

Her mother dropped her head in her hands and cried deep, ugly tears that dripped onto the floor.

My own eyes pricked to think how similar I must've seemed to Pim. How my commandments to know her mind must've petrified her. How my demands she speak and give me everything must've overridden so many terrible memories of Alrik demanding the same fucking thing.

I'd done exactly what that rapist had done.

I'd saved her and delivered her to yet another battle of wills.

I might not have physically hurt her, but I was just as bad. Just as cruel.

Just as fucking evil.

Christ!

I wanted to punch something.

I wanted to throw my chair across the room and tear myself apart.

I wanted to get on my knees and put a gun to my head for ever thinking I had a right to Pim's innermost thoughts.

Who the fuck was I to demand her secrets for safe passage on my yacht?

Who the fuck was I to expect her innermost thoughts in return for taking her from that disgusting white torture chamber?

I was nothing.

I was no one.

I'd already earned everything she'd kept from others by reading her letters like the thief I was.

Once a thief, always a thief.

And Pim had stolen my humanity.

I struggled to breathe, spiralling in on myself, drowning in regret as Pim's mother said through her sobs, "I couldn't be more proud of you, Tasmin. Never. Not a day went by that I didn't beg for your forgiveness for how I treated you. Not an hour ticked past when I wished I could rewind and hug you instead of berate you. Kiss you instead of scold you. And show you just how much I cared."

She scrambled on her knees to her daughter's side, clutching Pim's hands. "I loved you so much it scared me. Me—the woman who spent her entire career manipulating humans as if they were bugs under a microscope—was petrified of you. I thought love was weak. I believed if I let myself show how much you meant to me, I would be just like the people who came to me broken and begging for answers." She shook her head, tangled hair flying. "I was wrong. And I found that out far too late."

Her face turned black with memories. "I need you to know I hunted the same people I tried to help. I tortured people to find you, Minnie Mouse. I wanted so much to kill Kewet the moment I found him, but I held back just in case he knew more than what he said. I ransacked his apartment. I found the Disney watch Daddy gave you. I still have it— wishing I could give it back to you—even knowing how many times I badgered you to stop wearing such a juvenile thing. So many things I did, but when that killer tried to run, and I visualized you dead or worse, I snapped."

Her tears slowly stopped as her breathing evened out. "I will never apologise for what I did to him. For taking his life. I'd do it all over again. I would do it for you. I don't care if it means I'll rot in here. I have no remorse. I feel no regret." She squeezed Pim's fingers. "I would kill an army if it meant you were never taken and never had to live the life you did."

She brought Pim's fingers to her mouth. "I'm so damn proud of you. So heartbroken that I made it harder on you. I hope one day you can forgive me. I hope one day your father can forgive me. If you never come visit me again, this is enough. I will happily serve my time knowing in some small way, I showed you how much I care. How deeply sorry I am. For everything."

Pim sniffed, her own tears evaporating into salty tracks, leaving her skin white and limbs shaky. "I do forgive you, Mum." Her voice was achingly soft. "But after everything...do you forgive me?"

Her mother sucked in a wet sob. "Oh, Min, do you even need to ask?"

Pim collapsed, bending in her chair to fall into her mother's embrace. The two women clutched each other, and fuck, I couldn't stay here anymore.

I shouldn't have witnessed any of this.

I wasn't worthy after everything I'd demanded of Pim.

I would never be worthy or have enough breath in my body to apologise for being the same as the monsters she'd endured.

Her mother should kill me too for how cruel I'd been.

How callous and motherfucking selfish.

I wanted everything about her but not at the expense of her happiness.

Not anymore.

My eyes fell on Pim's form still wrapped in her mother's arms.

I can't do this anymore.

My legs bunched, hurling me upright from my chair.

I had to run.

Before I exploded.

The ticking in my brain was obsessing.

I was regressing.

I would snap soon and take my misery out on the woman I loved.

My legs forgot how to work as I moved on painful instruction to *run*. As I stepped toward the two on the floor, my eyes locking on the door and escape, Pim's fingers lashed around my wrist, injecting me with yet more self-loathing.

"Elder?" The way she looked up, glossy-eyed and trusting, hair spilling over her shoulders, and such fucking love glowing, I couldn't do it.

My voice cracked as I jerked my arm away. "I'm so fucking sorry, Pimlico."

Her mother jolted at the name. The name I knew I shouldn't keep calling her. It was a name linked to slavery and pain, but to me, she wasn't Tasmin.

She was Pim.

She was Mouse.

Once again, hindsight sucker-punched me in the chest.

No wonder she flinched whenever I called her Mouse. No wonder she grew pissy and pained when I demanded she tell me why that nickname affected her so much.

A watch.

A watch from her childhood stolen the night she was murdered.

Goddammit, I'd been such a heartless *fool*.

With a shaking hand, I bent and cupped her cheek. With tortured lips, I kissed her forehead wishing against hope she could feel my agony through my touch. That she could understand how I wished I could undo who I was, who I'd been to her, and every single way I'd treated her.

How I begged for self-discipline that I'd never touched her. How I wished I could undo the fact I'd manipulated her into talking to me and giving me things she'd wanted to keep private.

Her embrace by the submarine.

Her confession of liking clouds over stars and rain over sun.

How she hated toast—

They were things I hadn't earned. Things I'd stolen.

I had to get out of there.

Immediately.

I never spoke in my mixed heritage. I chose English over Japanese as a way to honour my father rather than my mother. But in that moment, English seemed woefully unable to convey just how damn sorry I was.

It wasn't enough.

The English language only had one way of apology.

Japanese had over twenty.

I'd use all of them if it meant the heaviness in my chest would ease.

I would murmur them forever if I could somehow find redemption.

But for now, all I could offer was one.

Kissing her again, I breathed into her hair, *'Owabi shimasu.'*

The translation: please accept this apology from the bottom of my heart.

"El..." Pim reached for my neck, but I swooped back, bowed low and sweeping to the woman I loved more than anything, then stalked from the room.

I didn't look back.

Pimlico

WHO KNEW FIFTEEN minutes had the power to completely change a person, a life, a relationship?

Stepping into that room, I knew it would be hard and emotional, but I had no *idea* I'd run the gauntlet, dredge up every agony, and swim through so many historical and present wounds.

I'd done that.

No one had forced me.

But as I touched my mother after a lifetime of shoulder pats and cool nods instead of hugs and kisses, everything I'd been harbouring, everything I didn't even know fermented deep inside me, gushed forth in noxious honesty.

I didn't do it to hurt her.

I didn't say such things to be spiteful or cruel.

In fact, I'd made a promise not to mention a thing about it.

I just...couldn't stop.

My childhood desires rose from nowhere, impulses took over, and I spilled things I never dreamed of spilling, *especially* to a mother who'd killed for me in front of a man who'd killed for me, too.

Two people who'd willingly stolen a life so I might live.

Two people who had a stain upon their souls for eternity.

I owed them more than I could ever repay.

I should protect them from unneeded memories and be ever so grateful.

They didn't deserve to hear what I'd endured before their sacrifice made my existence better.

That was my cross to bear—they had far too many others and all because of me.

I *knew* all that.

I hated myself that it hadn't stopped me.

And bringing forth such evil, spreading its darkness to the people I loved the most, hadn't made any of it easier.

It didn't make me better. It didn't cure me. Purging myself in such a way didn't release the filth still wriggling deep inside me like a snake I couldn't catch.

It only made me sad and mad and tired.

So, *so* tired.

And when Elder murmured Japanese into my hair then bowed as if he was a knight laying his sword at my feet, my heart had fallen upon his blade in terror.

I didn't understand what he said, but by the anguish on his face, it wasn't good.

I'd tried to grab him...to ask him to explain...to introduce him to my mother now that dirty laundry had been aired, washed, and hopefully clean enough to fold away, but he'd kissed me and bolted from the room as if he would die if he stayed another moment.

If my heart had impaled itself on the hypothetical sword he'd laid at my feet, then it well and truly ran itself through in misery as the door closed on him, shutting us apart.

My insides curled up as horror splashed through me like sour wine.

What have I done?

How had I forgotten that he was listening too? That everything I'd tried to hide from him just vomited into reality and tarnished everyone in the room.

I wanted to chase after him.

I wanted to console him.

I wanted to erase that crucifixion in his beautiful black eyes.

Unthinkingly, I untangled myself from my mother's embrace and climbed unsteadily to my feet.

I took a stumbling step toward the door, my mind consumed with fixing what I'd just broken, but then I looked back at my mother. At the way she drank me in. At the way she kneeled on the prison floor with such love and admiration and awe—three things I'd longed to see on her face since I was born—and no matter what I'd just ruined with Elder, I couldn't ruin this.

Not now.

Not when it was so brand new.

I slowly sat back down again, nodding at my mother to join me on chairs instead of dirty linoleum.

She stood with a wince and sat, planting her hands in the middle of the table, her fingers waggling for mine.

Once again, I glanced at the door.

Elder...

Is he okay?

What *happened?*

My loyalties were divided. Indecision kept me stationary.

"You can go after him." My mother's voice wrenched my head up. "I understand."

I had her approval.

My weight shifted from my butt to my toes, ready to launch me from my chair, but once again, I glanced at her face—to the regret and sadness and strange, messy pride—and settled back into position.

I had to accept that Elder was hurting but so was my mother.

So am I.

I couldn't split into two and soothe both. I had to remain here, for now, and give my entire attention to her. I had to do that so I could at least bandage up some of my own pain by curing some of hers.

Then, once I wasn't such a wreck, I could find Elder and do the same.

Knowing I had to cure others before patching myself up added another gruelling tax.

I'm exhausted.

Wrung out, mind blank, heart bruised.

But this was *my* fault.

No one wanted that trip down terrible memory lane.

I had to be the one to fix it.

Taking my mother's hands, I sighed heavily. "I'm sorry. I didn't mean to hurt you by telling you such things."

A soft squeeze followed by a motherly scoff. "Min, you could cut out my heart right now, and you couldn't hurt me any more than I did when I realised I failed to love you."

We shared a tangled smile, letting silence fill the holes inside us.

Finally, she grinned, somehow switching such awful topics and choosing a much easier one. "He seems nice. Strange...but honourable."

My bones ached as I looked at the door. "He saved me."

"Is he good to you?"

Speech became thick with tears, so I nodded.

"In that case, he's got my undying welcome to the family and thanks."

I nodded again, biting my lip to staunch yet more liquid. There was so much to say, so many better things to discuss. Things like Morocco and Monte Carlo and the Phantom and swimming with dolphins. So many magical moments all granted by the man who'd bought me a genie bottle from a dusty, toothless vendor so many weeks ago.

He was my true genie.

Better than any guardian angel or lover combined.

I'm so lucky.

And I hurt him so terribly.

A knock sounded on the door, cracking wide to reveal, not Elder as my heart had hoped, but the guard who'd presided over this meeting. "Fifteen minutes is up. Time to say goodbye."

So soon?

So fast?

Who knew fifteen minutes not only had the power to change a person, a life, a relationship, but also ticked faster than any other time on a clock?

My mother squeezed my hands again. "I can't tell you how much this means to me to see you. To see you healthy and alive and with a man you obviously care deeply for." She sighed. "I wanted so much for you, Tasmin. University, a career, a calling...but I'm wiser now than I was then. Looking back on my life, only two things stand out to have any real importance."

"What two things?" I didn't really want to ask. I feared she'd say her clients and awards she earned in her chosen field, but I wanted to be supportive, so I would plaster on a smile and nod brightly when she admitted it.

"You and your father," she whispered.

I froze, my ears ringing with shock.

"Nothing else mattered. I see that now, and it's too late. I loved your father very much, and he was taken from me far too young. And you, my precious girl, I loved too much, and I pushed you away only to lose you, too." Her shoulders rolled as tears once again filled her gaze. "I'm still your mother, so I'm going to give one more piece of advice...if you'll let me."

I hid my amazement that she'd put family above career and smiled uncertainly. "Of course."

Pointing at the door where Elder had run, she said firmly, "If you care for him and he cares for you, then ignore everything else. Forget everything I ever told you. Disregard everything society forces on you. You want kids; you do it. You want cake; you eat it. You want to go to the Olympics, by God, you have fun kicking ass." She laughed at the last one, deliberately lightening the mood even though my heart smarted with yet more truth. I couldn't have children so that point was moot—no matter how terrorizing.

"Under no circumstances do you let the *should-dos* dictate and steal your life. It's too short, Min. It's too easy to screw up. Be true to yourself and follow your heart. Only then can you look back and have no regrets." She stood, keeping my hands in hers, pulling me to my feet.

Moving around the table, she pulled me into her arms.

Mother to daughter.

Woman to woman.

Her wiry frame fit against mine as if it were a mirror image, both of us paying for our choices with different battle scars.

"I love you, Tasmin." She kissed my cheek, her dark hair mingling with mine for a second. "Stay in touch…if you want to. But don't stay in England if it's not where you want to be. Travel, explore, find where your soul is happiest."

"But what about visits—"

She tapped my nose, stepping away. "Phone calls and Skype. I'm in prison, but they allow liberties for loved ones and family. Up until now, I had no one to put on my register. I'll fix that today."

She blew me a kiss as the guard waited for her to present her wrists to slap the cuffs back on. "I'm so proud of you, Minnie Mouse. *So* proud."

I pressed my fist against my heart to prevent it from cracking under the pressure of such a gift. I couldn't stop the trickle of tears as she was led away.

Only, these tears weren't caustic and burning.

These tears were fresh and mending.

I was still exhausted.

I was still drained and crippled and frazzled from the day.

But for the first time, I unbuckled a piece of my past and deposited the terrible weight. Discarding one tiny piece of luggage—throwing away a satchel or a duffel filled with screams and silence—and finally had the courage to stroll away

---

without it.

* * * * *

I'd expected to find Elder waiting outside the room, but instead, I found a fresh-faced officer who led me silently back the way I'd come.

I couldn't argue about being escorted from the prison on my own, but I couldn't stomach the thought of Elder leaving without me.

Nervousness pooled in my belly. Anxious heat hissed over my skin.

Where is he?

What had happened to warrant him leaving me alone in jail?

Even though fear pressed and tiredness fogged my mind, I held my head high and followed my guide. Passing through security, I signed out and pushed open the doors to return to freedom. The irony that I'd been a captive along with my mother wasn't something I found humorous. I had my freedom now but how long would it be until she got hers?

My heart swelled with affection rarely felt toward her.

We'd both entered this calamity and survived with different habits and become someone entirely new.

In a way, I was glad. Perhaps this new mother-daughter existence would have a much closer bond than the previous version of ourselves. For once, I was looking forward to talking to her, answering her prying questions, and remembering how to be a member of a family.

Family…

Elder.

He was my family. He was the one I loved above all others—including myself.

Yet…he'd vanished.

Squinting in the newly appeared sunshine making a last hurrah before dusk fell, I spotted a black clad figure standing beside the sedan that travelled with the Phantom.

My heart leapt then plummeted as I recognised him.

Not Elder.

Selix.

Moving toward him, I struggled to contain the worried flutterings in my belly. "Where's Elder?"

Selix cocked his head as he opened the back door for me. "He told me to inform you something urgent came up, and he had to attend to it." His eyes flickered with the lie. "He'll meet you in a couple of hours and escort you to Hawksridge Hall where the ball is taking place."

Part of me wanted to stomp my foot and demand to be told the truth. To figure out why Elder had run and left his friend to feed me fibs. Yet the other part of me understood why.

I could understand how watching my mother and me rekindle our strained relationship could be taxing to anyone. What I'd said in there wasn't nice or sugar-coated. My tears hadn't been controlled or pretty.

But he *knew* me.

He knew where I'd come from. He'd been there. He'd waded through the blood and patched up my broken bones.

If he could do all that—stand beside me unflinching until today—then what had set him off? What made him run when we'd faced so much worse together?

Perhaps he regretted doing what he did for me. Maybe he second-guessed his willingness to get involved and needed some time on his own to revaluate his commitment now he knew more.

Or maybe... *he wasn't thinking about me at all?* Maybe he'd sunk into his own private agony—his pain at never having an open-armed reunion with his family. My mother had withheld her love but had killed for me. His mother had lavished her affection and then banished him.

I was so lucky.

He was still alone.

My heart twitched and tore at the thought.

I'd been so selfish. Of *course*, he would be distraught at

seeing two people who had never been close overcome their differences and unify.

I'm an idiot.

I rubbed my chest, doing my best to calm the lovesick muscle as I nodded at Selix. "Tell him to take all the time he needs." I placed a leg into the car. "If you speak to him between now and tonight, can you please tell him I'm eternally grateful for everything he's done for me. That he's my family just like I hope I'm his, but if he's reached his limit and needs space, then…" I looked away, fortifying myself for such traumatising words. "Tell him I understand, and he's under no obligation."

He smiled stiffly. "Will do. Now get in the car."

I slid into the vehicle and held back the wobbliness of sadness and exhaustion as Selix slammed the door. That was what I liked about him. He was no-nonsense. He saw I was upset but didn't take it upon himself to cajole or soothe.

His loyalties were to Elder, though I didn't understand why as their bond bordered violence with a sprinkling of mutual respect.

At the start, I'd believed Selix was a servant loyal to his employer. That he was nothing more than paid help.

There was no way I thought that now.

Now, I believed Selix was there for his own purpose, and Elder would prefer them equals instead of the second-in-command role Selix preferred to play.

That's all it is…a role.

A pantomime.

Just like Elder was playing the role as my protector.

He had his lines and delivery—following the script he wrote himself. However, I doubted abandoning me inside a prison while emotionally distraught was planned.

He must be hurting terribly.

I wish I was with him.

I wish he would let me help him.

Selix climbed into the driver's seat, and, without a word,

drove me to wherever I was meant to be.

* * * * *

The hotel room was opulent, but it wasn't private.

As I entered the suite at some luxury establishment, I expected to have some time alone. Selix had checked me in and given me the keycard. He'd escorted me up in the elevator and left me to my own devices once I was safely deposited outside the room.

I'd happily accepted the reprieve. Readily looking forward to a bath, a nap, and perhaps some time to write a letter to No One.

My fingers itched to put my thoughts on paper after speaking them aloud for so long. Plus, the need to erase what I'd penned about my mother was the one thing keeping me going instead of collapsing into lethargy.

Yes, a note would help.

They always do…

As the door closed behind me and I entered the lounge, I froze.

Do I have the wrong room?

This one already had guests, and not one of them was Elder.

"Hello?" My voice sounded hollow to my ears. Mild shock that I'd spoken without thinking almost made me wish to be mute once again.

I didn't want words.

I wanted letters.

I wanted No One.

I want Elder.

Living with trauma was a sneaky thing. Some days I was invincible—able to take on Elder and every obstacle in my path. And some days…some moments…those strengths vanished, leaving me shaking, panicking, and seeking all exits to flee.

This was one of those moments.

Backpedalling, all I saw were two women who weren't

invited, who I didn't know, who could be part of any trafficking or racketeering scam.

"Get out." I cursed the wobble in my tone.

A woman, with coiled brown hair and red lipstick, stood smartly from where she perched on the grey and navy couch in the window bay. "Ah, you're finally here." Clapping her hands, she summoned her friend to stand. They wore matching cream blouses with tailored black skirts and aprons with needles, tape, and chalk peeping from their front pockets.

"Who are you?" I grabbed a letter opener from the desk beside me, brandishing it. "What do you want?"

The women shared a look. The older of the two with ginger hair styled in a French twist held up her hands. "We're not here to hurt you. You can put that down."

"I'll put it down when I know who you are." I glanced behind me, eyeing the door. Selix had vanished into the room two doors down. If I was fast enough, I could run there before they could grab me. "Tell me. Right now."

The older woman with ginger hair pointed at herself and then her friend, followed by the embroidered sigil on their matching breast pockets. "I'm Mel, and this is Nat. We're from Social Art."

"Social Art?" My hand grew slippery around my weapon. "What's that?"

The red-lipsticked lady giggled. "Obviously someone didn't pass on the message."

When I gave her a blank look, she added, "We were hired by Mr. Prest to help you get ready for the masque."

"Oh."

A reply I could handle.

A response my flight or fight desires could accept.

Slowly, I put the letter opener down, my fingers creeping to my throat where prickling anxiety remained.

The masquerade.

I'd entirely forgotten about it.

All I wanted to do was rest. To somehow regroup from

this afternoon and figure out what had happened to Elder. God, the thought of mingling with strangers…all of them wearing masks?

I gulped.

I can't.

I wasn't in the right headspace. If my ever-present fear had sprung up from two women, what would happen in a ballroom full of hundreds?

I had a better handle on my panic attacks, but what if one found me in the middle of a crowd? What if I collapsed and sobbed and screamed and Elder had to drag me away? I'd ruin his reputation and his meetings with whoever he planned to do business with.

Shaking my head, I bypassed them, spying a bathroom beyond. "I-I'm not feeling all that well." I kicked off my ballet flats and made my way past a small table where a pad and pen embossed with the hotel logo begged me to scribble on it.

Pilfering the stationery, I didn't care which hotel Selix had brought me to or whereabouts in London we were. We were in England, and that was all I knew. Back in the country I knew better than any other and I still found myself completely lost.

"Do you think you could call Mr. Prest and give him my apologies?" Inching toward the bathroom door—backing over the threshold and almost free from their sharp gazes—I shrugged. "I'm sorry, I'm really not feeling—"

Something whispered over my scalp, warm and heavy.

Oh, God.

Terror sprang. Self-preservation kicked in. I spun around ready to attack whoever had attacked me, only to bury my face in a billow of tulle.

"Ah, you found it." Mel came forward, her heels silent on the carpet. "Your dress."

Hugging my notepad and pen, I backed away, my lips parting as I studied the gown hanging from a collapsible wardrobe. Small shelving with the most delicious blood red heels and a box with Victoria Secret's emblem rested beside the incredible creation of satin and lace.

"It's one of our signature pieces," Nat said as my arms went lax and I dropped the pad and paper. My entire body went floppy with awe. Shock. Amazement.

A rustle sounded behind me; followed by a soft voice. "That's the dress he ordered. It's from a collection called Bruised by Beauty by Nila Weaver."

Mel chuckled. "Well, it's a Weaver creation, but the designer of the company changed her last name a few years ago. In fact—" A light hand fluttered on my shoulder. "You'll meet her tonight at the masque. She's married to the owner—Jethro Hawk."

Even being touched by a stranger couldn't stop my wonderment as I studied the dress. It hung impersonal and lifeless, but it *glowed* with magic. Sorcery that promised whoever wore it wouldn't be mere mortal anymore but someone transcended from mankind. Someone ethereal.

The bottom of the skirt was oversized and bell-shaped with acres of elegant swathes of every colour on the red and blue spectrum. Ochre to blood and midnight to forget-me-nots. The colours twisted and turned, smudged and battled to look exactly like a bruise upon human skin. Slowly, the colours stopped fighting, creeping up the dress until the war ended and red was the true winner.

Red—the colour of passion.

Red—the colour of pain.

It shimmered and beckoned and beamed with the richest, deepest crimson I'd ever seen—as if blood had cascaded right from someone's heart. Off the shoulder with sashes of beadwork, navy and blue-black lace webbed like veins.

It was the most beautiful thing I'd ever seen.

And the most morbid.

Whoever wore this gown was shouting to the world she wasn't pure. She wasn't innocent. She was raw and bloodied and bruised and was so much stronger for it.

I choked on overwhelming love for Elder—that even

running away he'd somehow found a way to tell me how proud he was.

The hand on my shoulder squeezed gently. "Whatever tiredness, worry, or illness you're suffering, we have to find a way to fix it. This dress demands to be worn. *You* must be the one to wear it. It would be a sin not to."

Nat pushed past me, clipping toward the vanity where rows of makeup already rested on black velvet runners. Bottles and brushes, palettes and creams all ready to paint their chosen one.

"Oh, I almost forgot." Mel plucked a large box from the floor and held it out to me, cracking open the lid. "This goes with it. The whole ensemble is called Queen Who Bled."

With my heart lodged in my throat, my eyes fell on the final ingredient. And for the first time, I felt faint for all good reasons instead of bad. The familiar closing of my lungs and rush of panic in my veins only brought wonder and a touch of anxiety that I could never be beautiful enough to pull off such a mask.

A mask undoubtedly chosen by Elder.

A mask that would grant me protection, beauty, and queenly power.

I would go tonight.

I would wear the dress.

I would find Elder and thank him for everything he was.

And then I would kiss him.

Because gifts such as these...they deserved a hundred kisses.

A thousand.

More.

"I'm suddenly feeling much better," I whispered.

"In that case." Mel smiled. "Let's get you ready for the ball."

ELDER

LIKE A COWARD, I hid.

I shirked all responsibility and ran so I could somehow get my head together and not take my self-loathing out on Pim.

I meant to return to the hotel and collect her. I had a big plan to meet her in the hotel foyer, decked out in my black tux with black cravat, black waistcoat, and black mask and wait for her to descend the stairs as any novel-hero would.

That was before my escape from the prison refused to settle my nerves. That was before my stalk through English suburbs left me worse than I'd been before.

I'd constantly checked my watch, plagued by questions. Where was she? What was she doing? Would Selix have taken her back to the hotel? Would she permit the Social Art crew to dress her or would she refuse—too hurt from my disappearance and too tired from the truth?

Run ragged and desperate for a joint, I found my way to the hotel and dressed. I let the magic of marijuana turn me as normal as possible and waved off Selix's lecture of how dangerous it'd been roaming the streets without protection with the Chinmoku on the hunt.

I had enough to torment myself without including the mess of my past.

It didn't help that the instant I was mentally and physically appropriate for the unwanted masque, I couldn't stop pacing my hotel room.

Only a few doors down from Pim and all I wanted to do was interrupt her and demand she hear me out. But I didn't know what I'd say to her—the jumble in my brain too messy to configure.

I couldn't outrun the hatred for all I'd done, the pressure I'd put her under, the frustration with her silence, or the rancid desire that led me to force myself upon her the first time.

Who was I?

And why the fuck had she put up with me?

Me.

I didn't deserve a damn thing.

I'd made her steal for me.

I'd made her come for me.

I'd overstepped every fucking boundary I could.

So no…with the way I was feeling, I couldn't wait for her like a gentleman. I had to run like a beast and lick my self-inflicted wounds in private.

I travelled to Hawksridge Hall on my own—encased in a car without Pim for over an hour.

I glanced unimpressed at the giant estate as I arrived at the bottom of an incredibly long driveway to one of the oldest holdings in England.

It made me anxious to have so much permanency on land. The ocean lived in my veins and I missed it already.

I didn't care about turrets or copper cupolas or the lattice-work of grass growing up impressive spires. I didn't smile as I nodded thanks to my driver and entered the warm welcome of such an ancient hall. I didn't glare at the tapestries of prior lords and ladies or try to figure out the many secrets beckoning to be uncovered.

My fascination with secrets had gotten me into this mess. It wasn't my right to dig for answers about anyone; I intended to stop such a nasty habit this very moment.

Moving through already tipsy crowds, ducking around ballgowned women and nodding tersely at tuxedoed men, I made my way to the pop-up bar complete with decanters and goblets and allowed myself one drink.

Just one.

My rule of tasting a drop to refrain from the entire bottle.

As I sipped the neat vodka, I couldn't tear my eyes away from the entrance as I waited for her.

The girl I owed a thousand apologies.

How was I supposed to clear my conscience? What if she didn't turn up? What if she vanished into her home country, deciding for both of us enough was enough?

You know she won't do that.

The connection between us was too strong to falsify. We were committed—whether we'd voiced that commitment didn't matter.

I knew in my bones Pim wouldn't vanish, just like I knew I'd never be able to atone for my needs to master her body and soul.

The elegant ballroom with its stately pillars and monogramed mosaic floor was made to house an event such as this. The curtains glittered gold, and the guests looked every bit as splendid as the wealth dripping from crystal chandeliers as they danced in sync to the orchestra.

But I didn't care about any of it because it meant nothing to me.

The only thing that meant something was late.

My drink was empty, but my fingers remained tight around the warmed glass—needing to clutch something…waiting.

I thought I'd be prepared for her arrival. In the time it took to drink my vodka, a hastily scribbled script had formed. I was prepared with my apology and explanation.

But when she finally arrived?

Fuck me.

My knees turned to water and my breath to stone.

I couldn't move.

Christ, I couldn't move.

She appeared with Selix trailing behind her. Her eyes skittered over the dancing, mingling crowd, squinting against rubies and diamonds glinting in the low-hung chandeliers.

The large ballroom with its marble and four-story windows paled to nothing but brick and mortar as I drank her in.

If I didn't have a soul connection with her and imprinted every nuance—if I hadn't studied every twitch and mannerism—I might not have recognised her.

The mask.

It hid her eyes and forehead entirely, delivering her from woman to queen.

The time it took five nights ago to go through the one-of-a-kind designs thanks to my host's wife's fashion line was entirely worth it.

She was no longer anyone's prisoner...she was no one's princess.

The mask gleamed a deep, rich red to match her stunning blue and red dress, wings of the mask hid her cheekbones, flaring up to her hairline in a regal tiara. Red gemstones dangled beneath her eyes like blood tears while midnight feathers adorned the lacy crown.

Her gown swayed as she moved forward, her gaze seeking something, someone...me.

When I'd ordered the dress, I'd rolled my eyes at the name Bruised by Beauty. Yet another gimmick employed by a store to sell their underwhelming product.

How fucking wrong I was.

Pim looked as if she bloomed from a bruise. A pretty flower opened and still standing even after every petal had been damaged by plucking human fingers.

She looked draped in pain and blood; a queen of agony and everything she'd lived through.

I wanted to fucking bow to her. To take her hand in mine and kiss her knuckles with reverence. To pledge my loyalty, fealty, fortune, and heart.

And then she saw me.

And she transformed once again.

Her sin-red lips tilted into a nervous smile. Her green eyes glowed uncertain behind her mask, and her hair stole the candle light, absorbing it, glowing like liquid chocolate twirled and bound with a blue-black ribbon.

I'd never seen someone so beautiful or been so broken by it.

Instead of collapsing in homage, my legs moved toward her.

I couldn't breathe as I cut through the crowd, moving ever closer, bound within her spell. When we met in the centre of the ballroom, the music switched to a heart twisting waltz and couples began to merge into one, swirling around us as if we'd stepped through time and entered a ball centuries earlier.

I had so much to say to her and no words worthy.

I had so much to feel and no heart capable of such things.

So I did the only thing I could.

I bowed with my arm tucked over my waist. I bowed right to her skirts and waited for the fluttering of her hand upon my head. The moment she touched me, I couldn't stay apart any longer.

Sweeping my arm around her, I tucked her close. Grunting at the perfect sensation of her slim body encased in miles of satin pressing against mine, I swung her into a waltz.

I didn't know how to dance.

I'd chosen music over footsteps, but my OCD, for once, served as a gift instead of a flaw. Every movie I'd ever watched and show I'd ever seen, I recalled the rhythm, the flow, and my feet fell effortlessly into beat.

And just like I'd been winded and awed by Pim, I was once again blown away by how my brain quieted better than any joint.

One, two, three.

One, two, three.

The waltz rhythm ran through my veins and ears and blood.

One, two, three.

One, two, three.

A perfect box, our feet moving in unison, every move in threes.

I shuddered at the relief of moving in sync instead of fighting to stay within restrictions. My brain stopped being so chaotic. I sighed as everything made rational, comprehensible sense.

My fingers wrapped tighter around her waist as I threw my all in to the dance and clutched her hard.

The softest moan fell from her lips, her mouth parted, eyes bright as stars. She moved with me, entirely river-smooth and willing to be my marionette. For me to guide her, teach her, take complete control.

I forgot about where we were or why we were here and let myself fall the final way. To finally admit there was no bottom when it came to falling in love. That each time I thought I'd reached the end, another crevice appeared to trip into.

How many times would I tumble for this woman?

And how many times could I say sorry?

Gathering her closer, my body hardened with how delicate she smiled, how beautiful she was, how strong. Rubbing my lips over her ear, I murmured, "I'm sorry for leaving you this afternoon."

I started with the easier apology, my voice rough and ragged. The music was loud, but my whisper overrode it, delivering straight and true.

She jolted, then the smallest smile appeared. "I want to know why…if you'll tell me."

A chocolate curl came loose as I swung her into a spin. Tucking her back into my embrace, I reached up and brushed it behind her ear. My fingers tingled from her heated skin, nudging her mask a little, hinting that the girl I loved was beneath that crown and she'd chosen me despite how I'd acted.

"I'm a foolish, selfish son of a bitch."

She shook her head, the rhythm of the waltz keeping me centred with its one, two, three.

"You're many things but never that. I've never known someone as unselfish as you are."

I chuckled darkly and didn't reply. What argument could I deliver where I didn't have to prove my faults while begging for forgiveness?

"I'm sorry for demanding your voice, little mouse." I focused on her lips. They twitched at her family nickname—the same nickname I'd stolen just as I'd stolen her. The same name that complemented the one I'd shed so long ago in ways I couldn't bear. "I'm sorry for pushing you before you were ready to be pushed. I'm sorry for expecting things you weren't ready to give. I'm sorry for not finding you sooner. I'm sorry for demanding your thoughts. I'm sorry for believing I had access to your secrets. I'm sorry for not bringing you home from the start." My head hung. "I'm sorry for so many things but most of all…I'm sorry for being like him."

That was the main apology festering in my heart. The one thing I knew without question but wanted to ignore.

By stealing Pim, I'd become just like Alrik. I hadn't abused her physically, but I had continued to abuse her with my demands.

Never again.

If she didn't want to tell me a single thing about herself, fine.

If she wanted to build our life on shared experiences, so be it.

I would work on my stupid needs and never ask her to share herself with me again.

Because I loved her.

I couldn't imagine letting her go. If I never saw her again or never knew the true Pim, then it was a price I was willing to pay.

The music built to a crescendo, and I used the pace to

twirl and spin and throw her into a dip. She had no chance to reply, and my aching heart had more time to believe things could be repaired.

Then the song ended.

We slammed to a halt.

And our host for the evening officially welcomed us into his home.

Pimlico

"THANK YOU FOR attending tonight."

A deep, brooding voice jerked my attention from Elder toward the dais at the front of the ballroom.

Stupidly, I thought the music had come from a CD or music player, but I couldn't be further from the truth. A full orchestra sat on stage. Players relaxed and cleaned their instruments while the host smoothed his tux and prepared to deliver his speech.

Piano, violin, cello, and flutes.

The knowledge that Elder could pick up a cello and become part of them gave me goosebumps on top of the ones he'd already given me.

I hadn't had time to reply. I wasn't given the opportunity to cup his cheek and eradicate the self-imposed hatred in his gaze.

Why on earth was he apologising? And what made him think he was like *him*?

He isn't.

At all.

My mind ran riot; I had to find a reply that could fix Elder's shame. We'd skirted around each other for too long. It was driving us insane instead of allowing us to grow closer. The loose paperwork and unfiled experiences of my short life didn't have the necessary wisdom to repair us once and for all. I had no one to ask what was the best thing to do or say.

I only had myself and my confident then terrified then confident topsy-turvy thoughts.

"Welcome…" the host said in his dark baritone, cutting through my thoughts, demanding my full attention.

The ballroom quietened as hundreds of people focused on the man dressed in an impeccable tux. He wore a simple mask of plain black like a villain, similar to Elder's ebony velvet mask, not wanting to be known. However, topaz eyes gleamed from the shadows, dancing over his family standing beside him.

A woman in the most incredible gown I'd ever seen— minus the one I wore—smiled encouragingly. She looked like a raven transforming into a swan with her white chiffon and black feathers scattered all over the skirts. Her mask was different to everyone's and only covered one eye, cutting down her face to her chin in an intricate scrollwork of pearls.

But it was her necklace that set her apart.

Candlelight and chandeliers made it almost impossible to study the heavy diamond choker glittering around her throat. It cut her in half, almost overshadowing her beauty, if not for the royal way she held herself—taming it rather than wearing it.

I'd never thought as jewellery as *becoming* someone, but I had the strangest sensation that the necklace meant far more than just simple frosting for an elegant evening.

Tearing my eyes away, I looked at the two children standing well behaved in front of the host and hostess, holding hands. A boy who I guessed would look like his father with a matching black shroud over his eyes and a little girl who was the swanling born to the swan.

"Tonight is a significant occasion for us, and we're honoured you could be here." Our host, Jethro Hawk, flicked a glance at his wife. "This is the first time the ballroom has been used for happier festivities, and I'm sure it won't be the last." His throat worked as if such a simple sentence carried a private weight.

His wife reached out and took his hand. They stayed linked as he continued, "We invite you into our home and look forward to talking with you throughout the night. You are more than welcome to walk the grounds, visit the stables or orchard, or explore the many rooms at Hawksridge. While you are our guests, we do ask you respect the locked chambers and do not believe such gossip that has long since circulated our hall."

A slight ripple of murmurs tracked around the room.

A feminine laugh rang out, guiding my attention to a woman dressed in a turquoise gown dripping with sapphires and a mask that gleamed opalescent with moonstone. She was just as stunning as the hostess; only she sat in a chair with wheels wrapped in gemstones and ribbon, holding the hand of a tall, dark-haired man who favoured a white tux over the usual black.

She laughed again, surprising the hall into silence. "Come now, brother. I think the gossip is far more entertaining than the truth, don't you?" She smiled at the crowd. "Why else are so many here tonight but to hear the tale of debts turned marriage?"

"Here, here," someone said, raising a glass as waiters and waitresses made their way through the masses handing out champagne. "We'll happily listen to a bedtime tale or two."

Everyone laughed apart from Elder and me.

It was as if everyone knew something about this family that we didn't. Elder stiffened as his eyes locked on the host. Mr. Hawk's back straightened at the joke, an odd look crossing his face. He stood buffeted by the laughter, and it wasn't fun for him but painful.

His voice quietened the ballroom with strained command. "Tonight, there are much better things to entertain ourselves with than listening to stories. We have business to attend to, after all." He warmed to his speech. "Diamonds that are currently for sale with clarity and colour certifications are on display in the drawing room. A Mr. Elder Prest is here to discuss yacht orders with those nautically inclined. I, myself, am available to talk to anyone wishing to purchase a well-bred polo pony or two, and I believe a Mr. Sullivan Sinclair is here to help with any luxury island travel you may wish to book at his many locations."

With a curt bow, Jethro Hawk said, "For now, enjoy the music and champagne. Make the most of your night, everyone." The second he'd finished, he pointed to the orchestra who struck up music immediately. Squeezing his wife's hand, he guided his family off the dais and vanished from the ballroom through one of the many doors.

Elder's hand landed on my lower back.

I shuddered at his touch; slightly amazed that I was capable of lust so quick and powerful, I became instantly wet for him.

Turning to face him, I prepared to tell him things I didn't believe in but assurances he needed to hear. I wanted to grant him my forgiveness for all the things he apologised for—not because I believed he had anything to be sorry for but to hopefully grant him a smidgen of peace.

His onyx eyes burned into mine, full of complex love and hate, desire and regret, his voice just as tangled. "Let's find somewhere quiet. I need to talk to you."

I took his hand and nodded.

* * * * *

We didn't get far.

The moment we stepped from the ballroom and avoided perfume, tulle, and finery, we found ourselves practically bumping into our hosts.

Mr. and Mrs Hawk stood in corridor shadows, her hand on her husband's cheek, his forehead touching hers. Their children were nowhere to be found, and my skin flushed for the intimate moment we'd stumbled upon.

"Focus on me and only me," his wife murmured. "I told you this was a bad idea, Jet."

He groaned under his breath. "I'm sick of the fucking whispers, Nila. You know as well as I do this should stop them for good. Kes and Emma don't need this shit growing up."

"They'll be fine. They know the truth. What does it matter what the gossip mills are still saying—" Mrs Hawk noticed us. Pulling back, she dropped her touch from her husband's cheek and smiled brightly, friendly, entirely professional in her role as hostess. "Ah, hello. Out for an explore already? The drinks have just started circulating."

Jethro Hawk blinked, shook his head slightly, then hid his strained look with one of smooth elegance. "Ah, Mr. Prest." He came forward, his hand outstretched. "Pleasure to meet you in the flesh."

Elder tightened his fingers around mine as he reached with his other to complete niceties. He bowed his head respectfully. "Same, Mr. Hawk. Thank you for the invitation."

"Jethro, please." He smiled tightly. "We're lucky enough to mingle in the same circles of wealth and decadence. I intend to make acquaintances with all of them now that I'm in charge of my family's estate." Turning to me, his smile warmed. "And you must be Pimlico. The plus one."

I nodded. "I am."

"Do you have a last name?"

Elder tensed. "She has both a first and a last name, but for now it's just Pim."

Jethro studied us as if Elder had given up a lot more than just my name. He opened his mouth to reply, but two children streaked up ahead, miniature ballgown and tux flying as they bolted through the labyrinth of corridors, squealing in joy.

Jethro's face softened with absolute affection.

The same newfound agony that'd hit me in the police station found me again.

I gasped at the yearning in my heart—the way it held out its arms for something I never wanted and now would give anything to deserve.

I'd never had anything against children before—not that

I'd been around many. They were just tiny humans who belonged to other people. Even seeing the love Jethro held for his offspring didn't make my heart patter with hunger.

But that was because I wasn't in love with Jethro Hawk.

I was in love with Elder Prest, and I made the mistake of glancing at him thanks to the vice-clench of his fingers around mine at the sound of children's laughter.

His face turned white, his eyes black as pitch. One look and I knew where his thoughts had gone: to his younger brother who burned. To his cousins he wasn't allowed to contact. To his family he'd stocked an entire yacht with gifts for.

Elder came across so solitary—sailing the seas, content as long as he was away from land. Only his aloneness ate giant holes in him, infecting me, making me wish I could snap my fingers and give him everything he was missing.

The newness inside blinked into an all-encompassing *craving*. And this time...it was even worse. A crippling. A maiming. A terrible, horrible knowledge that if I could have such an awakening to wanting children...imagine how awful it would be for a man who put family above everything.

I wanted to join us together. I suddenly desperately, *torturedly* needed to merge and give him a child of his own.

That thought shocked me stupid.

I wanted children.

Elder wanted children.

I can never give him children.

I could never give him back the family who'd ostracized him, and I was too damaged to give him a new one—one that belonged entirely to him.

My heart wept even while my eyes remained dry.

Conversation carried on around me, but I lost track.

All I could think about was how irrevocably I'd just changed and how quickly it had happened. How swift I'd gone from singular to plural. How Elder was mine now, through and through. And I didn't deserve him because I could never give him what he ultimately needed.

My love would never be enough.

I'll never be enough.

Oh, God…

The pain of it.

The unfairness—

"And you? Are you enjoying Hawksridge Hall?"

The question wriggled its way inside my mind, interrupting my steamrolling thoughts. I tried to latch onto it, but I was dragged back down again.

I'd known pain. Immense, earthquaking pain.

But I'd never known something quite as sharp or quick as the heartbreak of knowing I could never give Elder a child. That this new ticking inside me was counting on a broken clock. A clock that would never be able to tell the time or deliver what I suspected was the one thing Elder wanted most in the world.

What if he eventually resented me?

Tears trickled from my heart to my eyes at the thought of not being whole. Of not being able to give him everything he needed and more.

I need to leave…

The pain just kept getting worse.

My fingernails dug into the dense fabric around my waist.

Common sense tried to snap me out of it.

Even if I *could* have children, I was young. Didn't I want to continue being young? There was no rush.

I almost scoffed at the thought. For two years, I'd lived wanting nothing more than to die. Now I was living I wanted to *live*. I wanted to laugh every minute and smile every hour. I wouldn't let right or wrong timelines sway my life.

Never again.

Even my mother had advised the same.

And I can't do a damn thing about it.

"Pim?" Elder brushed his lips over my ear, wrenching me back into my exquisite gown, drenching me in threads of orchestra music, and leaving me standing before the lord and lady of this ancient manor.

I gasped, rubbing at the burning in my heart before dropping my touch protectively over a stomach that would forever be flat and useless.

Get it together.

Forget it.

You're alive. Focus on that and stop asking for more than you deserve.

"Sorry? What?"

Elder scowled. "Are you okay?" He pulled back, planting his hands on my shoulders. "Panic attack?" His eyes scanned over my head to the ballroom still chaotic with dancers and partiers. "Shit, I didn't think. Crowds—they'll be too much for you."

How funny that I hadn't even thought about it.

I'd arrived with Selix protecting me and found Elder's stunning face half hidden behind a rich velvet mask, and I'd been happy, not fearful.

I'd had nothing to be frightened of until this moment, and the one person I was most afraid of was *me*.

I was afraid of losing him because I wasn't whole.

I was afraid of the things I would do to ensure he never knew my horrendous secret.

I was afraid of the insidious whispers of seducing him to see if the doctors were wrong. Of using him to find out one way or another if I was truly damaged beyond repair.

How far would I go if I let myself tumble down that path?

Not waiting for my reply, Elder grabbed my elbow and stomped toward the exit. "We're leaving. This was a bad idea."

Leave?

I couldn't.

Not yet.

Not until I'd had time to plaster my holes together and render over them to hide the cracks.

"No, wait." I leaned against his tug, dragging us to a

standstill. "I'm fine. Sorry, my mind just drifted."

Don't see my lies.

Elder scowled, disbelief on his face as he peered into my eyes. "Are you sure?"

His black gaze, as usual, was far too perceptive and had an uncanny way of deep sea fishing into my soul, hooking the truth even while it did its best to wriggle away.

Forcing a smile, I nodded. "I'm sure." I touched his wrist gently. "I keep thinking my ailments are private, but you were there when I had that panic attack on the stairs." It wasn't the right thing to do—bringing up our first meeting at Alrik's once again, but I'd rather cast his mind to that terrible place than this new one I couldn't formulate. "You gave me your jacket. You started my heart beating again. I promise on that moment that if I have another attack, I'll tell you and beg you to take me far away where it's just the two of us."

And possibly never three or four.

I crushed the voice of barrenness.

His eyes tightened. His teeth sinking into his bottom lip with deliberation. He made me weak and wanting, encouraging me to fib.

"You know…" I lowered my lashes, letting some of my pain show. "You might be right. I might've had a tiny panic attack, but I'm fine now." I looked up, forcing every courage and falsehood onto my face. "Truly, El."

It took him an eternity—an eternity where I wanted to perish for deliberately lying to him—until he nodded gruffly. "Fine."

My tongue fluttered for more fibs, needing to patch up the awkwardness between us. Only our host stepped forward, inserting himself into our conversation.

"I'm sorry for overhearing, but did you say you struggle in crowds, too?" Jethro Hawk asked in a deceptively bored voice.

My eyes narrowed, hearing more than I should in his tone. No matter the aloof politeness on his face, he couldn't hide the sudden interest hiding there.

His wife scowled, floating closer and placing her hand on his arm as if in some subtle code to behave.

Forcing my eyes from the golden inspection of her husband, I shrugged as if this whole thing was a huge waste of time and misunderstanding. "Like anyone, I have moments of fear as well as every other emotion. Who doesn't?"

Jethro rubbed his chin, his salt and pepper hair turning him ageless as well as wise. "Everyone does but some more so than others."

He spoke as if he were ancient and not in his early thirties as I suspected. He phrased things in a way that hinted he wasn't just talking about our current topic.

He unnerved me.

"Just like fear, some unlucky people have endured more trauma in their past than others." I shot back, unwilling to let him win. I didn't know why my hackles rose when he stared at me. My back prickled as if he could see more than he should. As if he understood exactly why I'd gone so quiet and why my heart raced so sickly now.

"Trauma can come in many forms, no doubt about that." His wife smiled.

My chin rose. "I agree. Only there is no such trauma now." Pressing close to Elder, more for my benefit than for his, I added, "Elder is the reason I no longer endure that word." Feeling far too studied and stripped bare, I turned ever more defensive. Jethro's question repeated in my mind. The fact he'd asked if I struggled in crowds *too*, meant he had issues himself.

He might be the master of this castle, but I wouldn't let anyone unsettle me again. "Why do *you* not enjoy crowds, Mr. Hawk? If you prefer smaller company, why invite so many guests tonight?"

Mr. Hawk kept his face indifferent. "It's not that I don't enjoy crowds. It's that they provide too many opportunities like this one." He waved his hand as his wife cleared her throat. Shooting her a glance, he said, "Anyway, that is another subject for another time. To answer your question simply, I prefer the company of those I trust far more than those I don't."

His wife stepped forward, taking the limelight and her husband's hand. Her laugh was bright after so much dark. "We all have secrets and histories, don't we? If everyone spoke the truth, I'm sure we'd never leave the comfort of homes for fear of what could happen."

Elder chuckled under his breath, accepting her end to this strange corridor conversation. "You are right, Mrs Hawk. The world is infinitely dangerous."

The awkward tension faded as Jethro smiled easier and less complicated this time. "I almost forgot." Untangling his fingers from his wife with a loving glance, he moved to an elaborate sideboard with hundreds of little drawers and scrollwork. Sitting on top was a brass candelabra holding at least thirty flickering candles.

Pulling a key from his pocket, Jethro inserted it into one of the drawers and pulled it open. Palming whatever it was, he relocked the cupboard and turned to face Elder. "This is yours, I believe."

Elder cocked his head but accepted the long, narrow box. The deep blue velvet held a silver stitched diamond on the top—the logo of the Black Diamonds. Now I'd seen it, I recognised it from posters in jewellery shops around London. I'd even seen it advertised in train stations with dripping diamonds billboards and their simple but powerful logo in the corner.

My eyes strayed to Mrs Hawk's choker; memories flooded me.

I'd seen that necklace before—or at least a replica of it on a billboard in the Pimlico subway station. A magazine had released an article about some fantastical rumour that an heiress to a family fortune in textiles had been kidnapped and held captive to serve debts to her kidnapper's family.

Was that what people were hinting at in the ballroom? Trying to pry into this couple's private world? No wonder they weren't at ease in crowds if they'd been plagued by such gossip.

"Thank you, Mr. Hawk." Elder tucked the box inside his tux breast pocket. "I appreciate the fast turnaround."

"Please, as I said, call me Jethro. And you're welcome." Glancing at me, he smiled sharply. "I see why you wanted it made so quickly."

Elder frowned. "Yes…well." He searched for a change of subject. "We've taken up enough of your time as it is." Cupping my elbow, he tilted his head. "We'll leave you to enjoy the rest of your party."

"Before you go—" Jethro extended his hand down the corridor. "I wouldn't mind discussing a few things about potentially purchasing a yacht from you. Do you mind? I believe Sullivan Sinclair wanted to meet you, too."

Elder looked at me reluctantly.

My eyes strayed to the box now hidden in his tux jacket. I wanted to ask what the hell it was, but I held my tongue. Things had happened in the space of a few moments that successfully made me wonder where I stood with him and what it all meant.

Elder's forehead furrowed, his eyes darkening with frustration. He'd accepted this invitation for business. And business was calling him away. "Will you be okay if I leave you alone for a little while?"

I beamed, doing my hardest to seem like a normal woman who didn't care in the slightest at being left alone with total strangers. Just because I hadn't seen evil in this resplendent manor or peered into the faces of masked guests with suspicion didn't mean I was strong enough to be left surrounded by people I didn't know.

But I'd already been a terrible person tonight. I wouldn't add more shame by guilting him into staying with me. Eventually, I had to face circumstances such as these, and tonight was as good as any. "Yes, of course." Already I itched at the thought of being vulnerable to another attack, another strangling, another selling.

That won't happen.

Because as much as I'd patched up holes with my mother, I wasn't as naïve as I once was. I would listen to my instincts over her tutelage. I would kill before I willingly danced with another murderer.

And besides, this was Elder's business.

Under no circumstance would I mess that up or be a weak invalid ruining his successes.

"Go. Honestly, I'll listen to the band until you come back."

Wrong. I'll hide in a corner somewhere where my back and sides are protected, and I can see anyone who comes near me.

Jethro shot me a curious glance, his nostrils flaring as if he could taste my lie.

Elder pulled me close, whispering in my ear, "I know you're lying, but I won't diminish you by dragging you with me or calling for Selix to guard you. Instead, I'll give you a task to keep your mind busy and idle hands occupied."

I gasped as his breath turned hot with command. "Steal me something, little mouse. We're in the hall of diamonds, after all."

I jerked back, studying his black gaze. "You can't be serious."

"Deadly."

Last time I stole, I ended up arrested.

And that was from an aborted attempt on a wallet. What the hell was the penalty for stealing an expensive diamond from the very family who mined them? Maybe they'd cut off my hand if the rumours were true that they favoured medieval punishments for crimes?

I didn't know why but the thought made me laugh nervously, anxiety threading through me. I went to shake my head, to tell him there was no way in hell I would do what he asked. But Jethro cleared his throat, ending our staring war. "If you will, Mr. Prest."

Elder released me, a sly smile on his lips. "Do what I ask, Pim, and the item Mr. Hawk just gave me is yours." He tapped his tux pocket. "You do want to know what's inside that pretty box, don't you?"

Damn him.

Before I could argue and reach into his pocket myself, he and Jethro turned on their heel and left.

The moment the men disappeared around the corner, Mrs Hawk sighed sweetly. "I have to make sure my children aren't up to something they shouldn't be. Will you be okay? Feel free to explore wherever the doors are open."

I nodded, swallowing hard at the thought of being left alone in a giant place with so many nooks and crannies for crime and pockets of darkness for horror. "Thank you, Mrs Hawk."

She patted my hand on her way past. "Please, call me Nila." Smiling with a touch of conspiring charm, she added, "By the way, you look exactly as I hoped someone as pretty as you would in that gown."

"Excuse me?" I smoothed the blue and red bruised bodice self-consciously.

Nila sighed wistfully. "I designed that only a few months into my stay at Hawksridge. I stole it actually from an ancestor who sketched in the same journal given to me at the time." Her gaze cleared. "I hope you like it. I find bruises rather beautiful…the range of colours fascinates me even though the pigmentation is the body's way of healing from pain. Maybe that's *why* I love them."

I didn't know what to say. The women who'd dressed me at the hotel mentioned the creator of this dress would be here tonight. I'd planned on complimenting her on her attention to detail and foresight of fashion, but Nila shook her head and switched subjects as quickly as she'd started this one. "Whatever task your man just set for you? It's worth doing. I love designing clothes and get a thrill seeing women wear my creations, but it's nothing compared to the intensity of seeing a Hawk diamond find its forever home."

She lowered her voice as if the portraits of long dead

relatives eavesdropped on us. "I've seen what your man requested Jethro to create. You'll want to see it for yourself, so do whatever he asks. It's worth it…trust me."

With that cryptic encouragement to rob her, she glided back into the ballroom and left me.

Alone.

ELDER

THE MEETING WITH Jethro Hawk didn't last long.

In an odd way, it seemed as though he was listening more to what I wasn't saying than to what I was. As I listed statistics and figures of my yachts, the accolades we'd won, and designs we'd accomplished, he stood tapping his finger against his lips, making me feel like a goddamn zoo exhibit.

By the time he nodded and admitted he was interested in a smaller size yacht for recreational fun rather than ocean travel, I was drained from doing my best to keep my mind on work and not on Pimlico.

Every time I thought about her, the agony of how I'd treated her rose all over again, swiftly followed by the love she'd crippled me with.

I'd apologised yet it wasn't enough.

I hadn't earned a response.

I hadn't given her time to give me one.

But I'd underestimated my need to have her accept my apology and absolve me of my sins.

Fuck, I should never have left her.

She'd zoned out in the corridor, but it was different from her other panic attacks. I was used to displays of physical terror—of holding her as she sucked in useless air and seeking out the monstrous beings who threatened her.

This time the enemy she fought was one I didn't understand. She hurt because of something unknown. Something I couldn't see or hear or touch.

I need to know what it is.

I needed to tell her to stop lying to me.

More time passed as I listed the smaller vessels available instead of the five-hundred-million price tagged thirty-room extravaganzas, and Jethro chose a few blueprint examples from the photos on my phone for a mock-up.

He excused himself once we'd arranged to discuss his requirements via email.

The moment he slipped from the meeting under the guise of finding his wife and children, I tapped the box burning a hole over my heart and stalked to the door myself.

I hadn't opened the gift.

I didn't want to. It was made for Pim, and it was only right she was the first to see it.

This meeting had been twenty minutes too long, but now I was free and had every intention of finding her. She'd be fucking terrified after what'd happened the last time she was at a large function.

Why the hell did I leave her and what the fuck possessed me to ask her to steal again?

I'd had no intention of doing such a thing. She'd ended up in prison, for Christ's sake. Her name had been entered into their database and her file found by whoever was hunting girls from the QMB.

She'd become known by people I wanted to hide her from.

And it was my fault for ever introducing her to the idea of thievery.

Goddammit, you idiot.

The moment I found her, we'd leave. I'd tell her to ignore any future idiocies of stealing on my behalf and ban her from ever taking what wasn't hers again—not just to save her karma and reduce any chance of her being jailed again but because she had no reason to steal.

I would provide for her.

I would be proud to care for her in every way she needed. *If she'll let me.*

The only thing she needed to steal was my apology. And then, once I knew she'd forgiven me, we could both move on and decide where to sail from here.

Africa, America, China? Where would be safe and where was the best place to wage war on the Chinmoku?

As I swept from the small morning room where Jethro and I had talked, I almost collided with another gentleman.

He stuck out his hand, a flash of sharp white teeth threatening as well as respectful. "Mr. Prest, I presume?"

I shook his grip reluctantly. "You presume correctly. And you are?"

"Sully Sinclair. Hawk told me you're in the business of creating custom yachts?"

I forced the urge to rip off the stranger's mask. I'd tolerated Jethro's black decoration because I'd seen photos of him and knew enough of his history to do business with him.

This man I'd never heard of or met.

A masquerade wasn't an ideal place to discuss work or acquisitions and not because liquor was flowing and there were much better things to do than talk facts and figures but because I had no idea what this guy looked like.

Was he good or bad?

Enemy or trustworthy?

About my height, he wore a mask that covered his entire head in smoky grey. A row of ivory beads decorated his forehead, forming into horns down his skull. His tux matched the smoke of his mask, turning him metallic, mysterious, and foreign.

His blue eyes were the only thing visible along with his jaw.

"Are you in the market?" I forced myself to ask, keeping up appearances when all I wanted to do was shove him aside and stalk after Pim.

"As a matter of fact, yes. I own a few islands in the Pacific, and my clients are used to a certain level of luxury." He flashed a shark-like smile. "Let's just say...I like to keep them happy."

The level of darkness in his voice told me everything I needed to know.

He dabbled in business I probably wouldn't approve of. He was a typical client—a scoundrel of the underworld who hid in dark shadows and paid in blood money.

A client I willingly sought because they paid better than white-collar billionaires, which meant I could clear my debt faster and fund my vengeance better.

Hiding my disdain for his occupation, I faked interest. "So you're after smaller vessels?"

"I'm after quite a few. Large and small. If you have time to discuss."

Every inch of me wanted to tell him that, no, I didn't have time. Not tonight. I wanted to tell him if he planned to do business it would be on my terms when my mind wasn't on my woman.

I'd set up another meeting—preferably online after I'd investigated who he was, what islands he owned, and what business he ran. I'd probably hack into his bank accounts to see if he had the funds before asking him to email me the shopping list he had in mind.

But I'd come tonight for this very reason.

And this gentleman might buy more than one—if he had money.

It could be entirely worth my while.

Hoping that Jethro Hawk had done enough vetting on his guests that I was safe to waste my time on Sully Sinclair, I kept my temper and smiled politely. "I can spare ten minutes."

Pimlico

I STOOD SURROUNDED by diamonds.

All loose and ripe for the picking like strawberries nestled in straw. Only these berries were made of faceted age-pressured beauty and nestled in black velvet.

Where was security? Why were there no locks and keys?

For the past twenty minutes, I'd stood gobsmacked at the wealth just scattered around the trestle tables like cheap glitter. From tiny gems to large baubles, anyone could come in, pick up a diamond, and leave.

It petrified me for some reason—how could the Hawks trust their guests not to pilfer? It horrified me at the lack of care, hinting at the amount of wealth they must have to write off this entire room if someone did get sticky fingers.

How much were they worth if they could give up a room full of diamonds to masked men and women in their home? And how much did they put on a human life to justify mining so many stones? Did they practice ethical mining techniques or were these blood diamonds I'd heard so much about?

You're running out of time again.

Just like at Elder's warehouse deliberating over what to steal, I found myself leg locked in the centre of the room, entirely suspicious and not in the least willing to take something that didn't belong to me.

I'd been cured of that stupid calling.

I'd made a promise to quit my unsuccessful career as a thief.

So ignore him.

My hands balled, and I nodded.

I would do that.

He'd requested a task, but for once, I wouldn't obey.

I wouldn't steal anything. I refused to do it again.

Turning in place, I held my chin higher, happy with my decision to ignore Elder even though I still struggled with outright insubordination.

A figure captured my gaze, slamming my heart into a brick wall. I levitated for a second as every muscle jumped.

Holy hell.

The man in the door frame remained cloaked in shadow; a slight chuckle filled the space. "Sorry, I thought you saw me."

Instantly, biting needles and creepy crawly legs worked over my skin.

Safe or dangerous?

Nice or Nasty?

Either way, I was alone with a strange man in an empty room in an unknown house surrounded by masked guests.

No.

My heart shook its head violently, deciding this scenario couldn't be permitted. Not again.

I would gladly accept my shortcomings about crowds and foreign spaces. I would work on my leftover flaws from my past.

But not here.

Not now.

Backing up, I glanced quickly over my shoulder to another exit that led to somewhere I didn't know. It would be somewhere in the hall at least—somewhere away from this stranger, sparkling diamonds, and potential threat. "I, eh…I was just leaving."

My feet sweated in my high heels, making me stumble. My

hands clutched my voluptuous skirts, wishing I could tear them off and *run*.

The man stepped forward, pushing his hands into his tux trousers. He shook his head, his mask quivering a little. "No need to worry. I mean you no harm."

I quit retreating.

I recognised him now he'd stepped into the light. Diamonds painted tiny rainbows over his black attire making him seem almost dreamlike.

The host of this masquerade.

Jethro Hawk.

I looped my fingers together to hide the residue shakes from his arrival. "Mr. Hawk, I'm sorry you startled me. I was just admiring—"

He tilted his head with a sharp smile. "I know what you were doing."

He can't possibly know.

I giggled. I never giggled.

I positively hated the way he made me nervous and jumpy and so aware every exchange was so much *more*. He wasn't just here to discuss diamonds, just like he wasn't just a man who'd inherited his family's fortune.

He was someone I didn't trust.

Even Elder, when he first stole me, didn't make me this uncomfortable.

Coming toward me, Jethro plucked a mid-size diamond from a tray and tossed it in his palm. "You're not here to admire." He gave me a dark look through his mask. "Are you?"

I shrugged. "Of course, I am. That and hiding from the crowds."

"Ah, yes. I seem to remember you saying you'd return to the ball and listen to music—"

"Am I not allowed to change my mind?" My fingers twitched in my skirts.

"Everyone has the right to change their mind; although, you'd already changed yours while lying to Prest."

How could he possibly know that?

I swallowed hard, determined not to let him see how rattled he made me.

"Why would you voluntarily go back into something you hated?" He cocked his head. "You're avoiding the ballroom just like I am, though for different reasons. There was no need to lie."

"Who said anything about lying?" I narrowed my eyes, desperate to turn this strange conversation onto him and ask what his reasons were for avoiding the very guests he'd invited. I couldn't see him being afraid of anything—not with his title and majestic hall and incredible family.

He didn't move, watching me far too perceptively.

The silence stretched on and on, adding more flutters to my belly. I couldn't stand it. "Well…I suppose, despite my reluctance to mingle, I've been rude enough." Moving toward the exit, I shot him a thin smile. "It was a pleasure to see you again. Thank you for your hospitality."

I needed to get away. I didn't like the nervous bubbles in my blood. I didn't like being watched as if he knew so much more than he should. And I definitely didn't enjoy the way he came off so cultured while my instincts whispered he wasn't always so well behaved.

I had an indescribable need to find Elder and sail away on the Phantom.

The salty waves of the sea had infected me just as they'd infected him. The steady firmness of soil beneath my feet was no longer comforting. I wanted the constant ebb and flow and freedom found from the movable sea.

"He loves you, you know."

I slammed to a stop, scarcely breathing.

"I think you know that, but I doubt it's because he's told you."

Turning slowly, I faced him with wide eyes. "How do you know he loves me? Did he talk to you about me?" How else could this stranger know the inner thoughts of the man I'd fallen for?

Jethro shook his head with a languid elegance. "He spoke, yes, but not in the verbal sense." Moving closer, he stopped a couple of feet away, giving me the sense of privacy while creating an intimate space between us. "I made a promise a long time ago not to eavesdrop on people. It's bad for me and the person who catches my interest. However, I also can't stand by and not tell the truth when neither party is doing so."

His lips quirked almost in apology. "Prest loves you as much as I love my wife. He's wracked with it, tormented by it, so fucking twisted with it, he's drowning in guilt for something he's done." He cocked his head. "I have no right to ask...but what has he done?"

I bristled, standing up for Elder while this man believed he could be capable of harm. "He's done nothing."

"Someone has done something." He scanned me head to toe. "You speak, too. Fairly loudly, I might add."

I crossed my arms. "I've hardly said anything to you."

He merely smirked and looked at the diamond as he balanced it over his knuckles before capturing it in his palm. "If he wasn't the one who hurt you, who did?"

My heart stood still, poised like a deer ready to bound into the safety of bushes. "Why do you think anyone has hurt me?"

His gaze hardened. "Are you saying they didn't?"

"I'm not in the habit of lying—even if you think I am. Nor am I in the habit of telling such things to strangers."

He nodded respectfully. "And I'm not in the usual habit of prying into people's privacy. My apologies."

I huffed, unwilling to forgive him and this crazy conversation.

Clearing his throat, he held out the diamond. "Please...take this."

I uncrossed my arms, letting them fall by my side. *"What?"*

"Please," he urged. "Take it."

My hand came up, accepting the gem before I could argue. I expected it to be warm from his touch, but it was just as cool as the others glittering on the table unloved. He'd given it to me but why? Perhaps it was to borrow, to hold, to put it back with its brothers and sisters.

I turned toward a trestle, ready to drop the gemstone onto a tray.

He shook his head. "Don't. It's for you."

"For me?" My mouth hung wide. "You're *giving* me a diamond?"

"The diamond is for him. The gift is for you."

My head ached trying to keep up with him. "What…what do you mean?"

"I mean the task he set you."

My veins turned to solid ice. "How do you know about that?" My skin broke out in goosebumps, matching the ice in my blood. Was this man telepathic? There was no other explanation for his knowing about Elder's sinful request of a robbery.

What is going on here?

He stepped back, placing his hands into his pockets. "I overhead him in the corridor. He told you to steal a diamond."

My cheeks flared with heat. "Oh, my God, of *course*." My insides gushed with relief for a rational explanation. "I'm so sorry. I wasn't going to…I swear. I was about to leave when you—" I dropped the diamond onto the closest tray, opening my hands wide in evidence of returning what wasn't mine. "There, see…it's back where it belongs."

Footsteps sounded behind Jethro. He didn't turn to see our visitor, but his entire body relaxed, his mouth became less taut, his shoulders less tense. "Hello, Nila. I was just having a conversation with our guest here."

His wife glided into the room with her swan and raven dress. She could've been on a catwalk with how stunning and modelesque she appeared. I had no doubt she'd designed the dress she wore, just as she'd designed mine. She was a magician with cloth and organza. "Jethro, I thought we agreed you wouldn't terrify anyone."

He chuckled as she slotted herself into him and kissed his cheek.

"Not terrifying. Merely tormenting." He tilted his chin at me. "Ms. Pimlico here won't take the diamond I gave her."

"Ah yes, the one Mr. Prest told her to steal."

"You heard that, too?" I asked, mortified.

Nila nodded. "Hard not to when a man's voice carries as much pain as yours does."

The muscles in my back relaxed a little. So *that* was how Jethro had known things about us. He must be a dialect master or hidden body language expert.

My God, what my mother would do to study him and learn his skills at reading people.

Jethro wrapped an arm around Nila, his fingers sinking into her dress as if touching her wasn't just about love but also about support.

She glanced at him with such adoration in her eyes, I was uneasy at intruding.

Tearing his gaze back to me, Jethro murmured, "Take the diamond, Pimlico. It's yours. Trade it for the item Mr. Prest had my staff urgently create." Guiding his wife toward the exit behind them, he added, "Also, my advice…if you love him back, I wouldn't wait for him to screw up whatever you have. It's been my experience that men overthink such things. Sometimes, all it takes is for a woman to show them that no matter how bad things are, forgiveness is easy if there is love."

Nila smiled at me, a mixture of excitement and understanding on her face. "Whatever it is my husband mentioned to you, trust him. Talk to your man, or if that doesn't work…seduce him."

Laughing quietly with their heads bowed, they left the room leaving me alone once again with their priceless stones.

Only now, I didn't have the task of stealing. I had the momentous quest of accepting a diamond that'd been gifted.

I truly didn't want to claim it.

But now I felt rude if I didn't.

Would they know if I left it?

Would they care if I did?

So many rainbow pebbles were scattered around the room, I doubted they'd even know.

As I headed toward the exit, I scooped up the diamond and clutched it tight.

Whatever Jethro meant about Elder loving me, whatever wrong he believed Elder had done...I couldn't permit it to continue.

Elder left me at the prison because he thought I hated him for making me speak. He'd heard what I'd said to my mother about Alrik wanting to control my mind and twisted it onto his own actions.

He wasn't innocent in that regard.

He *had* forced me to talk.

He *had* layered me with ultimatums and timelines.

But he'd done it all while falling in love with me.

He loves me...

I drifted through the door in a trance.

Was it wise to trust Jethro's declaration? How could a complete stranger know?

But he was right—Elder *was* overthinking and ruining what was simple between us.

Love was simple.

It was *life* that made it complicated.

And I was done waiting for him to figure it out.

I'd find the courage to ask him if he loved me because I loved him, and it wasn't some sort of platonic or patriotic or problematic kind of love.

It was honest and true and completely entwined with lust.

I loved him as my friend and protector.

I loved him as my romantic partner.

I loved him as any wife would love her husband.

If I could stare him in the eyes and make him believe that...maybe then he'd be able to accept whatever he was running from.

Jethro's voice repeated as I floated down the corridor beneath massive gold-stitched tapestries: *"He loves you, you know."*

As much as I would love confirmation from Elder, I didn't need it.

I *knew* he loved me every time he touched me. I felt it in his stare, his touch, his voice, his kiss. Even in his refusal and rage.

I knew he loved me every time he apologised or pushed me away or hurt my feelings by trying to protect me even when we both *throbbed* with barely restrained desire.

I knew he loved me before *he* knew.

He loved me.

I loved him.

I didn't need anyone else to tell me.

I know.

I trust.

It's true.

He loves me…

And that was the most incredible thing of all.

ELDER

I FOUND PIM drifting down the corridor with her hand clutched tight and a faraway look upon her face. Her mask hid yet more of her secrets; her dress draping her in the many bruises she'd survived.

Once again, the drive to know her thoughts ripped through me. Questions demanded to be asked. An interrogation whispered to be performed.

Her crown mask drove me insane. I hated that it hid parts of her from me. I despised that her stunning face was barred.

I knew my tension was due to my racing, complicated brain, but I couldn't stop blaming her for doing this to me. For getting inside my heart where I had no defences left. For making me fall when I couldn't afford to.

I would never be free of her; therefore, I deserved to know all of her. But if I was to ever know all of her, I would have to pry her secrets out one by one.

And I'd made an oath never to take what wasn't mine again.

No matter the pain.

No matter the pressure.

I would stand by my decision to love her but from a distance. Sex would only undermine my control. I wouldn't be able to stop myself from rifling through her memories. I wouldn't be able to stop myself period.

Add any more temptation or closeness between us and I had no doubt I would break all my promises and be just like the monsters of her past.

Slamming to a stop, I waited for her to look up and see me.

It took a few steps; her eyes focused on something I couldn't understand before she blinked and came to a halt. "Elder." The parts of her beautiful face not covered by her mask switched to a sensual smile.

I became instantly hard.

"I was just coming to find you." Her fingers tightened over whatever it was she held.

Where had she been? Who had she encountered? Had she done what I'd asked?

Please tell me she didn't.

"I'm sorry for asking you to steal again, Pim." Unlocking my knees, I ignored my instantaneous desire for her and stalked forward. Curling my hands, I made a conscious effort not to reach for her or bark questions about what she was thinking before I found her.

Was it this house? Was it the tapestries and histories whispering down its many halls? Or had something happened while I was gone? Something I couldn't control or prevent by leaving her alone?

The box inside my tux—the box meant for her—turned into an anchor weighing me down. The breathlessness in my lungs made it seem as if I were drowning on dry land. I should've glanced at the craftsmanship of Hawk's jewellers. I should've studied the gift before giving it. For all I knew, it could be a terrible tragedy and huge mistake.

Meeting her in the middle of the cavernous corridor, I stopped myself before I could touch her. As long as I kept physical distance, I could maintain propriety and fairness.

Unfortunately, she didn't operate under such self-denying rules. Leaning forward, she captured my hand with cool fingers, smiled gently as she uncurled my fist, then dropped a glittering diamond onto my palm.

Ah, shit.

She nodded resolutely as the diamond rolled a little in my hold. "There. All yours."

She'd stolen again.

All because I'd asked.

Goddammit.

My shoulders slumped with remorse instead of pride. "I'd hoped you wouldn't."

Her green gaze met mine. "You did?"

Clenching my fingers around the diamond, I hated myself for the added stress and torment I'd layered her with. "Never again, Pim. I won't ask anything of you that you're not comfortable with."

Including sex or secrets or anything else inappropriate.

I would atone from here on out.

A soft smile twitched her lips. "I didn't steal it."

I ran a thumb over the facets of the stone. "This is real. How else am I holding it if you didn't steal it?"

Her eyes tangled with things I hadn't been a part of. "I admit I wasn't going to. I was going to disobey you. But as I headed out of the room, Mr. Hawk found me."

My back stiffened at the thought of her alone with the owner of this estate.

"He told me to take it." She rolled her shoulders as if negating other things he'd told her—things I desperately wanted to know. "So I did. It's yours. Given freely, not taken."

Why had he given it to her?

Why did she carry a glow that hadn't been there before? Christ, I couldn't do this anymore.

The questions were too much. The need too strong.

"Come." Grabbing her wrist, I tugged her forward as my legs chewed up the ground. The music from the ball was too close. The lilts of laughter and people too near. My head ached, and my cock throbbed. I was losing to my lust, and Pim was making it so damn hard to say no. "We need to talk. Alone."

She didn't speak as I dragged her away from the strings of music, storming down passageways I'd never seen. Scanning rooms left and right, I had no idea what I was looking for. Drawing rooms and day rooms. Parlours and solars. On and on until a quaint sitting room appeared with a large, oversized paisley couch, warm floor lamps, and a crackling fireplace with fawns and fairies carved into its mantle.

It had space to pace. It had privacy to put myself back together again.

Pulling Pim inside, I closed the door and twisted the old-fashioned key resting in the lock.

I didn't expect the mechanism to work in such an old hall, but it turned as effortlessly as if it were new. Having a barricade—a lockable barricade—between us and the rest of the occupants of Hawksridge allowed me to finally suck in a breath and relax a little.

The only person I tolerated was Pimlico. And she was making my life intolerable.

Ideally, my façade would hold until we were back on the Phantom. I would wait until we left port and sailed away from human society. I would ensure we were safe and armed and had a joint to calm the irrational clawing in my veins.

But as she drifted deeper into the room and her dress whispered on the carpet, and the red of her mask obscured all the pieces I needed from her, I struggled to stay human.

I forgot how to ignore the fascination and compulsions of my brain.

I regressed enough that images of sex and nakedness and pleasure were more than just a temptation but an outright desperation.

My fingers clutched at the stolen-donated diamond. I struggled to understand the truth. To guess how she was truly feeling. Why she was softer and quieter in the way she studied me? Why did her eyes glow with conviction as well as hesitation?

It was as if she'd come to some conclusion while we were apart—a conclusion I didn't know and couldn't ask for.

My hands trembled as I shoved the heavy rock into my pants pocket then pulled out the box from my blazer. She'd given me a diamond on my request. She'd given me everything I ever fucking wanted, and it still wasn't enough.

The guilt would eat me alive if I waited another minute.

I had to give her something to balance the scales in my deformed brain and fight the overbearing lust quickly turning into wildfire inside me.

I would give her my gift.

I would make tonight equal.

And then I would take her home where tomorrow was a new day with stronger rules and regulations.

Pim looked at me over her shoulder as her fingers trailed over the polished lacquer of a nesting table, glided around marble busts of men long since deceased, and touched ancient easels with half-finished needlepoint. She never took her eyes off me as she floated around the room, staring in a dare, in acknowledgement, in agreement that everything we'd been running from had found us here.

Somehow, there was no more road, no more avoiding the crushing weight of seduction.

She knew it.

I knew it.

I didn't understand how it'd happened.

Why here, why now?

What was the catalyst to this suddenly heavy, heady invitation to forget, to let go, to be free?

No.

Shaking my head, I tore my gaze from hers.

That wasn't what this was about.

This was about balancing our relationship.

She'd given me something. Therefore, I had to give her something.

I had every intention of preventing the rampaging,

quickening desire from making me do something we'd both regret.

The box creaked in my hands as I gripped it hard. All I needed to do was give her this so we were even. So she wasn't in my debt for stealing me the diamond. So I wasn't in her debt for all the pieces I'd stolen this far.

A gift given purely because she was the most beautiful creature on earth.

Without a word, she settled on the inviting couch.

Her dress billowed around her, filling the room with the soft rustle of satin. The multi-coloured paisley print clashed with her bruised gown, making it seem like she'd turned joy into torment.

I wanted to stay on my side of the room. I wanted walls between us and chains around me. But I had to trust I had self-control. To be human long enough to ignore the body-breaking desire and get her back on the Phantom where she belonged.

Swallowing hard, I moved stiffly toward her. With aching joints from denying what I truly wanted, I sat slowly on the couch. It enveloped me, cradling us both, the age-worn cushions compacting together so our knees touched and gravity tried to sprawl us onto one another.

Christ, touching her…even with miles of dress between us was enough to make me shatter.

We locked eyes but didn't say a word.

We both fought to stay sitting and not give up on the rules we'd wrapped ourselves in. I *desperately* wanted to kiss her.

She licked her lips, her gaze latching onto my mouth.

I swallowed a groan as everything else faded. Nothing else had the same weight or importance as kissing her.

It was *everything.*

Kiss her.

I swayed closer.

She breathed quicker.

My heart burned with need.

Kiss her…

Fuck, it was the hardest thing I'd ever done—hovering in that tingling magic of an almost-kiss.

Kiss her…

I can't.

It took everything in me, it cost every pain, but I pulled back. The way my moods were tonight, I couldn't guarantee I could stop at one kiss.

I know I can't.

One kiss would turn to two.

Two would turn to ten.

Ten would turn to me inside her and every rule snapped and broken.

I pinched the bridge of my nose, counting my breaths, focusing on my heartbeat.

Most of the evening, I'd focused on things I could control. Counting the drapes, the mosaics on the floor, the champagne glasses discarded around the room. Little tricks I'd long since mastered to stay sane.

Counting wouldn't help me now.

Nothing could help me.

The box.

Give her the box.

Even that didn't offer the same safety as it once did.

Shit, I should've stayed standing. I should've thrown it to her from across the room.

Silence stretched, growing thicker by the second as I pushed the long rectangle from my lap and onto hers. I ripped my hand back before I could crush her dress in my fingers and hoist it high. Before I could strip her bare and take her. "Open it."

She still didn't speak as if the swirling desire had stolen her vocal cords. She reminded me all over again of the woman I'd saved. The slave with her sliced tongue and tattered bravery.

I shook from passion and pain. I crippled with need and nastiness.

Christ…

Her fingers quaked a little as she stroked the velvet casing before cracking it open. One hand flew to cover her mouth while the other quaked harder, distorting the jewellery inside. "Oh…"

How could one little sound reach into my trousers and fist me?

How could one woman reach into my chest and rip out my goddamn heart?

A tightness wrapped around my neck that had nothing to do with the awkwardness of giving someone a gift or the agony of preventing lust from winning.

Did she like it?

Did she hate it?

Would she wear it, or was it too steeped in painful memories?

The tightness dropped into my heart, wrapping bands of cold anxiety around the smoking muscle. The same pressure entered my lungs and legs and fingertips. A pressure demanding I touch her, kiss her, comfort her.

What sort of lover was I when I couldn't even kiss her forehead without fear of demanding more? What sort of man was I when I couldn't control myself around the woman he loved more than anything?

I pursed my lips as she touched the bracelet. My hands clenched together, finding another thread of strength to sit beside her and not explode into a million pieces of want.

I needn't have worried about the Hawk's craftsmanship. It was as if he'd reached into my brain and stolen the idea directly from the source.

Pim's fingers ghosted over the bright gold pennies dangling from the bracelet. Not copper or brass or any other unprecious metal. These pennies were pure gold to resemble how, even at the start when I'd tried to give her a penny for her thoughts, she was worth every wealth in the world to me.

Inlaid in the face of the perfectly stamped pennies sat a diamond. The glittering stones distorted the pennies' face, changing the numerical value from one cent to untold value.

Because that was how I saw her.

Her freedom was priceless.

Her secrets were invaluable.

Every part of her treasured and coveted.

No matter how much money I had or how much time I could steal, I could never show her how much I'd fallen in love with her.

Her eyes glossed with shock as she looked at me—truly looked at me and saw past my guards and barriers to the agony I was in. "I don't know what to say."

Even my teeth ached from sitting so close and not having her. "Then don't say anything at all."

"But…I have to. I have to find a way to thank you. To show you how grateful—"

Gravity was the last element to smash my self-control. The couch cushions, long since broken in by prior sitters, collapsed beneath me. My hipbone collided with hers; our legs flush against each other.

And that was it.

My hand ignored my half-hearted command not to touch and soared up to capture her cheek. "I'm the one who's grateful."

"But—"

"No buts. I need to say this…" My fingers tightened on her skin, already craving more. I denied those urges. I hadn't planned on this. I didn't want to strip myself down to the bone. But holding her cheek, staring into her mask-rimmed eyes with rubies dangling like tears beneath, I couldn't hold back anymore.

"I need to tell you how sorry I am. That I ran from the prison because I finally saw how you must see me." I shook my head in dismay. "After so long in silence, why did you give me what you never gave him? Why let me do the exact thing he was trying to do?"

She frowned as if in a dream she couldn't understand or

control. "You were never like him. Ever."

"I was. I *am*. I told you at the start I was after your mind rather than your body. I didn't know why at the time. I blamed it on my need to conquer things I didn't understand, but now I know different."

Her skin heated beneath my palm. "Know what?"

Running my thumb over her bottom lip, I whispered, "Isn't it obvious?"

The tip of her tongue tasted my finger, sending a full convulsion through me. Her voice echoed with every desire I felt. "Not to me."

I squeezed my eyes, fighting every bellow to kiss, to touch, to take. I'd started this. I had to finish it. I had to tell her the truth. "It's because I'm in love with you."

She gasped, jerking in my hold.

I could stop there.

I could kiss her and show her through actions just how true that was. But now I'd opened the vault, I had to tell her everything.

Everything.

Pressing my forehead against hers, our masks crinkled and joined. Feathers from hers and silk from mine, both of us disguised but still so aware of who the other was. So aware that we'd found each other, despite all the shit in the world.

My voice thickened as she grabbed my wrist, holding me while I held her. "I think I fell in love with you the first moment I saw you. When you refused to shake my hand. When you stood naked and daring me to hurt you. When you pushed away my penny for your thoughts. Fuck, Pim…"

She trembled, the penny bracelet on her lap dancing with light from the fire. My voice reverberated around the room, not fading. The damning words that I was in love with her echoing in every corner.

"I fell in love with you when you swam with me in the dark. I fell when you shared the storm with me. I fell so many fucking times for you, Pimlico, and I don't know how many times I still have to fall."

I scrambled for other things to say—things to fill the terrible silence of her not saying anything. I was weak. I'd just flayed open my heart, and I didn't know if she was happy or upset.

Pulling back a little, I studied her.

For once, there were no answers or secrets for me to claim.

Caressing her cheek, I dropped my gaze to the penny-diamonds nestled in her skirts. "I just told you I'm in love with you, yet you say nothing. Is my loving you a bad—"

Tearing her face from my hold, she slammed the jewellery box closed, tossed the bracelet onto the floor, and crushed her mouth against mine.

One second, we were separate.

The next, we were one.

Heat.

Wet.

Connection.

My brain forgot letters and language and reverted to touch and taste.

Goddammit, she shouldn't have done that.

I lost it.

Well and truly lost it.

My self-control from the past few days broke, and I kissed her back.

Fuck, I kissed her back.

Grabbing her jaw, I angled her closer. Her mouth opened, her tongue welcomed, and we fell together. She tumbled backward; I tumbled forward, smothering her on the couch.

Our mouths fought, our tongues danced, our breath threaded together. I'd never been so diabolical in the way I attacked, and she'd never been so ferocious. We battled, we fought, our legs tangled in her dress, her hands everywhere at once.

I kissed her deep.

I kissed her hard.

My hips thrust of their own accord as I climbed on top of her and pressed every inch of my agonising body against hers.

I needed her.

Goddammit, I needed her.

Our lips slipped and bruised. Our teeth nipped and gnawed. We devoured each other, uncaring about dresses and tuxes and the fact this was not our house.

Shit, this isn't our house.

We weren't free to do this here.

We weren't alone.

We weren't safe.

It was the only thing that saved her.

Saved me.

With a feral groan, I pulled away. My breathing was wild, my cock punching the waistband of my trousers. All I wanted to do was take her. Over and over again. The obsession had sparked, and no way in hell was I satisfied from one kiss.

I wouldn't be satisfied from one touch or thrust.

I wouldn't be satisfied until we both passed out from sexual exhaustion.

That can't happen.

I couldn't hurt her in that way.

Sitting up, I cradled my head in my hands, digging fingers into my temples to hold off the addiction.

The cushions shifted as Pim moved from lying to sitting. She didn't touch me even though I tensed for it. For the longest moment, she stared while I kept my eyes locked on the rose and gold carpet beneath my shiny leather dress shoes.

Our kiss was a living, breathing thing, far too alive and just waiting for a spark to rekindle.

My muscles begged me to grab her and finish what we started. Screw the fact that this wasn't our home. Fuck the fact that hundreds of guests partied down the hall.

But I couldn't because who knew what state I'd be in if I let go. If someone heard Pim's screams when I took her again and again. If a Hawk family member had to break down their own door to save Pim from my addictive rutting.

The pain of not having her was brutal. But it was better than the pain of taking her with no way of stopping.

Pim rustled beside me, but I didn't look. I focused on the swirls of gold thread, following the handmade carpeting—

But then the carpeting was obscured by red and blue satin as Pim slid to her knees in front of me, ducked beneath the cage of my arms and wrapped hers around my neck. "You just told me you're in love with me, and you only kiss me once?" Her voice caressed my lips as she added strength to her touch, guiding me down toward her. "Is kissing me such a bad—"

It was my turn not to let her finish.

My arms lashed forward, crushing her to me as my lips crashed against hers.

She moaned as I dragged her closer, her on her knees before me, the couch digging into her belly as I dragged her harder between my legs.

This kiss was wilder than the last. And she knew why. She knew my self-control had broken before and only a quick patch up of glue remained. I had precisely three seconds to kiss her before I had to break away.

One second, I kissed her deep and loving.

Second second, I kissed her rough and condemning.

Third second, I kissed her savage and begging.

Then I pulled away and pushed her away at the same time. I managed to do it.

I kept my promise.

I pinched my eyes closed so I wouldn't see the red wetness of her mouth or the flushed desire on her skin. I kept them shut so I wouldn't lock onto everything I wanted and say fuck off to the consequences.

Even without vision, it didn't stop her breath from hitting my ears with rampant need or her voice wobbling with lust. "Please, El…don't stop."

I swallowed a tattered groan. "Don't ask me that, little

mouse."

Her small hands landed on my thighs, wrenching every sinful craze to the surface. "Please, El…" Her fingers slid up the silkiness of my tux trousers, not teasing or slowing as she cupped my erection and squeezed the twin aches of agony beneath it. "I'm telling you not to stop."

My fingers latched brutally around her hand. I meant to shove her away. I meant to chide her and stand up. I meant to end this.

Instead, I pressed her hand harder against me, making me hiss with how goddamn good it felt.

She rocked against me, her fingers fluttering with maddening intoxication.

My eyes flared wide, my jaw clenched tight, the first wave of release rippled up my length. "Stop, Pim." Even as I gave the command, I kept her hand locked against my cock, digging her touch deeper into me, finding punishment and pleasure.

"You stop." She panted. "Stop fighting this. *Us.*" Her voice filled with bite. "Stop fighting *me.*"

I was so damn close to giving in. To letting her tear down my zipper and doing whatever she damn well pleased with me. But I *loved* her. Couldn't she see that? She'd transformed from a girl I barely knew to a girl I'd do anything for. She was just as much family to me as my own flesh and blood, and I had a history of hurting my family.

Killing my family.

Fuck.

Tearing her grip away, I buckled over at the clawing emptiness inside. The lacerating lust shredding me apart. "Get away from me, Pim. We need to leave. Right now."

I struggled to stand. The room swam. My head pounded.

And still, Pim rested on her knees before me looking like the perfect sacrifice. Lips parted, cheeks flushed, eyes begging.

She undid me—life, love, and sanity.

"I'm not leaving. Not until you kiss me again." With liquid beauty, she rose from the carpet, removed her mask, and let it dangle from her fingertips. Seeing her face for the first time tonight, seeing how beautiful she was, how innocent but so worldly, was the last nail in my self-control coffin.

She needed to know.

One last warning.

She needed to understand what would happen if she did this.

Ripping off my own mask, I threw it on the floor. "You're pushing me too hard, Pimlico."

"I'm not pushing you hard enough." Letting go of her mask, she rested a hand on my chest. "If I was, I'd be beneath you right now, and you'd be inside me."

I shuddered, gritting my teeth against the image. "And I'd hurt you when I couldn't stop. So *you* stop. Before I can't—"

"Can't what? Fight anymore? Deny me anymore?" Her lips whispered over mine, her small frame balancing on her tiptoes, guiding me into temptation. "Give in, Elder." Leaning close, she murmured in my ear, "I've never said these words to anyone. I never thought I would. But then you went and fell in love with me, and I fell in love with you, and you made it possible for me to say them." She swallowed before licking my earlobe with her tongue.

I convulsed. I almost came.

"All of this is because of you and me and the undeniable need to be together; I can say such things because you brought me back to life and therefore you have to honour them."

My ears burned to hear the things she could say now but couldn't say before. I positively died to hear them.

But she paused, panting against my cheek. Denying me at the worst possible time.

I shouldn't buy into her tricks, but I was too far gone. Too lust drowned. "What things…"

She kissed my cheek. Her fingernails dug into my chest. She inhaled quick and confident and with a commanding whisper utterly annihilated me. "Fuck me, Elder Prest. Be a man and *fuck me*."

340

And that was the end.

There was no more fighting.

No more negotiation.

No more right or wrong.

I lost.

Obsession won.

She won.

My body moved of its own accord, freed from the prison I'd put myself under. My hands latched around her waist, my fingers digging into her ribcage. "You just had to keep pushing, didn't you?"

A flicker of worry crossed her face before rebellion replaced it. "Yes."

I crushed her to me, wrapping her tight in my embrace, claiming her mouth with savage cruelty.

I kissed her possessively, brutally, quickly, callously.

I kissed her in gratefulness for shoving me past decency.

I kissed her in rage for proving I had no control.

"Fuck me, Elder." Her lips moved under mine, whimpering as my arms banded tighter. "Please, fuck me. I *need* you to fuck me."

"Oh, Pim…" Tearing her away, I turned and threw her on the couch behind me. "You never should have said such things."

Standing over her, cock hard, heart fast, mind a mess, I growled. "I'll fuck you. I'll fuck you until you can't stand to be fucked anymore.

"And then I'll fuck you again. And again. Because there's no earthly way I can stop now."

Pimlico

HE FELL ON me.

That was the only way to describe it.

He stopped fighting.

He tumbled.

He trampled me between desire and cushions and tore my legs apart beneath my dress to wedge his hard heat between them.

And then he kissed me.

And it was different from all the other kisses in the world.

Different to how he kissed me in Monte Carlo. Different to how he kissed me on the Phantom.

Different good.

Different bad.

Just *different*.

His lips were hot. His tongue wet. His teeth hard. His breath fast. His taste downright addicting.

I'd instigated this. I'd finally been the one to demand sex, not the other way around, and the thrill inside quickly faded for paralyzing passion.

I'd told him to fuck me.

I'd used crude language to shatter his final restraint.

And I was glad.

I was ecstatic beneath him.

I was joyous pinned below.

There was no fear of what would happen or thoughts about my healing. I would fuck Elder as surely as he would fuck me.

This was mutual, not one sided.

I wasn't afraid.

I'm not afraid.

I was breathless as he kissed me deeper.

I was squirmy and hot and wet and achy and so, so impatient for more.

There was no holding back this time. No ropes around his hands to prevent him from hitching up my gown. His touch messy and jerky as he gathered handfuls of satin, up, up, up, billowing around my waist, letting air kiss my thighs and hipbones. No chains to stop his fingers from clawing at the garters and blood red lingerie the two women from Social Art had dressed me in.

Nothing to tamper his incredible touch or slow down our manic pace. This wasn't making love or even the crude term of fucking—the same term I'd thrown in his face as a dare and demand.

No, this was urgency at its finest.

It infected him and me.

It was all around us, blocking us from the world, turning this room into ours and this moment into forever.

As Elder yanked at the lace between my legs, snapping off garters without caring, tearing pantyhose without looking, growling at the miles of fabric between us, I fumbled with his clasp and zipper on his trousers.

There were no sweet words or whispered sentiments. No gentle kisses or sensual seduction.

We had one goal.

One need.

Join.

Join.

Join.

The metal clasp came away; his zipper caught on my dress only for him to grab it and yank it down with a rip of cloth.

I had no idea what broke. I didn't know if my dress was in pieces, or his trousers were in shreds, but it didn't matter.

Nothing mattered.

All that mattered was

him

inside

me.

Nothing else was in my mind; no other thought permitted in my body.

I needed him more than I needed water or food or air.

I needed him to stretch me, fill me, bruise me.

I needed him to claim every dark part of me and bring it into the light because I *wanted* this. I wanted to be sexual. I wanted to be a deviant. I wanted to be wanton and abandoned and utterly free to scream as he entered me and bite him when he thrust.

The overpowering lust thickened and heated and burned. *God*, it burned.

Faster.

Quicker.

Hotter.

Our hands fumbled to the same command, tearing off clothing, pushing away barriers.

I couldn't explain it or even bother to understand it, but if I didn't have him inside, connected and joined, I would die.

Literally and spiritually die.

I'm dying.

I'm gasping.

I'm so...so...

"Elder...now." I arched, seeking his cock, revelling in the pure pleasure of being myself. Of not second-guessing or censoring. Of not worrying about fists or abuse. Of not being afraid of rape or molestation.

Elder was perfect.

He was mine.

He's not inside me.

"Elder..." I clawed at him, opening my legs wide, my head falling back as I moaned my desperation. *Please...*"

"Fuck, little mouse. You're driving me insane." His voice mingled with kisses as his mouth latched on mine. My lips turned raw from his five o'clock shadow. The sting of his affection righteous with the pain in my core demanding to be addressed.

Now.

Now.

God, now!

My fingers worked on his trousers, pushing and shoving them down his waist. My fingernails scratched him in their rush. My temper snapping at my insides at how much longer I had to wait.

His back bowed as I pushed faster, messier, completely out of my mind with need. The moment his trousers were mid-thigh, I battled the elastic cotton of his boxer-briefs.

He groaned as his cock sprung free.

I cried out as I finally, *finally* touched hot skin. Finally, *finally* caressed naked and hard him.

He shuddered as I grasped his erection, pumping it hard. A primal growl fell from his lips as he kissed me mercilessly, ripping my knickers to my knees then contorting himself to drag them off one foot.

They caught on the heel of my blood red stilettos only for him to tear off the shoe along with the lingerie. Both vanished over his shoulder, never to be seen again.

Once, I'd believed I was Sleeping Beauty awoken by his kiss and Snow White freed from the poisoned apple. Now, I was Cinderella missing a glass slipper, but unlike that fairy-tale, I knew exactly who my prince was and precisely what I intended to do with him.

I wriggled deeper beneath him, spreading my legs

unashamedly as he pressed heavily on top of me.

His hips scorched my inner thighs.

His lips never stopped kissing.

His hand disappeared under my dress.

His tongue never stopped dancing.

His fingers latched around his erection.

His mouth never stopped claiming mine.

His knuckles bruised my tender skin as he arched his hips and searched for my core.

And then we both froze.

Indescribable moment.

Blissful. Breathtaking. Brutal.

We hovered in that second with the tip of him at the entrance of me.

A second where nothing and no one could hurt us.

And then he thrust.

I moaned.

He groaned.

The world fractured in two.

I was used to violence. I was used to being taken quickly. I was used to being empty then full. Alone then ridden hard and fast.

What I wasn't used to was the lightning bolt of perfection as Elder stabbed inside me vicious and completely unapologetic. I wasn't used to my reaction as my legs scissored around his hips, and I arched up to meet him, brutalising us with bruises, demanding more, commanding him to go harder, faster, deeper.

It felt so right.

So good.

So true.

More.

More.

More.

Our mouths spread wide against each other, struggling to breathe through the indescribable pleasure of joining, struggling to stay alive with oversensitive flesh and scattered minds.

We ceased existing as our bodies adjusted to being joined and heat rushed from him to me in the form of heartbeats and understanding that we were together now, but this wasn't over.

The race had just started.

If I didn't have my suspicions about Elder's addiction, I might've become scared. Terrified at the black gleam in his gaze and the determined set of his brow. This wasn't just sex to him. This was a competition to be bested only to be undertaken again and again.

I was willing to be that competition—to allow him to use me to find his release with the hope of proving him wrong.

I believed he could stop.

He believed he couldn't.

At this point, I didn't care who was right.

He thrust again, and all my thoughts turned to willow-the-wisps.

He drove into me, burying me into the soft cushions, clamping his teeth into my neck.

I rode with him, flying up, tilting my throat so he could bite me harder. At no point did I suffer panic or terror or anything but the overwhelming sensation of being owned by Elder and being utterly contented by it.

His pace turned frantic.

Thrust.

Thrust.

Thrust.

The couch bumped and scraped on the carpet. My dress fluttered around us, spilling to the floor in red and blue waves. His black hair clung to his forehead, sweat decorating his brow as we fucked each other with rage and frenzy.

His hips trapped a bunch of my dress against my clit and every thrust made sparkling promises build in number.

My spine tickled.

My hips loosened.

My legs tightened for the release they whispered.

I was close.

So close.

So fast.

So ready.

Elder switched from mayhem to inferno, his hands locking in my hair, holding me prisoner as his hips drove faster, harder. "I'm sorry. Fuck, I'm sorry." He rode me as if the seconds counting down were seconds to his death.

He didn't touch me. He didn't kiss me. He just fucked me as I'd dared him.

Fucked me because he had to.

Fucked me because we had no choice.

And with each thrust, I climbed higher, teetering on the pedestal of an orgasm I furiously wanted.

My eyes popped from the pressure. My head ached from the need. My insides knotted and tangled, ready to explode in delirium.

Only, he reached the finish line before I did.

Throwing his head back, his spine hollowed as he thrust again, and a gruff animalistic groan wrenched from his lips. Warm wetness spilled deep inside me, making my body clench for things it knew it could never have.

Collapsing on top of me, he breathed hard in my ear.

He didn't speak, and I didn't mention how tingly and tight I was—on the knife edge of release. I wasn't worried. I would come. He wasn't finished.

I waited.

I waited some more as his heartbeat clamoured against mine.

I worried I might have it wrong.

That Elder had somehow figured out how to sleep with me once and only once. Perhaps that was why he went so furiously fast—to get it over with before he truly gave in.

Disappointment swelled in my chest; a touch of anger that I hadn't come and probably wouldn't if this truly was a fast coupling for him to get control again.

Only, his cock never softened inside me.

His body never moved to stop crushing mine.

His fingers never unlatched from my hair.

Slowly, his hips rocked again, gently at first with a hiss hinting at sensitivity. "Did you think I was finished with you, little mouse?" His growl seared my blood, my nipples, my clit.

I shivered as he drove upward, nudging against the innermost part of me, bruising me with pleasure.

"I'm not finished." His fingers tightened in my hair. "I'm not done." His teeth nipped at my jaw. "I'll never be satisfied while fucking you."

My sizzling orgasm sat up and paid attention. "Take me. As many times as you need." My hands walked down his back, loving the rippling power of his muscles as he drove again and again. "Once isn't enough."

His eyes gleamed. "You want more of this?" He thrust up, grinding into me.

I gasped as starlight filled my vision. "Yes. God, yes." I grabbed his ass, intending to pull him harder against me. To rub against him and find my release but in one jerk he withdrew, leaving me empty and clenching for more.

"El—" I pouted and clawed the air for him to return.

His fingers grabbed my waist, plucking me effortlessly from the cushions. In one deliciously primal move, he manhandled me to the arm of the couch and pushed me against it.

I breathed hard as his hands turned to claws and tore at the tiny hooks holding my bodice in place. "I need to see you, Pim. Need to taste you."

He scratched and broke, shredding my dress as each hook and eye pinged free. The bodice slacked around my torso, quickly revealing I might've worn red knickers, garters, and stockings beneath the dress, but I wore nothing above it.

The corset was all I needed to push my breasts up.

And now that corset was ruined and hanging like torn wings at my sides.

"Christ, Pim." His eyes locked onto my breasts, his tongue darting between his lips. His head ducked, and his mouth captured my left nipple and then my right.

I stood swaying with one hand clutching his hipbone with his trousers around his thighs and the other swooping up to tangle fingers in his hair.

"Oh, God." I cried out as teeth tangled with tongue.

He kissed and suckled, drawing more tingling need through the invisible cord from core to nipple. My knees wobbled as he bit me harder then stood to his full height and kissed me just as feral.

With one hand cupping my throat, he spun me around and pushed me over the rolled top of the couch arm. Something sounding like an apology fell from his lips as his fingers pulsed around my neck. "Remember I tried to stop this and you wouldn't take no for an answer."

Sweeping up my dress, he slotted his naked hips against my ass, his hand fumbling between heavy fabric and slippery bodies to once again find my entrance.

"I tried to fight you, Pimlico, but you're just too fucking beautiful."

The head of his cock found me.

I sucked in a breath, my belly squished and lungs struggling in the prone position he'd placed me in.

"I tell you I'm in love with you and instead of accepting my gift…you make me do this to you."

I whimpered as he speared back inside me, forcing me to bend fully over the couch, thrusting so hard my toes came off the floor.

With one shoe on and the other foot balanced on tiptoe, I gave in entirely to his mania. His hands captured my breasts swinging unhindered and untrapped by my fallen bodice. His teeth nipped at the back of my neck, and my hair that had been painstakingly done by my dressers tumbled around us.

There was nothing alluring or beautiful about this moment.

He rutted into me like a monster.

And I bent over and took it.

God, I took it.

I *craved* it.

I loved how inhuman he was, how barbaric and consumed.

His thrusts were short and sharp, his grunts in time with every claiming of my body. We were untamed and messy, him driving into me and me arching back into him.

My orgasm built even stronger, a steady drumbeat in my clit and core and nipples.

I had to come.

Had to.

Had to.

Had to.

Letting the couch hold my weight, I buried my hand under my dress, fumbling and digging to find myself beneath so much frustrating fabric.

The moment my fingers found my clit, I sobbed with sex.

Sex was a noun, but here, now, it was a verb, an adjective, a living, breathing entity that filled me up and made me burst.

I didn't think about how foreign it was to touch myself after never doing such a thing. I didn't ponder on what Elder would think of me chasing my own pleasure.

All I focused on, all I *could* focus on, was the pummelling of his hard size in my pussy, the rapidly building pressure of muscles being hammered by his lust, and the spike of blissful insanity as I rubbed my clit with my fingertips.

Him and me together.

Chasing the ultimate paradise.

I wasn't programmed for soft loving. Whether a by-product of my past or I'd always been built that way, I needed to feel the thrum and not just a tickle.

I punished myself as surely as he punished me and I loved it.

Fucking loved it.

Elder grabbed my hips, holding me steady to drive into me harder. "Fuck, that's it. Christ, Pim. Make yourself come while I fuck you. Feel my cock in you. Feel me hold you down and know you can't go anywhere. You're mine. You belong to me. My cock belongs in you. Your orgasms belong to me. Everything about you belongs to me." His pace turned crazed, his sweat dripping onto my spine as he drove into me faster, harder. "Come with me, Pimlico. Come. Now. Christ…*come…*" His voice switched to a lupine growl, and I rubbed so hard, a cramp shot down my arm and into my fingers.

The pain only added another dimension.

And this time…this time, I reached the finish line before him.

I screamed loud and uncaring as the crescendo found me, rippling down my core, squeezing inner muscles, shooting me into utopia as my legs gave out and I puddled over the couch arm.

The rush of liquid heat ensured my body was ready for deeper penetration.

Elder took full advantage.

He reared up, hands clamped on my hips, burying himself as far as he could as he roared out a second release.

On and on he thrust, feeding me his pleasure.

His cock throbbed with its own heartbeat, and residual clenches from my orgasm battered both of us.

He'd taken me twice.

He'd ravaged every part of me.

I was boneless, breathless, mindless.

But it wasn't over.

Once more should be the key.

Lucky number three.

I honestly didn't know if my heart could stand another. It bashed against my ribs as if it'd torn free from veins and arteries and suffocated in a pool of pleasure.

I gasped and gulped, my hair over my face, my dress in tatters.

I believed I had a few moments of reprieve while he gathered himself together.

Not this time.

Almost angrily, Elder withdrew and stumbled away. I turned in time to see him clutching his head, shaking and mumbling, his eyes squeezed shut.

He was resplendent in a tumbled tux and glistening cock spearing out from beneath his black shirt. His trousers still clung to his muscular thighs—neither one of us nude even after two bouts of passion.

Not bothering to hide my breasts or rub at the trickle of his seed on my inner thigh, I moved toward him.

He was still hard.

Still ready.

He couldn't stop now.

Three was the magical number.

I would survive another.

I had to.

He had to.

We had to do this if my theory was ever to be tested.

Elder held up his hand. "Stop, Pim. I'm trying so fucking hard—"

"No, you stop." If he was back to fighting it, this wouldn't work. He had to give in because I needed to know if this experiment would work. If it didn't, then Jethro and Nila Hawk would stumble upon us tomorrow gasping for water and bruised beyond recognition from marathon sex all night. But if it *did* work, then we could finally find peace as well as pleasure and find a way forward we both could live with.

I got to indulge in this new side of me.

And he got to have me knowing there was an end in sight.

Come on, Elder.

Don't stop.

"I want more." Swaying toward him, I cursed the weakness of my voice—the scratch of being well used. But I wasn't lying. I *did* want more. I wanted this now, and I wanted more in the future.

I wouldn't let him ruin it.

He said I belonged to him.

Well, for the first time, I *wanted* to belong to someone, but only if I could have him in return.

He had to do what I wanted… *he has to*.

Tackling him, I climbed his body and reached for his mouth. But he grabbed my wrists in one hand and my cheeks with the other, his eyes blazing into mine. "What are you doing to me?"

"Trying to free you." Dangling in his grip, I fought to get free. "Let it happen."

"Stop."

I managed to wriggle out of his grip, swatting away his touch, and darting in to kiss him. "Fuck me, Elder Prest. You're not finished yet."

He snapped again.

This time, he fell to his knees, dragging me with him.

His mouth claimed mine, my dress whooshing up to surround us in red and blue.

Pushing aside my gown, he somehow managed to free me from the material to settle me on his lap. Our bare skin was intensely hot and slippery with combined sex and sweat.

We were no longer human, just animals desperate to mate.

Squirming on his lap, I moaned like a cat searching for cream—searching for him, entirely unshackled from propriety and self-awareness.

I was empty.

Empty.

"Fill me, fuck me…Elder…*please*."

"You're going to kill me, Tasmin."

My eyes flew open at my real name just as he stabbed up and his cock impaled me all over again—both enemy and victor over swollen-sensitive flesh.

He called me Tasmin.

He glowered as if I were a conquest as well as his mistress.

He hated me as well as loved me in that moment.

I gasped and groaned as he drove exquisitely deeper.

"This is what you get. Are you happy now? Happy that I'll just keep fucking you until I can no longer stand?" He punctured his growl with his rampaging hips, bouncing me in his arms, jerking me down to spear deep, deep, deep.

My breasts jiggled before his hands captured them, forming a bra from his fingers, squeezing me depravedly.

A barely there memory scrambled through my mind of the first time we'd had sex. He'd been on his knees, and I'd been in his lap. Only he hadn't moved when he'd entered me. He'd been rigid while I burst apart in his arms.

Now, I pushed his shoulders, causing him to clench his belly only for his legs to kick out and lie down with my pressure.

The moment he was on his back, I gave him everything he wouldn't take that first day.

"Yes, I'm happy. Yes, I'm glad you're fucking me. But now, it's my turn." Digging my fingernails into his chest, I rode him.

I took him.

I moved with him as he guided my hips to a faster beat.

I studied his face as his jaw tightened and eyes blackened and hair tangled on the carpet.

I arched and revelled in the way he locked onto my bare breasts.

I gasped and preened at how gorgeous he was wearing a rumpled tux with my dress all around him.

I rode him while he rode me, and I took back every last piece of my sexuality on the floor of Hawksridge Hall.

With our eyes locked and bodies joined, my hand vanished under my dress for the second time. I couldn't finish this without coming again. I needed to stare into his eyes and shatter. I needed him to see just how much he'd broken through my bounds and created a bold sexual lover who would never tire of him, never deny him, never ever leave him.

My dress trapped my hand, layers upon layers of satin preventing me from finding where we were joined.

Elder's jaw clenched as his nostrils flared, inhaling the scent of us, his face drenched from exhaustion. One hand left my hipbone, burrowing through my skirts, finding me swiftly.

His thumb latched onto my clit with reckless precision, burying me under an avalanche of heaven.

"Let me." His voice was a cross between a snarl and thunder.

His face turned to stone as his thumb rocked me in the perfect way and his cock drove into me in ultimate rhythm.

I gave up being self-conscious or worried or tender or shy.

I threw myself into the carnage we created, my knees heating from carpet burn; my heart well and truly expired. "Elder…El…*God*, El."

My head fell back, my eyes closed, my body swayed as my hips rocked, forcing myself down and onto him, filling me with him, consuming him, riding him, buying him, forging him to me for eternity.

I'd never been so free, so liquid, so dazed.

It was a dance.

A waltz.

A fucking on the floor with my lover panting and writhing beneath me.

"Come, Pim. Ride me." He grunted and groaned. "Fuck, yes, ride me. Take me. Fuck, I want to come. I want to watch you break apart. I want to feel you."

His face twisted into something demonic. "Ride me, Tasmin. Fucking ride me."

So I did.

Time lost all meaning as we merged into one. We no longer fought to stay in sync; we *were* in sync. Our breathing, our thoughts, our bodies, our orgasms.

We drove each other up and up and up. We drove each other insane and crazy and wild.

And when there was nowhere else to climb and nowhere

else to venture, we fell.

Ripple after ripple turned into a tide which turned into a waterfall.

His hand on my clit pushed me from orgasm to bitter splitting, and I jerked as if someone cut all my strings, crumpled me up, and threw me down to earth to forever be his.

He roared.

I screamed.

We rode out the waves, his heels driving into the floor to climb higher into me and my knees bleeding from rocking so hard.

We were determined to mark each other. Blinded and deaf to anything but crawling inside each other in every way possible.

And when the last clench wrung us dry, and there was nothing more than agonising echoes, we crashed together—boneless, broken, and utterly burned out.

Slowly, his cock softened inside me.

Slowly, the angry drive diminished from his eyes.

Slowly, his touch turned soft and adoring instead of rageful and controlling.

Finally, he kissed my forehead and brushed sweat-tangled hair from my eyes. "It's time for us to go home."

I nodded, too weak and sated to speak.

I stayed in my sex daze as he rolled me off him, and we both winced at him pulling free. My body mourned him, but my heart was glad for a reprieve.

Doing up his trousers and smoothing his shirt, Elder gently scooped me into his chest and pulled me to my feet. I allowed him to do his best to fix my broken dress, smiling as he used his cravat to wrap around my bodice and keep my corset together, so I didn't flash the masquerade guests.

I snuggled into him as he wrapped his arm around me, plucked the penny bracelet from the floor where I'd tossed it, found my shoe and discarded knickers, and unlocked the door.

Guiding me through Hawksridge Hall, I feared we'd bump

into the master and mistress in our current state of undress. We looked as if we'd gone to war and both sides had lost.

But both sides won instead.

I hugged that happy lucky conclusion.

I was right.

He was wrong.

My theory on three was cemented.

As we stepped into the cool English night and kept to the shadows to avoid peering eyes, I whispered, "You owe me an apology."

His eyes flashed, knowing full well what I meant.

I'd promised this would happen, and I'd promised the loser would owe the winner commiseration.

I waited for him to deny he'd been able to stop willingly. That we'd slept together and stopped without the need for any third party interference.

He merely guided me down the steps and onto white gravel. "I owe you nothing. Don't try that again, Pimlico. Do you hear me?"

He was back to calling me Pimlico.

I was glad.

For a second there, I'd been two people blended into one.

I was back to one.

The better one.

The stronger one.

The one who had just won.

I smiled and made no promises.

Because we both knew I'd proven a point.

He'd stopped at three.

We'd found our middle ground.

And we both knew what that meant...

There would be no denying me now.

ELDER

WE DIDN'T SAY goodbye to anyone.

It was the height of rudeness, but with my blood coursing through my veins and overwhelming tenderness commanding me to care for Pim, I couldn't bow to social niceties.

I couldn't waste time finding Jethro Hawk to thank him for his hospitality. I wouldn't be able to look him in the eye knowing full well I'd broken every rule of guest etiquette. He must never know we'd christened his quaint sitting room not once, or twice, but three fucking times.

So uncivilized but so ridiculously good.

Even now, with rational thinking part of my arsenal again, I couldn't understand how I'd stopped. All I could remember was the driving obsession to claim again and again. She'd felt so good, so hot, so wet. All other thoughts apart from quintessential fucking didn't factor in my brain. I was utterly obsessed, one-tracked, consumed. Yet when I'd done my best to stop after the second time, and Pim had chased after me, denying me the right to protect her, the sense of calm after my third release shocked me stupid.

All my life I'd known three was my tic, my twitch, my go-to number.

But why had Pim dared risk her well-being to see if it

worked in sex too?

How did she know?

Silly woman.

Silly, incredible, sexy-as-fuck woman.

Sitting beside her, I wasn't raging with regret for hurting her but comfortably exhausted—almost at peace for indulging in what I'd wanted for months and finding both of us survived.

She'd tested her theory...just like she'd warned me. I only wished she hadn't done it in someone else's home.

But then again, in a way, I was glad.

We'd crossed boundaries at Hawksridge Hall. We'd gone to battle and come out a little bloody, a little banged up, but with better awareness of our opponent.

Pim had known the risks and broken me anyway.

She'd opened her heart and body and trusted me.

Trust.

That one terrible gift.

If I'd known she'd throw that back in my face after I gave her the penny bracelet, I would never have taken her to Hawksridge. I would never have let myself be alone with her.

Stepping into that room, she'd given me no choice— almost as if she'd heard my fleeting thoughts about leaving her somewhere in England. Of putting her in a safe house, surrounded by guards, and preventing her from being beside me when the Chinmoku hit.

The idea had come to me while talking to Jethro. He was a man who'd lost a lot to gain so much. I understood the lengths he would go to protect his wife, and it made me aware how selfish I was being by keeping Pim by my side.

I loved her...therefore, it was my duty to protect her.

And I can't do that with her on the Phantom.

I clutched her closer, cuddling her into my body where we sprawled on the back seat of the car.

Once again, my heart burned for the peril she'd put herself in by seducing me. The danger she'd willingly endured, purely to knock some sense into me—to prove my libido wasn't something to be terrified of—merely something to be treated like every other thing in my life.

By rules and regulations and specific repetitions.

We'd been driving for over an hour. Another twenty minutes or so and we'd be back in South Hampton and on the water.

Selix drove, and I trusted him not to have overstepped in liquor. It didn't mean he hadn't mingled with guests and, judging by his own rumpled appearance and a few pieces of hay in his hair, I'd say he'd had an eventful evening with some mystery woman.

The knowledge we were going home ought to make me happy.

It didn't.

If I took Pim away from England, there was no telling what sort of shit would find us.

If I was a good man, I'd leave her at Hawksridge where the well-known Black Diamonds would protect her. I'd leave her guarded by my own men and hunt the Chinmoku to ensure she remained safe.

I couldn't trust her not to pull another ridiculous stunt like disobeying me with the coastguard.

This wasn't fucking Romeo and Juliet.

I didn't want to die for her, and I sure as hell didn't want her to die for me.

I've had enough death of loved ones.

Pim rested her head on my shoulder, breathing quietly. Her warmth and slender weight clutched my heart with right and wrong.

If I was a better man, I'd leave her here.

But I wasn't.

I loved her. I'd miss her. I couldn't fucking walk away from her—especially now.

As tyres hummed on highway, taking us closer to the ocean, Pim raised her arm and twisted her wrist. She smiled at the gentle clink of gold and diamond pennies dancing on her new bracelet.

My stomach clenched again, second-guessing my choice to give her something that represented money after so much talk of currency and debts.

"I'm sorry for tossing it on the floor when you first gave it to me." She looked up, pushing away a little to see me. "I love it so much. But when I saw it...I couldn't stop myself from kissing you."

Opening my arm, I waited until she'd snuggled back into me before I kissed the top of her head. She smelled like champagne and sex and me.

The best smell in the world.

"I'm glad you like it."

"*Love* it."

"It certainly earned a reaction from you."

She laughed quietly in the dark.

Selix flicked me a glance in the rear-view mirror, raising his eyebrow. He wasn't stupid. He knew we'd done something. The intimate bond webbing Pim and me was too strong to ignore.

I *burned* with it.

We couldn't keep our hands off each other and not for sex but for connection.

My fingertips never stopped stroking her. My lips never far from her skin. Her ruined dress and my dishevelled appearance couldn't hide what we'd done to achieve this new level of intimacy.

I gave him a smirk as he returned his attention to the road.

Another fifteen minutes of quiet, companionable driving and South Hampton pier appeared, slumbering under a blanket of stars. Boats hovered on crystal water, their inhabitants asleep at this time of the morning. The smooth sea reflected the half-moon on its calm surface, welcoming us home.

The Phantom, being oversized and unable to dock in the regular bays, floated in the distance in a spot reserved for cruise ships. Luckily, it was away from the main hub and private with its own driveway and ramp.

Selix drove us through the complex off-shoots and warehouses around the port then parked beside the gangway and waited for me to open the door and help a tousled Pimlico from the backseat.

Her bracelet glinted on her wrist and her knickers and heels dangled from her fingers.

I winced. We'd forgotten something. "Ah, shit, our masks. We left them on the floor."

Pim glanced up with a sly smile. "Oh well, I have no doubt the Hawks will know what happened in there. It's not like we were very discreet." She rested her palm over my heart. "We were loud, Elder."

I clamped my fingers over her hand, squeezing with all the fucking love I felt for her. "There was an orchestra, Pimlico."

She smirked. "I don't think an orgasm scream can be likened to any particular instrument."

"Oh, I don't know." Tucking her hand in mine, I slammed the door and guided her toward the ramp. "I'm sure I could mimic you on my cello."

"Is that right?" She tiptoed over the gritty pier, her feet bare and vulnerable.

I wanted to scoop her up, but that damn dress of hers would probably suffocate me if I carried her up the gangway.

"I might need you to recreate said scream to get it perfect, though." I chuckled under my breath.

Her eyes heated. "I'm sure that could be arranged."

I'd never indulged in banter like this. Never hovered in the sexual joy of falling in love and being so fucking happy just talking to a person.

Not that Pim was just a person.

She was my reason for existing now.

She'd taken reign of my misery and loneliness and given me something to hoard and worship. I missed my family, but for once in my life, I wasn't crippled by it.

How could I ever have thought about leaving her here? I

didn't care if it took me months or years to eradicate the Chinmoku, I would find a way with her by my side. She would remain *safe*. She was my newest addiction, and unlike my other unhealthy obsessions, I was determined to stay level-headed and sane even as my heart twisted into a lovesick fool.

The car engine revved. I glanced back at Selix who wound his window down. Pointing down the length of the Phantom where the garage to store the car was open, he said, "I'll park up for the night. Catch you on board."

I nodded. "Thanks."

He grinned. "Expect an early wake-up call, Prest." He waved, sending a silent message that he'd want to know what the hell happened when we had our regular sparring season.

I'd tell him pieces, but I'd also tell him I'd had enough of him being second best. He was never my staff—he was the one who chose that role. I wanted him as my equal if we were to fight the Chinmoku together. That was my war...not his. If he was to be a part of it, then he needed to accept my terms.

Mainly inheriting half of my company once the lottery debt was paid.

Squeezing Pim's hand, I guided her up the ramp, inspecting the looming giant of the Phantom. Its bulk far outshone any of the smaller crafts around the pier. Her hulking presence granting a false sense of invincibility.

A chilly breeze whipped around us as we reached the top. My tux's fly was broken, allowing air to circulate around yet another growing erection. My shirt and jacket flapped around my waist, untucked.

I wanted a hot shower and fresh sheets.

I wanted them with Pimlico.

I wanted her beside me instead of behind a lock and key a deck below.

Climbing on board, I spun her to face me, desperate to kiss her.

She smiled as my lips touched hers, her cheeks pinking with the same desire infecting me.

Forcing myself to break the kiss before I took it too far, I breathed, "Spend the night with me."

Her eyes flared. "Are you asking for more sex or...?"

I fucking loved that she gave me the choice. That she didn't turn me down, beseeching that three times was enough for one evening. She merely smiled so pure, so sweet, and gave me anything I needed.

Christ, this woman.

What could I do to ever repay her...to ever deserve her?

Tucking wild chocolate hair behind her ear, I laughed quietly. "Sleep with me."

Her lashes fluttered, her gaze dropping to my chest seductively. "Sleep, sleep?"

I laughed harder. "Sleep. You know? Where you let me hold you, and we both try to rest so we're not zombies tomorrow?"

"Ahh, sleep! Yes, I've heard of it." She wrinkled her nose. "Then again, it is rather boring, don't you find?"

Nuzzling into her neck, I groaned. "God, don't tempt me again, Pimlico."

She pressed against me, her arms whipping around my waist. "Where's the fun in stopping?"

My fingers captured her jaw, holding her still as I pressed my mouth to hers. The kiss had a life of its own, managing to somehow stay innocent but dirty at the same time. Our tongues touched then retreated; our hearts swelled then softened.

I was so fucking in love with this girl.

Kissing the corner of her mouth, I murmured, "I'm sure another kind of sleeping could be arranged."

She shivered in my arms. "Let's go then."

Breaking apart, we stumbled over the main deck, impatience and desire turning our limbs jerky. She glanced at me with my flapping ruined tux and laughed. I looked at her in her rippling, torn dress and didn't know if I'd make it to the room.

Laughing together was one of the best things in the world.

I was enraptured by her, completely addicted, and for once, I didn't care or try to break the spell.

She was all mine.

I would never get over that fact.

Never take her for granted.

Never let her go.

I couldn't remember the last time I'd been so content.

And that was my utter downfall.

She'd taken over my senses.

Every. Single. One.

I didn't pay attention to my surroundings because all I cared about was the sea breeze coiling her hair and how her smile made my heart fucking stop. I didn't notice the stillness or wrongness because all I saw was a goddess who'd somehow managed to bring me back to life.

I really should've paid attention.

I should've noticed how deathly quiet the Phantom was.

I should've found it odd that no staff greeted us.

No captain to inform us of tides.

No music floating from the kitchen.

No deck hands checking the rigging.

Nothing but empty decks and vacant rooms.

I didn't notice any of that as Pim and I stayed wrapped in each other, drifting toward my bedroom, stopping to pull each other close for another lust-quick kiss.

The pennies on her bracelet were the only noise in the dense early morning air.

The sliding doors to my quarters were open—nothing unusual as I often left them wide. The lights were off—again, nothing unusual as I wasn't there to require them to be on.

My room was quiet and still.

My bed untouched and white in the moonlight.

My instincts dulled and focused on Pim and only Pim.

But as I turned to close the doors and flicked the switch to turn the glass from clear to opaque, and Pim drifted forward to turn on the floor lamp by my desk, and the sound of her dress was replaced by the click of a gun, and the lamp flooded the empty space revealing it wasn't truly empty, I was gripped with ice cold rage and lava hot panic.

My life fucking ended before I could even yell. "Pim—*no!*" Too late.

Too motherfucking late.

A man's arm shot out in the receding darkness, wrapping around her neck, holding her in front of him. His smile leered over her shoulder, heralding my worst fucking nightmare.

Two seconds in my domain and I'd lost my woman to my enemy.

Fuck!

How had I let my guard down so badly? What sort of idiot had I become?

My hands balled as I stalked toward the man holding Pim.

A Japanese man.

A man with thin lips and a red birthmark on his cheek.

A man I'd fought with so many years ago.

"Let her go." My voice was nothing more than a thunderous snarl.

"I don't think you're in the position to give instructions."

My blood froze as another man switched on the overhead lights, drowning the bedroom in light.

Shit, shit, *shit.*

He moved toward his colleague holding Pim, his steps elegant and controlled. His head was bald—as it had been in my youth. Tattoos ran over his skull and around his ears, ending in whips of Japanese characters at the tips of his cheekbones.

He was a scary son of a bitch and a cold-hearted killer.

Pim's eyes turned wild, but she didn't utter a sound. Her muteness might help in this situation. As long as she stood still and didn't antagonise them, they would keep their focus on me.

Please let them keep their focus on me.

If they killed her—

My heart wrenched itself into pieces at the thought.

I couldn't go there.

I wouldn't.

Gathering my strength, I calmly did up my tux button and stood to my full height. I wouldn't be intimated. Not by him. Not by anyone.

This was *my* yacht.

They were trespassing and would die a slow death because of it.

I bared my teeth. "Hello, Kunio."

The second-in-command of the Chinmoku stood smiling, knowing full fucking well he'd bested me. He should never have gained access to my boat, let alone put his goddamn hands on my woman. "Hello, Miki-san."

I shuddered.

I wasn't Miki anymore. I hadn't been him for a very long time.

My mother had given me a Japanese name, calling me after the moon. I'd changed it to the name my father had wanted when she'd banished me.

It wasn't a name I ever wanted to hear again.

The fact that Kunio was here and not the master of the Chinmoku was grotesque disrespect.

They didn't see me as worthy enough to be addressed by their leader before killing me.

My fists tightened, but I did my best to keep my full temper from showing. My hands craved the samurai swords I trained with. My heart *howled* for their blood.

"Let her go." I did my best to keep my voice bored when really it was lethal with hatred. "She's not part of this."

Kunio glanced at Pim with a condescending smile. "Not part of it...just like your brother and father weren't part of it? Just like the rest of your family aren't a part of your blood debt?"

Every muscle locked in pure fury. "Exactly. You've already claimed two innocent lives. You don't need another."

"They were never innocent." He moved slowly around the

room. "They were yours. You let us down. They were ours to punish."

Pim stood with her chin high and chest barely moving. She stared at me with trust even while fear etched her face.

I hated, positively *hated*, she was in danger yet again. She'd lived through enough. She shouldn't have to put up with yet more bullshit all because she'd chosen to love me.

What a stupid, terrible choice on her part.

I'm so sorry, Pim.

Storming forward, I made sure to enunciate clearly and with authority. "Let her go, and we'll do what is necessary."

Fight until one of us is dead.

More men materialized from the shadows around the room, standing beside their leader. Seven in total. Seven plus Kunio. Once again, an uneven fight against the Chinmoku.

They were never ones for equal odds.

That was how they destroyed other gangs, took over turfs, and created a reputation of bloodthirsty inhumanity.

And once upon a time, I'd fought for them.

I'd been so fucking naïve and too wrapped in my obsessions to care.

This was my karma.

I deserved it.

But Pim didn't.

"You disappointed us." Kunio ran his hands over his bald head, stroking his tattoos. "You know how we hate to be disappointed, Miki-san."

Oh, I knew.

I'd seen their disappointment first-hand.

I'd smelled their disappointment from my father and brother burning.

Even though the Chinmoku ran illegal operations, trafficked women, manufactured drugs, and corrupted everything they could get their hands on, their faction wasn't huge.

They didn't trust easily and only welcomed the tried and

proven to join their ranks.

When I'd been invited into their family, there'd been seventy-nine fully fledged members. That number might've grown over the past decade, but I had no doubt if Kunio only brought seven men with him, then they were seven of his best.

Seven men who liked to inflict agony on others in unique and imaginative ways.

Kunio dragged a finger down Pim's arm.

She hissed but remained steadfast and silently seething.

"I approve of your taste in women. Perhaps, instead of killing her, we'll make her one of us."

The thought of Pim belonging to the Chinmoku enraged me to the point of blacking out and killing everyone in my path.

She would never again belong to anyone. *Especially* them.

Hatred lodged in my throat. "Let her go."

"As I said before—you're not in a position to give instruction." Kunio looked at his men.

They were all identical replicas with the Chinmoku uniform of black trousers and t-shirt, black bandana, and red fingerless gloves.

Long ago, the leader had told me they wore red gloves to symbolise the blood they were about to shed. Already bathing their flesh in the life force of their enemy.

I'd once worn a pair of those gloves.

Now, I wanted to cut off their hands.

Scanning the men, I took note of the many different weapons strapped to their bodies—some favoured simple guns while others had knives buckled to their legs and back. They might wear the same wardrobe, but when it came to their chosen method of killing? Anything was permitted.

Where the fuck was Selix?

My staff?

How had the Chinmoku taken custody of my ship without my goddamn knowledge?

Folding his hands in front of him, Kunio cocked his head. The atmosphere changed from poised to prepared.

I'd once been on the other side and understood what that subtle shift meant.

This was never meant to be a conversation of my betrayal and punishment. This wasn't a drawn-out negotiation for Pim's life or mine.

This was an extermination.

My limbs loosened, my knees ready to unlock and fight at a second's notice.

Kunio smiled. "You know as well as I do how this night will end. Your woman is now ours to do with as we please. Your life is now ours for your disobedience. Your very existence belongs to us. Tonight, we collect."

My heart rate slowed. My eyes sharpened. My breathing shallowed.

Kunio looked at the black-shrouded man beside him. There was no nod, no command, no signal.

But it didn't matter.

My room went from silent threat to all-out homicidal war.

Four men pounced on me at once.

Their blows struck my head, my chest, my back, my kidneys.

Their swiftness put me on the back foot even though I'd seen it coming.

I was drained from three bouts of sex.

I was tired from shame and worry.

I was livid at Pim's imprisonment.

I was too many things and not focused.

Emotion should never be part of a fight.

First rule of combat: the mind must be pure of all thoughts. The body vacant apart from the dance of violence.

An uppercut shot stars into my vision, my jaw howling under vicious knuckles.

And that was the last invitation I needed to lose myself.

I bellowed in fury, hunkering down to become more than me, more than human, more dragon than animal, more monster than man.

It'd been too long since I'd fought to maim. I'd grown too used to holding back, of locking down my true nature.

The four Chinmoku didn't care.

They hit and kicked and struck.

Each punishment I deserved as I was too slow to drop my pretences and meet them beast to beast. But as agony flared and panic swelled and Pim screamed my name, I sank the final distance and found the mindlessness of precision.

I welcomed the cutthroat bloodthirstiness I always carried.

I nursed the mania of winning.

I threw myself head first into the crystal clarity of how to inflict the most damage.

I turned off my conscience and worries...

And went rogue.

Pimlico

I'D ALWAYS KNOWN Elder could fight.

I'd sensed his power that first time in the white mansion. I'd witnessed it when he killed Darryl with one twist of his neck.

But this...this wasn't Elder.

This was a demon dressed in a tux. There was no humanity left in his eyes as he delivered blow for blow. He kicked and pummelled. He broke bones and knocked out men without a second thought.

But no matter how many times he bested the bastards determined to kill him, they never stopped striking.

When one fell, a fresh one joined.

When one screamed, another one rushed to deliver like for like to Elder.

Elder was a machine. Inhuman. No matter how many swings he took, no matter how much blood gushed from his nose, he never made a sound.

He was the ghost his family called him.

He was the dragon inked on his chest.

I fought the man holding me. I ignored the enemies all around.

All I saw was Elder and the impeccable deadly dance he

invoked.

I was desperate to go to his aid, to help...*somehow*. But tight hands never let me go, the sharp muzzle of a gun against my ribs never waning.

I daren't cry out in case I distracted Elder. I enlisted my silence and forbade tears from tracking.

The battle continued terribly uneven with Elder vanishing amongst a cloud of opponents only to reappear with a perfectly aimed upper-cut.

Everyone focused on the fight in front of us. The crash of falling furniture and rip of bedding as they brought destruction to every inch of the suite.

I couldn't take my eyes off the man I loved—the man I wanted to keep forever being hammered closer and closer toward death.

There were so many of them and only one of him. No matter how magical Elder looked fighting for his life— eventually, he would tire. Eventually, he would lose. Eventually, he would be dead and then...*oh, God.*

I couldn't think about what would happen.

My heart was already broken.

My mind already fractured.

I didn't breathe as Elder threw a man across his quarters, ducking as another fighter leapt onto his back. A sob plaited with a curse as Elder stumbled beneath his weight, twisting and clawing, tearing the Chinmoku away then round-house kicking him in the chest.

As the man soared to the floor, something caught my eye.

It took everything in me to tear my attention from Elder, but my heart restarted in sick, disgusting hope as the doors to the deck slowly slid open, cracking apart silently, hardly noticeable thanks to the opaque blackness of the glass matching the darkness of night beyond.

Oh, my God.

Selix.

Please, let it be Selix.

At least two would be better than one—no matter the never-ceasing tidal wave of agony Elder endured. At least he might have a weapon to combat the glint of knives flying around the room.

Only, Selix didn't appear…two other men slipped into the room.

Two men I'd never seen before.

Both dark-haired and wearing black suits, they moved like shadows themselves. For a second, a scream percolated in my throat.

Were they more Chinmoku? Yet more assholes who wanted to murder the man I loved?

Elder had to know.

He must be prepared to somehow become immortal because he couldn't die—not like this. I couldn't watch him be murdered.

I can't!

My mouth parted; my breathing manic as the two men stuck to the perimeter of the room, cloaked in obscurity. My teeth clacked together as they pulled out matching guns and pointed them at the Chinmoku. Not pistols or anything small, their weapons were big and automatic and carnage inducing.

They pointed them at the enemy and not my lover.

The minuscule faith that they were here to help rather than hinder kept me quiet.

I glanced at Elder.

He stood in the throng, hitting wildly, his face cold and concentrating even as blood rivered over his temple and cheek. Bruises decorated his skin. His hair wild and torn.

Even if these men were friends, he still needed to be warned.

They pointed their guns at the Chinmoku, but Elder was in the centre of their target.

He was in their line of fire—

They'll kill him, too.

I opened my mouth to scream. *"El—"*

Too late.

A spray of bullets cut through the fight, ending it as suddenly as it had begun.

My scream turned into a cower as the man holding me automatically ducked for cover. The man named Kunio skittered out of the path of death as his warriors all tumbled like plucked weeds.

"Fucking vermin," a French accent spat as another ricochet of bullets broke apart the group, sending men sprawling with multiple wounds.

"No!" I wriggled and fought, my eyes strained on the blood bath in front of me.

I can't see him.

I can't see him!

For a second, no one moved. The scent of gunpowder hung heavily in the room.

Then, slowly, the pile of body parts moved. I sobbed in relief as Elder shoved off dead Chinmoku to stand on wobbly feet.

Being in the centre of the throng had saved his life.

I didn't know if he was unscathed, but he was alive.

He was alive, and they were not.

My heart turned nasty with hate.

How *dare* they try to hurt him?

How *dare* they try to kill him?

I wanted to grab a gun and finish what these two strangers had started.

Elder breathed hard, one hand fisted and another with a finger bent the wrong way. He stood as straight as he could but one leg didn't bear his weight, and his face was an artwork of violence.

He glowered at the new interlopers, his black gaze menacing and assessing.

He didn't recognise them.

He wasn't glad to see them.

Not that the two men with their guns cared. Ignoring him

as if he were nothing more than a beetle about to be squashed, they trained their guns instead on the man holding me and the remaining Chinmoku beside us.

The slender man of the two who'd reaped carnage licked his lips as if desperate for more bloodshed but willing to play human...for now. "Let her go."

My heart coiled and hissed. I fought harder to be released. My eyes shot past the men demanding my freedom and latched onto Elder.

He gave me a pained look, a thousand apologies in one glance.

The man holding me tightened his grip, shaking me to behave. "Who the fuck are you?"

"None of your business," the bulkier man of the two snarled. "You heard him; let her go."

Reluctantly, the Chinmoku looked at his boss and loosened his hold. I immediately darted out of reach.

"You'll pay for this," Kunio snapped. "You don't know—"

Two more shots rang out, the bullets flying so close, the slipstream rippled over my skin.

Two more thuds echoed through the floor as the last two Chinmoku toppled into silence. They fell like fallen trees, soundless and dead as old wood.

It was over.

Whoever these sinister angels were, they'd saved Elder's life and returned me to him.

I couldn't stand to be apart any longer.

Uncaring that the two men still held smoking guns, uncaring I didn't have answers to who they were, I bolted to Elder, my gown fluttering in red and blue as I cringed and climbed corpses to reach him.

"Pim..." Elder tripped toward me. "Fuck, Pim."

My toes slipped on warm blood. My stomach curdled at the stench of death, but as I stepped into Elder's arms and pressed my forehead to his heart, I didn't care about anything.

He was alive.

This was my fault. I'd distracted him. I'd turned his mind from survival to seduction.

"Elder...I'm so sor—"

His lips landed on my hair. "Don't. Please, don't. This is my fa—"

Hands latched around my arms and waist, pulling me away, yanking me into the embrace of a lemon-sandalwood scent.

"Wait!" My tears fell harder, hating to be torn from the one man I needed.

The slender, dangerous killer who'd just committed countless murders in a fight that wasn't his held me as if I weighed nothing. He growled at Elder. "Don't fucking touch her." Backing away, he trained his gun's muzzle on him.

"Don't!" I scratched at my captor's arm. "Don't shoot."

"Stop." Elder clambered over bodies, baring his teeth as he stalked us. He raised his hands in surrender even as one arm looked suspiciously broken. "Don't hurt her. She's mine."

My new captor chuckled with a blackness I'd only heard in my nightmares. "Not anymore."

"Wait!" I squirmed in his hold, unable to fully face him with the grip he had on my body. This damn dress gave way too much fabric to be used as a leash. "He's my friend. He's—"

Friend was woefully unjust.

Lover was woefully unfair.

He's my reason for living...purpose of existing...

The man didn't give me time to sort out my scattered thoughts. Moving backward, he kept his gun high and me tucked tight. "As entertaining as this has been, we're leaving now." French accent thickened English vowels, making my ears twitch. Wasn't French supposed to be the language of love? What the hell were these men doing here and what did they want?

"I'm not going anywhere with you." I fought again only for the man to drag me close and breathe in my ear. "We're taking you somewhere safe. Don't fear us."

His concern shocked me stupid, long enough for him to drag me toward the exit and further from Elder.

"No, wait! I *am* safe. I'm with him." I pointed at Elder. "El…please. Tell them."

Elder stepped forward, his body bleeding and his limp unable to be disguised. "Take your hands off her. I won't tell you again. We're together. She's mine, goddammit."

"Wrong." The man holding me raised his gun.

"No!" I threw myself into him, knocking him off balance, sending the splatter of bullets into the cupboard holding Elder's cello. The bulkier man with his dark suit and even darker soul pointed his gun at Elder. "Don't fucking move."

With strength that squeezed the life out of me, the French man plucked me into his arms, swung his gun strap over his elbow, and carted me from Elder's suite.

I looked over his shoulder as he jogged onto the deck.

I kicked. I screamed. I punched. I didn't care anymore. "No. Stop. I don't want to go! You've got it all wrong!"

Who the hell were these men? Why had they helped stop the Chinmoku and then kidnapped me?

I couldn't understand. I didn't *want* to understand. I wanted all this to end and for Elder and me to do exactly what we'd planned—curl up in bed side by side and find peace in dreams together.

I wanted to be safe.

I wanted this to be a mistake.

"Wait!" Elder gave chase. Tripping with injury, holding his side as he ambled into a run, he skidded to a halt as he approached the man holding me.

The guy's arm tightened, bruising my ribcage as he backed toward the railing where part of the banister where Elder had swum and a ladder existed to the water below was raised.

Out the corner of my eye, I glimpsed a speedboat bobbing beside the Phantom. White sleek lines with wooden embellishments with a beautiful sparrow painted in full flight on the bonnet.

Elder gasped, his face manic, his fingers slippery with blood as he held the brass balustrade. Blood darkened his tux to glisten a sick maroon. "Stop. I *love* her. You're making a huge fucking mistake."

The French man chuckled harshly. "I'm not the one who's making a mistake. You did that the moment you thought you could buy women for pleasure." He muttered something in French followed by a growled, "Too fucking bad you don't know the meaning of love." He raised his gun, wedging me between the banister and his hard body. "You're all the same. *Filth.*"

Tears spilled down my cheeks as Elder glanced at me with horror in his eyes. "I don't know who you are, but you've got it wrong. She loves me back. We're—"

"I've had enough of this bullshit." With a squeeze of his trigger, the man holding me shot the man holding my heart.

"*No!*" My scream, my wail, my screech tore apart the night sky, punctured the moon, and sent seagulls flying into the stars.

The loud boom of a bullet soared from gun to Elder, shoving him backward, slugging him hard, spinning him up and over the railing and down, down, down.

He fell overboard.

I screamed as a wet splash gobbled him up, the sea claiming a victim like the kraken with its next meal.

One second, Elder was alive…here.

The next, he was gone….fallen.

It took a heartbeat to understand what had happened.

It took another for the sheer pulverising agony to crack me wide.

It took another to gather up enough air to scream.

And scream.

And *scream.*

"No!"

No, no, no.

"*No!*"

I fought.

My God, how I fought.

I hated them.

I loathed them.

I would *kill* them.

Kill, kill, kill them.

He had to be alive.

He knew how to swim.

He'd survived fists and kicks and pain.

He has to be alive.

Please, God, let him be alive.

Nothing in this world made sense anymore.

There was nothing keeping me sane. Nothing to fight for. Nothing to understand.

The man holding me murmured French nothings under his breath.

I *despised* him.

Turning me to face him, he cupped my cheeks with such tenderness, he flayed open my already threadbare heart.

His thumbs soothed my scalding tears; remorse filled his face, kindness replacing the killer in his eyes. Shame and regret almost twin mirrors of Elder's whenever he'd done something to hurt me.

"Shush, girl," he whispered. "It will all work out, you'll see. You're free now. You're safe."

I was ice cold.

I was frozen solid.

I was borderline catatonic with grief.

Shaking my head, I begged him to understand. To save Elder. To fix the damage he'd done. "Don't you see? I *was* free. I was safe. I was with him. I *love* him." Sobs clogged my throat. "I love him. I love him, and you killed him!"

The man shook his head sadly. "You *think* you love him, but you don't. Men like that twist minds. They hurt women and make them believe it's normal." His lips pulled back into a feral snarl, terrifying me all over again. "He won't do that again. You have my word."

"You don't understand!" I struck him. I slapped him. I wanted to rake my fingernails over his sinning awful face. "He saved me from that. He wasn't—"

The other man tapped him on the shoulder. "Q, we'd better go."

"*Tu as raison. Allons-y.* We'll sort her out when we get home. Tess will know what to do."

"No, I'm not going anywhere with you!"

I had to get to the water.

I had to get to Elder.

"Let me go!"

Something pricked my arm, sending warmth and harsh stinging through my blood.

A needle glinted in the moonlight.

Convulsive vehemence filled me as my eyelids fluttered. "You—you *drugged* me?"

The man who smelled of lemon and sandalwood smiled sadly. "*Je suis désolé.* But it's for your own good."

Nothing was for my own good.

This was everything against what was good for me.

They'd taken Elder.

They'd taken me.

They're taking...

My mind skated and slipped as if ice skates were now my foundations and a frozen puddle my brain.

I wobbled, my knees forgetting how to hold me up.

I felt sick.

I felt woozy.

I felt lost.

Cursing him, I collapsed into his arms, dangling in his embrace as my body vanished from my control and a bone-chilling lethargy crept over me.

I cried for Elder.

I cried for me.

I cried for everything we were so close to claiming.

I couldn't let him do this.

I couldn't let this stranger steal everything I ever wanted.

He had to have a name.

I had to know him.

So when I woke up, I could curse him and hex him and make him feel a tenth of the despair he'd caused me. "Who...are you?" My ability of speech was waning. "Why are y-you doing this?"

Just before the clouds crept over me, just before the moonlight blotted out on the worst evening of my life, the man cuddled me close, stroked back my hair, and gave me the answer to the question I'd carried for weeks. "My name is Q Mercer, and I'm saving you from the life you were sold into from the QMB. I've been hunting the men who bought women and giving them back their life. You're the last one." He scooped me into his arms, my ballgown whispering over his arms. "You were the last, but now you're found. No one is going to hurt you again. *Je promets.*"

No one will hurt me again? But you are...

This dark avenger who thought he'd rescued me had totally destroyed me.

This was the man who'd accessed my file at the police station.

This was the man hunting me not the Chinmoku.

This was the man I would hate for eternity.

My mind blanked out.

My body disappeared.

I remembered no more.

Preorder Millions, the last book in the Dollar Series for $3.99 (ebook), read Jethro Hawk's tale about debts and diamonds, and meet Q Mercer's tale about slaves and secrets for free

at
www.pepperwinters.com

PLAYLIST

Kesha - Learn To Let Go
Rag'N'Bone Man - Human
Rag'N'Bone Man - Skin
Clean Bandit - Symphony feat. Zara Larsson
Sia - To be human
Ed sheeran - Shape of you
Alessia Cara - Stay
Martin Garrix, Troye Sivan - There For You
Shawn Mendes - Mercy
Scars to your beautiful - Alessia Cara
Don't Let Me Down- The Chainsmokers ft. Daya
Rag'N'Bone Man - Life In Her Yet

ABOUT THE AUTHOR

After chasing her dreams to become a full-time writer, Pepper has earned recognition with awards for best Dark Romance, best BDSM Series, and best Hero. She's an multiple #1 iBooks bestseller, along with #1 in Erotic Romance, Romantic Suspense, Contemporary, and Erotica Thriller. With 20 books currently published, she has hit the bestseller charts twenty-eight times in three years.

Pepper is a Hybrid Author of both Traditional and Self-published work. Her Pure Corruption Series was released by Grand Central, Hachette. She signed with Trident Media and her books have sold in multiple languages and audio around the world.

On a personal note, Pepper has recently returned to horse riding after a sixteen year break and now owns a magnificent black gelding called Sonny. He's an ex-pacer standardbred who has been retrained into a happy hacking, dressage, and show jumping pony. If she's not writing, she's riding.

The other man in her life is her best-friend and hubby who she fell in love with at first sight. He never proposed and they ended up married as part of a bet, but after eleven years and countless adventures and fun, she's a sucker for romance as she lives the fairy-tale herself.

THANK YOU FOR READING!

Printed in Great Britain
by Amazon